THE NORSE QUEEN

THE NORSEWOMEN BOOK 1

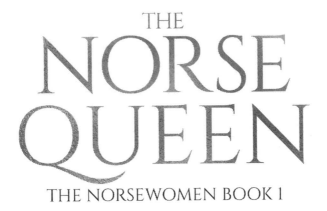

JOHANNA WITTENBERG

ISBN 978-1-7345664-0-6

Published by
SHELLBACK STUDIO

Cover design by Deranged Doctor
Cover art by Bev Ulsrud Van Berkom

Author Website: JohannaWittenberg.com

For my mother, who first introduced me to Åsa and her world

North Sea

Skagerrak

Borre
Skirinssal
•Tromøy

Hedeby
•

Kattegat

Bornholm

Öland

Gotland

Eastern Sea

Birka•

Lake
Ladoga

Svir

Lake
Onega

•Aldeigja

Itil (Volga) River

Bolgar•

CHAPTER 1

The thrall takes instant vengeance, the coward never.
—*Grettir's Saga*

Tromøy, Norway
August, AD 818

Asa was hanging off a cliff raiding swallows' nests when she sighted the sail, a striped patch against the glittering sea. She dropped the eggs into her sack and swung out on the rope, squinting into the glare.

The sleek hull knifed through the waves, bearing directly down on the island.

Friend or foe?

Too narrow for a merchant's knarr. This was a dragon ship, built for war. Painted shields crowded her rails, curved prow reared out of the waves. Coming fast.

Heart pounding, Åsa scrambled up the rope and sprinted for the steading.

Across the fields, the sentry headed in from his lookout. The cursed boy had sprouted like a stalk of wheat, and the way his long legs ate up the ground, he was going to reach Father before she did.

Åsa spotted her father in the sheep pen. She cut through the barley field, the ripening stalks slapping at her legs, and threw herself onto the fence a heartbeat ahead of the sentry.

"Father, a ship!" she managed to croak.

"My lord," the lookout gasped behind her, "a longship, thirty men."

Her father blinked at them mildly. He was culling the new lambs, some to be raised for wool and breeding, some for slaughter, and some for sacrifice to the gods. His big hands gently separated a bleating lamb from its mother.

He gave the nervous ewe a pat and straightened to his full height, towering over both Åsa and the sentry. His boots were muddy, and tufts of straw stuck to his wool shirt with what was no doubt manure. Harald liked to dress this way in spite of being a king. In his youth, he had been a great warrior, or so the old húskarlar liked to tell as they drank their ale around the longfire. Nowadays he ruled sheep herds and barley fields.

"Åsa, get my horn," he said.

Her heart beat triple-time. This was real. A raid. A battle.

She tore into the great hall's entryway and seized the ram's horn from its place on the wall. It was a beautiful thing, silver-chased and rune-carved, handed down in the family for generations. Cradling it under her arm, she dashed back to her father. He was already striding toward her, the sentry at his heels.

King Harald put the horn to his lips and sounded a call that echoed throughout the farmstead. Men and women alike snatched up axes, cudgels, pitchforks, and scythes—anything with an edge—and ran toward the hall.

Åsa followed her father through the hall entryway and into the main room, blinking while her eyes adjusted to the gloom. In the longfire's red glow, the húskarlar were already donning their ring-studded leather armor and fetching their painted wooden shields from the wall. Her brother, Gyrd, was among them, strapping on his mighty sword, Wolfbane, looking like a young god in his helm and chain-mail brynja.

Åsa's hands trembled as she lifted her own shield from the wall. She turned to meet her fóstra, Brenna, who was huffing under an armful of chain mail.

"What have you done with your hair?" Brenna dumped the brynja on the floor and took hold of Åsa's braid. "It looks like the tail of a billy goat." She whipped an antler comb from her belt and attacked the red-gold frizz.

Åsa wrenched out of Brenna's grasp. "There's no time for that! Help me into my brynja."

Grumbling, Brenna hefted the chain-mail shirt over her mistress's head. Åsa braced herself as the heavy rings cascaded down her torso. She had spent all winter in the smithy painstakingly forging each link, and hours practicing to get used to the weight of it. Now she was donning it for battle.

Gritting her teeth, she held still while Brenna settled the helmet over her hair. Finally, Brenna held out Åsa's sword. Forged by Ulf, their smith, Lightning was smaller than Wolfbane but every bit as sharp.

She snatched it from Brenna's hand and slashed the blade through the air. "We're ready for them."

Gyrd eyed her sourly. "You look like a lad. You've fifteen winters now, you should dress like a lady."

"Make me." Åsa glared at her brother.

He scowled, and she could see he was about to press the issue when their father strode in.

"Stay in the back row," Gyrd muttered.

Harald towered over his men, chain mail and helm gleaming,

great sword swinging from his belt in its rune-carved scabbard. He looked like a warlord. He sounded like one.

"Form up!" he bellowed.

The húskarlar fell in behind their king and stormed out of the hall's great entry doors. Harald's sworn men flanked their king, shields poised to lock in a defensive wall at his command. Åsa shoved her way in beside her father, jutting her chin at Gyrd's frown. Next came the archers, bows in hand, quivers of arrows over their shoulders. Behind them the common folk gathered, armed with their pitchforks and scythes.

All eyes were trained on the harbor.

The longship's crew had furled their sail, and now the slender oars sliced through the waves. One final pull, and the oars sprang straight up as the sleek hull glided onto the beach. Åsa shivered as warriors leaped over the side and splashed ashore. Helmets flashing in the sun, bristling with swords and spears, the strangers marched up the long hill. Their leader stood a head above them all. He strode with a lanky grace, bearing his weapons as if they weighed nothing, battle helm in the crook of his arm. Behind him, a warrior bore a red banner that snapped in the breeze.

"A little small for a raiding party," Jarl Borg remarked. The aged jarl was Harald's long-time friend and mentor, and nowadays he spent more time on Tromøy than on his own lands.

Harald nodded. "Gudrød's men," he murmured, gazing at the banner's emblem. He touched his sword hilt uneasily. "I haven't seen him in twenty years."

The tall leader halted his party within shouting distance of the hall. "Harald, king of Agder, I am Olaf, son of King Gudrød of Borre. My father sends greetings to his old friend."

Olaf was fair-haired, strongly built, and handsome, somewhere near Gyrd's age. Åsa found herself hoping they wouldn't have to kill him.

"Welcome, Olaf Gudrødson," Harald said. "I've had no word

from your father in many years. What brings you and your war party to my island?"

Olaf turned to survey his men. "We are no war party," he said. "These are only my escort. Sea travel is perilous these days."

"Perilous indeed," Harald agreed, and waited. Åsa's hopes for battle began to fade.

"My father sends us in peace, with offers of friendship and goodwill," Olaf continued.

"Well, then," said Harald, "lay down your arms and enter my hall as guests." He turned and nodded to his men.

Åsa's heart slowed to a trudge. A feast was required, and she would have to prepare it. She bit back her disappointment and relinquished her weapons to Brenna, who had been behind her all along.

Stepping forward, she pulled off her helm and forced a smile.

She found herself gazing up into hazel eyes framed by lush blond lashes. A flush crept over her face as she tried not to stutter. "Welcome to our hall, Olaf Gudrødson, I am Åsa Haraldsdottir."

His gaze locked on to hers, and she saw him swallow, a blush rising up his throat. He lowered his eyes and swept into a bow.

"Lady." His blond hair, bound around the brow with a silver cord, swung gracefully across his face. Åsa caught her breath.

"Please refresh yourselves while we prepare a meal," she managed to blurt, then turned and fled into the hall. She paused in the shadows while her breath returned to normal and her cheeks cooled. Then she bellowed for the kitchen staff.

She dispatched two women to deliver hot water and towels to the guesthouse, where Gyrd and her father would entertain the guests while she organized refreshments. Her mind worked furiously on how to feed thirty extra warriors while giving the meal the hallmarks of a feast. Preparations for the evening meal were already underway. There was no time to spare.

This was not the first feast Åsa had supervised. She had

become lady of the house three years ago when her mother had died, the duties tainted with loss.

She set her jaw. Olaf might have been accustomed to the riches of Vestfold, but here on remote Tromøy, they knew how to entertain. She set two women to fill the whale-oil lamps while five burly men hauled the trestle tables down from the rafters. The others followed in her wake as she strode out to the storehouse.

She unlocked the door with a key from the great ring at her waist and thanked the goddess Freyja for the newly butchered hog hung in the rafters. The women filled baskets with cheese, root vegetables, and a sack of barley to be ground for bread. In the brewhouse, she tasted the new ale and deemed it ready for serving.

When all was properly in motion, Åsa retired to her bower where Brenna waited to help her dress.

The old fóstra's expression was triumphant as she gripped the offending braid. She yanked the leather tie off and sank the antler comb into the wild curls. Åsa danced with impatience while Brenna gave her a thorough grooming. When Åsa's hair shone in a burnished cascade that rippled down her back, Brenna swiftly recaptured the glinting torrent in a fashionable knot at the back of the girl's head, then combed the length into a silky ponytail.

Brenna had laid out Åsa's best gown, of soft red wool woven by her mother, trimmed with strips of precious silk from the East. She felt ridiculous in it. Where Queen Gunnhild had been dainty and beautiful, Åsa took after her father: tall, rawboned and gawky, blue-eyed with fair freckled skin and a storm cloud of red-gold hair.

The gown had a wide tablet-woven border added to the hem and sleeves to accommodate Åsa's long arms and legs, but she still felt her limbs stuck out like sticks. Longing for her rough breeks and shirt, she fidgeted while Brenna forced her into the dress. But she held still when Brenna brought out her mother's necklace of amber and crystal beads and fastened it around her neck.

"You are beautiful, lady," said Brenna, gazing at her with moist eyes.

Åsa snorted. *This should meet with Gyrd's approval at least.* He was always trying to get her to dress up and act like Mother, maybe because he missed her so much. Well, Åsa missed her too, but wearing her mother's clothes wouldn't bring her back from the dead.

She took a deep breath and marched to the rear entryway of the hall where Tromøy's steward, Toki, stood beside the ale vat holding her father's prized drinking horn. Taking up the silver dipper, Åsa ladled ale into the horn. Toki placed the brimming heirloom in her hands, and she peered into the great room where the guests and her father's warriors assembled. She closed her eyes and took a deep breath.

When she entered the hall, the men fell silent. Carefully following precedence, she approached her father in his high seat and offered him the horn, saying, "Drink, Harald, king of Agder, and welcome our guests from Vestfold."

After her father had drunk, she proceeded to her brother. Both kings' sons, Gyrd and Olaf were of equal rank, but as the host, Gyrd took precedence. She led him to the seat beside their father and held out the horn. "Drink, Gyrd, heir of Tromøy, and welcome our guests."

Her eyes met her brother's over the rim of the horn. Gyrd waggled his eyebrows at her, making her choke. She could feel the flush rising in her cheeks. She jerked the horn out of his hand, giving him a scowl that promised she would settle the score with him later. She composed her face and turned to Olaf.

With a distinct quaver in her voice, she forced out the required address. "Olaf Gudrødson, we welcome you to Tromøy.

Please partake of our ale in good health." She could hear Gyrd snort as she conducted Olaf to the guest seat beside her own. Her hand shook just a little as she held out the horn. "Honored guest, please accept this horn."

Olaf inclined his head as if she were the most gracious hostess. "Thank you, good lady." As he took the cup, his fingers grazed hers, and she felt a lightning thrill jolt through her.

Åsa refused to make eye contact with Gyrd as she seated Jarl Borg and the great skáld Knut. Wiry and wizened, the famous poet's vigor belied his true age. Knut traveled the land year-round with only his serving boy for company, visiting each hall in turn to relate the tales of ancient kings and famous battles.

Olaf's men had settled themselves beside Tromøy's húskarlar on the benches around the longfire. Åsa took her place next to her father, in the chair that had been her mother's, and gestured to the servers to fill the warriors' cups.

Harald turned to her and smiled. "You are lovely, Daughter."

"I feel like a scarecrow," she muttered, plucking at her sleeves. "I wish I were like Mother."

Her father regarded her with glistening eyes. "Oh, but you are very like her," he said. Then he quickly turned to his guests.

Åsa could not help casting sidelong glances at Olaf. He looked up and caught her eye. A blush flooded his face, and Åsa recognized the same confused excitement she felt. He quickly averted his gaze.

Gyrd smiled at their guest. "We must be close to the same age," he said. "I suppose your father has taken you raiding many times?"

Olaf kept his eyes on his drink as the flush crept up his cheeks. "Not really."

"Well, neither has mine," Gyrd declared, looking directly at his father. "I think he will keep me in the practice yard until my beard is gray."

Harald scowled at his son. Åsa signaled the servers to make a round, distracting attention by refilling horns and mugs.

The rich smell of meat wafted into the hall, commanding everyone's attention. Serving men staggered beneath platters piled high with pork and fowl. Other servers scurried around the benches serving bread, steaming bowls of turnips and greens, and an ever-flowing river of ale.

Silence fell while every warrior attended to his food. Åsa sampled the meat and bread, surveying the room with satisfaction.

When the company had done justice to the meal and the servants removed the wreckage, the sated warriors stared over their drinking horns, watching the fire's glow. Sparks rose with the smoke, vanishing into darkness. The massive peeled tree trunks supporting the lofty roof displayed carved and painted scenes of the gods who leaped to life in the flickering light.

Åsa knew she must start a conversation with Olaf, but her mind was empty.

She cleared her throat. "You are far from home."

"Yes." His voice cracked a little, sending a rush of compassion through Åsa. He was shy.

She struggled on. "You are very brave to sail so far." She wanted to ask him about the trip's purpose, but that was not proper at this time. It would seem like a challenge. Instead, she said, "I have never been to Vestfold. I have heard that Borre is a great hall."

"Yes, it is larger than Tromøy." Olaf's eyes widened as he realized the implied insult. "But your father's hall is very grand. Do you run it all yourself?"

Åsa looked down at her hands. "Yes, since my mother died."

"I am very sorry for your loss," he said. "My mother died too, last year."

"I am sorry." Åsa hurried to fill the silence. "What was she like?"

"She was beautiful, kind, brilliant," he said softly. "She taught me the runes herself."

"I learned the runes from my mother too. You must miss her very much."

"I do." He met her eyes, and she glimpsed a sadness in them to match her own. "As you must yours." His eyelids hooded and he stared into his ale horn.

Åsa's throat constricted, and she could not tell Olaf how her mother had understood her like no one alive did now.

They sat silently, companions in grief, while the din rose around them.

King Harald stood and the revelers quieted. "My humble hall is graced by the skáld Knut," he announced, raising his horn, with a pointed look at Åsa. "I hope he will favor us with a saga."

Åsa realized her father's purpose was to distract Olaf from his gloom. She flushed at her own bad manners. It was her responsibility to make her guest merry, not bring him close to tears.

She was glad when the old poet stepped onto the floor and began a long performance of King Harald's exploits in his youth. In these tales Olaf's father, King Gudrød, played a more heroic role than Åsa could remember hearing in the past. Deeds that had been previously attributed to Harald were now credited to Gudrød.

The skáld's subterfuge, along with the drink, seemed to work its magic on Olaf. As the evening wore on and the ale flowed, his eyes met hers more frequently. She thought she detected a sparkle in them. He even began to smile. Åsa smiled back with real warmth, glad that Knut's performance alleviated the need for conversation. She didn't want to bring that sadness to his eyes again.

While Knut was in the midst of a lengthy telling of the succession of kings in Vestfold, Olaf shoved the horn into Åsa's hands and got unsteadily to his feet.

"I claim the floor," he blurted.

There was a shocked silence at the young man's audacity in interrupting the great skáld. The warriors' eyes went round, and Harald's eyebrows arched up toward his hairline. Åsa reddened in consternation.

But far from being angry at the interruption to his diatribe, Knut looked relieved. He bowed to Olaf. "Of course, my lord, I have gone on too long. The floor is yours," he said, and took his seat. Åsa was surprised at the deference the skáld showed the younger man.

A hush fell over the hall as Olaf stepped into the firelight. Straightening his tunic and rising to his full height, he lifted his chin and, in a voice that resounded through the hall, began to recite.

"Three maidens through Mirkwood flew, fair and young..."

An approving murmur arose as the audience recognized the opening lines of "The Lay of Völund."

Olaf skillfully set the scene in which the legendary smith and his three brothers built their hall in the woods by Wolf Lake, and how they captured three Valkyrie maidens by stealing their swan cloaks. The brothers married the Valkyries, and the three couples lived happily for seven years until the Valkyries discovered their swan cloaks and flew away. Völund's two brothers set out in search of their lost wives, but Völund stayed home, certain his bride would return. While he waited, he forged seven hundred golden rings for her.

When the evil king Nidud heard that Völund was alone in his hall, he sent his men to capture the renowned smith. Nidud had Völund hamstrung and imprisoned on an island, forcing the smith to make all manner of precious things.

Through magic and cunning, Völund took his revenge on Nidud and escaped.

Riveted by Olaf's resonant voice and dramatic gestures, Åsa

listened avidly with the entire company to the story they all knew by heart.

As Olaf came to the end of the tale, when Völund flew over the king's hall in the form of a bird, Åsa's voice rose with the others as they all shouted out the closing lines.

The warriors pounded the boards in approval. Their applause thundered through the hall, followed by utter silence. With tears in his eyes, Knut threw his arms around Olaf. "The years I spent at Borre teaching you have paid well. You have always been my best pupil. When I am in my dotage, you can come and entertain me, young lord of skálds. Now I have developed a powerful thirst. Let's drink."

Åsa clapped her hands and called for mead, the poet's drink.

As the longfire slowly subsided to embers, Olaf and his men stumbled off to the guesthouse while Tromøy's húskarlar wrapped themselves in their cloaks and lay down upon the benches. When all was quiet but for a few drunken snores and snorts, Åsa retired to her bower.

Flushed from the mead, she reflected on the evening. Nothing had been lacking, all of the guests were sated, and the company had been congenial. This was not always the case with a group of hard-drinking warriors. Disagreements often sprang up, and for this reason, weapons were never allowed in the hall. The peaceful evening was due largely to Olaf. His captivating performance had formed a bond between the two households.

Brenna helped her out of the red wool dress and carefully folded it away in its trunk. "Oh, lady, why do you think this handsome young lord has come here?"

Åsa's pulse quickened while she shrugged off the question and climbed under the down quilt. Tired as she was, her mind buzzed with questions like a hive of bees. Could Olaf be here for her? A thrill passed through her, tinged with dread. Olaf's plans might well include a marriage proposal. There had been other suitors. She knew some had sought her hand in order to form an alliance with her father and his strategic holdings, but Harald sent them all packing.

She firmly cleared the questions out of her mind and willed herself to sleep. There were many reasons for a king to send his son to see an old friend, many boons this young man could ask of her father. She would have to wait to find out.

CHAPTER 2

Åsa rose early next morning to hunt with her brother and their guest. She donned her leather jerkin and hawking glove, and coaxed her falcon, Stormrider, from her perch. Stormrider rode the glove serenely into the yard where their horses were saddled and waiting. Gyrd and Olaf were already mounted. Gyrd carried his own falcon, sister to Stormrider, on his fist, while Olaf bore Harald's goshawk. The old hawk sat the stranger's fist with a veteran's aplomb.

They set off across the sun-dappled meadow, followed by three men on foot to serve as beaters. Olaf rode between Åsa and her brother, his hair glinting silver next to Gyrd's rose gold.

She cast a sideways glance at her guest. *What really brings you here to our island?*

He looked up and met her eye. Flustered, she groped about for conversation. "Do you hawk much in Borre?" She immediately regretted her stupidity. Of course they did.

But Olaf smiled. "It's one of my favorite sports. I love to watch a falcon stoop on its prey."

"I raised Stormrider," she said proudly. "Gyrd and I got our nestlings from the cliffs together, and our mother taught us to man them and train them to hunt." Under Gunnhild's expert tutelage, Åsa had spent nearly every waking hour with the young falcon. Stormrider still lived with her in the bower room. "A falcon is a very special blessing from the gods," her mother had told her.

Olaf regarded the falcon's snowy breast and dark-barred flanks under a hooded cloak in dark gray the color of thunderclouds. "A beautiful bird, and well named." He smiled his shy smile.

The ground turned marshy, and Gyrd called a halt as the beaters sloshed out into the tall grass. He turned to Åsa. "You can fly first."

She released Stormrider's jesses, boosting the falcon into the air. As Stormrider ringed up high into the sky, Åsa felt a pull in her chest as if part of her could soar with the bird. She knew Stormrider did not share this bond. "A falcon is not a dog," Gunnhild had cautioned her. "If ever she returns to the wild, the tie is broken. She'll never come back."

A flurry on the ground claimed their attention as the beaters flushed a wood duck. It rose up from the grass in a bluster of wings. The hunting party watched raptly as Stormrider spotted the duck. She seemed to hang in the sky for a heartbeat, then folded her wings and stooped, plummeting toward her prey. Åsa could almost feel the pressure of the wind rushing by her face, then the stomach-dropping jerk as Stormrider swung upright and threw out her wings to brake as she struck the duck, knocking it sideways in a flurry of feathers. The strike was slightly off, and the duck squawked, flapping away.

The duck winged over the meadow, Stormrider in pursuit. Åsa spurred her horse after them. Hoofbeats sounded close behind, and she glanced back to see Olaf following.

They galloped across the open land, Åsa whistling for her bird. The silvery jingle of the peregrine's bells led them to a copse where Stormrider struggled with the injured duck. Finally she managed to get her notched beak around her prey's neck and broke it with a snap. She began to tear at the duck's throat, her beak bloody.

Åsa dismounted and approached Stormrider with a tempting bit of quail meat to lure the falcon from its kill. The raptor cocked its head up to catch her gaze, and the recognition in the golden eye sent a shiver up Åsa's spine.

Murmuring endearments, she set the falcon on her glove, tying off the jesses and pulling the leather hood gently over the bird's head. She looked up to see Olaf smiling down on her, and again she felt a stirring in her chest.

"Well done," shouted Gyrd, riding up and bagging the duck.

They hunted until late afternoon, arriving home with a dozen ducks for the kitchen staff. Åsa gave the meal's preparations a harried glance.

"You'd better hurry," said Toki. "Brenna's in a fine rage."

Åsa rushed to her chamber, where Brenna brandished a comb with pursed lips. The fóstra gave a little shriek when she saw Åsa's state. Her hair had come out of its braid and was snarled with branches and leaves, her arms and legs were scratched and bleeding, and she smelled of horse sweat and falcon droppings.

"Strip off those rags," Brenna commanded. Åsa shrugged out of her hunting clothes and submitted to Brenna's brisk ministrations.

The staff seemed to have managed quite well without Åsa's presence. The evening was an even greater success than the previous night. Keen from a day of hunting, the visitors greeted the food with enthusiasm. From the high seat beside her father, Åsa listened to Olaf and her brother recount the day's hunt. As Olaf laughed at something Gyrd said, she felt a pang at their comradery. But then Olaf's eyes strayed to her.

She was glad that, thanks to Brenna's torture, her hair gleamed, the gown's long sleeves covered her scratched arms, the dirt was scrubbed from under her fingernails, and she smelled of soap instead of sweat. For the first time, she took pleasure in looking her best.

Knut, backed by the entire company, urged Olaf to give another performance. He had not imbibed quite so much tonight, and he rose stiffly to take the floor. Åsa sat on the edge of her seat as he stammered the first lines. But soon he shed his nervousness and his spellbinding voice took over. He had chosen the tale of the star-crossed lovers, Sigurd and Brunhild. When Olaf spoke of the shield-maiden, his gaze strayed to Åsa and a little flutter stirred in her belly.

When the story ended to thunderous applause, Olaf took his seat beside her and drank gratefully from the horn she offered him.

"Thanks," he said.

"You're welcome. You were wonderful, again."

He flushed and kept his gaze on the drinking horn.

"They must love you in Borre."

He said nothing.

"I envy them, getting to hear you speak all the time," she went on. Then she noticed that he was silent, staring into his mead.

His eyes flicked up to hers. "I don't speak at home."

"But you're as good as Knut."

"My father doesn't like it."

"He what?"

"He doesn't like it when I speak. He thinks it's unmanly."

"Does he think Knut is unmanly?" she demanded indignantly.

"No, of course not. Just when I do it."

Åsa could see that she had embarrassed him and quickly stopped speaking. She was grateful when Gyrd came to her rescue and took control of the conversation. In a few moments, he had the three of them laughing. Olaf's eyes sparkled, and he met her gaze with smiles once more.

Åsa floated to her bower. Brenna beamed as she helped her out of the fine gown and packed it carefully away in its chest. "Your father was very proud of you tonight," she said.

Åsa hardly heard the praise. Her mind was filled with Olaf.

There was a tap on the door, and Gyrd sauntered in.

"Sister, I think you have your eye on this handsome young lord from Borre," he said.

"Don't be silly," said Åsa. She was glad the room was lit only by the fire so her brother couldn't see her blush. "I treated him with the honor due any guest of our father's."

"I know you better than that, Åsa," Gyrd teased. "You never took your eyes off him. When he recited 'The Lay of Völund,' I thought you would swoon." Åsa glared at him, and he hurried to add, "And I think you have good taste in men."

Åsa ducked her head. "He's a very nice young man."

"A very nice young man," Gyrd agreed. "Intelligent and well educated. And I think he is here to ask Father for your hand."

Åsa stared at him. "Do you really think so?"

"What better motive could a young king's son have for visiting our humble kingdom?" said Gyrd, taking her hand. "I think he'd make a very good brother-in-law. A poet. A learned man. Our kingdom would be allied with Borre, and the jarls in Vestfold and the Uplands." He looked at her slyly. "And the children would be very pretty with such good-looking parents."

Åsa kept her eyes fixed on the fire as she turned a fine shade of red.

"Well," said Gyrd, "I think you should accept his proposal."

Panic rose in her. "But who will be mistress of Tromøy? I can't leave you and Father."

"Don't worry about us. Father could marry again," said Gyrd.

"He's old! Who would marry him?" Åsa blurted.

Gyrd laughed. "I expect there might be a few women who would be willing to become mistress of Tromøy and queen of East Agder, even if she had to marry an old man like Father. Of course, I could look for a wife myself. Olaf and I are near in age. If his father is ready to let him marry, why not me? Father would have to agree. I can think of a girl or two…"

"I don't want to marry," Åsa said. "I want to be a shield-maiden and fight beside you and Father."

"What is the matter with you?" Gyrd said. "You must marry. This would be a good match, perhaps the best offer you will ever get. An alliance with Borre would benefit us greatly. I have no doubt that Olaf would be good to you. You would be mistress of a great hall. And when the old king dies, which can't be too long, you would become the queen of the most powerful kingdom in the land. Gudrød is king over most of Vestfold, the Uplands too. All he has to do is throw the Danes out of Skiringssal and he would have all of Vestfold. You'd have riches we can only dream of here in Agder."

When Åsa said nothing, Gyrd sighed.

"Sleep now. You may feel differently in the morning. Good night, sister." He kissed her forehead and departed.

Åsa lay awake long into the night, thinking of her mother. Her father had taken Gunnhild in a raid in Lista and made her his queen. Until Åsa was twelve, they had shared this room. Now all she had left of her mother were those things she had inherited: the amber necklace and finely woven wool dyed in jewel colors.

If her mother had lived, Åsa and Gyrd would have been fostered out to a jarl's household, but after Queen Gunnhild's death, Harald had kept his children close. In the three years since her mother's death, Åsa had kept busy filling the void, learning as fast as she could from whomever she could.

Åsa had been barely twelve, but that was old enough to be present in the birthing chamber and learn what she could of the ways of childbearing. She couldn't forget what she learned from that grim, bloody childbed.

They had never been able to speak of that day. She'd staggered from that awful room, covered in her mother's blood. Gyrd, still a boy himself, sobbed in the shadows. Her father, looking white and somehow shrunken on his high seat, had silently handed her the ring of keys to the great hall. Without a word, she'd hung them on her belt.

When she thought of leaving Tromøy for a strange new kingdom, her stomach churned. She knew every tree, every brook, every person and animal on the island. They were as much a part of her as her own eyes, her own heart. How could she ever leave? Borre was so far. When would she ever see her father and brother again? Her stomach burned at the thought of some other woman ruling her beloved island in her place.

Yet when she closed her eyes, she saw Olaf's smile, his gentle eyes. She imagined what it would be like to touch him, to thread her fingers through his long blond hair, to kiss him.

But that led to childbirth and pain and blood. The thought jolted her out of her romantic reverie. She did not want to become a wife or a mother, trapped in a house, endlessly pregnant, with death looming at the end. If she were lucky, she would have a few years with her children until she died or they did. And always another pregnancy swallowing up the future. Better she stay a maiden, and die a clean death on the battlefield with her father and her brother.

Åsa tossed in her bed. The goose down bunched under the ticking like fists.

No man could understand. She needed a woman's counsel. She needed her mother.

She grabbed her shawl and walked barefoot into the summer night. Hurrying through the fields, she waved to the sentries, who were all accustomed to her nighttime wanderings. The dew-laden barley stalks chilled her bare legs, a soft breeze rustled the trees.

Queen Gunnhild's burial mound presided over the steading. Åsa climbed the grassy hill as she had so many times. Perched at the crest, she looked back over the dark hulk of the timbered hall.

In the moonlight, she made out the turf roofs of the granaries and smithy, and the byres where the cows and goats wintered. Beyond, the fields flowed down to a sea that shimmered like steel beneath the moon.

Åsa lay on her back in the cool, damp grass, pressing her body into the mound. Far below lay her mother, buried with the baby who killed her. They lay together in the timber burial chamber, tucked into her mother's bed made up with down-filled linen, surrounded by treasures. Åsa remembered her father performing the rites of death. In a grief-fueled killing frenzy, he'd sacrificed his favorite horses and two dogs along with mixed livestock to accompany his wife and child into the afterlife.

When the ceremonies were complete, men assembled early with shovels, ready to close the mound. Åsa had stumbled away from the raw new hill that loomed over everything, wandering blindly through fields ablaze with wildflowers. She had ripped flowers out of the ground until she was exhausted. Her father, still splattered with gore, had found her clutching a ragged bouquet. He led her back and helped her climb onto the platform that was nearly engulfed by the mound. Sunlight streamed through the opening of the burial chamber, lighting her mother's face on the pillow. Åsa rushed to her side, but the dank smell of death overwhelmed the space. She thrust the flowers into her mother's hand and fled.

Now she looked up at the stars. They seemed to hang very close in the luminous sky. "Mother, I don't know what to do," she whispered. "I am so afraid. I want to do right, but I don't want to suffer as you did. I don't want to die."

She remembered a song her mother taught her when she was very young, a vardlokkur, in words humans could not understand. It was a song to call the dísir, the loving spirits of the dead. When women died, sometimes their spirits remained close to earth to watch over their families and help them in troubled times.

Closing her eyes, she imagined the warm breeze was her mother's soothing hand. It seemed as if she could hear soft voices on the wind speaking in the words of the vardlokkur. If she just concentrated a little harder, she would make out the words.

Focusing all of her attention on the voices, she followed them into the spirit world.

CHAPTER 3

The early sun poked Åsa awake. Cold and stiff, she pulled her shawl around her and staggered off the mound to the well. She drew a bucket of icy water and splashed her face until the blood returned to her head. Brenna found her there, face raised to the sun.

"Lady, your father and your guest are waiting." She pursed her lips. "Come, let me see what I can do with you."

Brenna led her back to her bower, where she combed out the rat's nest of red-gold hair and marshaled it into a knot. Shaking out a blue linen overdress, she brought it over Åsa's head. Brenna frowned at her foster daughter's bloodshot eyes.

"There's no time," she said. "You will have to do. Go."

Åsa hurried to the great hall where her father presided from his high seat. Olaf stood before him, clutching a carved wooden box. His blond lashes were lowered, resting on ashen cheeks.

Her father cleared his throat. "Åsa," he said, "young Olaf here has something he wishes to say to you."

Åsa turned to the Olaf, fighting panic mixed with an odd flutter of excitement. *You can do this.* She steeled herself to recite the prescribed acceptance in a suitably modest fashion.

Olaf knelt and held up the carved box, opening the lid. Gold glinted in a nest of wool. The bride price.

A shock jolted through her. *This is really happening.* Her chest squeezed and she wanted to run.

Then her eyes met Olaf's, and her panic drained away.

"Lady Åsa, your father has given me permission to present this offer to you," he began in a faint voice.

Her heart went out to him. He was so shy and gentle. She wanted to wrap her arms around him. Maybe it would be worth it—the pain, the fear. Other women thought it was. Perhaps she could bear it, for someone like Olaf.

"As you know, my mother died last year. Our kingdom has been without a queen," he went on. "The völva Heid has been performing the sacrifices and ceremonies, but she has duties elsewhere. We need someone to look after the household."

His approach was more practical than she had expected. Still, perhaps he had been schooled in what to say, to lay it out before her.

"My father has sent me to ask for your hand," he said. Åsa felt a flush beginning in her cheeks. "He offers this gold arm ring as bride price. He wishes to make you his queen."

Åsa stared down at Olaf. Acid rose in her belly as she struggled to grasp what he was saying. His *father* wished to marry her. An old man, as old as her own father. Not this beautiful, gentle boy but a brutal old king. He'd already put one wife in the grave, and he wanted her to be the next.

"No!" she cried. "I won't marry that old man." She saw the color drain from Olaf's face. She glanced wildly at her father, whose mouth was open as he rose from his chair. "I won't do it," she blurted, backing away. Olaf stood there, holding the oaken chest. Her father drew a great breath and took a step toward her.

She turned and bolted from the hall.

Åsa ran straight to her tree and vaulted into the branches.

Through stinging tears, she stared out over the sea. She wished Olaf had never come to Tromøy.

She watched her father's húskarlar escort the visitors to their longship and launch it into the sea. The oars ran out, pulling the vessel from the surf's grasp, then the sail flared. The ship dwindled into the distance, tacked north, and vanished behind an island.

She couldn't face her father after what she'd done. She would stay up here until everyone had forgotten about her, and then, tonight, run away. She'd take her arms and armor and travel the land, finding service with another king like the shield-maidens in the sagas.

Pins and needles crept up her legs. It was almost a relief when she spotted Gyrd coming across the field. Although she stayed motionless behind her cloak of leaves, he knew she was here.

"Well, you caused quite a drama," he said as he climbed up beside her.

"Is Father furious?" she asked.

"I can't imagine that he's happy," he replied, settling comfortably against the trunk. "You left him in a very awkward position."

"I know. I felt very wrong, but I just can't do it." She wished she could explain to her brother the dread and panic that boiled inside her.

Gyrd whistled. "You made that abundantly clear. Poor Olaf was truly shocked. I wouldn't like to be him, going back to tell his father that he had failed in his mission."

Åsa stared at Gyrd in horror. "What will happen to him?"

"Olaf is Gudrød's only heir, so I doubt he'll do him any permanent harm. But he won't be easy on him either. I can just about imagine what Father would do to me. Now, come home."

"I can't," said Åsa. "I've ruined everything. I have to leave home. I have to run away and take up the shield."

"Åsa, if you were to leave, you would hurt Father far more

than you already have. And you would hurt me too." He put his arm around her. "It will all be all right."

"Really?"

"Yes, really. It's not Ragnarök. The world won't end just because one girl refused an ancient, ugly king."

Åsa rested her head on his shoulder, and the two of them sat while the evening sounds rose up around them.

"Come on, you can't stay up here all night. Brenna will roast my tail." Gyrd gave her a nudge. "Don't worry, I'll stick by you until things blow over with Father."

Åsa looked at her brother gratefully. "Thank you, Gyrd. I don't know what I'd do without you."

"Well, it looks like you won't have to find out for a while," he said. "Come on, now." He climbed down from the tree, gently pulling her with him, and caught her as they reached the ground. Together, they walked back to the great hall.

Åsa went straight to her bower and to bed where she tossed and turned, feeling guilty for disappointing her father. But she knew in her heart she had done the only thing she could. She could not force herself to give her life to an old man she had never met.

IN THE MORNING, Åsa dragged herself from her bed and fastened the house keys to her belt. She supervised the breakfast and saw to the rest of the day's provisions, ignoring the curious stares of the servants. At midmorning, she led a cleaning party to the great hall. The daylight glared on the remains of the feast. Mead-stained cups stood on the trestles, spilled over onto the benches, and congregated in the corners. Scraps of leftover bread and vegetables that the dogs had missed were strewn over the rush-covered floor. Gathering up the cups, she set women to scrubbing the boards before the men hoisted the trestles into the rafters. Women and children swept the old rushes out to the hogpen where the pigs would pick through the fodder for scraps and bed in the rushes.

A shadow blocked the light from the door. She looked up to see her father and quickly lowered her gaze.

"Åsa," he said. "We need to talk."

"I'm sorry, Father," Åsa began, but he held up his hand to silence her.

"Walk with me, child."

Without a word, she followed him.

It was to her mother's mound they both went when in need of comfort, and they wandered there together now. Åsa followed her father, ascending the grassy hill in silence. At the top, he stopped and gazed out over the steading to the sea. The wind ruffled his hair, blowing the grass and wildflowers flat.

"Gudrød and I were great friends when we were young," he said. "Together, we went raiding and trading every summer until we each married. He was with me when we took your mother."

"Yes." Åsa knew by heart the famous story of her father and Gudrød's younger days of raiding together. "She was the daughter of the lord of Lista, south of Agder. You took her from her father's hall, along with great treasure."

Her father nodded absently, staring off in to the distance. "There is more I must tell you," he said at last. He looked at her and sighed.

"What you don't know is that Gudrød claimed her first. To Gudrød, she was just a prize, but to me...we loved each other. I tried to buy her. I offered him everything I had, but he refused." Her father paused again, remembering. "So I took her. We sailed away in the night. I left behind my share of the booty we had taken in the season's raids, hoping it would be enough to satisfy him, but Gudrød never took defiance well.

"For a long time, your mother and I lived in fear that Gudrød would come for revenge, but the years passed and he didn't come." He smiled. "Your brother was born, then you. Everything I have done in this kingdom, I did for her. For your mother's sake, I gave up raiding. We were not rich, but we had many years of happiness.

"Being queen of Borre is no small thing. You would have wealth and power you could only dream of. I am proud of you for refusing his offer. I couldn't imagine you with that old brute. I wouldn't let him have your mother, and he can't have you either."

Åsa threw her arms around her father and felt safe in the strong circle of his embrace.

CHAPTER 4

Borre

The longship cut through the sparkling chop, leaving Tromøy far behind. Olaf's dread grew with every mile under the keel. His mission had been a complete failure, a humiliation that brought shame on him and his father. He could not understand how it had come about. King Harald had been a generous host, while Gyrd had confided his hopes and dreams like a brother. And Åsa. When he closed his eyes, he still saw the red-gold braid tumbling from her helmet, his first glimpse into those startling blue eyes.

Now reality crashed in. He had failed his father once again. What had he done wrong? Had he not presented the offer correctly? When she ran from the room, he'd been shocked. King Harald had seemed shocked too. He stood there for a long time, staring after his daughter.

"I'm sorry, boy," he'd said. "When Åsa makes up her mind, that's the end of it. You'd best go pack."

29

Gyrd had met him outside. "What happened? My sister ran out of here like a hunted deer."

Olaf had been too ashamed to say anything. He'd continued to the guesthouse, leaving Gyrd mystified.

King Harald had met him on the beach, and seen him off in silence. Olaf's crew caught his mood and plied their oars without their usual banter. The wind on the coast was fair. They raised sail and made good time on a passage Olaf wished would never end.

He understood that Åsa didn't want to leave the place she'd known all of her life, the people who'd raised her, her family. He sympathized with her fear of traveling far from home to wed a man she'd never met.

But Gudrød wouldn't understand. Father was never pleased when something thwarted his will. Olaf quailed at the thought of his father's rage, shortly to be directed at him.

When they made camp on a deserted beach that night Olaf kept to himself. He slept fitfully in his sheepskin sleeping bag, imagining the crew's scorn at his failure, a precursor to what he would face at home.

The gray morning dawned, with a chill wind that hurried their passage up the coast. By noon, the massive burial mounds loomed, dominating Borre's shoreline. The biggest hill contained Olaf's grandfather, Halfdan, interred in his longship to watch over his hereditary lands through eternity. Near the patriarch's mound rose a smaller hill, where Olaf's mother, Alfhild, lay. It was a year ago that he had kissed her icy cheek and watched the only person who had ever understood him vanish under tons of earth.

Beyond Alfhild's hill stood three lesser mounds. Two contained the remains of his father's brothers with their horses and gear. The third mound was empty, raised as a memorial to kin lost at sea.

The helmsman laid the ship alongside the north seawall.

Lacking a natural harbor, Borre's fleet sheltered in the arms of two man-made stone jetties. Olaf stepped carefully onto the massive stones, planting his boots solidly on the wet surfaces. He could not be seen to slip when disembarking.

He trudged up the trail beneath the shadow of the mounds as if he carried one of the jetty's big stones in his stomach. The timbers of Borre's great hall rose dark amid the trees. From the gables of the broad roof, carved dragons' heads jutted to challenge the four directions.

Olaf passed the practice yard, which was bounded by a fence of hazel branches. The highborn youths of Borre were hard at their wrestling throws. Keeping his face impassive, Olaf cringed inwardly under his half brother's jealous stare. Although Hrolf was not a legitimate son, he was Gudrød's kind of boy. Time after time, Olaf had fought off Hrolf's challenges with sword and axe, besting him in contests of wrestling, swimming, and horseracing. But somehow Hrolf's rough manners and careless words pleased Gudrød in ways Olaf feared he never would. Olaf's edge over Hrolf was a precarious one. It was not unheard of for a king to make a bastard son his heir.

He reached the great hall and stopped at the door to prepare himself, his hand tracing the writhing serpents carved into the oak. He took a breath, pushed open the massive door, and stepped across the threshold, pausing again in the entryway while his eyes adjusted to the gloom.

Within, Gudrød waited on his high seat before the fire, a cup of mead in his hand. Beside him sat the völva Heid, the great sorceress and priestess of Freyja. A woman of forty winters, her riot of bronze hair was now threaded with silver. Some terrible accident in her youth had hunched and twisted her back, yet she moved with a determined vigor.

Heid had been summoned during Alfhild's illness, but her spells had failed to save the queen. The völva and her entourage had stayed on after Alfhild died. She now performed the rituals and sacrifices that were the queen's duty and spent her time by Gudrød's side.

Gathering his courage, Olaf approached the high seat. His father's eyes, cold as agates, fixed on him from beneath shaggy straw-colored brows.

"Well, boy, where is my bride?"

Olaf couldn't meet his father's eyes. "She refused." He choked on the words.

"What's that?" bellowed Gudrød. "Speak up, boy."

The völva, whose ears missed nothing, narrowed her eyes.

"She has refused your offer," she announced.

A flush began to creep up Gudrød's neck. His eyes snapped.

"You idiot," Gudrød shouted, leaning forward to aim a cuff, which Olaf dodged expertly without looking up from the floor. "You should never have allowed her to speak. That's what comes of entrusting you with anything. You're just like your grandfather."

Face now a deep shade of red, Gudrød drew a threatening breath. Olaf kept his eyes fixed on the ground. He knew better than to interrupt.

Gudrød was just getting started. "He let those Danes just move in, take our hall at Skiringssal. The Danes established a trading port right on our doorstep, and he did nothing. He demanded no tax. Took no action. He was a coward, just like you." Gudrød slammed his fist onto the arm of his chair.

Head down, Olaf absorbed the familiar accusations like blows.

"Halfdan the Mild, they called him. When I married your mother, I didn't break his mound to get his sword for you, and you don't bear his name. I didn't want my son to take after that old coward, but you did anyway!" Gudrød glared at Olaf. "Thanks to your grandfather, the Danes now hold the land where our great forefathers raised their mounds. *They* are all buried at Skiringssal."

Olaf risked a glance at his father, sensing the rant was near its end. "That's why old Redbeard thinks he can turn down my offer. He thinks I won't take action against this insult. He thinks I'm like my father." Gudrød leaped to his feet. "Well, I'm not mild. Bring me my sword!"

"Hush, you fool," said Heid harshly. "You've already made a mess of things. Let me handle this. I will pay a visit to Tromøy and bring the girl back."

"What makes you think you will succeed?" Gudrød sneered.

Heid returned his look with disdain. "My vision was clear when I went under the cloak. What I saw there will come to pass."

"It had better," Gudrød growled, returning to his mead.

The sorceress hoisted herself out of her chair, wrapping gnarled fingers around her brassbound staff. "Leave this to me," she said haughtily, and called for her thralls. "Ready my ship. Gather my acolytes, we sail for Tromøy."

THE GREAT HALL of Borre bustled with preparations for the voyage.

The völva gathered her retinue, the sacred number of nine maidens. Under Heid's critical eye, the young women packed her herbs and magical tools into a chest that the völva locked with an iron key. Pocketing the key, she hobbled after the thralls as they carried the chest to her wagon. Lavishly carved and painted, each panel of the cart portrayed a magical scene from the legends, the four corners guarded by the likeness of a fierce warrior carved in oak. The bed of the cart was removable, lashed to the wheelbase with leather ropes.

Two of the biggest thralls wrestled Heid's chair of prophecy into a farm cart. Painted with runespells, the völva's seat was believed to have magical properties. Likewise, slaves had disassembled the völva's traveling bed and loaded it along with her down mattress, cushions, and piles of fur. Another cart carried tents, cooking gear, and provisions for the two-day journey.

Harness bells chimed while thralls struggled to hitch up Heid's two matching white horses. When all was finally ready, her acolytes crowded around the sorceress to help her into her cart.

"Have a care, you idiots, I'm not made of wood." She slapped their hands away. "No! Leave me. I said, leave me be." Grimacing, she hoisted herself into the cart. She picked up the reins impatiently while an apprentice tucked a blanket around her knees.

At last, she set off, her entourage falling into line behind the cart. Their voices rose in song as Heid drove down to her ship.

Named for the goddess Heid served, *Freyja* was a karvi, a class of small, fast longship crewed by thirty warriors and a helmsman. Red and blue paint picked out the entwined beasts carved along the length of the vessel's graceful stem, which terminated in a serpent's coil.

The sorceress lowered herself down stiffly from her cart into her apprentices' arms. She fretted and scolded as they bundled her onto the ship, wrapped her in furs, and settled her on down-filled cushions. Thralls dismantled the cart for loading and coaxed the skittish horses onto the boarding plank. At last, everything was on board. The rowers ran out their oars and the helmsman shoved off. The acolytes raised their voices in song.

By midday, cat's-paws dappled the water, and a following breeze filled in. The crew shipped their oars and hoisted the sail. Catching hold of the dangling lines, they brought the vast woolen square into trim. *Freyja* surged through the sparkling seas as the young women took up their song once again.

Near sunset, the völva instructed the crew to beach the ship in a cove she favored. They feasted around a roaring bonfire, making merry late into the evening while thralls set up camp. One man was sent ahead in a small boat, rowing through the night to alert Tromøy of the völva's impending arrival.

CHAPTER 5

Tromøy

C lad in her chain-mail brynja, Åsa grabbed her wooden practice sword and ran to meet Gyrd in the yard. Jarl Borg stood waiting to supervise.

Åsa flew at Gyrd full force, shield down and sword slashing. When Gyrd pulled his blade back just before it bit into her, she ducked under his guard and let him have a vicious whack with the flat of her sword.

"You don't play fair," Gyrd complained, nursing his bruised rib.

Jarl Borg could not quite stifle his grin.

"Huh! I need every advantage I can get against a big brute like you," Åsa retorted.

Jarl Borg turned away, his shoulders shaking.

"You are a demon, not a girl."

"That's how it appears to a man who wears a large-size shirt and a tiny little hat." Åsa grinned, nimbly eluding her brother's swat.

Gyrd frowned. "You're getting too old to play at being a boy. You're a king's daughter, it's time you acted like one."

"Make me," Åsa said. "I can dress like I always have and still run the hall. Just because I wear the storeroom keys on my belt doesn't mean I have to give up all the fun. I'm not going to sit inside embroidering for the rest of my life. I'm going to be a shield-maiden."

"Shield-maiden!" Gyrd said. "There are no shield-maidens. Those are just stories."

"How would you know?" Åsa said. "You've never been anywhere."

The look on her brother's face stopped her short.

"It's not my fault father's a coward," Gyrd blurted. Åsa gasped.

Jarl Borg fetched him a cuff on the head. "What's that you say, boy?" the big warrior bellowed. "Your father is not a coward, and if I ever hear you say such a thing again, I'll cut off your ears."

Red-faced, Gyrd drew his sword. Jarl Borg's shield was already there to meet it. Steel clashed on wood, and they glared at each other over their shields.

"He never raids," Gyrd cried. "By my age, other boys have been out a-viking a dozen times. I've never been on a single raid. If he wants to sit at home shoveling pig shit, he could at least have fostered me to some jarl who would show me some action."

Jarl Borg shoved him aside with his shield. "You puppy, you don't know anything."

The old warrior turned his back and stalked out of the practice yard.

Åsa's cheeks burned under her helm. Why had she blurted the words she knew would cause her brother the most humiliation? He was sixteen years old and still without battle experience. He was falling behind the other highborn boys his age, and he was worried about his future. Who would follow a king who had never been on a raid? No matter how much he practiced with his father's jarls and house guard, it did not make up for being in a real battle. Why did she have to point it out?

Outside the hall, she heard the lookout shout.

Åsa scanned the shoreline and spotted the rower pulling the small boat up on the beach. She ran down the trail to meet him, the lookout hard on her heels.

"Lady," the messenger gasped with a low bow, "I have rowed through the night with news of the völva Heid. She is on her way here, and expects to arrive this evening."

Åsa caught her breath. The völva's visit was a great honor and an important event. Heid made a regular progress through the land every few years, and the last time she'd visited Tromøy, Åsa's mother had still been alive. Åsa vividly remembered the aura of glamour that clung to the sorceress and her followers, and how she had dreamed of running off to become one of them.

It was true that the little island was remote, and there had been no noble marriages or births. Perhaps it was just time for a visit?

A tiny knot of worry niggled in Åsa's stomach. Olaf had mentioned that Heid had been staying in Borre since his mother's death.

The messenger was still recovering his breath. "The völva asks you to erect the seidr platform, and prepare a meal for her and her retinue."

Åsa had assisted her mother in the preparations for the völva before, and she remembered the ceremony well. This would be the first time that she had been in charge, and she was determined to do everything properly.

She brought the messenger into the hall for some food and a well-deserved rest, then went to inform her father. Harald raised his eyebrows but said nothing, setting men to erect the seidr platform in the hall while Åsa directed the household staff in preparing the sacred meal the sorceress required. Observing the proper ceremony, Harald and Gyrd killed a boar, sacred to the goddess Freyja, and brought its heart to Åsa.

She took the gory organ and set it to seethe in a cauldron over an outdoor fire, singing softly to the land spirits to alert them to the upcoming ceremony, and silently entreating them to gain the völva's favor.

Circling the cauldron three times in a sunwise direction, she added each of the sacred ingredients. The magical stew simmered for hours while Åsa returned to stir it regularly, picking up her chant. While the stew cooked, the boar's meat roasted on spits over another fire.

The knot of worry tugged at Åsa's stomach.

Late in the afternoon, the lookout sighted the völva's longship. Gyrd led a contingent of farmhands to help the ship's crew unload while Brenna dragged Åsa to the bower to fuss over her hair and coax her into a good dress. By the time Brenna let Åsa go, the sorceress had boarded her cart and gathered her retinue. The völva shook the reins, and the procession set off up the hill.

Mindful of her good dress, Åsa watched from the doorway, transfixed by the beautiful young women who walked before the cart strewing flowers in the völva's path. Their soft singing drifted up the hillside, accompanied by the horses' silvery bells. In brilliantly dyed dresses, the girls glowed like jewels in a precious necklace strung along the trail.

As the völva's cart drew up to the hall, King Harald, freshly bathed and robed, stepped forward to hand her down. Heid descended and preceded him into the hall, her dark cloak flashing with gems. She carried a distaff made of iron and set with gemstones. From her belt dangled a leather pouch rumored to contain her witch's tools: poison herbs, owl droppings, magic runes, bones of the unborn, teeth of her enemies, and the gold of the dead.

King Harald led her to the place of honor across the longfire from his own high seat. From her lofty chair, she scrutinized the folk of Tromøy, who stood frozen, awed to silence.

"I have come here because of a vision that concerns those who dwell here," she declared, her voice resonating in the hall. "Tonight I will consult with the spirits of this place, and tomorrow I will prophesy."

Åsa carefully carried in the sacred boar's heart and placed it on the board before the sorceress. While the apprentices sang softly in the background, the völva tasted the heart, eyes closed in concentration as if to hear what it had to tell her. She drank only water. Åsa watched nervously, trying to discern the sorceress's reaction to the dish. Had it turned out right? Why had she come to Tromøy? What would the spirits have to say?

At length, the sorceress looked up and nodded, conveying her approval and permission for her entourage to be seated. The apprentices filled the benches alongside Tromøy's húskarlar. Ale and mead flowed with the poetry and song.

Åsa and Gyrd knew most of the young people from past visits. They brought news and gossip of the countryside, and told enthralling tales of magic and adventure. Heid's followers were the best and brightest daughters of the land, chosen for their intelligence and deep-mindedness. Their life was a coveted one of rigorous training and constant travel. Those who could look into the future and consult with the gods held rank equal to the nobility, of whom many of them were born. Some of the girls would go on to become sorceresses themselves, others would marry well. Women trained by the völva were much in demand as wives in lordly houses. The mother of every house was responsible for the spells that protected their homes and families, and for the rituals and sacrifices to the gods that ensured prosperity and good fortune.

"Sit beside me, Astrid," Åsa called to a tall girl whose long brown hair was done in a fashionable knot at the back of her head. Astrid had fostered at Tromøy until Queen Gunnhild's death, and the girls had been close as sisters once.

"May I join you?" Gyrd appeared, sliding onto the bench beside Astrid.

"By all means." Astrid smiled as she moved over to make room for him.

Soon Gyrd and Astrid were completely absorbed in each other. Åsa watched as the couple laughed with their heads together, sharing a drinking horn. She wished Olaf were sitting here now, his head bent to hers the way Gyrd's was to Astrid's. Why couldn't he have been her suitor?

As the longfire burned low, the völva laid down her fork and clapped her hands. At once her nine apprentices put down their cups and rose. Gripping her staff, the sorceress levered herself up. She descended from the high seat and hobbled out of the hall, her retinue filing out behind her.

They made their way to the burial mounds, where they would perform sacred rituals until dawn, calling upon those not of this world to help the völva see the future. From the doorway, Åsa and Gyrd watched them disappear into the mist, listening to their voices rising softly as they called to the spirits.

IN THE MORNING, the women of Tromøy gathered in the hall with the sorceress's apprentices to ring the seidr platform. The men took their places in a circle around the women. The völva entered, staff in hand, jewels flashing. A girl hurried to help her mount the dais and settle her on her chair of prophecy. Another apprentice beat a hypnotic rhythm on a skin drum as the women crossed their arms in front and raised their voices in the vard-lokkur, the spirit-summoning songs they had all learned in child-hood. The men raised their arms to the heavens and swayed with the haunting, otherworldly songs of ancient words whose meanings had long been lost. The words were not easy to follow, spells in the language of the álfir, ancient magic passed down from mentor to apprentice through the generations. Each participant sounded the chant, merging into a single voice that resonated in the hall.

As the vardlokkur came to a close, the völva spread her arms, raised her eyes to the ceiling, and declared, "Let them come who wish to come, let them go who wish to go, and do no harm to me or mine."

Casting a seed of cannabis into the flames of the small brazier, she inhaled the smoke deeply and fell instantly into a seidr trance, eyes rolling back to reveal the whites, head lolling to the side. Then, as though gripped from above, she sat straight up and spoke in an unearthly voice.

"The daughter of this house has a proud destiny in the web of fate. She was born to be a peace-weaver, the mother of great kings," she intoned. "But she has disturbed the web with her will-fulness and disobedience. She has angered the Norns." The völva paused and drew a deep breath in the silence.

"Great misfortune will come upon her house if she continues on her course." Heid's voice rose until it resonated in the rafters of the great hall. "She must restore the balance, and submit to the will of the gods."

Åsa gasped aloud. Tears of regret sprang into her eyes. She stepped forward to kneel before the völva and repent.

"That's enough!" cried King Harald, striding to the platform. The völva's eyes snapped open. Åsa caught her breath as utter silence fell in the hall.

"My daughter has made her decision, as is her right, and no one can gainsay her," Harald declared.

For a moment, Heid appeared to reel in confusion. Then she gripped the arms of her chair and drew a great breath.

"How dare you! How dare you interrupt the gods when they speak." She struggled to her feet, trembling with rage.

"Get out, you hag," Harald roared. "Get out of my hall."

"You will regret this, Harald Redbeard. You will pay." The sorceress glared around her. "You and all your house will pay."

Heid's apprentices rushed to help her as she stumbled down from the platform. The onlookers parted as the sorceress hobbled to the door, her body jerking with fury. Her acolytes fell in hastily behind her while her thralls scrambled to collect the magical paraphernalia.

At the threshold, the völva turned and struck the doorframe three times with her staff. She uttered what was undoubtedly a curse and was gone.

Everyone in the hall was stunned to silence, staring at each other in horror.

Harald was speechless with rage, his face turning from red to purple. Åsa overcame her shock and took his arm, trying to lead him to his seat.

He shook her off and shouted to Gyrd, "Follow her, make sure she does no more mischief." Gyrd gathered the warriors and rushed after the völva and her entourage.

Åsa stood by her father's side, afraid to utter a sound. She trembled at the thought of what she had brought down on her house with her willfulness. It was bad enough that the völva had paid them a special visit. To interrupt the sacred trance as her father had done was tantamount to challenging the gods. The insult was unthinkable. And the völva had cursed them.

Harald's color faded to an unnatural gray. He allowed Åsa to lead him to his chair, where he collapsed, breathing hard. Åsa hurried to get him a cup of small beer, which he drained and handed back to her with a shaky laugh.

"That old hag roused my temper as it has not been stirred in many years," he said faintly. He looked at Åsa's worried face and patted her hand. "Don't worry, child. Her curses are nonsense. They have no power against our swords."

In spite of her father's words, dread coiled deep in her stomach.

CHAPTER 6

Borre

Olaf forced himself to stride past the hazel branches marking the bounds of the practice yard where his half brother, Hrolf, waited. A dozen other youths loitered in the yard watching the rivals, but Olaf was acutely aware of his father seated beneath the great ash tree, flanked by the warriors of his hird.

He took a deep breath and advanced. With all his will, he brought his eyes up to meet Hrolf's mocking stare.

They took up their stances for wrestling. Leaning forward, they gripped each other's arms, waiting for the master-at-arms to blow the horn.

"So that girl sent you packing," Hrolf taunted. If it was meant to undermine Olaf's confidence, it was working. Olaf began to sweat. He knew that, any day, Hrolf might best him. Today could be that day. To win, Olaf must throw Hrolf to the ground while keeping to his own feet.

Hrolf was a year older than Olaf, not quite as tall, but he was the heavier of the two. He also possessed an arrogance that Olaf could never hope to match. So far, Olaf had held his own by the skin of his teeth. He could not afford to lose that edge now.

Determined to keep his face expressionless, Olaf shifted his gaze to stare over his half brother's shoulder. Meeting the eye of your opponent was not proper.

The horn sounded, and the two boys started circling sunwise, keeping their hold on the other's arms. Hrolf tried to hook his leg around Olaf's in the traditional tripping throw, but Olaf twisted out of the hold and brought his own leg around his half brother's. Hrolf managed to get out of the hold, and the two circled, jerking their legs up like two crows hopping.

After several feints, Hrolf's hook managed to take hold, and he jerked Olaf's leg out from under him. Olaf landed hard on his backside. He could not lose in front of his father. In desperation, he grabbed Hrolf's leg and yanked him to the ground. Olaf's move had changed the match from formal style to loose hand, a free-for-all version in which the first to regain his feet won the match. From the corner of his eye, he saw his father lean forward with interest.

They struggled in the dirt, trying to twist out of each other's grip. Hrolf jerked like a gaffed fish, but Olaf hung on desperately. He could feel the sweat collecting under his palms. Any minute, he would lose his grip. He had to be the first on his feet.

Then Hrolf gouged him in the eye, momentarily blinding him. Olaf could feel his half brother slip from his grasp. He lunged upward, clenching his arms around Hrolf's chest in a crushing bear hug, forcing his opponent to drag him along as he gained his feet. As he was pulled up, Olaf scuffled his feet in the dirt, scrambling for traction. Blinking furiously, his vision finally cleared enough for him to see that they were both standing again.

Still gripping his brother, Olaf snapped from the waist, shaking Hrolf like a rag. Hrolf pressed both thumbs into Olaf's

45

eye sockets. Olaf jerked his head back, but Hrolf hung on, applying pressure.

"That will be enough," roared the master-at-arms.

But Hrolf did not let up. Olaf realized his brother truly meant to blind him. He choked down panic and brought his hands up to gouge at Hrolf's eyes.

"Enough!" The master beckoned three burly trainers. The big men grabbed the brothers in bear hugs and held them as they glared and struggled to break free.

"You young fools! Never lose your temper," the old master admonished. "That's enough for today."

The trainers dragged the boys in two separate directions. Olaf blinked desperately, searching out his father. Gudrød had gotten to his feet, and his face looked toward Olaf, but he could not make out his father's expression.

"A ship!" came the cry from the lookout. "It's the völva."

Olaf's stomach tightened. She was far ahead of schedule. Heid must have driven her crew through the night to get here this soon. How had Åsa taken the sorceress's visit? Had she reconsidered Gudrød's offer? For her sake, he hoped so.

Even from the practice yard, Olaf could tell that things had not gone well. Heid slapped away the thralls that tried to help her off the ship. Without waiting for her cart to be assembled, she stormed up the hill, her followers scurrying in her wake. There were no songs or flowers this time. Olaf's stomach knotted as he thought of Heid's fury unleashed on Åsa.

The völva arrived, red in the face, breath rasping in her chest. She smote the ground with her staff.

"Damn the girl," she shouted. "And damn Harald Redbeard. He will regret this."

"So, you've failed too," said Gudrød with a snide grin. "Now it's time to let a man handle things."

"He insulted you, Gudrød," Heid spat. "He said you were too

old and feeble for a spirited young girl. He said he would not waste her on you."

A flush spread over Gudrød's face. This was not good. Panic snaked up Olaf's spine.

"Old, am I? Well, this wolf still has his teeth," he snarled. "Redbeard has been sitting down there on his island, laughing at me all these years. I'll make him wish he'd never betrayed me. Never made off with what was mine in the middle of the night like a coward. Now he's found the courage to defy me, thinking I'm too old to make red war." A grin spread over his face, making Olaf's stomach churn again.

"Hrolf," Gudrød shouted. Hrolf turned toward his father. "I wish to see my warriors assembled here, sooner rather than later."

"Yes, Father," said Hrolf. He flung a triumphant look at Olaf.

An hour later, Olaf was sitting in the hall in his place on the warriors' bench, awaiting his father's command. Gudrød ignored him, his attention on his mead cup.

Warriors began to arrive, taking their place on the benches. Hrolf blustered among them, giving orders that no one heeded. When the benches were filled, Gudrød rose. Hrolf snapped to attention at the head of the assembly.

"We raid Tromøy," Gudrød barked.

Hrolf raised a cheer that all the warriors joined. All but Olaf. A heavy weight settled in his stomach, pinning him to the bench.

"Crew all the ships," cried Gudrød. "I want a full force. Be ready to sail at dawn." He grinned. "We will attack under cover of night, before Redbeard knows what hit him."

With that, he called for food and ale. Slaves scurried in to serve the warriors on the benches. While the others feasted, Olaf stayed frozen in his seat like a wood carving. He had been an honored guest of King Harald, drunk their mead, eaten at their board. In Gyrd, he had found a kindred spirit, and Åsa filled his waking dreams. How could he now fall on them like a wolf and spill their blood? Yet it was what his father required.

When the slaves had cleared the remains of the feast and the fire burned low, Gudrød rose. "Hrolf, you will sail with me on *Dragonlord*." Hrolf threw a triumphant glance at Olaf, who sat in rising misery.

Gudrød turned on Olaf. "There's no place for a boy on this raid." His voice dripped with venom, like the poison drops on Loki's head. "I won't have your bad luck infecting mine. You stay home with the women and keep the fires burning."

Olaf's humiliation was complete. He didn't look up, but he could feel his rival's scornful grin. Yet his relief was greater than his shame. He thanked the gods that he would not make war on Tromøy.

That night, he lay uneasy on his bench, listening to Hrolf's boasts and the excited talk of battle.

Before first light, Gudrød's húskarlar loaded their sea chests with chain mail and helms, swords and axes, and lugged them down to the ships. Olaf sat alone in his seat. He rose and, pulling his cloak close around him, wandered into the predawn gloom.

Skirting the yard, he kept to the forest's shadows. He drew near to the harbor like a ghost from the mound, watching the warriors mount the dragons' heads on the ships' prows. Heid stood on the beach, leading her apprentices in a war chant.

"Let Harald Redbeard's blood redden his land. Let his hall be consumed by fire. Let this day's work be his end."

The air seemed to shimmer as the chanting stilled. Dread burned in Olaf's veins. He had failed his mission and now their blood was on his hands.

Dawn glimmered as the warriors racked their shields along the rails and took up their oars. Voices rose in rowing chants, filling the air with a foreboding rumble as Borre's fleet thrust out into the choppy seas and headed south, bearing on Tromøy.

CHAPTER 7

Tromøy

Åsa wondered if she would ever sleep again. Even though her father had sent Heid packing, she feared the völva's curse. After hours of tossing, she pulled on her breeks and shirt and ran barefoot into the summer night, to the one place on Tromøy where she was welcome at any hour—the forge.

Here it was always warm, and Åsa had spent many hours with Ulf. He had been blacksmith on Tromøy since before Åsa was born. Once a warrior, Ulf had been crippled, and so had turned to making weapons for others to use. He'd been with her father on the famous voyage to the eastern lands, where they survived the long river passage south and fought off the ferocious tribesmen who sought to sink their ships and rob them of their goods and their lives. Ulf had been captured in the southern lands and enslaved to a Serkland sword maker. The sword maker freely shared the secrets of his trade with his slaves, for he worked them all to death. It was he who had crippled Ulf's legs so that he could not escape.

But against all odds, Harald had rescued Ulf and brought him home, where he survived and healed to become the most skilled smith in the North.

Ulf was also said to be a wizard, like the legendary smith Völund, with knowledge of the runes and spells to enchant the weapons he made. He was famous for both his skills and his magic, and much honored by King Harald.

Ulf's old wounds kept him from sleeping much, and it seemed no matter what time of the day or night Åsa came, he was always awake and making something. Tonight she found him, as usual, working in the glow of the forge. His young apprentice sleepily trod the double foot bellows, pumping air through the blowhole in the soapstone slab that protected the bellows from shriveling in the fire. The stone was carved in the likeness of Loki, god of mischief, being punished for one of his many crimes.

Åsa's cheeks flushed in the blaze of the forge as she watched Ulf. It took many days of hard, careful work to make a sword.

Judging the temperature by the iron's red glow, he drew out the stack of hot metal bars and laid it on the anvil. Sparks hissed up and vanished into the darkness of the ceiling. He raised his hammer and struck the iron three blows. As the stack cooled and hardened, the blazing red dulled and the tone of the hammer blows changed. Then back went the iron into the fire until it glowed red again.

"Do you think I was wrong?" Åsa asked him. Of course he had heard about her refusal, and the völva's curse; everyone on the island knew by now.

Ulf looked at her seriously. Åsa loved him because he never treated her like a child.

"You have the right to make the choice," he said gravely. "Your heart spoke for you, and you must follow your heart."

"It will cause trouble for Father."

"Your father can handle a little trouble," he replied.

Ulf brought out a silver brooch in the shape of slender animals intertwined. "Do you know who this is for?"

Åsa smiled at him. "No," she said, although they had played this game many times before.

"It's for my favorite girl," said Ulf, pinning the silver brooch onto Åsa's wool cloak. "I made this for your wedding gift," he said. "But I think you need it now."

A horn sounded, then another. Åsa's heart beat hard in her chest as her eyes met Ulf's.

"Raiders!"

Ulf hefted his axe. He tossed her a sword and pushed her out the door.

Inside the hall, confusion reigned. Folk bustled about bearing armor and weapons, lighting lamps, stoking the red embers of the longfire. The carved timbers danced in the firelight. Loki leered out of the shadows while Odin's single eye gleamed.

"Arm yourselves," Harald commanded, striding through the hall. Short-legged Toki scurried in his wake, attempting to lace up the king's chain-mail brynja as he walked. Åsa handed off the extra sword she had brought to a warrior and joined Gyrd in donning chain mail and helm. She found Brenna waiting with her armor. Ducking into her brynja, she held still long enough for Brenna to set the helm on her head before seizing her sword and shield.

"Show no lights," Harald cautioned.

Heart pounding, Åsa followed Gyrd and their father outside where Jarl Borg already waited. "Here they come," he said, nodding at the trail.

In the darkness, a line of torches snaked up the path from the beach, their lights glinting on ring mail and helms. But for the sound of their footfalls and the clank of metal, they were eerily silent.

After years of training, a real raid, Åsa thought. Although they drilled regularly and were always prepared for trouble, no attacks had ever come. Harald Redbeard's reputation had kept raiders away. *I've always dreamed of my first battle, but I never thought that it would be here in my home.*

It was good that the sentry had spotted the enemy, Åsa thought with a shudder. She had heard tales of hall burnings. A favorite tactic of raiders was to set fire to a hall at night, trapping the occupants inside as they slept. The attackers would wait outside, slaughtering anyone who tried to escape the flames.

"We can see them by their torches, but they can't see us in the darkness," Harald said in a low voice. "We'll hit them with arrows before they get close enough to make us out."

Gyrd drew his sword and took his place beside Harald and Jarl Borg. Åsa stepped up beside him.

"Stay with Ulf," her father said to her. "You will not fight in the shield wall." Åsa felt the bite of disappointment, but she knew that during battle she must follow orders. Slinking back behind the front lines to join Ulf and the archers, she sheathed her sword and unslung her shield. She took up a bow and quiver of arrows and waited for the signal.

"Nock," Harald said in a hoarse whisper. Åsa fitted an arrow into her bow, nerves as taut as her bowstring.

"Draw." She drew back the string and held. It took real strength to hold the arrow at the ready. Åsa was proud that her arm never quivered.

"Loose!" her father cried. Aiming high, she let go her shaft with the others, sending invisible missiles hissing through the darkness.

Cries went up from the raiders as the arrows found their marks. Torches fell and smoldered in the wet grass. *Take that.* Elated, Åsa waited for her father's next command.

"Nock!" came the shout from the darkness below. "Draw!" There was whisper of bows. A dozen points of light sprang up in the darkness.

Flaming arrows.

"Loose!" From the enemy ranks, a flight of burning arrows pierced the night.

"Shields up!" Harald shouted. Åsa shouldered her bow and picked up her shield in one motion, locking it to Ulf's as they flung them overhead. Flaming arrows struck the wood with a *thwack*. A stray shot hit the cow-byre roof, and the dry thatch burst into flame, casting an eerie light. Panicked cows lowed and crashed against the walls of the burning shed.

The attackers halted a hundred yards from the hall, roaring and beating their weapons on their shields. Her father's húskarlar raised a war cry in answer. Blood surging, Åsa shouted with Tromøy's warriors as she clashed Lightning's hilt on her shield boss.

From the enemy ranks, a tall warrior stepped into the firelight, chain mail gleaming, helm picked out in silver. Tall enough to be Olaf. For an instant, Åsa's heart clutched in her chest. But as soon as he moved, she knew he was not Olaf. This man moved with more experience, more confidence. An older man.

"Gudrød," Ulf breathed.

The name seared through her like a firebrand. He was here for her. Åsa scanned the enemy ranks anxiously, but there was no other helm towering above the rest. Olaf was not there. A flood of relief washed through her.

Then Gudrød drew his sword.

"What in the name of Odin..." Ulf said softly, eyes riveted on the sword. It had a wicked, curving blade that bore a pattern of swirling dark and light bands. The steel shimmered like water in the firelight.

"The Serkland sword," Ulf muttered. "I wondered what happened to it."

Gudrød cried, "Form the Swine Horn!" His guard mustered to him, locking shields into a wedge formation designed to penetrate the enemy defenses.

"Shield wall!" bellowed Harald. Gyrd hoisted his shield and locked it to his father's. Harald's hird instantly locked their shields to form a barrier, each one overlapping the next. *Now is Gyrd's chance to prove himself,* Åsa thought. *The enemy will soon be wishing they could run back to their ships.* Her fingers twitched on Lightning's hilt.

Gudrød barked a command. Roaring, his wedge surged forward to charge Harald's shield wall. Over the thunder of feet, her father shouted for the house guard to brace for the impact. By the light of the burning thatch, the war bands clashed. The air rang with the crash of blades shattering wooden shields, the thud of spears, the cries of rage and pain.

Shield to shield, the two armies shoved each other. Åsa watched them use the familiar tricks she had learned in practice. Warriors hooked their axes on the top of the enemy's shield, then pulled down and thrust with a short sword. They slashed down low with their blades, under the shield wall, to catch unguarded calves and ankles. But this was not practice. Men screamed and fell. The air took on the taint of slaughter, of blood and entrails.

The shield walls disintegrated. In the chaos, warriors hacked with axes and thrust with swords. Metal clashed on wood, blade bit bone, battle cries mingled with shrieks.

Jarl Borg worked his sword and shield furiously, holding three men at bay. The old lord was breathing hard but kept his form. Gyrd, lithe and graceful as he slashed and whirled, crushed his opponents with powerful sword blows. *He is in his glory*, Åsa thought. She sighted her father's helm bobbing above the melee. Blood racing, she raised Lightning.

A few attackers broke through to the rear ranks, and at last Åsa had her chance to fight. Side by side with Ulf, she hacked at the enemy. Free of the restraints of practice, Lightning bit flesh and tasted blood for the first time. She whirled and bashed with sword and shield. *Like practice, only better.* Nimbly, she managed to get under a big man's guard when he threatened Ulf. She pricked his armpit with Lightning, then danced away as he rounded on her. Ulf struck him from the side with his axe, and the big man went down.

The battle glow warmed her blood as she eagerly sought the next opponent. She slashed a tall, thin man across the hamstring, and he went down with a satisfying shriek that Ulf cut short with his great axe.

Then the enemy was gone. *Have we won?* Looking around, she saw the warriors on both sides had drawn back to form a ring.

Breathing heavily, Ulf rested his axe on the ground and pointed with the tip of his beard.

Gudrød stood in the firelight, his unearthly sword in hand.

"Redbeard," Gudrød shouted, "you owe me a bride."

Åsa stood motionless in the crowd. In spite of her mail and helmet, she felt exposed. *All this is because of me.*

"Gudrød," Harald called back, "that was a long time ago."

Gudrød sliced his sword through the air, firelight dancing on the blade's pattern. His voice rang out. "Give me your daughter, and I will spare your miserable kingdom."

"Come and claim her," Harald roared.

"As you will," Gudrød replied. "Stop hiding like a woman! Come and face me."

"Here I am!" Harald charged out of the ranks. Red-faced, blue eyes glaring out from beneath his helmet, his voice carried like a war horn. The gentle farmer was transformed.

The warriors cheered.

The two kings clashed. Åsa's heart leaped when the impact sheared a big chunk of wood from Gudrød's shield. Her father chopped his sword into the opening, but Gudrød lurched away. Pressing his advantage, Harald bore down on his opponent. Gudrød took the next blow on his shield's metal boss, giving ground. Harald's sword hacked down again, forcing his opponent back. He was breathing hard, eyes glittering with rage. Battle lust had changed her father into someone Åsa had never seen before. *This must be what he was like when he was young.*

Gudrød charged, and Harald went down on one knee to take the brunt on his shield. The night rang with the shattering impact, and then both men were on their feet. Harald thrust inside Gudrød's guard and pierced his mail. Bellowing, Gudrød went down, and Harald raised his sword for the killing blow.

Gudrød rolled abruptly and brought up his sword. Steel rang out as Harald's sword met Gudrød's wicked blade.

And shattered.

Shards of metal shot out like sparks. In the shocked silence, Åsa heard Ulf catch his breath. "How…" he muttered.

Horror burned in her chest like molten lead.

The völva's curse.

Harald brought up the jagged shard that still jutted from the hilt. He made a desperate slash, but Gudrød swung his sword in a glittering arc, slicing into Harald's neck. Blood spurting from his throat, Harald dropped like a stone. Gudrød knelt on his chest and drew his knife to finish the butchery.

A fire roared in Åsa's veins.

"Åsa, no!" Before Ulf could stop her, she flung herself at Gudrød and drove Lightning into the tall king's spine. The rings of his brynja stopped the blade, but it gained his attention.

Gudrød rounded on her with a roar, swinging his sword. Åsa dodged the blow, leading him away from her father's body. The big man swung at her again, and she ran under his guard, ramming her sword into his gut. She heard him huff, but the pain only enraged him. He grabbed her helmet and tore it off her head, seizing her braid as it tumbled out. He yanked hard, bending her head back to expose her throat. Åsa glared up into his eyes, burning with rage. She jerked Lightning up at the eyes staring so coldly into hers. Gudrød flinched away from the blow, but the edge of her sword slashed his cheek. Blood welled from the wound. He roared, shook her by the hair, and raised his sword.

Gyrd barreled into him. The tackle propelled the big man backward, but he managed to keep his feet and his sword. The impact threw Åsa to the ground, and one of Gudrød's warriors grabbed her by the arm, jerking her to her feet. She slashed him with Lightning, drawing a thin weal of blood, but another warrior got hold of her and smashed her arm against a pillar. Her sword dropped from nerveless fingers. Her attacker held her hands together while the man she had cut bound her wrists in front, yanking the leather rope tight. Holding her in an iron grip, he turned to watch the fight.

Gyrd grappled Gudrød in a wrestler's hold. With the younger man inside his guard, Gudrød could not land a sword's blow. The two struggled, each trying desperately to throw the other. Gyrd had the strength and youth, but experience was the victor. Gudrød managed to fling his enemy away. He drew back the Serkland sword, and this time there was no one to stop him.

The curved blade pierced Gyrd's mail as if it were a linen shift. Blood gushed from the slash, cascading down his chest. He sank to his knees, his gaze finding Åsa's and holding it while the light dimmed. Gritting his teeth, he pivoted on his knees and collapsed at Gudrød's feet, facedown.

The onlookers gasped, for Gyrd's last act was a sign from the gods that vengeance was sure to be taken. To Åsa, it was a message to her from her brother in his moment of death. *Avenge me.*

And I will make it true, she swore to herself.

Gudrød laughed at the curse. "There is no man of this family alive to take vengeance," he said. He turned his stare on Åsa. "You are the heir to Tromøy. And you belong to me."

~

GUDRØD BENT over Harald's corpse to finish sawing through the neck. He grabbed the hair and held up the dripping head, raising a cheer from his men.

They turned to looting the hall of its treasures. Gudrød found Harald's silver-chased drinking horn. Åsa's face burned as the men cheered again. They stripped the fallen warriors of Tromøy of their weapons and armor, and rounded the living up to become slaves.

They picked up Harald's body and sat it on his high seat, placing the bloody head in the corpse's lap, the shattered sword in his hand. Gudrød looked at him, then turned and stalked toward the door.

"Burn the hall," he ordered.

"No!" cried Åsa, kicking the man who held her.

Gudrød looked down at her, a glint of pity in his eye. "They are all dead, girl," he said, gesturing around the ruined hall, which reeked of blood and was strewn with bodies. "Harald's hall will be his funeral pyre, to carry him to Valhöll with his son and his warriors."

Åsa glared at him. "And I will send you there to join them."

Gudrød's eyes hardened and he gave a short laugh. He signaled his men to set the fire and strode from the hall.

Åsa fought her captors all the way down to the ships. She took grim satisfaction from the blood and bruises her kicks and bites dealt the warrior who dragged her to the shore.

"Come help me with this hell bitch!" he cried.

Laughing, another warrior grabbed her legs. "Can't handle a little girl?" he jeered.

Åsa ceased her struggle and stared back at her father's hall. The fire had taken off. Flames roared against the sullen backdrop of the forest. With a resounding crack, the ridge beam broke and the roof collapsed. Dark shapes ran for the woods, silhouetted against the fire. *Hide,* she willed them. *Wait for my return.*

A piercing cry split the night. Against the blazing sky, a winged shape took flight.

Stormrider.

Go.

She felt the surge of joy at the falcon's escape and the wrench in her chest as she let go.

Her captors flung her hard into the bow of the ship. She landed on her back, the wind knocked out of her, and lay staring up at the snarling dragon's head while the pain lanced through her.

The keel grated on gravel, and the warriors' chant rose as they heaved the sleek hull into the surge. The men thudded in over the sides and took up seats on their sea chests. They racked their shields over the gunwales, ran out the oars, and thrust the ship into the chop.

Ulf lay nearby, bleeding and pale, but breathing. Gritting her teeth, Åsa eased herself onto her belly and dragged herself to him with her elbows.

"How are you?" she whispered, struggling to her knees. His leather jerkin was soaked with blood, but it was hard to tell the extent of his wounds. She flexed her bound hands, and the pain of the blood flowing back into her fingers made her gasp. Taking a deep breath, she grasped the torn layers of leather and wool and pulled them aside. The blood had not yet dried to the wound, but still it pulled on the skin. Ulf moaned faintly and stirred.

What she saw heartened her. The slash appeared to be fairly shallow, and no organs were visible. As long as it did not fester, he should survive.

Ulf's eyes fluttered open. "Forgive me, lady," he whispered.

"What have you got to be sorry for?"

She had to bend down to hear his words.

"The blood of your father is on my hands."

"He died by Gudrød's hand," she said.

"Lady," he said. "Harald died because his weapon failed, and I am the maker of that blade. If I had made a better sword, he would still live."

Åsa carefully pulled his jerkin closed again. There was nothing she could do here except keep him warm and still. "Your weapons are the finest in Agder," she said. "You have nothing to be sorry for. It was the völva's curse."

"The Serkland sword..." Ulf muttered. He closed his eyes, deaf and blind in his misery.

She turned to the weeping women and children, and a few wounded men like Ulf. Her eyes searched the captives. She saw Toki and Brenna huddled with the children, little Yrsa sobbing into Brenna's lap. Joy flickered in her to see them alive.

Brenna looked across at her, anguish in her eyes. Toki's face was battered and bruised.

They had been Tromøy's free folk. All slaves now. She dared not think about what would happen to them in Borre. "I will take care of you, and take vengeance," she heard herself say. *And how will I keep that promise?*

Cold and trembling, Åsa struggled to her feet. Clinging to the gunnel, her bound hands numb and raw, she stared at her father's hall blazing across the water. The scent of smoke carried on the wind.

She watched the light dwindle into the distance until it was no more than a dot. It disappeared behind a wave, popped back up briefly, then winked out of sight.

The seas roughened as the ship came out from behind the headland. Åsa let go of the gunnel and fell back into the bottom of the boat, where she lay staring at the horrors in her mind.

CHAPTER 8

Borre

Asa bolted awake when the longship grated on stone. She lay on the floorboards in a slime that smelled of blood and brine.

At first, she could not grasp where she was. But then it all came back. Scenes of the battle hammered at her mind. Her father's headless corpse aflame on his high seat, Gyrd's body at his feet.

She had slept through an entire day at sea. This was Borre.

The ship surged as Gudrød's warriors heaved their sea chests onto the jetty and vaulted over the side, laughing and calling to each other. She tried to sit up, pain jolting through her head. Her hands throbbed, swollen in leather bonds that cut her wrists. A huge man plucked her out of the bow and tossed her over his shoulder like a slaughtered sheep. The sudden pain forced a cry from her. She bit her lip and peered out through tangled hair as the warrior lugged her up the trail.

A sullen sun lowered over a field of burial mounds. Beyond, the great hall brooded among the trees, its timbers stark and gray. The massive oak door yawned open like the maw of a great beast, framed by carved and painted creatures that gripped and clawed and swallowed each other. The warrior carried her through the entryway and into the hall, where he dumped her on the floor.

She found herself staring up at the völva Heid, who looked down on her with menace and disdain.

"So, girl, here you are to meet your fate after all. You could have saved your father and your brother if you had just obeyed your destiny."

Åsa looked away and gulped air through her mouth to stop the tears that threatened to choke her.

Gudrød strode in. He wore a fine red cloak over his chain mail, soft leather boots on his feet.

"It took a king to do the job, in spite of your magic," he said.

Heid grinned up at him. "Let's hope that you are up to the task the fates have set you. Perhaps this child is too much for you, after all."

Gudrød grabbed Åsa's arm and jerked her to her feet, making her gasp with pain.

I will kill him before I let him take me, she vowed. But she did not believe her own promise.

"Stop!" Heid commanded. "You must first hold the wedding feast."

Gripping Åsa firmly by the arm, Gudrød turned on the völva.

"I paid no bride price for her," he said. "I took her without the consent of her father or her brother." He laughed. "She has no male relatives left alive to take revenge or restore her status. She is nothing but a thrall, my thrall. Why shouldn't I take her like one, and cut her throat when I am done with her?"

From her seat, the völva spoke slowly, as if to an idiot. "You know you must marry her to lay claim to Harald's lands. You need her alive, and you need her son, born to a queen, not a slave."

And once I have produced a child, they will have no further use for me.

"What do I care?" said Gudrød. Fear shot through her as he dragged her toward the door. With shame, Åsa knew he could feel her trembling. She squeezed her eyes shut.

Taking up her embroidery, Heid said evenly, "Gudrød Half-danson, you would be a fool to let this chance go by for a few hours' entertainment."

Gudrød hesitated, fingers digging into Åsa's bicep.

Without warning, he shoved her away. She landed hard on the rush-strewn floor as he strode from the room, calling for his horse.

Relief made her shake all the harder. She turned her eyes to the sorceress to see what her new captor had in store.

The völva hoisted herself from her seat, leaning heavily on her staff. From the floor behind her chair, an old woman rose and scurried to assist. "Sigrid, bring her to my bower," the sorceress commanded as she hobbled toward the door. The old thrall gripped Åsa's arm and helped her to her feet, pulling her firmly in the völva's wake. Åsa wanted to resist, but what was the point?

The door opened onto a yard of packed earth. Åsa scanned the yard, hoping to catch sight of the other Tromøy captives. What had befallen Brenna and Toki? Where was Ulf? She worried about his wounds. They were nowhere to be seen.

But she glimpsed Olaf watching from the shadows of the trees. He looked as forlorn as she felt. Their eyes met for an instant, and he quickly looked away.

Sigrid led her to a two-story timber building. The oaken door was carved with bind runes, and on it hung the brass ring of sorcery. It had no doubt once been the dead queen's bower hall, but now it was a sorceress's lair. Heid pushed the door open and went inside. Sigrid gently guided Åsa across the threshold.

The low sun filtered through the gable ends, supplemented by firelight. Pine smoke scented the air. The far reaches of the room were lost in shadow, but there was a spacious feeling.

Around the longfire, Heid's female apprentices sat on benches, spindles whirling as they gossiped. They fell silent as the völva entered the room.

Heid hobbled past them without speaking, Sigrid leading Åsa in her wake. With a shock, Åsa recognized Astrid among the women. Of course, she was an apprentice. Their eyes met, and Astrid nodded at her, kindling a tiny flare of comfort.

At the far end of the room, they came to a wall with an iron-bound door. Åsa's stomach clenched again as the völva produced an iron key from her belt and fitted it in the lock. Pushing open the door, Heid stood by while the old woman ushered Åsa inside.

A small brazier burned cheerily, warming and brightening the high-ceilinged room. Sigrid drew a rush from the floor and lit it on the brazier, carrying it to light the oil lamps that hung in the corners.

When the room was a blaze of warmth and light, the thrall poured a cup of water from a pitcher and offered it to Åsa. She reached for it with shaking hands and guzzled until her stomach gave a warning lurch.

"Fetch some hot water to bathe her," the völva commanded. Bowing her head, the old woman backed out of the room, drawing the door closed behind her.

"Sit down," Heid said to Åsa, nodding at a stool by the fire. She drew the knife that hung from her belt. Åsa flinched, but the sorceress only cut Åsa's bonds and stepped back, looking her prisoner over. Åsa met her eyes defiantly. No one stared at Redbeard's daughter.

"Where are my people?" she demanded.

"I would be more worried about myself right now, if I were you," said Heid.

"I must see them," Åsa insisted.

"You are in no position to make demands." The völva sat down on a chair. Her voice softened a little. "I knew your mother, child. She was a good woman, and I'm sorry she's dead."

Åsa glared at her captor, rubbing her wrists to ease the pins and needles as the feeling flooded back.

"Are you sorry my father and brother are dead?" she retorted.

"That was payment owed," snapped the völva.

"What do you mean by that?"

Heid laughed. "Never you mind, girl. Just do as you are told."

A tap sounded at the door.

"Enter," said the völva.

Two men rolled in a wooden tub, which they set by the brazier before scurrying out like a demon was after them. Behind them came Sigrid, bent beneath a yoke with two wooden buckets full of steaming water.

The sorceress heaved herself out of her chair and busied herself setting a small pot to boil over the brazier. "Clean her up, Sigrid. Give her a robe."

Sigrid poured hot water into the tub and cast some herbs on the surface, filling the room with fragrant steam.

"Come, lady." Sigrid gestured to a three-legged stool. Åsa sat and raised her arms to let the old woman haul off her chain-mail brynja, sighing as the heavy rings pulled away. Sigrid unlaced the leather jerkin and padded undershirt, then peeled off Åsa's wool trousers and helped her climb into the wooden tub. Åsa sank back in the steaming water, letting the heat soothe her screaming muscles and bruises.

Her hair was a salt-encrusted rat's nest. Sigrid gently untangled the ratty braid, then eased Åsa's head into the warm water. She gave herself over to the soothing waves that lapped over her aching head. Sigrid coaxed her back into a sitting position and lathered her hair with lye soap. After dunking her head twice to rinse, Sigrid scrubbed her with a rough cloth, bringing the blood to her skin. The old woman helped her out of the bath and dried her with a linen towel, then pulled a clean shift over her head. Seated once again on the stool by the brazier, Åsa let the old thrall tackle her hair with a pot of scented oil and a bone comb.

Heid sat drinking an herbal-scented concoction, gazing into the fire.

"Poor lamb," Sigrid murmured as she worked out the tangles. Åsa looked up to meet the old woman's sad eyes, one slave to another. The tears rose, and this time, Åsa let them cascade down her cheeks unchecked.

The old woman stroked her hair, singing softly in a language Åsa had never heard. Gradually her sobs subsided, leaving her limp.

The sorceress looked up from her tea. "Sleep. You will be safe —for now."

Sigrid led Åsa to the bed and helped her lie down, tucking the furs around her. Exhaustion swept over her, and her eyes closed, though she struggled to keep them open. The last thing she heard was the key clicking in the lock.

OLAF HAD WATCHED from the shadows of the burial mounds as his father's ship came alongside the jetty. He'd seen Hrolf throw Åsa over his shoulder and followed on the fringes of the forest as his brother lugged her up the trail. Was she hurt? He could not help her now that he was out of his father's favor. He watched from the trees as Hrolf carried her into the hall. He dared not enter, but he couldn't leave.

The warriors dragged the other captives up the hill and shoved them into the slave quarters, drafty hovels no better than animal byres. Their wails rose in the chill air.

Eventually, the back door of the great hall creaked open. Heid stepped into the yard, followed by the old slave Sigrid, leading Åsa. As they crossed to the bower, a little of the weight lifted from Olaf's stomach. Heid would keep her safe.

For now.

ÅSA JOLTED UP IN BED. A finger of daylight streamed through the gable end, picking out the intricate carvings of slender creatures writhing up the bedposts. Above her, the great headboard bore a valknut, the corpse knot, sign of Odin.

Memories flooded back. Again, she saw the shimmering blade slash her father's throat, the life running out of Gyrd's eyes like water through a sieve, the crashing beams of her home against the flames. Everything she had loved turned to smoking ash.

Yesterday I was the daughter of a king. Today I am the slave of his murderer.

I thought being lady of Tromøy was a burden, but if I could have Gyrd and Father back, I would wear the keys with joy. I wish I'd never picked up arms. I wish I'd done as I was told. If I'd been the peace-weaver I was meant to be, Father and Gyrd would be alive.

The furs began to vibrate. Green eyes peered out at her, and an enormous black cat burrowed its way over, nuzzling her with a soft head and purring, giving her a moment of comfort. She looked around the room, but she seemed to be alone. Where was Heid?

She threw back the furs and rose. This might be her only opportunity to search for a way out. The cat jumped down from the bed and followed her, still purring.

A floor-to-ceiling wall of solid timber sectioned off the room from the main hall. In the wall was the only door. Beside it hung Heid's gem-encrusted cloak, with her catskin cap and gloves. In the corner squatted the völva's chair of prophecy, carved and painted, the seat well padded with feather bolsters. Shelves ran along the walls, holding lidded jars, feathers and bones, queer-shaped stones, and rune-carved staves brown with blood. Bundles of herbs dried in the rafters—lovage, parsley, mint, thyme, and marjoram—their scent mingling with the woodsmoke of the brazier, over which a small pot steamed. She could see no other way out than the single door.

The lock clicked. The door opened and the völva entered.

"I see you've met Flosi." Heid nodded at the cat, who left Åsa's side to nuzzle the sorceress's leg. Heid crossed to the brazier. She ladled liquid from the pot into a cup, added a pinch of something fragrant from a leather pouch, swirled it three times sunwise with her index finger, and held it out.

"Drink this. It will give you strength."

Åsa shook her head, clamping her mouth shut and glaring at the völva. Her mind whirled with a hundred questions.

"Have you seen my people?" she demanded. "How do they fare?"

Heid nodded. "They are alive."

"When can I see them?"

The sorceress did not answer.

"Why are you helping me?" Åsa said.

"Your mother was a friend," said the völva. "But don't push it too far."

TWO WARRIORS DRAGGED ULF, bound in chains, into the smithy. With effort, he lifted his head and focused stinging eyes on his surroundings. The workshop was much larger than the one on Tromøy. An enormous forge stood in the center, kept alive by a boy treading a double foot bellows. From the walls hung tools of the finest quality—metal shears and hammers, tongs, fullers, and saws.

Gudrød stood by the forge beside a stout man whose muscular shoulders spoke of many hours swinging a hammer. Undoubtedly the resident smith, he fixed Ulf with a cold blue stare. He did not appear to want to share his tools. Ulf met his eyes and held.

Gudrød said, "Arne, meet Ulf, the famous smith of Tromøy. He will be working here with you now."

Arne bowed his head without breaking eye contact with Ulf. "Yes, lord."

Gudrød nodded to one of his men. "Release him."

Ulf braced himself to take on the weight of the chains as the warriors let go. He straightened up, broke off the staring match with Arne, and turned his eyes on his captor.

Gudrød drew the curved sword from its scabbard.

"Did you ever think you'd see this again?" he asked.

"The Serkland sword," Ulf said. "I wondered what became of it."

"One of the treasures Harald left behind the night he made off with the woman," Gudrød said.

"That woman was my queen. And it was Harald who killed the Serklander, in a fair fight. The sword was his by right."

"At the time, I did not consider it adequate compensation, but now it has gained me everything that once was his. His daughter, his kingdom, his son, his life." Gudrød looked at the sword with satisfaction, then held it out to Ulf. "What do you make of it?"

Lifting his chain-laden arms to take the sword, Ulf examined it carefully. The surface of the metal swirled with a pattern like waves in the sea.

"This blade was forged with greater skill than any Northern smith possesses. It is far lighter than any of our swords," Ulf said, hefting it. "The metal is hard yet flexible. Even after battle, the edge is still razor sharp, without a chip or a nick."

Gudrød took the sword back. "If I had an entire army with such weapons," he said, turning the blade in his hand. "I could take back Skiringssal, and rid our land of the Danes—a king with such an army would rule the North." He looked at his resident smith, who still glared from under bristling eyebrows. "Arne has tried and failed many times to make such a weapon." He fixed Ulf with his gaze. "I know you learned many secrets when you served the Serkland sword maker."

Ulf considered his reply, not wanting to give away too much. "It is true I learned to forge swords such as these," he said slowly. "But they were not made from bog iron. They were made from wootz steel, a metal we do not have in the North."

Gudrød smiled. "Then you shall make this wootz."

"Even the Serklander did not know the secrets of making the wootz," said Ulf. "The ingots were imported from another land, where the process was closely guarded."

Gudrød's eyes glinted, hard as the blade he held. "If you want to live, you will find a way to forge a sword to match this."

CHAPTER 9

The sorceress set Åsa to work in the bower hall. Surrounded by chattering girls, she sat like a rock in a merry stream, heavy and dark. Her gaze was lost in the fire, distaff slack in her hand, spindle dangling near the floor.

Astrid slid onto the bench beside her. "I am so sorry."

Åsa's throat constricted as she struggled for breath.

"I had hopes for your brother," Astrid went on sadly, "but now I will follow the völva's path."

Åsa could not reply. What good were words? The tears trailed down her cheeks.

Astrid tended to her spinning in silence, but her quiet presence seemed to form a buffer of calm between Åsa and her memories.

She wondered about Olaf. He had not been part of the raiding party, but he must know what his father had done. The thought dragged her spirits even lower.

After the evening meal of soup and bread, the apprentices burrowed under the furs on the benches, still chatting as the longfire burned low. Heid bade Åsa follow her to the bower room and locked the door behind her with the iron key that hung on her belt.

The völva brewed a potion over the brazier, poured two cups, and offered one to Åsa.

"Here, child, this will ease your pain and help you sleep."

Åsa shook her head again, mouth shut tight. If she let the old witch drug her senseless every night, she'd never escape. Heid shrugged and set the cup aside. She let out a faint groan as she made herself comfortable on her chair, gesturing to the stool beside her. After Åsa was seated, the sorceress sipped her own cup, then took up her distaff and spindle.

"Spinning soothes the spirit, and helps the potion to take effect sooner," she said.

After a while, the distaff began to droop, and Heid's eyes fluttered. The old sorceress rose with a groan and tottered to the bed. She lay down with a sigh, propping herself on down bolsters and pulling the linen coverlet up to her chin. The cat, Flosi, leaped onto the bed and burrowed under the covers. Åsa could hear her purring vigorously from across the room. Hand buried in the cat's fur, Heid began to breathe in the even rhythm of sleep.

The soft feather mattress invited Åsa's aching body, still battle sore. She forced herself to stay sitting on the stool, her back against the wall. Her eyes drooped with exhaustion, but as soon as she closed them, visions intruded: her father's headless corpse, the life going out of Gyrd's eyes, the hall in flames. Åsa bolted awake, trembling and covered in sweat. She had slipped off the stool and lay on the cold floor. There she stayed, tossing restlessly all night.

∼

IN THE MORNING, Åsa woke alone and dragged herself into the bower to join the apprentices around the longfire. She sat, distaff idle in her hands as she stared into the flames, struggling to push down the grief that welled up into her throat.

Don't look. Just take one step, then another.

Astrid sat beside her that day, saying nothing. When she went outside, she coaxed Åsa into the sunshine with her. The harvest was underway, and the Tromøy captives were working the fields. Toki and Brenna toiled with the other slaves, filthy and ragged, the adults scything the barley while the children gathered the gleanings behind them. The reeve backhanded little Yrsa for spilling her load. Brenna ran to the crying child, and the reeve knocked her to her knees. Åsa gasped and started toward them, but Astrid grabbed her arm.

"Are you mad?" she hissed. "Keep out of matters that do not concern you."

"But they do concern me," said Åsa. "They are my people."

"Not anymore. Now they are Gudrød's slaves," said Astrid, dragging her back into the hall.

AGAIN, Åsa tried to sleep sitting on the floor, her back to the wall. She shifted uncomfortably, a groan escaping her.

Heid sat up, rubbing her eyes.

"Child, I am old and crippled. You cannot keep me from my sleep. Sigrid!" she shouted. The old thrall rose from her pallet by the door. "Make this girl a pallet by the fire."

Åsa watched, shamed by guilt, as Sigrid took straw from her own thin pallet and made a bed by the fire. She thanked the old woman, who nodded wearily and trudged back to bed. Åsa crawled onto the linen-covered straw, wrapped herself in her cloak, and slept.

For once, no nightmares awakened her.

After a night's sleep, Åsa felt stronger, though her will was still low. She spent her day sitting silently with the apprentices in the bower, the spindle idle in her hands. Astrid stayed by her side, maintaining a barrier between her and the other women. They eyed Åsa curiously but did not try to talk to her.

Astrid spoke little words of encouragement to her in low tones, seeming to expect no answer. Åsa's bruises and sore muscles had begun to heal, but inside she was numb.

A week passed, then two.

When Åsa's monthly blood began to flow, Heid knew it immediately.

"The girl will be fertile at the equinox, as I had hoped," Heid said to Gudrød triumphantly, marking the primstave that tracked the changing seasons. "It will be the ideal time for her to conceive the child. I will sacrifice a sow to Freyja on the wedding day for the fertility of the marriage. You must choose a good horse to send to Odin."

I will be the sacrifice, Åsa thought. *He will rape me until I am pregnant.* She stared at Gudrød's blunt fingers. *Those hands murdered my father and my brother, burned my home, and made me a slave. I will cut them off before I let them touch me.*

As the days shortened and the fall equinox drew near, Åsa slept less and less. Gudrød never came into the bower, where men were all but forbidden, but she felt his eyes on her wherever she went. She could not shut out the vision of being trapped alone with him in the wedding chamber. She lay awake in the night, planning.

She had to get away. But how could she leave the enslaved folk of Tromøy behind? Yet, what could she do for them here? She had no power to help them. If she escaped, if she returned to Tromøy, she could rally the scattered warriors from the hinterlands of Agder. She could raise an army and attack Borre to free her people, and rule in her father's place.

First she must get away.

Åsa stared into the darkness and allowed herself to imagine that she was back on Tromøy in her own bed. She would be tired from a long day in the fields. Sleep would come over her easily, secure in the knowledge that her father and brother and the warriors of Tromøy protected her, knowing in the morning she would rise to see all the people who had loved her since she was a baby. She would meet them in the kitchen to prepare the breakfast porridge and set out the cold meat and cheese and boiled eggs. She imagined herself at the long table in the yard where everyone she knew and loved gathered, laughing and chattering as the morning sun warmed their shoulders. Her father sat at the head of the table dressed in the old work clothes he preferred to wear, his face already flushed from the sun. Gyrd was beside him, blazing with energy, bragging about the adventures he planned.

With a shudder, she realized that this was the afterlife she visited. What was really left on Tromøy now? Blackened fields littered with bloated corpses of cattle and sheep. Ragged, starving people picking through the wreckage of their homes, struggling to stay alive. She saw her father's charred bones, still clutching his shattered sword in the wreckage of the great hall. Her brother's skeleton, facedown, picked clean by animals. Jarl Borg, undoubtedly nothing but bones himself, burned and scattered. Her throat constricted when she thought of all she had lost. Breath came hard, and she forced her mind to look away.

When she did fall into a restless sleep, she dreamed of lying on a bed, unable to move, Gudrød leering down at her. As he reached out for her, she bolted awake, trembling and drenched in sweat.

She had to get away. Now.

The völva stirred in her sleep, shifting her crippled body. Flosi woke and crawled in beside Åsa. The purring calmed her. She lay awake, stroking the cat's soft fur and making plans.

The sorceress slept with the iron key suspended from her belt on a leather thong. If Åsa could increase the dose of herbs in Heid's nightly brew, the völva might sleep heavily enough to enable Åsa to get the key without waking her.

Every day brought her closer to the equinox, closer to the wedding. Closer to snowfall. She must get away while the weather was good. Once winter set in, she would be trapped here at Gudrød's mercy until spring. He would get her pregnant, and then she would be trapped for life.

In the morning, she surprised Astrid by accompanying the women on a berry-picking expedition. As they wandered in the woodland near the shore, Åsa eyed the boats drawn up on the beach. Nestled in the loom of the great dragon ships lay some smaller skiffs. If one should disappear in the night, it might not be missed right away.

She picked out one that was just the right size and wandered down to get a better look. Easy to handle for one person, easy to hide. It had no sail, but inside lay a pair of oars.

There were moments when the thought of taking to the sea alone in a tiny boat, to return to her ruined, burned-out home seemed mad. But she couldn't stay here, the thrall of her father's murderer. That was a thousand times worse than anything that awaited her out there. She had to get free of this place. Better she die in the attempt.

I am the daughter of Harald Redbeard, she told herself. *I was born on an island, I grew up on the sea. I know how to handle a boat, I know how to hide. Alone, I will be quick and hard to spot. I can get there. Some of my father's men must have survived. When they hear I have returned, they will gather to me. I will raise an army, and we will come back and free my people.*

I just need to get hold of that boat.

There were too many people watching during the day. She had a better chance at night. She observed the lay of the land, memorized the trail through the trees and the movements of the lookouts. There was a man stationed at the hall at all times, as well as one patrolling the beach. But he was watching the sea, not looking for someone coming from the hall.

She tracked the waning moon anxiously, waiting for the

darkest night. When it was no more than a curving sliver in the sky, she implemented her plan.

That night, when the völva brewed her pain-killing concoction, Åsa managed to purloin a handful of the sleeping herbs and hide them in her pallet. Then she waited.

Two more evenings passed, and finally the moon was dark. Åsa sat by the fire, fearing the völva would feel the tension emanating from her core. Her spinning, always poor, was impossible tonight. The wool came off the distaff in uneven clumps, her fingers making lumps of the fibers or breaking them off entirely.

Her nerves were stretched to the breaking point when at last the völva rose, took her soapstone pot down from the shelf, and hung it over the brazier, adding a pinch of her sleeping herbs. While Heid's back was turned, Åsa drew out the extra sleeping herbs and tucked them in her sleeve. She held her breath as Heid hobbled over to lock up. While the sorceress made her painful way to the door and turned the key in the iron lock, Åsa leaned forward and dropped the herbs into the pot, gave it a quick stir with her finger, and resumed her spinning before the völva turned around.

Heid grimaced with each step back to the pot. She leaned over, sniffing the rising mist as the strong aroma of the sleeping herbs filled the room.

Åsa froze as the blood drained from her face. She had not considered the strong odor of the herbs she had used. How could it possibly escape the völva's expert nose?

Åsa tried to focus on her spinning. The wool rasped between her fingers. She held her breath as Heid tipped the pot, pouring the brew into two clay cups. She handed one to Åsa, and took a deep inhalation of her own. As she brought it to her lips, Åsa stared, unable to move.

Heid paused, cup halfway to her lips. Åsa's stomach knotted.

"You must drink your potion, girl," said the sorceress, fixing her with a penetrating gaze.

Åsa blinked, a rabbit in a snare.

"It is natural for a bride to be nervous," continued the völva. Åsa looked away. The hint of sympathy in the sorceress's voice made tears rise up.

"But, like many a woman before you, you have no choice in the matter. You need to drink this to help you sleep." Heid nodded at the cup.

Åsa's throat constricted. Her heart raced as she stared at the earthenware cup in her hand.

"Drink it," the völva ordered.

"No, I will be all right," Åsa faltered.

"Girl, you are disturbing my sleep. I am old, and cannot afford to go without my rest. The brew will not harm you. Drink it."

Åsa wrapped trembling fingers around the cup. The clay was warm to her touch, the potent steam enveloping her face as she brought the cup to her lips.

"Flosi!" Åsa cried as the cat approached them lazily. She reached down and scratched her ears. Flosi let herself be petted before moving on to rub against Heid's leg. When the sorceress bent down to pet the cat, Åsa quickly spilled half of the brew into the rushes beside her stool. Bringing the cup back to her mouth, she pretended to swallow.

When the völva straightened up, Åsa set down the cup. To her relief, Heid smiled and drank her own in one gulp. Heaving another sigh, the sorceress leaned back heavily in her chair, took up her distaff, and began to spin.

Soon the tip of the distaff began to droop. The spindle whorl spun slowly to a stop. When the völva's head bobbed and her mouth sagged open, Åsa rose and gently coaxed the sorceress to her bed. Heid burrowed under the furs without opening her eyes, and soon was snoring.

Åsa picked up the sewing shears and crept over to the bed.

Gently lifting the key from Heid's belt, she cut the cord. At the table, she gathered the remains of the evening bread and cheese in a cloth, slipped the knife from the board into her belt, and slung the waterskin over her back. She threw her gray wool cloak over her linen shift, drew the hood over her hair, and glided to the door.

The iron key slid into in the lock and turned with a sharp click. Åsa held her breath, watching the sorceress, but Heid did not stir.

Clutching her bundle, Åsa nearly tripped on a body. It was the thrall Sigrid, sleeping in the shadows. The old woman's eyes flew open in fright.

With a pleading look, Åsa held her finger to her lips. Sigrid stared at her, then closed her eyes and turned to the wall.

Åsa opened the door a crack and peered out into the great hall. Her eyes had not adjusted to the darkness, but hearing soft snores, she crept out, turning back to lock the door behind her. She set the key near the door and stared into the gloom. This was the most dangerous part, venturing out of the shadows and crossing the center of the bower hall, fully exposed. The dull glow of the smoldering longfire picked out the forms of the women lying on the broad benches that lined the walls. Listening intently, all she heard was the soft sound of regular breathing. Nobody stirred. Åsa strained to catch any sounds. She fixed her sight on the floor and took a careful step out into the open. Placing one foot, then another, silent in soft leather shoes, she made her way past the sleeping forms.

At last, she gained the exit to the bower. She lifted the hide that covered it and slipped into the darkness of the entryway.

The hammering of her heart slowed. She wrapped the cloak tightly around her and tucked her skirts up into her belt so that her legs were free. She longed for her breeks, but they had disappeared after her bath that first day.

Sending a silent prayer to her mother for luck, she eased the oaken door open a crack. The hinges groaned, and she froze, listening, but all she heard were snores from the hall. She slipped out into the night and pressed herself against the wall.

Gradually her eyes adjusted. The sentry approached, making his rounds. Åsa kept to the shadows, skirting the hall in the opposite direction. *Let me not meet him at the other end.* Breath caught in her throat when he materialized out of the gloom. She shrank against the wall, bowing her head to hide her face beneath her hood.

If he turned around, he could not miss her.

He stood there for an eternity, looking and listening, his attention focused on the sea and forest. Åsa held her breath, trying to melt into the wall.

Finally, he turned his head to the south and moved on. As soon as he rounded the corner, she sprang from the safety of the shadows and darted across the yard. Gaining the cover of the trees, she crouched behind a trunk to catch her breath.

The thick brambles snagged at her cloak and caught her hair, but it was better than being exposed on the trail. Skirting the burial mounds, Åsa could feel the evil haugbui that haunted them. Gudrød's ancestors would bear her no good will.

Worming her way through the forest, she hoped the sounds of her movements would be taken for wildlife. The beach seemed impossibly far away.

At last, water gleamed through the foliage, and the dragons' heads of the longships reared up, the skiff invisible in their shadow.

Crouching in the undergrowth, she watched the lookout patrol the shoreline. Like the sentry at the hall, his attention focused toward the water, scanning the horizon for the flare of a war beacon, the loom of a ship. He never glanced in her direction. When he headed down the beach away from her, she darted across the sand for the cover of the boats. Creeping along in the shadow of the ships, she felt her way to the skiff.

Keeping low in the shelter of the longships, she eased her weight against the boat's stem. The stout little vessel was heavier than she had anticipated. She gritted her teeth and pushed harder.

The boat didn't budge. Taking a deep breath, she shoved with all her strength, and the keel broke loose. It shot out from under her, rasping across the gravel, and she pitched onto her face. Pain washed over her, and she lay still, hoping the waves lapping on the beach had masked the sound. There was no time to pause. The skiff was already drifting away. She heaved herself to her feet and waded into the water. She caught hold of the boat and squirmed over the side, where she lay in the bottom, calming her breath and listening.

Her heart lurched.

There were no oars. Yesterday they had been in the boat. Where had they gone? There was no sign of them on the dark beach. She had to go back.

The boat was drifting quickly with the current, out of control. She dropped her cloak into the bottom of the skiff and eased her leg over the side, slipping silently into the water. She choked off a gasp as the icy water closed over her chest. She gripped the bow and towed the boat back to the beach.

The sentry had started back. Any minute, he would catch the movement of the skiff and her shadow plodding through the shallows in her sodden shift.

She shoved the skiff up onto the gravel, wincing as the keel grated, and dove into its shadow. She lay shivering, trying to quiet her breath as the sentry's boots crunched nearer and nearer.

The chill took hold of her as the sentry inspected each of the longships. She shrank under the curve of the skiff's hull, praying that the shadows would conceal her.

She was shivering so hard, she feared the movement would catch his eye. His boots appeared in the space below the stem. He must be able to hear her heart thudding. She shut her eyes and prayed to her mother.

Her mother must have heard, for when Åsa opened her eyes, the sentry's boots were striding away. Only after his footsteps had faded into the distance did she dare to sit up.

She chafed her hands and legs until the feeling returned, then she forced herself onto hands and knees and crawled between the hulls, searching for the oars. There—they shone white against the dark gravel, high on the beach out of reach of the tide. How had she missed them?

There was nothing for it. She wormed her way across the gravel, watching the sentry's back, willing him to keep going. He stopped and half turned. She curled up into a ball, hoping her gray cloak would pass for a rock. Her heart froze as his eyes flicked over her, but after a moment, he began his trudge down the beach again. She resumed her tortured crawl.

At last, her hands closed around the oars. Hugging them to her, she crabbed her way back to the boat. She eased the oars over the side, managing to land them without a sound. Crawling to the bow, she straightened up halfway and took a grip on the stem. A jolt of fear coursed through her as she realized how weak she was.

The dark form of the sentry moved at the far end of the beach. Now was the time to go, before he turned back toward her. Concentrating her will, she shoved with all her strength, hanging on for dear life as the boat slid free. She drove it into the water and flung herself over the side.

Keeping her head low, she eased into a sitting position and picked up an oar. The blade entered the water near the stern without a splash. She sculled with a single oar, propelling the skiff silently. There was no help for her telltale wake but prayer and luck.

She skirted along the shadow of the breakwater, hoping that would hide her passage and that any sound she made would mingle with the waves lapping on the rocks. Her sodden smock chilled her and chafed at her skin. The salt water would never dry, she knew, but cling in a sticky mess.

The end of the breakwater loomed ahead. The guard's head jerked up. He got to his feet and stared in her direction. Heart in her throat, Åsa grabbed at a jetty rock to stop her movement.

She clung to the rock, keeping her head low.

They hung silently in the water. Åsa peered over the side, watching the sentry, who was straining to see into the darkness.

Finally he sat down beneath a tree, opened a bundle, and began to eat.

Åsa pulled the skiff from rock to rock in the shadow of the bulkhead, sliding through the water like silk, leaving no wake. The craft was exposed for a moment at the end of the jetty, and she peered anxiously at the shore. The guard was leaning back against the tree trunk, engrossed in his food. Åsa grabbed the next rock and pulled herself around the end of the jetty, into open water.

She took her seat cautiously, picked up the oars, and pointed the small craft south, stroking smoothly through the water, careful not to splash. She stayed close to the shore in hopes that the boat's dark shape would blend into the shadows of the trees.

Once she had rounded the headland and was out of sight of the jetty, she rowed hard to put as much distance between herself and Borre as possible. With any luck, her absence would not be discovered until morning. Even so, she hugged the coast, keeping a sharp eye to the north. Of course, they would guess her destination was Tromøy. A longship could easily catch her small craft, but the tiny boat had the advantage of blending into the wooded shoreline. As long as she sighted them first, it would be easy to disappear into one of the small estuaries that riddled the coast.

Rowing warmed her blood, and new energy surged into her limbs as the trembling subsided. Borre dwindled into the distance, and Åsa's spirits rose for the first time in weeks. Still, the wet smock chilled her, and the imbedded salt crystals chafed her skin raw. She boated her oars and struggled out of the sticky linen shift, laying it out in the bow in hopes that it would dry. She wrapped her dry cloak around her torso, tying it tight across her chest. It covered her body warmly down to her feet, leaving her arms free.

She picked up the oars and stared in wonder. Countless stars reflected in the still water so perfectly, it was like dipping her oars into the sky. As each oar stroke parted the stars, the small craft glided through the heavens. A song rose up in her throat as the hypnotic rhythm of the oars took over.

Home, she thought, and rowed toward it through the night sky. *Gyrd and Father and Mother are gone. My father's hall is gone, but my tree will still be there.*

As the night wore on, her bravado thinned and doubts rose. What did she know of making war, of ruling a kingdom? She thought of her father. It took more than courage to show that kind of strength, that kind of wisdom. She had not appreciated all he'd accomplished until it had been reduced to ashes, and she was the spoiled fool who had brought it down.

But she was the only hope Tromøy had.

When they see that I have returned, my father's sworn men will come to me. They will come against Borre with me, and free the captives. We will rebuild the hall, and everything will be as it was before.

Except that her father and Gyrd would not be there.

At some point, her grasp began to slip on the oars. Her hands felt sticky. *Blood.* Her palms were raw and bleeding, but she had not felt them. She tore strips from her shift to wrap her hands and kept rowing.

Eventually, the sky began to turn rosy. Shafts of light flared and the sun burst out from the horizon, turning the water to gold.

It was time to make for shore and get out of sight. Her arms were leaden. She rowed close in and chose one of many tiny inlets that flowed into the sea, bringing the little boat as far up as possible. Hidden among the branches, she tied off to a tree. The first thing she did was plunge her raw hands into the icy stream and soak them until they were numb.

She ate a little bread and drank some water. After draping her clothes on a branch in hopes the morning sun would dry them at least partially, she wrapped her cloak tightly around her and lay down in the bottom of the boat. Sleep took her instantly.

CHAPTER 10

Gudrød roused Olaf with a cuff to the head. "The girl is gone," he shouted. "She took a boat. Go get her. Don't come back without her this time."

Olaf stumbled out of bed, trying to comprehend. Åsa had escaped. For a moment, he was glad. Then it dawned on him.

He's giving me another chance. Don't ruin it this time.

He struggled into his breeks and leather jerkin, sheathing a hunting knife in his belt. No armor for a boat journey. It would just slow him down. He picked up his sword and spear.

He stopped at the cookhouse for a bowl of porridge. While he ate, he considered his options. There could be no doubt where she was heading. Tromøy was the only place she would go. He didn't doubt that she knew how to get there, but she was out there alone and probably unarmed. Anything could happen on the way.

Bolting the rest of his porridge, he snatched some dried meat, flatbread, and a flask of ale, lugging it along with his weapons down to the beach where his small sailing craft lay among the longships. Searching the row of boats, he saw that the missing one was a rowing skiff. With a decent breeze, he should be able to catch her easily with the advantage of a sail.

And bring her back to Father, against her will.

He shoved the thought aside and focused on launching the boat. The beginnings of a breeze kicked up a small chop on the water. In the cold gray morning, he set his sail for Tromøy.

Olaf made good time along the coast. With this wind, he should catch up with her by midday. Even if she had rowed all night, without a sail, she could only travel about a third of his speed. But she could be hiding in one of the hundreds of tiny estuaries that punctuated the coastline. He worried that he might pass her by and never see her.

He hugged the shore, letting the current's back eddy carry his craft along, peering into the dense forest that crowded right down to the water.

He couldn't fail his father again. Gudrød was not a patient man. It was a miracle that he'd given Olaf another chance. No, if he couldn't recover Åsa now, he'd best not return to Borre.

What did she hope to accomplish by running away? She would never make it all the way to Tromøy on her own. Even if she did, what could await her there? Her father's hall was burned, the crops ruined, the livestock slaughtered. She'd starve this winter, if she didn't freeze to death first.

A sound echoed from the shore. Deep, like a roar.

It came again.

He dropped the sail and fitted his oars, rowing toward the beach.

ÅSA WOKE TO A RANCID STENCH. The sheltering branches rattled as a powerful force ripped them away. Her little boat pitched violently under the weight of something huge and dark.

A bear.

Åsa grabbed her oar and swung it at the beast, connecting with a solid thud. The bear's roar deafened her, and a mighty paw knocked her to the bottom of the boat. She lay there, not daring to move, while a wet snout snuffled at her with interest.

Idiot! She realized that, in her exhaustion, she had forgotten to cache her food in a tree. Åsa drew her eating knife from her belt. The bear flicked a huge tongue across her arm and opened its maw, baring its gleaming teeth. Åsa gathered the shreds of her courage and leaped up, stabbing the puny blade into the huge body with all her strength. The knife barely pricked the thick pelt. The irritated bear roared again, his breath a foul, hot blast on her face. Åsa cried out and shrank away. The bear dropped to all fours and began woofing, preparing to attack her in earnest.

Åsa marshaled her courage. *To show fear is certain death.* She gripped her oar, took a deep breath, and screamed back at the beast with all her might, thrashing the oar high in the air with one hand, holding the knife low by her side in the other.

The bear looked at her uncertainly. Then it shook off its doubts and charged.

A mighty thwack sounded and the bear stopped short. The beady eyes widened, and it shrieked, pawing at the spear that quivered in its side. Drawing his short sword, Olaf climbed into the boat. The bear turned on him, one massive paw swinging through the air, each claw a dagger. Olaf dodged the blow, but it glanced off the side of his head and sent him reeling.

Åsa grabbed hold of the spear protruding from the bear's side and rammed it deeper. In a fury the bear swung back toward her, blasting her with its roar. She gritted her teeth and shoved the spear in with all her strength. The bear raised huge paws, claws poised to rake her.

Rising, Olaf forced his short sword up under the mighty ribs, seeking its heart. The beast screamed, its massive body writhing, trying to shake him off. The skiff heaved, throwing Åsa to the bottom of the boat. She got to her feet, keeping her grip on the spear that still protruded from the bear's side. Olaf's sword was buried to its hilt, but the bear managed to wrench it out of his grip. Drawing his hunting knife, Olaf went for the animal's throat, sawing through veins and muscle. As he breached the jugular, the bear's warm blood sprayed. The black eyes dimmed. Olaf shoved Åsa out of the way just as the huge corpse thudded to the bottom of the boat.

They stood panting over the bear's dark hulk. Their eyes met, and they both began to laugh unsteadily. Their gazes caught and held and the laughter trailed off.

Olaf reached a tentative hand out to touch her face, and she shivered. He bent his head and found her lips with his. She held on tight as he gathered her to him.

Lips still pressed to hers, Olaf lifted her to his boat rafted alongside. Together, they fell to the bottom, limbs in a tangle. She smiled up at him, her eyes reflecting the sky. He pulled the pin that held her cloak and let the fabric fall away. He stared down at her, heart beating fast.

She took hold of his linen shirt and peeled it up his torso. The sun warmed his back, and he raised his arms to let her pull it over his head, then flung it aside.

Her small hands pulled him down with a surprising strength, and a moan escaped him. Her eyes were closed, her lips parted, and a look of exultation swept across her face.

He shut his eyes and let himself go.

It was over too soon. Exhausted, they lay in the bottom of the boat, limbs entwined.

Åsa whispered, "Take me home. Take me to Tromøy."

Olaf froze.

"I will make you a king," she said, her voice rising. "You and I will rule my father's kingdom together."

His heart leaped. He could see it. A new life with her by his side. Far from his father, far from Hrolf.

"We could rebuild the hall together. Farm the land. Fish the sea."

For a moment, he believed in it. The new hall rose from the ashes. Crops bloomed in the field, cattle grazed in the pasture. Ruling from the high seat, beside Åsa.

Then reality set in.

He withdrew his arm and sat up.

"I cannot," he said. "If I took you to Tromøy, my father would pursue us. I cannot stand against him and his hird."

"Some of my father's men must still live," she said. "They would rise up to defend us and avenge my father."

"Not enough," he said. "Not enough to stand against my father. He would slaughter them to the last man." He quailed at the thought of how Gudrød would humiliate him. And what he would do to Åsa.

"Then just let me go," she said, her voice rising. "You are alone, no one need know that you found me." She stood and reached for her linen underdress, now dry and hanging from a branch. She pulled the dress over her head, the linen sliding down to hide her body.

He knew this was the biggest chance of his life. He had fulfilled his father's mission, and killed a bear. No one could never again scorn him, never again doubt his manhood, never again question his worthiness to be king. All he had to do was bring her back to claim his birthright once and for all.

"You are my father's now." His chest tightened. "You are his by right. I failed to bring you to him once before. I cannot fail again."

With unexpected speed, Åsa drew her dagger from the bear's hide and lunged at him. He dodged and caught the blade on the meat of his upper arm. Pain seared through him, and he let go of her reflexively. She leaped to her feet, tearing the knife out of his arm. She ducked out of his reach, keeping the dagger between them.

"Please don't make this harder than it must be." He picked up a rope and advanced on her, blood streaming down his arm. "Alone, you will never survive the trip. There are more bears and wolves out there, and storms, and ghosts, and sea serpents."

"I'd rather take my chances with the wild animals than with your troll of a father!" She thrust the dagger at him. On his guard now, Olaf sidestepped and reached for the knife.

Gritting his teeth, he closed his fist on the blade and jerked it out of her grip, tossing it over the side. Pain jolted up his arm, momentarily blinding him. Without losing momentum, he hooked his leg around her knees, hobbling her. Åsa kicked out and threw a wicked punch that connected with his cheek. Ignoring the pain, Olaf used his weight to force her to the bottom of the boat. He lay across her, struggling to bind her thrashing limbs.

Once she was immobilized, he stood up. "I'm sorry," he said. "I have no choice."

"Then you have condemned your father to death." Åsa glared up at him. "I swear on my father's corpse that I will kill him."

He rigged her boat in tow without speaking. With leaden arms, he hoisted the sail and steered for Borre.

THE LOOKOUT MUST HAVE SPOTTED them from a long way off, for a crowd had gathered on Borre's shore to watch Olaf bring in the boats. They cheered when they saw the bear's hulking carcass in tow. Hrolf skulked in the crowd, eyes boring into his half brother. Olaf allowed a small smile of triumph to flicker across his face as he beached the boats. Hoisting the bound girl onto his shoulder, he made his way through the crowd up to the hall.

The völva met him at the door. "Well, boy, your father will be proud of you." Did her tone hold a sour tinge? She conducted them to the high seat where Gudrød sat, the crowd spilling into the hall behind him.

Gudrød did indeed look pleased as Olaf set Åsa on her feet before him.

"Well done, son," he said. But Olaf's surge of pride turned bitter as his father glared at Åsa.

She returned his stare defiantly, and Olaf cringed. *Don't challenge him.*

"I know about your conspiracy. I know your folk aided your escape," Gudrød said. "They will be punished, you can be sure of that."

"No," said Åsa. "I acted alone."

A surge of admiration rose in Olaf's chest.

"Hrolf," Gudrød shouted. "Bring in the prisoner."

Hrolf dragged in a limp body and dropped him at Gudrød's feet. The man's eyes were tortured slits in a swollen purple face, his lips crusted with blood. Olaf shuddered as he recognized the steward from Tromøy, Toki, more by his clothes than by his mutilated face.

Åsa gasped. She dropped to her knees beside him and examined his wounds.

Hrolf gave a chilling smile. "I found him sneaking back. This man is guilty of stealing a boat and helping her to escape."

"The penalty for that is death," said Gudrød, looking down at the prone form with distaste. Dread rose in Olaf as he thought of the slaves his father had beaten to death for smaller crimes.

"This man is innocent," said Åsa, not looking up from the wounded man. "I acted alone."

Olaf winced. She was brave to take the blame, but she should not think her high status would save her from Gudrød's fury.

"How did you escape, then?" Gudrød demanded. "The völva had you under lock and key."

"I drugged Heid and stole her key."

Gudrød glared at the sorceress, but Heid ignored him. She had no fear of kings.

Hrolf sneered at Åsa. "How did you get the boat?"

"I stole it."

Hrolf smiled again, and Olaf's heart sank. "It's hard to believe that you managed to steal a boat alone. Are you saying that you drugged the völva, sneaked out of the bower without waking anyone, slipped past the guard, and stole a boat, with no help at all?"

"Yes," she said. Olaf quailed at the defiance in her eyes. *Don't fight them.*

"Impossible," Hrolf sneered. "You could never have done all that on your own. Someone aided you. This slave had the opportunity to help you get out of the bower, to steal the boat, and to help you escape." Hrolf nudged Toki with his boot, and the wounded man moaned. *Be still,* Olaf pleaded silently.

"Get him up," said Gudrød. Åsa cried out and scrambled to her feet as Hrolf hoisted Toki up roughly and held him there, swaying.

Gudrød glowered at the steward. "Perhaps your sacrifice will win the gods' favor."

"No!" Åsa lurched forward, hampered by her bonds. Olaf reached out to steady her, but she jerked away.

"Please," she said. "Spare him. I will do anything you ask."

Gudrød glared down at her, a cold smile spreading across his face.

"Kneel to me."

She stumbled to her knees and hung her head, her snarled hair shadowing the tears that streaked her dirty face.

"Your father was a fool," said Gudrød. "He thought he could take what was mine. He thought he could hide from me in Agder. Now he is dead, his son is dead, his hall burned. His daughter is my property. If you are lucky, I will make you my queen." He looked at Toki, who sagged in Hrolf's grip. "If you want this man to live, you will swear to me that you will never try to run away again."

Give him whatever he wants, Olaf urged her silently.

"I swear." Åsa's voice cracked.

"Swear that you will obey me in everything."

Åsa seemed to choke on the words. The hiss of steel snapped her eyes open. Hrolf held his dagger to Toki's throat.

"I swear."

"Send him back to the fields," Gudrød said. Olaf exhaled.

Hrolf sheathed his knife, gave Toki a vicious jerk, and dragged him out of the hall.

~

THE NEXT DAY, Gudrød ordered the bear ceremony in honor of Olaf's kill. The húskarlar gathered in the sacred grove beneath the tall wooden images of the gods: one-eyed Odin, god of war, poetry and magic; his son, mighty Thor, protector of mankind; and Frey, god of fertility and peace. Thralls kindled a huge bonfire in the clearing while Heid's followers sang praise to the bear's spirit.

Olaf watched his father plunge his knife into the rank corpse. Gudrød tore out the bear's massive heart and held it out to him. Olaf fought the impulse to shrink from the organ that dripped with gore in his father's hand. Choking down the bile that rose in his throat, he managed to take a bite, chew it, and swallow. He kept his lips firmly closed as his father roared his approval.

"Now you have the heart of a bear." Gudrød pounded Olaf on the chest. Olaf stood firmly against his father's friendly assault while the crowd cheered.

Then he saw Hrolf glowering from the shadows. The teeth of fear nipped at his happiness.

Slaves skinned the bear, carefully preserving the head and pelt for Olaf to wear in future ceremonies. They cut the meat from the bone and set it to simmer in a huge cauldron. The warriors gathered around the bonfire while the bear meat cooked, toasting Olaf with the ale Gudrød had supplied for the occasion. In Knut's absence, the younger men began to compose poems about the feat. Olaf stood among them, drinking, red-faced with pride. He realized with relief that his half brother was gone.

HROLF BROODED IN THE SHADOWS.

A hunched form wrapped in filthy rags detached from the trees and approached him.

"Boy," came a croak from within the rags. With the words rose an overwhelming stench.

Hrolf started, arm raised to strike the apparition.

A cackle emanated from the stinking form. A bony hand darted out to grasp Hrolf's arm and twisted it behind his back.

"I'm here to help you, boy," said the stranger, holding Hrolf in an iron grip.

"Get away from me, troll," said Hrolf, struggling to throw him off. "What could you possibly have that I want?"

The stranger laughed and turned him loose. "I know how you can bring your brother down."

CHAPTER 11

Early the next morning, Gudrød arrived at the smithy with Olaf, followed by a contingent of warriors carrying the bear's great bones.

Ulf struggled up from his pallet, dragging his chains with him. Gudrød bid the warriors lay the bones at Ulf's feet.

Arne appeared, combing his fingers through his beard. Behind him came his helper, a boy named Bram, who stared at Ulf with wide-eyed awe.

"Remove his fetters," said Gudrød, handing Arne an iron key.

Arne took the key, his eyes sparking rage. Ulf gritted his teeth and held his hands out. Arne fitted the key in the lock and turned it. The manacles dropped away, and Ulf's arms lifted in their sudden lightness. He rubbed them to quell their burning tingles while Arne bent to unlock his ankles.

From his scabbard, Gudrød drew the Serkland sword. The assembly gasped at the sight of the curved blade that shimmered in the light.

He held it before Ulf. "You are known as the most famous smith in the land, are you not?" Gudrød's voice grated. He did not wait for Ulf to reply. "You served a Serkland sword maker, learned his secrets, and lived to tell the tale."

"It is true, my lord, I was a slave in Serkland, and there I learned to forge swords from the wootz steel."

Gudrød gestured to the pile of bones. "You will burn these bones to forge a great sword for my son." He put his hand on Olaf's shoulder. The boy's eyes were wide, perhaps with excitement, perhaps with fear. "It will be the greatest sword ever forged in this land," Gudrød continued. "You must make it the equal of the Serkland blade."

Ulf showed no emotion as he replied. "Lord, without wootz steel, I will never succeed."

"Yet succeed you must," said Gudrød, "For if you fail, I will give Arne here a chance to succeed. And in his forge, he will burn your bones. Come, son, we have a feast to attend." Gudrød swept out of the smithy, pulling Olaf with him. The húskarlar followed.

Ulf regarded the pile of rank bones. Without a source of wootz steel, he had no hope of duplicating the Serkland sword. He would have to forge a pattern-welded sword and hope it passed muster. He could emulate the swirling pattern in the blade well enough to fool any eye. But could he make a sword strong enough to pass?

Gudrød would keep him alive as long as he had hope that Ulf would succeed. If he kept trying, he could draw his life out for quite a while.

But did he truly want to live? Harald was gone, with all Ulf's comrades. Like Völund, he was a crippled smith, enslaved to a wicked king. He smiled to think that his situation was so like that of the legendary smith. But he would not be sprouting a pair of wings. There was no escape for Ulf.

Except one.

There were plenty of sharp edges in the smithy. Chisels, saws, axes, knives, blades of every size and shape. He wouldn't need to give himself to Gudrød's tender mercies. One quick swipe, and he'd be on the Hel road.

Tempting.

But it would be a death without honor. If there was an afterlife, his would be spent in cold Hel with the sick and the lame.

Fitting.

He'd given Harald his oath to protect Åsa. He didn't see how he could keep his word, but he wouldn't leave her.

He'd live, for now. For Harald's daughter. And vengeance.

Under Arne's jealous glare, he heated bog iron in a clay crucible, boiling the slag out and producing a hard metal that he forged into billets. He forgot everything but the work as he layered softer iron with the hard metal, twisting and hammering them together into a single bar. The layers duplicated the rippling patterns of Gudrød's Serkland sword.

Ulf slept with the linen-wrapped blade beside him. Day after day, he painstakingly drew out the composite metal into a sword blade. He shaped it straight and narrow with a taper toward the edges and a fuller down its length. For the edge, he stacked and folded a hardened bar over and over, then forge-welded the hard edge over a resilient core.

He held the finished blade over the flames, watching the metal turn from red to orange. Now was the moment of greatest risk—the final quench. The quench was required to give the edge hardness, but this was when the brittle metal was most likely to crack. If that happened, days of work would be ruined.

Ulf pulled the red-hot blade out of the fire. Holding his breath, he plunged it into the quench, taking care that the entire blade entered the trough simultaneously. Steam hissed, enveloping him in a thick mist. He braced himself for the sound of cracking metal. As the steam dissipated, the air remained silent. He pulled the blade from the quench and exhaled.

He examined the blade from every angle. His stomach

clenched as he observed the slightest bend, enough that he must straighten it.

He passed the blade high over the flames to restore the steel's flexibility, watching the color carefully. He withdrew it from the fire and, holding his breath, gently forged out the bend, expecting to hear the crack of metal with every tap of the hammer.

When he was satisfied, he set it aside to air cool, and then began the labor of grinding the metal to make it shine.

Once the sword was ground, he etched it with apple cider vinegar to bring out the pattern.

It was the best weapon he had ever made, by far. But doubt nibbled at his mind. Was it a match for the Serkland sword? Was it as light, as well balanced? He pondered these questions as he polished the blade to a sheen and gave it a cutting edge.

Finally he fitted the bronze guard to the tang, riveting a grip of oak wrapped with silver wire and a pommel engraved with runes for protection and victory.

He swung the finished sword, testing its balance.

"Now?" said Bram eagerly.

Ulf nodded and handed him the sword. Grinning widely, Bram positioned himself, legs braced wide, the pommel gripped with both hands. He raised the sword with his skinny arms.

Bram brought the new blade down on the anvil with enough force to make the boy stagger. Grin never wavering, he repeated the batterings on every angle. The smithy rang with metal on metal while Arne looked on with a sour face.

Finally Ulf called a halt. He examined the edge minutely for nicks, testing for sharpness.

Satisfied, he sent word to the great hall.

Gudrød and Olaf burst into the smithy, húskarlar crowding the door behind them.

"Where is this miraculous sword?" Gudrød demanded.

It took all of Ulf's willpower to keep his hands steady as he presented the new blade to Gudrød. He could not breathe while the king inspected it.

Gudrød handed it back to Ulf. In an eye blink, Gudrød drew his own sword and slashed at the smith. Instinctively, Ulf flung up the new sword to block. Steel rang as the blow rattled down Ulf's arm to his very core.

He hardly dared to look.

When at last he did, he saw that his creation was still whole. It had withstood the Serkland blade without a nick. Ulf exhaled slowly.

Gudrød sheathed his own sword and grabbed the new blade from Ulf's hands. Holding it aloft, he declared, "This sword shall be known as Bear Biter." He turned and presented it to his son.

Olaf took the sword with both hands. Bowing his head, he said, "I pledge this sword in service to you, Father."

The húskarlar sent up a cheer. Gudrød clapped his son on the back, and they trooped out of the smithy, calling for mead.

Ulf's knees buckled. He turned his back on Arne's stare and stumbled to his cot.

CHAPTER 12

Gudrød's húskarlar followed Åsa wherever she went and guarded the bower door at night.

When she demanded to see Toki the day after his beating, Hrolf escorted her to a cow byre. He opened the door with a leering grin. In the gloomy reaches, she saw Toki lying on a straw pallet. Brenna knelt beside him, tending his wounds.

Åsa exchanged a tearful glance with Brenna and fell to her knees beside the wounded man. "I am so sorry. I did not mean to involve you."

"It wasn't your fault, child," he said. "I will mend."

"Perhaps I didn't hit you hard enough, slave," said Hrolf.

Åsa bit back her retort, afraid that might provoke him. She just touched her hand to the steward's face.

"Don't worry," he whispered. "Brenna is taking good care of me."

"Is there anything you need?" Åsa asked.

Brenna shook her head. "Heid is supplying me with medicine," she murmured, so low that Hrolf didn't hear.

As Hrolf trailed Åsa back to the bower, she glimpsed Olaf. He met her glance out of the corner of his eye, but he quickly turned away. Hurt and fury burned in her throat, nearly choking her. She was a fool to have trusted him, to have thought he was different from his father. A fool to think that he cared for her, that he would ever choose her over Gudrød. She fixed her gaze on the ground and kept walking.

Back in the bower, Heid had the apprentices in a frenzy of preparations for the wedding, stitching linens and sorting moss and herbs for dying and ale brewing.

The work went on for days. Sigrid sat on a stool in the corner making a tablet-woven band in the ancient pattern to trim the wedding garments.

Heid stood over the old woman as she worked, bone tablets clacking as the colorful threads flew. Without warning, the sorceress slammed her iron staff on the floor. "Fool," she cried. "You have the pattern wrong. You will bring down a curse on us all with your slovenly work!"

Sigrid winced and looked up at her, bleary-eyed. "I am sorry, lady. My eyes are not what they once were."

"It will all have to be redone. Get out of my sight." Beating Sigrid about the shoulders with her staff, Heid drove the old woman out of the hall.

Anger boiled in Åsa's chest. But what could she do about it? The other women kept their eyes focused on their work. A slave was only valued for the work they could perform and cast off when they were no longer useful.

Then Åsa realized that an opportunity had presented itself.

"In Tromøy, Brenna made all of my mother's clothing," she said to Heid, her words coming in a rush. "She knows the pattern of the wedding band perfectly, she has never made a mistake. Her eyesight is perfect."

"We can't bring in a field slave to weave the wedding cloth," Heid said tersely.

"Brenna was not a slave on Tromøy." Åsa's voice rose shrilly. "She has looked after me since I was born. She is the only one who can make my wedding robes. She is the only one left who knows my ørlög." Åsa glared at the sorceress, fighting back tears. Her cheeks burned and she couldn't catch her breath.

The völva stared at her, then turned to an apprentice and said, "Bring the thrall Brenna."

Åsa swallowed. "And her children," she said in a voice that trembled.

Heid compressed her lips, then repeated, "And her children."

WHEN BRENNA ENTERED THE BOWER, she looked so worn and tired that Åsa burst into tears.

Brenna took her in her arms, as she had so many times over the years. "There, little lamb. We all miss them. They wait for us in Odin's hall." They held each other for a long time, sharing silent tears. "Toki is nearly recovered," she said. "He bears his injuries lightly."

From that moment on, Brenna took charge of the robes, and the wedding as well. She insisted that all the Tromøy women be brought in from the fields to help with the garments, and of course they must bring their children with them.

"A woman works better when she knows her children are near," she said.

Heid did not argue that point.

Brenna knew how to work the system. "You have too much to do," she said sympathetically to the steward. "It's a shame they can't spare Toki to assist you. He's a devil for work. Back in Tromøy, his feasts were famous throughout the south land." The steward looked thoughtful, and the next day Toki was at work in the kitchen.

Toki brought in more Tromøy folk to help in the kitchens. Soon Åsa was surrounded by familiar faces, people she had known and trusted all of her life. Now she could to go to the kitchens and speak with the cook who had fed her since she was a baby. Every day, she greeted her people, and realized that, in a way, she was keeping the promise she had made to take care of them.

Their main topic of conversation was the folk left on Tromøy. *How will they survive the winter, with the crops burned and the livestock killed? How will they stay warm?* Åsa had no answer to that, but at night she lay awake, turning the questions over and over in her mind.

"We owe you our lives, and the lives of our children," Brenna said. "If you hadn't brought us in, we would have died in the fields."

If it weren't for me, you would not have been working in the fields in the first place, Åsa thought.

∼

TRUE TO ÅSA'S BOAST, Brenna's tablet weaving was perfect. All too soon, the women brought out the wool fabric for the wedding garments. Brenna began to fit the gown, assisted by old Sigrid, who had been forgiven. Åsa stood motionless for hours while they cut and pinned. Heid's highborn acolytes flitted about, getting in the older women's way and infecting the bower with their excitement.

When at last the gown was done, Åsa spent miserable hours under the völva's watchful eye embroidering the seams and neckline of her gown with an intricate pattern critical to the garment's magical powers. The needles pricked her fingers bloody. If she made the slightest mistake, Heid would make her undo every stitch and begin again.

Åsa was picking out her faulty embroidery yet again, letting the sound of the apprentices' chatter run past her ears. Even though they were the daughters of kings and earls like her, she did not feel like one of them. They were free, here by choice, living under the völva's protection, honored guests wherever they went. She was a captive.

Astrid sat down beside her. "I am sorry you have to go through with this," she whispered, with a glance to the apprentices. "They aren't really as unfeeling as they seem. They're just excited about the wedding."

Åsa choked on her reply as tears dripped onto her embroidery. Momentarily blinded, she nicked her finger on the narrow, razor-sharp blade. She cursed as a drop of blood spilled onto her skirt.

"Careful with that," said Astrid. "That blade may be small, but it is lethal!"

Small but lethal. Åsa fingered the blade thoughtfully. Half a dozen of them lay on the benches.

Raising her finger to her throat, Åsa located the pulsing artery. Here was where one cut an animal for sacrifice. Gudrød had such an artery as well. All it took was a good slash, and there was no stopping the bleeding. A shudder ran through her. She would have to let him get close.

She could stand it.

She laid the blade along the wide, embroidered side seam of her gown. It would fit invisibly. But it would not bear the völva's close scrutiny. From now on, her embroidery would have to be perfect.

~

AMID THE PREPARATIONS for the wedding and the equinox sacrifice, the skáld Knut arrived at Borre. Gudrød immediately ordered a feast in his honor. While the household was busy with preparations, Åsa found a moment alone with the old skáld.

"Have you had any news of Tromøy?" she whispered.

Knut looked grim. "I stopped there a few weeks ago. The people are making ready for winter. The jarls have sent them some stores, but I don't like their prospects."

Åsa finished what Knut left unsaid. Tromøy would remain hers as long as she lived, by right of inheritance, but her father's kingship had dissolved upon his death. Agder was no longer united. The jarls would vie among themselves, as they had before they'd made her father king years ago. Chaos would rule the land, and the people would suffer a continual state of war: killing, raiding, crops burned, homes destroyed. This would go on until the day that one warlord vanquished all others, as her father had, and was accepted as king by the rest. But Åsa knew that none of the jarls of Agder would choose to support another above their own claims. The fighting would go on for a very long time, and the people would suffer.

All my fault, she thought, turning away from the skáld.

AT DAYBREAK, Åsa woke to female voices singing outside the bower. For a moment, she thought she was home on Tromøy, and it was her childhood friends who sang. But they were Heid's apprentices, come to rouse her for her wedding day.

"It's time," said Astrid, gently pulling her from the bed and guiding her to the wooden tub that Sigrid and Brenna were filling with hot water from buckets. Åsa stepped into the bath and sat stoically while the women scrubbed her skin rosy. She did not let her mind focus on what would happen today.

Fighting down panic, she let them help her from the tub. Brenna dried her with a linen towel, and Astrid dressed her in the hateful gown she had so painstakingly embroidered. Åsa fumbled at the seam until she felt the tiny blade. She clutched it tightly for a moment, then forced herself to let go of it before anyone noticed.

Brenna combed out Åsa's long red-gold hair, arranging it loose and flowing over her shoulders in an unmarried girl's style for the last time. Crowning her with the gilded bridal headdress, she whispered fiercely, "This is what you must do to survive. And survive you must."

Singing once more, the girls escorted her to the sacred grove where hazel rods staked out the sanctuary beyond which no guest could bear weapons. Within its hallowed bounds the freemen sworn to Gudrød gathered with their wives and children. They greeted the bride with smiles and well-wishes, and some ribald suggestions for the wedding night.

Astrid led her beneath the carved images of the Frey and Thor, squeezed her hand, and stepped back. Heid came forward and grasped her shoulders, digging gnarled fingers into her flesh. Her breath reeked of the sacred herbs. The völva gave her the goddess' kiss and said, "May Freyja bless you and make you fruitful." Then she picked up a sword and put it in Åsa's left hand.

Åsa shook off her trance and looked at the crowd. Every man, woman, and child watched her. Olaf's blond head shone above them all. His eyes widened as they fastened on her. Something inside her sparked in answer but quickly soured into bitterness. She would not be fooled again.

As Gudrød approached, she forced herself to stay motionless, her face frozen.

Heid took her place before the wedding couple and called down the blessing of the gods. She turned to Gudrød, who held his own sword out to Åsa, hilt first. "Wife, I bid you take this sword into keeping for our firstborn son." By tradition, it should have been the sword of a great ancestor, but in the ultimate display of disrespect to both his dead father and his new bride,

Gudrød offered a nondescript weapon hastily taken up from the armory.

As Åsa reached out to take the sword with her right hand, she eyed the veins standing out in Gudrød's neck.

Wait, she told herself. *Your chance is coming.*

Mustering her self-control, she gripped the proffered sword and extended her own to Gudrød. "And this I give you in return, to keep us safe." Her father's sword lay broken and burned in Tromøy, so, like Gudrød's, hers was a castoff weapon supplied from the armory.

Having exchanged swords, the couple turned to the altar. It was an enormous, ancient stone, its top worn smooth from years of use. On it gleamed a massive golden arm ring. Within this ring, Heid placed two gold finger rings, and spoke a blessing over them. She picked up one of the rings and hung it on the tip of Gudrød's sword. He turned to Åsa and offered it to her. With shaking hands, she managed to take the ring and place it on her finger. She then raised her sword to receive the other ring from Heid. But her hands shook so hard that the ring fell to the ground. The onlookers sucked in their breath, for this was an omen that boded ill for the marriage. Åsa waited stoically while Heid bent and picked up the ring without a word and placed it back on the sword point. Gudrød snatched it and shoved it on his finger.

He turned his back on his new bride. "Let's drink some ale!" he shouted to his men, and led them to the hall.

Åsa fought the urge to run. Astrid put her hand on her shoulder as Heid and her acolytes closed in. "Frigg be with you," she murmured.

They ushered her toward the hall, singing and strewing flowers in her path. Åsa clutched her sword, preparing to use it on her new husband. But Heid took it from her with a stern look.

Clutching the tiny blade hidden in its seam, she arrived at the hall where Gudrød waited at the threshold surrounded by his men. Grinning amid suggestive comments, he picked her up roughly and carried her inside. He dropped her on her feet, drew his sword, and rammed it into the central pillar of the hall, where it stuck fast, quivering. The company sent up a mighty cheer.

Heid hobbled forth with the double-handled wedding cup of honey mead. She offered it first to Gudrød, who raised it in a toast to Odin. He drank and held the cup out to Åsa. She grasped the handles but could not bring herself to speak.

"To Freyja!" he shouted for her, and tipped the cup to her mouth. She managed to choke down the mead. The crowd cheered again as Gudrød gripped Åsa's arm hard and led her to the dais, where he firmly pressed her into the high seat next to his.

Then Heid limped forward, carrying Thor's hammer, Mjölnir. This she laid in Åsa's lap and cried, "May the marriage be blessed with many children." The crowd cheered again and shouted lewd advice. Then the drinking began in earnest.

While they waited for the food, Knut stepped into the center and recited the story of the Yngling clan from which Gudrød claimed descent. "Many years ago, Olaf the Woodcutter came from Uppsala in Sweden and founded the royal Yngling line here in Vestfold. It was he who built the Shining Hall in memory of his family's royal seat at Uppsala." At Gudrød's frown, Knut hurried on.

"There came a famine, and it was said that his people sacrificed King Olaf to Frey, that he might bless the land and make it fertile again."

Knut went on to relate the histories of other kings. King Sigurd sacrificed his son to Odin to turn the tide of a battle, bringing him victory. King Aud the Old was said to have sacrificed nine sons, one after the other, to prolong his own life. As the king aged, he grew weaker every year until his last remaining son turned the tables and sacrificed Aud.

Åsa sat beside Gudrød for hours, back pressed into the chair, worrying at the tiny knife in the seam.

The song and laughter swirled in the air like woodsmoke. When the tumult had reached a deafening peak, the thralls carried in platters of meat. As always, the hall fell silent but for the scrape of knives on plates while guests attended to the food with gusto.

Åsa stared at the meat on her plate, but she couldn't eat.

After the thralls had cleared away the food, more stories were accompanied by much belching and laughter. Gudrød signaled the musicians to play. At the sound of harps and pipes, the drunker guests got up to dance.

Gudrød raised his horn one last time. "To my bride!" he declared. The warriors banged their cups on the trestle tables.

Åsa had worked the tiny blade inside the seam until she had cut an opening. With her fingernails, she pulled the blade out partway, making sure it slid easily, then pushed it back into the pocket in the seam.

At last, Heid came forward and pried Åsa from the high seat. Laughing and making suggestive jokes, the women surrounded the bride once again. Astrid linked her arm in Åsa's and led her to the bridal chamber.

Åsa kept her eyes lowered as she tried to control her trembling. Her finger sought the pulse in her throat. *His or mine,* she thought.

She would have to let him get close. She would have to let him lay hands on her. But once she had driven the blade into his artery, he would bleed out quickly, losing control of his limbs and falling unconscious in seconds.

If she somehow failed, she would turn the blade on herself and be gone to the afterlife before he could take her.

She held herself still while the women undressed her, her grip tight on the blade. As they removed her gown, she pulled the tiny knife free of the seam. She stood in her pleated linen shift, clenching the seam ripper in her fist while Astrid served her a strong drink laced with a powerful fertility potion and Heid spoke spells over her. At the chamber door, Astrid kissed her and stepped outside. Without meeting her eyes, Heid grasped her with gnarled fingers and drew her forward, kissing her on both cheeks in the goddess's embrace. Then she gave her a little push toward the bed and backed out of the door.

Accompanied by lewd shouts, Gudrød reeled into the bridal chamber. He slammed the door on the raucous crowd and peeled off his shirt. Battle scars pocked his torso. He stank of mead from every pore as he reached for Åsa.

Gripping the knife, Åsa let him seize her shoulder and pull her close. She fixed her eyes on the pulsing artery at his throat. Blade clenched in her fist, she struck.

Even drunk, Gudrød was too seasoned a warrior. He dodged reflexively, and the blade missed his throat, nicking his shoulder. Blood welled and he roared in surprise. She slashed again, slicing a long cut down his chest, and caught a glimpse of fear in his eyes just before he backhanded her across the face. Her head snapped back, and he clamped her wrist in an iron grip, twisting until the pain forced her to let the knife drop. He snatched it out of the air and held it up.

"So you want revenge, eh?" he said. "You think you can kill me with a seam ripper? I slew your father, and your brother. I have taken your kingdom and enslaved your people. Everything that was yours is now mine. You are powerless. My property."

He dragged her to the bed. She kicked and writhed as he forced her down onto the mattress. Åsa fought panic as she lay pinned under his body, his breath hot on her face. Under his onslaught of fury and frustration, she quit fighting, focused instead on enduring the endless pain until she went deep within and found a safe place.

He struggled and strained for an eternity, but in vain. In the end, he was unable to consummate the marriage.

"If you tell anyone about this, I will kill you." His breath was hot against her ear.

Åsa lay unresponsive, coming back to her body from far away.

"Do you understand?" he said harshly. She nodded, rigid as a stick of wood, trying to control her breath.

Gudrød got off her. Åsa kept her face averted but watched him out of the corner of her eye.

"Keep your mouth shut," he warned as he pulled on his clothes and threw open the door. "Let's drink!" he cried.

The revelers poured in. Someone tore the linen off the bed with a triumphant cry. Clutching the tatters of her shift, Åsa allowed herself a faint smile as they caroused. The sheets were suitably spattered red, but all the blood was Gudrød's.

FOR THE BRIDE'S morning gift, Gudrød gave her back her mother's jewels.

Tears welled instantly at the sight of the familiar amber gleaming in its carved box, but Gudrød's taunting grin kindled a fury in her that burned the tears away. The wedding guests were utterly silent. Meeting his gaze with a flinty stare, she lifted the necklace from its box and fastened it around her neck. Face expressionless, she turned back to her breakfast.

The wedding feast went on for a week. Åsa retired alone to the bridal chamber each night while her husband drank with his men. She waited in the dark, sleepless for hours, stiff with apprehension, but he did not come. Perhaps he feared that he would be impotent with her again. As long as he left her alone, she was content.

Each day, Åsa took her place on the high seat beside her father's murderer, offering him the mead cup, greeting his guests, presiding over swimming and wrestling contests and horse fights. She smiled at the winners and awarded them silver arm rings, doing all she must to ensure her status as queen. Power was what mattered. It was her only advantage, her only weapon.

Olaf and Hrolf dominated the wrestling. Day after day, they defeated all challengers, fighting their way toward each other with hate in their eyes. The rivalry simmering between the half brothers was the subject of much gossip and betting.

At last, they were the only two standing.

The crowd buzzed with anticipation as they stood face-to-face, stripped to the waist. They grasped each other by the shoulders and began to circle, each trying to hook their leg around the other's while eluding the same hold from his opponent. After several seconds, Hrolf succeeded in taking Olaf down momentarily. Olaf arched his back and twisted out of Hrolf's grip, springing up and dancing away. Hrolf grabbed Olaf's leg and yanked him back down. The two rolled across the ground, each trying to pin the other with his body weight. Olaf scrambled to the top, but Hrolf clung to him, trying to flip him. Olaf bore down, shifting his weight to counter Hrolf's moves, trying to wear his opponent out, but Hrolf refused to let go. The test of wills wore on, the two thumping and straining on the ground as the onlookers hooted and shouted encouragement. At last, Olaf broke free. Hrolf grabbed at a leg, but his grip was weak, and Olaf shook him off, gaining his feet unhindered, thereby winning the bout.

As the crowd cheered and bets were settled, Olaf approached the high seat for his reward. Gudrød took a silver ring from his arm, then handed it to Åsa.

She rose to offer the ring to Olaf, and their eyes met. Åsa looked away, but not before a blush rose up to her face. From under her lashes, she saw that Olaf was red too, although it could have been a flush from his exertions. Sweat darkened the blond hair on his chest and arms, and he gave off an earthy scent. She controlled her trembling hands as she slid the ring onto his arm and resumed her seat with relief.

That evening, she sat beside her husband in the high seat while the local wits tried to outdo each other in outrageous insults and tall tales. She smiled at her enemies while imagining each head grinning back from a spike.

One by one, the guests took their leave, and Borre shrank to its normal population. As she served the last guest his stirrup cup of ale, Åsa longed to crawl into bed and sleep.

Borre's húskarlar still shadowed Åsa everywhere she went. It was silly. Where could she go now, with winter around the corner? To avoid them, she resumed her place among the women in the bower. No man dared to enter, for spinning was believed to wreak havoc on manly functions, and weaving was even worse.

THE WEEKS WENT by as fall gave way to winter. One morning, Åsa lost her breakfast. When it happened again the next morning, she caught the völva watching her with a satisfied look.

I'm pregnant, she realized, her mind reeling.

With Olaf's child.

Fear sickened her. *What will Gudrød do when he finds that I'm carrying another man's child?* There was no hiding it now that Heid knew. With a word, he could cast her aside, declare her a thrall and her child a bastard. He could have her killed outright. Even if she survived his wrath, she feared the long months ahead, a dark winter that would end in suffering and childbirth.

There was one way out, a way she considered long and hard. It was still easy to lay hands on a blade, they were everywhere— in the bower for sewing, in the kitchens for meat, so many different kinds were used for everything. She could end her life right now, and avoid all the misery that loomed in her future.

But she knew that was the coward's way, which Harald Redbeard's daughter could not take. And the choice was no longer just her own. She could not make that decision for her child. She must see this through to the very end.

GUDRØD SPENT much of his time with Olaf beaming by his side. Bitterness turned Åsa's stomach as father and son walked into the hall, arm in arm.

She managed to keep out of Gudrød's sight at first, but when the guests arrived for the autumn feast, Åsa knew she was trapped. The queen had to take her place on the high seat at her husband's side.

She dressed for the occasion in loose garments. Mounting the high seat, she hoped her slight thickening would not be too obvious. Gudrød did not spare her a glance, and for a little while, she thought she could escape notice.

Then the völva rose and called for silence.

Heid turned to Gudrød and announced, "My lord, congratulations are in order. Your seed has taken root. The queen is with child."

Åsa's heart lurched. Her gaze went to Olaf involuntarily before she dragged it away. Heid was beaming at her while the warriors cheered and banged their shields.

Gudrød's eyes widened. Åsa's stomach knotted as she watched realization came over his face. He turned his glare on her. Panic choked her. She was exposed, trapped there on the high seat in front of the crowded hall.

Then Gudrød's grim expression contorted into a smile. He laughed.

"I could tell she was fertile," he declared. "And I knew just what to do about it." He raised his horn. "To my future son," he shouted. The warriors cheered and drank to Åsa.

It was good that she was sitting down. Relief hit her hard. *He has as much to lose as I do,* she realized in a rush. The fertility of the king was the fertility of the land. Impotence and cuckoldry in a king brought pestilence on the crops, made women and livestock barren. Kings had been sacrificed by their people for less. If anyone suspected the truth, Gudrød would be a dead man.

She raised her cup and forced a smile that turned her stomach. *Your secret is safe with me, my lord.*

CHAPTER 13

Åsa held her despair at bay with work. She was up before the gray dawn to join the Tromøy folk in filling the storehouses for winter, smoking fish and salting meat, storing the wild hazelnuts and apples in wood buckets, rubbing the grass-wrapped cheeses. She joined Heid's apprentices in festooning the bower's rafters with bundles of lovage, parsley, mint, thyme, and marjoram, the clean scent of the herbs mingling with woodsmoke and filling the bower. The sheep got a final shearing, and the thick fall wool was blended with the weaker stuff from the spring shearing.

She started the winter ale, for it must be ready for the feast on winter's first new moon. This was the sacrifice to remember the dead and honor the álfir. It was the álfir who could cause the most trouble if they felt they had been slighted. It was they who caused the milk to sour, the crops to fail, the livestock to take sick. A careful lord did not neglect them.

On the eve of the dead, after the last sheaf had been blessed, Åsa burned dried flowers as offering to the dís. Watching the fragrant smoke curl up to the high ceiling and out the open gable ends, she imagined her blessings carried on the wind to Tromøy.

JOHANNA WITTENBERG

Perhaps they would reach her mother, deep in her mound. Perhaps Gunnhild would forgive her daughter for the destruction she had brought down on her people, and would intervene on their behalf.

It was all she could do.

For the first time since the day Heid had announced her pregnancy, Åsa took her place beside Gudrød. They did not meet each other's eyes. As was required of a queen, she stood at the altar as he made sacrifice to thank the álfir for the harvest, and led the prayers asking for their help surviving the long winter to come. Åsa received the well-wishes from the local farmers and Gudrød's húskarlar, gave them gifts, drank to the gods, and was relieved when it was over.

But all this was only a prelude to the great Jól feast. In the days that followed, Gudrød continued to avoid Åsa, staring over her head when they passed each other. She wondered if he had guessed who the true father of her child must be. It hardly mattered. As long as the fragile truce survived between them, she would be safe. Her status as a free woman and queen depended on his acceptance of her and the child, and she intended to do everything in her power to preserve it.

No one expected any love between them. They knew Gudrød had taken her by force and the consummation of the marriage was an act of rape. Kidnap was not an unusual method for a powerful man to obtain a wife, especially when land ownership was involved. Everyone knew she had no choice and must make the best of things for herself and her unborn child. She had little left to lose, and the power of a queen to gain. Some would think it a fair exchange.

But there were times when she caught Gudrød watching her with a calculating stare, and she knew she was not safe at all.

The first snow flew, filling the air with swirling flakes. Overnight, the dark forest shone white against the gloom. Back on Tromøy, Åsa had always loved the coming of winter with its promise of the Jól festivities. She relished the ease of skiing across the snow-clad fields, the dizzying speed as she flew down steep hills. When the ponds froze solid, she had joined the other children, strapping cow-bone skates to their boots and whizzing across the ice.

But in her memories, Gyrd was always there, racing her, throwing snowballs, building ice forts.

At night, she tossed and turned under her eiderdown quilt, tortured by visions of her childhood friends on Tromøy huddled in a freezing lean-to in the forest, gnawing on bare bones, bereft of hope. How would they get through the winter?

As snow blanketed the landscape, Åsa sat with Heid's women by the crackling longfire, spinning wool and flax.

Distaffs bobbed and whorls twirled while the women gossiped about the world outside. They spoke of endless battles between the thirty-odd petty kings who squabbled over the land like wolves. There were jarls who fought to become kings and kings who fell to the status of jarls, the only difference between them being who paid tribute to whom. They told tales of the famous sea kings, those landless second sons who swore no oaths to any lord but ruled the seas in their longships, harrying the coasts, taking booty and land.

True to his nickname, the Hunting King, Gudrød spent much of his time away in the forest with his men. He always took Olaf with him, the son basking in his father's approval. Åsa was glad to have them both out of her sight.

They would be gone for a day or two, returning with sledges loaded with game, to feast and drink themselves senseless. Then Gudrød would take to his bed. Once he recovered from the merrymaking, he would call up his men and embark on another hunt.

Sitting by the fire in the great hall after the evening meal, Åsa heard the stamp of horses and jingle of harnesses signaling the hunters' return. She wrapped her shawl around her shoulders and slipped out the back door to the bower. It was best to stay out from under Gudrød's eye.

She paused in the shadows to watch Olaf stomp into the hall arm in arm with his father. Rosy and laughing, he never looked in Åsa's direction. Bitterness twisted in her like a knife. He would not be enduring a long winter heavy with child or face the terrors of childbed at the end of it.

OLAF KNEW he should be ecstatic. All of his life, he had longed for his father's approval. After years of rejection, he had given up hope and resigned himself to the cuffs and jeers his father gave him, and the disparaging looks from his father's men who did not quite dare to voice their disdain for a king's son.

Now everything had changed. Instead of cuffs, he received Gudrød's manly clap on the shoulder. His father beamed whenever he saw him. Gudrød consulted Olaf on every matter, and if he never followed his son's advice, nobody mentioned it. There was no mockery in the húskarlar's voices now when they called him "lord." Hrolf still watched him jealously but held his tongue. He dare not challenge Olaf now. For the first time, Olaf felt adequate. More than adequate, really, he felt almost mighty. As if he might really take his place as king one day.

He spent the evenings entertaining those gathered in the hall with poems and tales, which gave him the excuse to drink moderately, just enough to lubricate his tongue. His poetry was much admired by all the warriors.

It seemed the women admired him as well. There were always girls waiting for him when he walked anywhere alone. Heid's apprentices vied for his attention. It was from among them he might one day choose a wife, and they were always friendly to him.

All but one. Åsa. Olaf did his best to brush her off, the way his father did, but he could not forget that day with her. He favored a slave girl whose hair was the same reddish gold. When he let his vision blur, he could imagine she was Åsa.

He could see the sorrow in her eyes. She had lost everything, her family, her home. She was a prisoner among hostile strangers. And he had betrayed her, had achieved his good fortune at her expense.

It was hard to watch her beside his father on the high seat, knowing she belonged to Gudrød when Olaf still longed for her.

And now she carried Gudrød's child. Olaf still daydreamed of what might have been if he had taken her to Tromøy as she had begged him to. He imagined them living together in her father's hall.

It was a fool's dream. If he had taken her to Tromøy, Gudrød would have hunted them down relentlessly and left no one alive. Likewise, if he had let her go alone, in that tiny boat, she wouldn't have even made it to Tromøy. Her first day out, she had nearly been killed by a bear. No, he had done the only thing he could. A man had to make hard choices sometimes, he was learning that.

He was learning other things as well. A king's authority must be maintained, sometimes with harshness. Olaf was learning a little of the bluff and bluster that men used to maintain their positions. He had not learned cruelty yet, or how to make men fear him. He did not think he ever would learn that. He hoped he wouldn't have to.

HROLF FOLLOWED the tracks that led deep into the forest. His skis carried him swiftly across the blue-shadowed snow. His shield was slung across his back and his sword at his hip, but he wore no armor. Over his shoulder, he carried a pack.

He came to the clearing and waited, exposed in the snow-muffled silence. He tried to slow his breath as the sweat began to chill his body. He could feel the watcher's presence.

"Hrafn," he cried. "Hrafn, I would speak with you."

Silence. Hrolf began to wonder if he were in the wrong place. But no, this was the place. The stranger had been clear.

An arrow zinged past his ear. He remained rooted to the spot. If he moved, he knew he would die.

Another arrow kissed his forehead without marking him.

A hooded figure emerged from the trees, advancing on Hrolf.

"Did you bring meat, boy?" The voice was a growl from deep within the hood.

Hrolf nodded, not daring to speak.

"Give it here." The stranger threw back his hood, revealing a frizz of white hair and a grizzled beard. From his leathery face, one piercing blue eye stared out. Where the other eye should have been, a mangled lid had been sewn shut crudely. It looked as if the old man had stitched it himself.

Hrolf tried to still the tremble in his hands as he withdrew a linen-wrapped haunch of mutton from his pack. The old man grabbed it and began to tear at the meat with his teeth, his one eye predatorily on Hrolf as if sizing him up for a meal.

"Ale!" the old man demanded. Hrolf brought out a flask. The old man seized it with one hand and guzzled, the ale mingling with the grease running down his beard.

When he had finished the mutton, he cast the bones aside and fixed Hrolf with his single eye.

"I have been outlawed to live in the wilds. Any man is entitled to kill me without penalty…if he can." The old man cackled as if this were the funniest thing in the world. "All men fear me, even Gudrød King. Once I was Hrafn Storm Sword, his greatest commander. But so great did I become that he came to fear me. Out of fear, he cast me out. Now, boy, tell me why you seek old Hrafn?"

Hrolf cursed his voice for quavering. "I wish to follow the ways of the berserk."

Hrafn threw back his head and laughed, a mad sound that sent a shiver down Hrolf's spine. Everything told him to run as fast as he could and never look back.

The laughter stopped abruptly, and the old man pinned Hrolf with his one-eyed gaze.

Hrafn circled Hrolf, who scarcely dared to breathe. "No metal can bite me," the old man hissed. "No fire can burn me. That kind of magic does not come easily. To gain it, I endured the kind of torture that would kill any normal man. It is the only way, Odin's way. Most who try do not survive it. What makes you think you can learn those ways, boy?"

"I am a king's son," Hrolf managed to say more boldly. "A trained warrior. I can meet any challenge."

Hrafn's stare raked over him. "A king's bastard, more like. But king's blood is king's blood. Hold out your arm."

Hrolf forced his forearm away from his side. In spite of all the effort of his will, the arm shook.

The old man didn't seem to notice. He grasped Hrolf's wrist and unsheathed a worn hunting knife, running the filthy black blade across Hrolf's forearm until blood welled up. The berserker licked the blood off the knife, smacking his lips reflectively as he gazed off into the forest.

"Hmmm…yes, yes," he muttered. "King's blood is king's blood." His single eye riveted on Hrolf again. "If I teach you, boy, you must do whatever I command."

"Yes, yes, I will. Anything."

"The way is hard. It might kill you. Why do you wish to undertake such a risk?"

When Hrolf forced the words out, they came in a whisper. "I wish to be king."

Hrafn once again threw his head back and laughed his insane laugh. Hrolf shuddered at the sound. "I will make you a king. But when I do, you must restore everything your father took from me. I will be the king's commander again. I will be a lord of men again. Feared and respected. And rich. You will make me rich, boy."

"Yes," said Hrolf. "Yes, whatever you want."

"Very well," said Hrafn. "Come back here on the new moon, and we will begin."

THE DAYS SPED BY, and the second new moon of winter arrived, marking the first day of Jól. Gudrød's sworn men flocked to Borre for the feast, for it was time to renew their vows to the king. Anyone who was absent without the excuse of illness or death risked being counted Gudrød's enemy in the new year.

The jarls arrived from the distant territories with their retinues, overflowing the guesthouses and setting up tents in the yard. As more and more arrived, a great camp arose around the hall. Borre was transformed into a temporary city of weather-proof deerskin tents. The smoke of a hundred fires curled into the winter sky, and the chill air filled with the sounds and smells of three hundred men, women, and children, and their livestock, as they churned the pristine snow to mud. Great vats of Jól ale were set out for the throng to participate in the ceremonial drinking.

Six warriors manhandled the trunk of a felled ash tree into the hall and onto the central hearth. This was the Jól log, and it would burn all through the twelve days of the feast. Adults and children alike fell on the enormous log in delight, festooning it with mistletoe and carving it with runes for good fortune.

In the queen's bower, Åsa stood patiently as the women dressed her in a pleated linen shift with a long train. Over that came a gown of wool twill the color of wine, the neckline and cuffs trimmed with a tablet-woven band. Astrid fastened the linen veil over Åsa's red-gold hair with silver pins, fussing with the headdress until it was to her liking.

Heid unlocked a rune-carved trunk and brought forth a linen-wrapped bundle, which she placed in Åsa's hands. Carefully pulling back the cloth, Åsa uncovered a charred length of wood, the remains of last year's Jól log. As the lady of the house, she must kindle the new wood with the old, ensuring the continuity of life. Her mother had trained her in this ritual since childhood, and she had succeeded alone after her mother's death.

But now she must perform before her enemies.

The merriment in the hall stilled when Åsa entered bearing the half-burned wood on its linen wrap. The women gathered around her, and even the men fell silent as Åsa knelt on the hearth. With her knife, she cut a notch in the log, then took the Jól stick from the linen and fitted the tip into the notch. She rubbed the stick hard between her palms until she began to feel the heat. With a burst of speed, Åsa ran her hands down the stick, producing a flurry of tiny wood flecks. She could hear the women breathing as they leaned in close. Her palms were already raw and she was beginning to sweat, but she kept up the friction, offering a silent prayer to the dís.

A wisp of smoke floated up. The men cheered and went back to their ale. The women watched, knowing the drama was not complete.

Gently blowing on the tiny flame, Åsa coaxed the fire to life, feeding it with wood shavings. When the fire bloomed on the Jól log, the women heaved a collective sigh. Åsa began the familiar chant. "The light of life continues, the light of life endures."

The company replied, "The light of life will return."

As the mighty log blazed, the warriors raised a toast to their favorite god, Thor, protector of mankind. Jólnir was one of Odin's many names, but it was a time of feasting to honor all of the gods.

Limp with relief, Åsa took a cup of ale and sat. She joined in the familiar songs she had sung around the Jól fire with her family as far back as she could remember. But the smoke made her throat constrict, and she choked on the words. Tears bit the corners of her eyes, and she rubbed them away.

Astrid was giggling, her head together with a visiting jarl's son, as she had once done with Gyrd. She seemed to have recovered from the loss, forgotten him and moved on. Åsa looked away to hide new tears. She would never forget her brother or her father or her mother. She would never forgive Gudrød for what he had done. Nothing could bring them back to her.

But I will have my revenge.

DURING JÓL, sacrifices were made to ensure the favor of the gods, as well as the álfir, the dís, and the wights, who were spirits of the land and dwelled in rocks, waterfalls, and groves. The people hoped if they sacrificed willingly now, during the long winter, the gods would not take their children, their spouses, their food, or whatever else they could not stand to lose.

In the sacred grove stood an enormous ash tree, representing Yggdrasil, the world tree, Odin's steed, the means by which the god traveled between the nine worlds. Beneath this tree, Åsa was required to perform the ceremonial duties of queen. Here she must lead the Dísablót, the sacrifice to the female ancestors who watched over the families.

At the base of the tree was an open pit the size of a grave. Years of sacrifice had saturated the clay walls with blood. Some of it was human, Åsa knew, from captives and slaves, and in times of famine or disease, even royal blood had been splashed on the walls. The people gathered around the pit. In the pit was tethered a sow, sacred to Freyja. Åsa must carry out the sacrifice.

In Tromøy, she had made sacrifice after her mother's death. But now she was three months pregnant; as she was led to the place of sacrifice, the tang of blood made her stomach heave. She turned aside and retched.

Heid, prepared for this, handed her a steaming cup. "Here, these herbs will settle your stomach."

"No!" Åsa cried, pushing the cup away. "This is not my home, this is not my family. I am not here by choice. I will not perform the sacrifice for my enemies."

The sorceress gripped her hard by the shoulders and stared into her eyes.

"Girl, would you give up the only power you have?" she said, giving her a shake.

Chest heaving, Åsa stared back. Heid was right. Biting back nausea, she took the cup and drank.

She descended the rough stairs cut into the side of the pit, unsheathing her sacred knife. Three of the sorceress's apprentices followed her down bearing bronze bowls. The sow stood quietly, drugged with Heid's herbs.

The women raised their voices in a vardlokkur. Åsa swallowed hard. Gripping the ceremonial knife, she approached the drugged animal and knelt, crooning the chant. She placed her hand gently on the sow's throat and located the pulsing vein. *Make it quick and painless.* She drew her knife across the vein. One apprentice stepped in to catch the spray of blood in a bronze bowl while the other two helped her ease the animal to the ground. The beast's tiny eyes cleared for an instant. Åsa stared into their depths, straining to see beyond life before death glazed them over like ice on a pond. Then she gathered her strength and rose.

Two apprentices helped her climb out of the pit; another carried up the bowl brimming with blood, taking care not to spill a single drop.

Entranced by the vision she had glimpsed, Åsa mounted the platform and took her place among the tall wooden idols. The women of Borre ringed the platform, the men forming a circle around them.

The three apprentices held up the bowls of sacrificial blood. Åsa's stomach no longer heaved at the smell. She took a cautious breath and gripped the tied bundle of fir twigs, anointing first the gods and then the worshippers. The women's voices joined hers in a chant, asking Freyja to bless the land, the livestock, and the women with fertility. Åsa dipped the fir bundle again and called on the dís to protect women in childbirth.

As she led the women in the vardlokkur to call the spirits, Åsa thought of Alfhild, who used to perform these rites in her place. She wondered if the former queen had been happy here with Gudrød. Had she loved him, and her son? Had Queen Alfhild, a woman rumored to be of elfin blood, become a dís? Did she watch over her son and husband still—and perhaps over the lonely young girl who had taken her place? Åsa sent a silent prayer to Alfhild for protection of the child in her womb.

Heid mounted the platform. Looking up into the smoke that rose to the treetops, she prayed to the gods to let her see the future of Borre.

She turned first to Gudrød. "I see success in all of your undertakings in the new year, lord," she said. "You will win all of your battles, and take much booty. Your land will be fertile"—she gestured to Åsa's swelling belly—"and your family will grow."

Gudrød beckoned the sorceress to approach. Amid the cheering throngs, he presented her with a silver ring.

Heid's apprentices mixed the remaining sacrificial blood with milk in great bowls and poured it into the álf cups hollowed into the rocks. The meat from the sacrifice seethed in great cauldrons for the evening feast, while the carcass hung in the sacred grove to honor the gods.

Knut had returned from his travels to spend the Jól season at Borre. From her high seat, Åsa watched him perform with Olaf, entertaining the company with new riddles and the old legends.

After everyone had stumbled off to bed, Åsa waited in the

shadows for the skáld. "Have you seen my people? Please tell me how they fare. Do they have enough food for the winter?"

"My lady," Knut whispered, looking grave. "I stopped at Tromøy on my way north and have seen some of your people. They survive by foraging, fishing, and hunting, and with luck, they will make it through the winter. They will plant their crops in the spring. But I must tell you the truth—I fear for them next year when the raiding season begins. Now that your father is gone, Tromøy is fair game. Without warriors to defend the crops, raiders will strip the land. Next winter, the folk may starve."

A hook of worry caught in Åsa's heart. She sent the skáld a solemn look. "I will do what I can for them."

The old man bowed his head.

No one was going to help them. The down mattress became a bed of iron as Åsa lay all night, trying to think of a way to help the people of Tromøy.

By the time she woke to the thralls reviving the morning fires, she knew what she must do.

THE JÓL FESTIVITIES reached their peak with the winter solstice. No wheel could turn as the old year became the new, and even spinning was forbidden. Gudrød led the wild hunt through the countryside, wearing the horned helmet of Odin. Olaf, of course, rode beside him. They came back roaring a hunting song, dragging a red-eyed boar that snorted and thrashed its tusks. This would be the oath boar.

The hall rang with cheers as the hunters paraded the glowering boar through the hall. Its fierce red eyes raked the room for some opportunity to attack its enemies. The huntsmen dragged the beast outside and wrestled it down into the pit, where it raged and bashed the earthen walls.

On that short day, the sun was no more than a running sore

on the horizon. It was a day when no one left their fires by choice. The dead were closer now to the earth than at any other time of the year except midsummer. Good and evil, the spirits of the dead walked the land.

The highborn gathered in the hall, where the great Jól log still blazed on the longfire. The benches were piled with furs, the walls hung with tapestries illustrating heroic deeds. Lamps flared against the dark, and in the flickering light, Loki seemed to grin and leap from the carved post.

Åsa filled the silver-chased drinking horn with mead from a pitcher of precious glass taken long ago on a raid in Francia. The bitterness of her heart flowed with the mead. As she carried the horn to Gudrød, she kept her eyes lowered to hide the hatred that burned there. He took it from her without looking at her, and rose to circle the fire in blessing.

Holding the horn aloft, he cried, "To Odin, for victory in war." He took a hearty swig from the silver rim, and as the warriors cheered, she imagined that he drank her fury. He held the horn out to Olaf, and it seemed that he drank her bitterness. The nobles passed the great horn around the room, drinking it dry and returning it to Åsa. Without looking up, she poured and handed it once more to her husband.

"To Frey and Njord, may they bring peace and good harvests," he declared, and drank.

Accompanied by cheers, the horn made its way through the hall once more, and Åsa filled it yet a third time.

Gudrød hoisted the horn and proclaimed, "To Thor, son of Odin and protector of mankind," and sent it on its way.

Now the kitchen staff stepped forward to fill everyone's cup, and the highborn rose and shouted, "To King Gudrød, long may he prosper!"

Then came quieter toasts, to the memory of departed kins-folk. Åsa took her place on the high seat beside the man she had sworn to kill, and silently drank to her father and Gyrd.

May I take vengeance soon.

Gudrød stood before his sworn men and raised his great horn. The hall fell silent. "I have an announcement to make." He looked at Olaf. "My son has grown to be a man, as you all have seen. He has proven himself to be brave, a good fighter. He has killed a bear and made the bear's power his own. He has yet to taste battle, but I believe he will prove himself in that as he has in all other things. Today, I declare him my heir." He raised his horn to Olaf, and drank.

Åsa brought her cup to her lips, but bitterness rose in her throat and she could not drink.

The company rose to their feet and roared, "Olaf!" and all the jarls drank to him. One by one, the jarls came forward and swore their oaths to Gudrød's heir.

All except Hrolf, skulking in a corner, his stare burning into his half brother in a way that kindled dread in Åsa's belly.

When the jarls had quieted, Gudrød spoke again. "My father built this hall after the Danes took Skiringssal, the Shining Hall, from him. He lies in his mound here in Borre. While it is true that Borre is a mighty hall, my forefathers are buried at Skiringssal. My ancestor, Halfdan Whiteleg, raised the shining hall there. Its roofs gleam with silver above the tree line. The power of my family lies at Skiringssal, with the spirits that guard them, and the luck of my ancestors." Gudrød's eyes took on a gleam as he spoke. "Long have I dreamed of regaining my inheritance, for the Ynglings to feast in the Shining Hall once more. We tried once, and failed. We will not fail again."

He looked around at his eager warriors. The great room was silent except for the Jól fire's crackle.

"Taking that place will bring us honor and the favor of the gods." Gudrød's voice rose. "Traders come there from the world over, bringing soapstone from Agder, iron from the inland bogs, amber from the Eastern Sea, furs and ivory from the north, glass from Francia, and silver." He paused, letting the vision sink in to his listeners. "Whoever rules Skiringssal rules the sea." His voice thundered, the rafters seemed to quake. "All its riches would be ours."

A cheer rose up from the men. Gudrød waited for the roar to die down, then raised his mead horn.

"Swear to me now that when the day comes that I send the war arrow, you will sail with me and we will take Skiringssal back from the Danes."

The men beat their cups on the tables, the sound rising to fill the hall like thunder. Olaf and three other warriors manhandled the huge oath boar into the hall. Though Heid had given the animal a calming potion, his tusks gleamed in the firelight and his red eyes shone with hate.

Gudrød approached the seething boar and laid his hands upon its bristles. "I swear by the gods that I will take back the Shining Hall, or die trying."

The warriors dragged the boar around the room. One by one, each of Gudrød's warriors and jarls laid their hands on its quivering hide and vowed to follow their king into battle.

Now Gudrød handed out gifts to the oath takers: silver rings, horse harnesses, fine armor and weaponry.

Åsa's time had come. She drew a deep breath, rose, and faced Gudrød.

"Husband, I beg a boon," she said, sinking to her knees.

The room fell silent, all attention riveted on her. She dug her nails into her palms to force herself to stay on her knees before him.

Gudrød scowled. "Ask, wife."

Åsa took another breath to steady herself. "Lord, I beg you to send warriors to Tromøy to defend my people. Raiders will come in the summer and take all of their crops and livestock. They will starve."

Gudrød stared at her, a flush spreading up his neck. Åsa strove to hold his gaze.

"Lord, you took my father's kingdom by force, and left its people without his protection. They are your responsibility now." She was betting that he could not find a way to refuse her request in front of all his sworn men without losing face.

His face darkened to purple, and Åsa held her breath.

Without taking his eyes from hers, he laid hands on the hide of the oath boar. "I will send warriors to Tromøy in the spring," he choked.

His furious glare warned her that while she had won this battle, the war was far from over. She rose, took her victory, and fled.

CHAPTER 14

After Jól, the farmers and jarls departed with their followers and families, leaving the grounds a field of trampled mud. Day after day, the snow drifted down, blanketing signs of the festivities until Borre drowsed under a soft white comforter. Gudrød and Olaf ventured out again with their hunting party, leaving the great hall in peace until they came stamping back to feast, sleep it off, and depart again.

It was the weaving season. All the raw flax and wool had been spun and dyed before Jól, and now every woman and girl able to stand would spend her waking hours before the loom until spring chores demanded their time. Men hauled in the big standing looms and nailed them to the bower walls.

Heid's apprentices warped the looms, measuring out the linen strands and weighting them with stones to keep them hanging straight. The most skilled among them wove the starter rows.

Åsa dreaded it. She hated all form of needlecraft, but weaving was the worst. The boredom of standing for hours at the loom, ham-handed and awkward, concentrating on getting every exacting thread perfect, made her back ache and her eyes water. As a child, she had escaped her mother's tutelage whenever she could, sneaking out and speeding across the snow on skis. Her mother often as not had smiled and let her go.

Heid, on the other hand, was a stern taskmaster. She kept Åsa and the apprentices standing at the looms all day, working by flickering lamplight. Under the sorceress's fierce glare, they created a fine cloth interwoven with mystical symbols. If even one thread was out of place, Heid insisted that it be meticulously unwoven and started again. It made Åsa want to scream.

The second morning, as the apprentices gathered before the loom, Åsa slipped out the bower door. The brilliant sunlight reflected off the snow as cold, pure air hit her lungs. She plunged into the pristine snow, making her way purposefully across the yard. Gudrød's warriors barely spared her a glance. A pregnant woman couldn't get far in the depths of winter.

She plowed her way through the snow to the smithy. It was a pit house, half its height dug into the earth, timbered walls rising up to support a sod roof. The building was twice the size of the smithy on Tromøy, boasting two furnaces and a wondrous assortment of tools. Fire crackled and hammer blows rang.

As Åsa stepped down into the building, Ulf looked up and a smile split his beard. She settled on the bench beside the forge and watched Ulf work. The scent of charcoal and hot iron mingled with the sound of hammer blows to banish all that had happened. She closed her eyes and became a girl again, safe on Tromøy.

Arne labored on the other side of the shop, back turned to his rival. The two smiths never spoke to each other, but Arne sent malevolent glares in Ulf's direction. Catching the look, Åsa rolled her eyes and grinned, glaring mockingly at Arne's broad back.

Arne was a plain, straightforward smith, competent enough, but with no knowledge of the runes or spell casting. Nor had he ever been called upon to use such things in the years he had served his king. He continued to produce and repair the everyday items needed at Borre: the scythes, shovels, hoes, and ploughs for farmwork, as well as the stirrups and bridles for horses and the cauldrons, lamps, braziers for the home. But it was Ulf who forged the new swords for the warriors of Borre. He made the axes, spearheads and arrowheads, shield bosses, chain mail, and helmets. If it was used for fighting, Ulf made it.

He worked constantly, forging new blades and experimenting with techniques, turning out fine weapons that bore the distinctive wave pattern on the steel surface. Gudrød bestowed these on his favored jarls and húskarlar.

"They look the same as the Serkland sword," he said, holding up his newest blade, "but they aren't. I can duplicate the swirling pattern by blending the soft and hard metals together to make a superior sword, but mine are heavier and lack the balance. I simply cannot make the same blade. It's the iron. Ours is not the same quality as the wootz steel, and I don't know how to produce it. Bear Biter is the finest weapon I have ever made, the lightest and the strongest, but it's not the equal of Gudrød's Serkland sword."

"Yet it withstood Gudrød's blade," Åsa said.

"Luck, perhaps, or the fact that it was but a single blow. My blades will stand up against any forged here in the North. But in a prolonged battle against another Serkland sword? I don't know."

Neither of them mentioned what had happened when her father's blade had clashed with a Serkland sword.

"Gudrød knows they aren't the same as the Serkland blade," Ulf confided.

Åsa sucked in her breath. "But, he said he would kill you..."

"He won't waste my abilities," said Ulf confidently. "Not while there's a chance that I might succeed."

But if Gudrød's threats didn't mean much to Ulf, the challenge consumed him. He barely limped as he scurried about the smithy. He seemed almost happy.

Åsa warmed herself at the fire, watching him work as he told her tales of the álfir. For a time, she let herself imagine that they were back in Tromøy, and all that had happened was only a bad dream. She could almost believe that her father was alive, that Gyrd would come bursting at in any moment to hear Ulf's tales.

The spell was broken when Arne slammed out of the smithy door, giving her a glimpse of darkness that told her the short day had passed. She needed to get back to the bower before the völva locked the door. The less of a scene she created coming in, the better the chance that she could slip away again. It would certainly make the winter more bearable than fighting with the loom every day while listening to a bunch of silly girls' gossip.

"I must go," she said, rising.

"Good night," Ulf said, glancing up briefly before returning to his work. Wrapping her shawl around her, she stepped out into the utter dark of the winter night.

The great hall loomed, blacker than the night, its gable ends glowing faintly with the light of the longfire within. She trudged through the snow, skirting the building toward the bower.

As she passed by the back door to Gudrød's chamber, the sound of voices caught her ear. She froze, then edged farther back into the shadows, controlling her breathing, willing herself to melt into the wall.

"Why should I feed them all winter?" Gudrød was saying.

"My vision was clear when I went under the cloak." It was Heid's voice, and her tone raised the hair on Åsa's neck. "For three days and three nights, I conversed with the gods. The prophecy was clear. Harald's daughter will bear a son of your seed."

"I have an heir. What do I need with another?" Gudrød said. "I didn't think Olaf could ever become a king, but he has changed. I am very pleased with him."

"A king needs many sons. Who knows how long each one might survive?"

"Bah!" said Gudrød. "It will probably be a girl. Another useless mouth to feed like her mother. I should sacrifice them both to Odin."

Åsa's heart lurched, and her hands went instinctively to her stomach.

Heid said, "The sacrifice of a babe in the womb is of no use. The child must first be born. Then you can decide what to do with the two of them."

Åsa stifled a gasp and plunged through the snow to the bower. She wrenched open the oak door and stepped into the entryway, her mind reeling. *A prophecy. All of this was because of a prophecy.*

The völva was behind it all. It was she who'd advised Gudrød to propose the marriage, she who'd urged him to take Åsa by force. She who'd bade him kill Åsa's father and brother.

Heid took everything from me, and now she only keeps me alive to fulfill her prophecy.

Åsa felt a flutter in her belly. She held her breath, and it came again. It felt like—a kick. *A boy,* she knew. *A little king.* A fierce surge of protectiveness swept through her, with a longing to hold this child in her arms and look into his face.

She put a hand on her belly and felt the kick again. She had to make sure the sorceress continued to want her, and her child, alive. Heid must never discover that this was not Gudrød's child.

Åsa was in her bed, cuddled up with Flosi, when Heid entered the bower. She feigned sleep, listening to the sorceress's steps drag closer. When they stopped, she struggled to remain still beneath the sorceress's labored, mead-scented breath as Heid stood over her.

After an eternity, Heid shambled back to her own bed.

THE NEXT MORNING, Åsa appeared at the loom beside Astrid, striving to focus through a haze of exhaustion on the mind-numbing task at hand.

"Where were you yesterday?" hissed Astrid. Her head jerked up as the völva entered. The apprentices fell silent, watching their mistress expectantly.

"I am glad you could join us," said Heid drily as she passed Åsa.

This is going to be a long day.

Heid took her place before the fire, the jewels of her robe glimmering like stars in the midnight-blue wool. When she spoke, her voice took on a singsong quality. "The Norns," she said, "weave the great web of life."

Åsa sighed. Her mother had taught her about the Norns, three giant sisters who dwelt by the well of fate at the base of the world tree.

Heid picked up a pair of shears. "The Norns hold the ultimate power over man, and even over the gods. Spinning the fate of each newborn child, they decide when to cut each life thread." She snipped a hanging thread, and the scrape of metal sent a shiver down Åsa's spine. "The völur represent the Norns at every birth celebration of consequence, to bless the child and foretell its future."

Heid pulled on a weft strand that dangled from the loom, setting the warp weights bobbing. "We are all connected, each of us a thread in the Norns' great web of fate. Every action we take affects the entire web, reverberating out to its furthest reaches.

"The wise know that the warp and weft of life can be altered by those who weave. This, I will teach you. However, be warned that these actions can cause unforeseen effects and unintended consequences." Heid looked sharply at Åsa.

Such as when I refused Gudrød. It cost me everything, yet here I am, his wife.

The sorceress turned away and resumed speaking. "The runes can give knowledge, they can heal, provide protection, and also cause great harm. Each rune has its own meaning, its own power, and can be used individually, or bound to other runes. We cut and color the runes, but the rune we carve is only a symbol. It is the *sound* of the runes that contains the power. When we chant the runes in a galdr spell, the sustained vibration of the voice creates the magic."

A tingle rose in Åsa's arms and legs as comprehension glimmered.

"For your weaving to have power, you must employ the art of galdr."

Utter silence reigned as the apprentices held their breath.

"The voice must be trained to achieve the proper resonance, the breath regulated for tone and power. Your stance must be strong." Heid stood with her legs apart, knees flexed. "Draw your breath in to fill your belly." Eyes closed, she placed her hands on her stomach and inhaled.

"Feeeeehuuuuuuu." She sounded the first rune, Freyja's rune, the symbol of abundance. Her voice reverberated in the bower's lofty ceiling, filling the hall with rich sound that faded into silence, leaving the air charged with power.

"Now, breathe in and chant with me."

Åsa placed her hands on her belly and took a deep breath. When Heid sounded the first rune again, Åsa opened her mouth and let the sound vibrate from her throat. Joined by the other women's voices, the chant swelled, sending a shiver down her back.

"Now, go to your looms," said the völva. "Take up the weft thread and draw it through the warp according to the pattern. Pull it tight and chant the runes."

All day, Heid kept them at it, chanting the entire twenty-four runes over and over, until Åsa's voice rasped and her lungs burned.

"The baby doesn't leave much room for air," she gasped to Astrid, wincing under another kick.

"I hope the day will come when I find out how it feels," Astrid murmured. "I long for a child."

"A husband first," said Åsa mischievously.

"Of course!" said Astrid. "It's just that I haven't met anyone… not since Gyrd."

"Gyrd is gone," said Åsa fiercely, blinking back sudden tears. "You must look to the future."

"I know." Astrid nodded, her own hazel eyes glistening. "But it's just that…I miss him."

"I miss him too." Åsa's throat was tight.

"Of course you do! How selfish of me. He was your brother, and you loved him all your life. I only knew him for a short time." Astrid sighed. "But what I knew of him I can never forget."

The two stood, united in grief, until Heid roused them. "Weave! Pick up your weaving sword. Chant the runes!"

The next days ran into one another, punctuated by a trance-like sleep. Åsa struggled on, bolstered by Astrid's presence.

One day, as the chant vibrated in her throat, Åsa felt a peculiar shift in her mind. Her shoulders dropped, her feet rooted to the floor. The blood seemed to vibrate in her limbs.

The world took on a different quality, as it had when she'd sat out at night on her mother's burial mound.

The trance had come on her.

In the days that followed, she entered the trance easily, like a dog trained to the call. Åsa had only to step to the loom and raise her voice with the others, and the calm settled over her like a cloak.

As the long, dark nights of winter set in and pregnancy slowed her down, Åsa began to take the symbols she wove seriously for the first time. Now, with hours of enforced confinement, she fell into the rhythm of the warp and weft. The magical quality of the art enthralled her.

For hours each day, they wove and chanted by firelight. Animated by the power in the room, Åsa loosed the runes into the air like arrows. Each session left her hoarse and breathless. But as she practiced day after day, the vibration in her voice grew in concert with the others until the air shimmered with power.

Little things began to happen. The copper bowls of the oil lamps would emit a faint ringing sound. The wooden beams of the hall creaked, a candle flared.

"Good, that is good," said Heid when these things happened.

~

AFTER TWO WEEKS OF WEAVING, every loom held a linen field patterned by figures of wool. Heid bade the women gather around her as she stood before the longfire.

She gave each apprentice a slender branch of ash wood.

"All highborn children should know how to cut and color the runes. Show me your skill at this. Runes are the symbols of galdr, and we chant the runes as we carve them."

Åsa drew the tiny knife she wore on a chain suspended from her brooch and carved off small, flat pieces from her branch. When she had twenty-four slips, she began to incise a different rune on each one, as her mother had taught her. For a moment, it seemed that Gunnhild sat beside her whispering the name of each rune as she carved.

Heid made the rounds of the room, inspecting their work. "Those who have passed on still walk beyond the veil that separates the living from the dead. You can feel them, sometimes hear them. They can see things that we cannot. They see our futures, they know our fate."

Åsa's throat constricted. Her mother was with Harald and Gyrd, together beyond the veil. All but for her.

"On certain days of the year, that veil becomes thin. It is then we sacrifice animals on the world tree and, at critical times, men, so that we can communicate with those beyond the veil and gain knowledge of the future. Odin gave us runes that can make the dead speak."

If Gudrød has his way, it will be me swinging from the world tree.
Åsa dug her knife into the wood and carved *Raidho*, the rune for
the letter *R*, which also meant journey, physical or spiritual.

Once they had carved their sets of runes, each girl made an
incision on the heel of her hand, squeezing a few drops of blood
into little wooden lot cups. They rubbed the blood into the rune
marks, etching the symbols in blood, dark against the white of
the wood.

"You all can read and write a line of rune script," Heid said.
"You know that the future can be told with the runes by those
who know the art. Some of you may have already experimented
with divination." She stared around the room, and some of the
apprentices looked down at their laps.

Heid dipped her hand into her linen rune bag, drawing three
slips and dropping them into a lot cup. Eyes heavenward, she
shook the cup and intoned, "Let the chips fall where they may!"

She drew three chips and laid them out on the linen cloth.

"We choose three runes, one for each of the Norns. See here."
She pointed to the rune on the left. "Urd's rune, What Once Was;
Hagalaz, the symbol of war. It lies across Ansuz, rune of the
divine, in the position of Verdandi, the Norn of That Which Is.
This could mean that past conflict interferes with the will of the
gods."

She paused, then indicated a third slip.

"But Skuld's rune, the rune of What Shall Be, is held by
Eihwaz, the potential of the yew tree." Heid gazed upon the rune
layout for a moment. Then she looked up at her apprentices.
"This is only an example. It isn't meant to divine the future. Now,
you try. Choose someone to read for."

The bower filled with chatter as the girls chose partners. Åsa
caught Astrid's eye and smiled.

"You go first," Åsa told her.

Astrid drew three runes from her bag, then dropped them in
her cup and shook them.

"What does my future hold?" she chanted, casting the slips onto her linen cloth.

Åsa leaned forward to examine the runes. "In Urd's position, you have the rune Gifu, the marriage rune. But it's upside down. Love lost." Astrid's eyes met hers. *Gyrd.* Åsa's throat thickened. She swallowed and scrutinized the layout until she could speak again. "The rune for Verdandi is Berkana, the birch tree. The birthing rune, and of romance and healing." She met Astrid's hopeful gaze. "Perhaps you will meet someone soon."

She looked down at the slips, blinking to read them through unshed tears. "Skuld's rune, the rune That Will Be. Inguz, the sign of Frey and Freyja. True love, fertility, a lasting marriage."

She smiled up at Astrid. "You will marry well and have many children. Sorrow is in the past, and all is happiness ahead for you."

Astrid closed her eyes. A tear squeezed out and trailed down her cheek. "I pray that you are right." Then her eyes flew open and a determined smile fixed itself on her face. "Now you," she said, nodding at Åsa's cup.

Åsa picked up her rune cup, foreboding like a lead weight in her stomach.

Astrid looked at her with pity. "Go on. It's better to know."

Åsa closed her eyes and cast her runes. She did not dare to look at them. Instead, she kept her eyes on Astrid's reassuring face.

"For Urd," said Astrid, "you cast Hagalaz, reversed. War."

Guilt coursed through Åsa like poison. War she had brought on, and her father and brother had paid the price.

Astrid had been watching Åsa with concern. Now she dropped her gaze to the runes. "Verdandi, That Which Is Becoming: Thurisaz. Thor's rune. Great strength in facing a powerful enemy."

Åsa shivered, thinking of Gudrød.

"And for Skuld. That Which Shall Be." Astrid sucked in her

breath. "Nauthiz. Destiny. To accomplish the impossible." She fell silent.

Åsa stared at the final rune. The impossible. For her, even to survive the winter qualified.

Heid clapped her hands to end the session. Åsa shook off the shreds of enchantment that clung like cobwebs. She and Astrid carefully put the slips in their white linen bags and stowed them in their chests.

They practiced reading the runes for a week, advancing to the nine-rune form, with a column of three runes representing the past, the present, and the future. Åsa's rune casts now seemed mundane, as if all the power had been used up in that first one.

In the second week, Heid moved them on. "You have all mastered foretelling. But the runes can make a spell. Carvings can be infused with runic power. The runes can be combined into bind runes, patterns to cure and patterns to curse, to bring love or death. There are love fetters to bind a man, war fetters to bind an enemy.

"Sequence is important," she went on. "Each rune modifies the meaning of those coming before or after. Secret marks can be placed to change the meaning."

Heid took up a wooden cup and swiftly carved a string of runes onto the cup. Then she filled it with clean water. "This appears to be an innocent passage of the runes," she continued. "But notice these three dots after the passage. They are not mere decoration. They tell the adept to look at the third rune. That is the rune of power, hidden within the phrase. These runes make the contents of this cup poison to anyone who drinks from it."

She held the cup to her thrall Sigrid.

"Drink it," she commanded.

Sigrid sat frozen, her eyes huge. Åsa held her breath. For a slave, it was death to disobey the völva's command. But in this case, to obey was death as well.

"Go on, go on," Heid urged her.

The habit of obedience won the inner struggle. With shaking hands, Sigrid brought the cup to her lips and drank.

Sigrid's face contorted. The cup fell to the floor, and her body began to tremble.

The apprentices gasped. Åsa felt as if she had been kicked in the stomach. She started to rise, but Astrid grabbed her by the shoulders and held her on the bench. "Wait," she hissed.

Heid beamed at them. She picked up the cup and with her knife altered one of the runes so that it became another. "Now, the same water that was poison has been transformed into the antidote."

Heid grasped Sigrid's head and forced a few drops between the thrall woman's chattering teeth.

Sigrid jerked upright, clawing her throat. The apprentices shrieked.

"There," said the völva triumphantly. "Works like a charm!"

A pitiful mewing came from Sigrid's throat. She huddled on the floor, rocking back and forth.

"Off you go," said Heid. The old woman still did not have control of her legs, so she used her hands to drag herself away from the sorceress.

"Now, was that cup really poisoned, or did Sigrid only convince herself that it was? We will never know the answer for certain, but there can be no magic without belief."

Åsa choked back the fury that rose in her breast. No matter what the truth was, it was a cruel thing to do to a helpless old slave.

I must learn all I can, and protect the innocents.

CHAPTER 15

Olaf followed his father as the hunting party moved silently through the forest, skis hissing over the snow's frozen crust, bows slung, quivers bristling with new-fletched arrows. A light dusting of snow flaked down on them from the trees. Hungry birds flitted among the branches, alert for seeds.

Gudrød moved fast for a man his age. Olaf and the rest of the warriors had to work hard to keep up. Cheeks flared red from the cold and exertion, breath rasped in throats. Even Hrolf was winded, his cheeks blowing in and out as he skied.

The hares wore their winter coats now and could only be seen if they moved, startled by the silent band of hunters bearing down on them. But they were after bigger game, tracking a deer. Borre's storehouses still held plenty of preserved meat and fish, a luxury that most steadings lacked deep into winter. Gudrød's love of hunting kept their winter table supplied with game, ensuring that he always had meat to give away this time of year to hungry folk whose larders had run out. His skill and luck at hunting was an important part of his reputation. The king's personal luck brought his kingdom good harvests, fertile live-stock, and successful hunting to ensure survival through the lean months of winter. Gudrød held no illusions about his fate if his people went hungry. Starving men had been known to sacrifice their king to the gods and choose a new leader with better luck. Gudrød's great-grandfather had been one. That fate would not befall Gudrød the Hunter King. He made sure his people never went hungry.

The weak sunlight struggled through the trees, casting dim light on the hunting party as they followed the deer's track. They traveled a familiar route across the icy crust.

Out of the corner of his eye, Olaf caught the movement in the forest at the same time as his father's head turned. Olaf swung his bow up simultaneously with Gudrød.

Bows rose in a wave through the hunting party, but only Gudrød and Olaf let fly, followed by Hrolf a heartbeat later. Three arrows quivered in the buck's side. Ears twitching, it looked up, startled at the hail of arrows as the rest of the company let loose. Two hit their target, others piercing the red-spotted snow. Not realizing its wound was mortal, the deer spooked and bounded into the trees, the hunters following. Swift as the buck was, the trail of blood on the snow was easy to follow. Olaf outstripped Hrolf and Gudrød, his skis whispering across the snow crust. He spotted the deer on the ground thrashing on a red snowbank. Drawing his hunting knife, he approached cautiously.

Olaf knelt in the snow a safe distance away, waiting for the panic to bleed out of the dying animal. As it calmed, he began the traditional hunter's chant to usher the deer into the otherworld.

He heard the snick of skis across the snow behind him. Without turning his head, he kept up his chant as the red circle widened around the buck.

Suddenly, Hrolf darted in front of him and grabbed the deer by its jaw, sliding in to slash its throat. Gudrød and the other warriors arrived in time to witness the blood spurting from the deer's artery, drenching Hrolf, who held his mouth to the stream, letting the blood spray down his throat while the others cheered him on.

Through the entire demonstration, Olaf remained on his knees, completing the chant.

Afterward, they gutted the buck and strapped the carcass onto the sledge. The hunting party towed it back through the woods, voices raised in a drinking song. Olaf hung back a little. The raucous singing of the hunting party seemed to clash with the death chant that still echoed in his mind.

They arrived at the hall in triumph, doffing their furs and hanging up their bows as the thralls fell on the sledge to take charge of butchering the carcass. Gudrød took his high seat before the longfire. Freshly split pinewood scented the room. Shadows danced on the walls, sparks flying up into the gloom of the ceiling.

Seated on the bench at the head of the house guard, Olaf accepted the mead horn from a serving woman, knowing she would warm his bed tonight. He averted his gaze from the empty seat beside his father. He was getting used to not seeing Åsa in the hall.

He brought the horn to his lips and tipped it back but kept his lips closed against the mead. He was not in the mood for drinking tonight. He was not so sure he was even in the mood for a woman.

That was nonsense. He had everything he had ever wanted. Only a fool would turn away from it. He gave his head a little shake and let the mead pass his lips.

CHAPTER 16

Winter began its slow surrender to spring. The sun bored a hole through the clouds and melted the snow in torrents, animating waterfalls and streams, filling the air with water music until the temperature dropped and frost paralyzed the streams again. Trees alternately glittered with icy coats, then thawed and dripped.

Gudrød's sworn men gathered at Borre's hall for the spring equinox feast in honor of the dawn goddess, Ostara. Åsa, heavy with child, took up the mead horn, offering it first to Gudrød before carrying it around the room in welcome. She was glad to see Knut among them, returned from his winter travels. She hoped he had brought news of Tromøy for her.

The skáld made his way straight to the high seat, not even stopping to doff his winter cloak or wash his hands and face.

"Lord, I have news of the Danes," he said with an intensity that got Gudrød's attention.

Gudrød gestured for Knut to continue.

"My lord, since they murdered their father, the Danish king's sons fight among themselves for the throne. They united only long enough to throw out the one strong leader they had—their father's brother, Klak-Harald. He lurks across the river in Saxony, under protection of the Frankish emperor, while the princes squabble over who will rule.

"Now Klak-Harald has raised a Saxon army to march against his nephews. The Danes have recalled their entire fleet to defend against his attack." The old skáld paused while the import of his words sunk in.

Gudrød bared his teeth in a grin and finished the sentence. "Leaving Skiringssal with minimal defenses." He raised his arms for silence in the hall. "This is our chance," he cried. "The old rooster defeated us years ago when we were young and untried, but we have many battles behind us since then. While Klak-Harald distracts the Danish pups, we can swoop in and take what is ours. We will not only take back the home of my fathers but take all that the cursed Danes have built over the years, their market and the seaport besides. Silver and gold, furs and ivory, silks and jewels. All those riches can be ours." He rose from his seat in excitement. "Who will follow me to retake the Shining Hall?"

The room buzzed like a hive as the highborn debated the merits and drawbacks of the plan.

Then a jarl from the Uplands stepped forward. "I will go with you."

A cheer rose, and one after another, the warriors lined up to swear to join Gudrød in battle.

Gudrød smiled and held up his hands for silence. "You won't regret your wise decision. Soon, we will feast in my father's ancient hall, and the riches of Skiringssal will be ours. Return to your homes. Sow your crops, and prepare for war. Muster here at the next full moon."

Åsa realized that she had to take action before the jarls left the hall. She approached Gudrød. His eyes flicked to her, and she seized his gaze. With her will alone, she gripped his attention as she stood before him.

"Husband," she said, loading her voice with power so that it resonated in the rafters of the hall. "I beg a boon."

He scowled at her impatiently. "What is it?"

"I remind you now of your Jól promise to me." Her voice carried to everyone in the hall. "Tromøy is your possession but also your responsibility. You have left the people undefended and leaderless. I beg you to send warriors to protect them."

Gudrød laughed. "I have the chance to regain my ancestral hall, and the great trading port as well. Do you think I would put that in jeopardy for your father's little kingdom?"

"But my people will not survive the summer raids if they are undefended!"

"They are your people no longer." Åsa flinched as his words cut deep. "I need every man I have to take back Skiringssal." Then he paused, a glint in his eye. "Once I win, I will send someone to Tromøy," he said, then strode from the room, followed by the departing jarls.

A wave of relief washed through Åsa, but it left behind a taint of worry.

GUDRØD KEPT both smiths busy repairing weapons and making new ones for his warriors. The smithy rang with hammer blows. Along with sword blades, Ulf turned out spear tips, arrowheads, and axe-heads, while Arne repaired chain mail and helmets and forged new shield bosses. The charcoal burners worked night and day to keep up with their needs. Every man that could be spared assisted the smiths, riveting spearheads to shafts, sharpening battle-axes, hauling wood and water, collecting scrap metal to be reforged. The boys vied for their turn treading the double bellows to keep the forge's dual fires white hot.

Gudrød took Olaf down to the beach where the longships lay, ready for action.

"Now, boy, you will learn the art of command. *Sea Dragon* is yours."

Olaf stared at the ship. *Sea Dragon* was a smaller version of his father's vessel in every way. With thirty oar ports, it was a real warship. The dragon's head on the stem matched the one on Gudrød's flagship, *Dragonlord*. Olaf could hardly believe he had a ship of his own to command. *What a change from a few months ago.* This was his opportunity to prove himself as a leader, to gain renown and attract followers. A man who wished to be king must show skill and courage in battle, and even more important, he must demonstrate his luck. Gudrød had never given him a chance like this before.

Olaf moved aboard *Sea Dragon* immediately. The comforts of the hall had lost their allure. He craved the salt air and the stars in the night sky. Scarcely sleeping, he sat up all night honing Bear Biter to a fine edge.

The next day, he passed the hazel poles of the practice yard with a confidence he had never felt before. For the first time, he was glad to see Hrolf waiting to challenge him. He met his half brother's searing stare and gave a brief nod before drawing his practice sword.

Olaf let Hrolf charge, dodging the blade at the last moment. Hrolf whipped around and stabbed up under Olaf's shield. Olaf slammed his shield down on Hrolf's sword arm with a numbing force. Before Hrolf could recover, Olaf fetched him a blow to the helm that sent him reeling, then swept the flat of his sword at Hrolf's legs, bringing him down to the jeers of the onlookers.

Hrolf lay on the field in defeat, but his glare promised revenge of such ferocity that it sent an icy shard of fear up Olaf's spine.

HROLF HAD BEEN HANGING from the tree for hours, maybe days.

He didn't know how long. It had been dark when the old berserker had dragged him here.

"You must endure Odin's trial to gain his blessing," Hrafn had told him as he'd harnessed Hrolf's chest and hips with a hemp rope, then tossed the end up over a high limb. With surprising strength, the old berserker had hoisted Hrolf up the tree and made the rope fast to a gnarled root. Then he shinnied up the tree and bound Hrolf tight to the trunk at the shoulders, hips, and ankles. He slid back down the tree and picked up the spear that leaned against the trunk and jabbed the tip into Hrolf's side. It hurt, but the wound wasn't deep, it was just enough to start the blood oozing.

"Here you'll stay until I come for you," Hrafn said with a leer. Then he'd melted into the forest, cackling.

At first, it had been torture, hanging bound to the trunk of the tree. Hrolf was sure that both knees had been dislocated, but he no longer felt anything in his shoulders or arms. Whether it was the cold or shock that numbed him, he could not tell. Maybe it was the foul brew the old man made him drink. His stomach roiled when he remembered the taste. Eventually the nausea had passed, but at the same time, all the strength drained from his limbs.

Now he had gone to a place beyond pain.

Hrolf could not be sure what time of day it was in the deep forest where light barely glimmered through the boughs. In addition to the strange sense of timelessness, he had lost all sense of space. He was nowhere, no longer attached to his body. He did not feel the thirst that had once consumed him. Hunger no longer poked at his guts. Was he alive or dead? Perhaps he didn't even exist anymore. Yet, somehow, his awareness lived.

All-father Odin had sought the power of the runes in Hel. To enter the realm of the dead, Odin had hung, wounded, on the world tree, slowly dying for nine nights.

Would the old man really leave him here that long? Would he come at all?

A breeze ruffled Hrolf's hair. Light sleet spattered him.

A raven landed on the branch above his head and hopped over to inspect him.

Hrolf shuddered. Hrafn's name—"raven."

Hugin and Munin, Odin's spies, were ravens. They flew around the world each day and returned every night to report the doings of mankind to their master.

Hrolf watched the bird anxiously. Odin had sacrificed an eye for knowledge. Hrolf wanted to shut his tight so that the raven couldn't peck them, but he was more afraid to take his eyes off the bird.

The raven hopped closer to him, cocked its head, and said, "Why do you do this? Why do you suffer?"

One word came to him. *Olaf! Olaf, Olaf, Olaf, Olaf...*

The raven looked at him with one glittering eye. "Olaf!" it croaked, and flew away.

HROLF WOKE to find himself lying on the ground at the base of the tree. Hrafn must have come and cut him down, but the old berserker was nowhere to be seen. Hrolf was alone.

And alive. He had survived the ordeal. He was an initiate. A berserker.

A feeling of power flooded him.

Hrolf sat up slowly, wincing as his sore muscles protested. He grabbed hold of the tree and hoisted himself to a standing position and waited while the strength returned to his legs. Then he set off through the woods toward home.

He would show them what he could do.

As THE WAXING MOON FATTENED, Gudrød sent out the war arrow. With the barley and flax fields planted, farmers took their weapons down from the wall and burnished the rust from the blades, and came flocking to Borre to seek their fortune in war.

The jarls arrived, their ships crowding Borre's shore. More rode in on horseback from the hinterlands, leading their troops. Borre became a small city again.

By day, the warriors held games in the fields, swordplay and archery, wrestling and spear throwing. By night, their campfires dotted the hillside like fireflies. Smoke-scented air that rang with song and laughter.

When the last ships had arrived, Gudrød ordered a feast. The great hall was jammed with warriors, their numbers spilling out into the yard, drinking and bragging.

The sun was just dipping behind the trees when Åsa trudged up to the hall to take her place beside her husband. She had lain in bed all that day and struggled to get ready for yet another feast. The past week of celebration had taken its toll. Her feet were swollen, and the child seemed to have gained several pounds recently.

Outside the door, a hooded figure detached from the shadows.

"Don't go in."

Åsa froze, gripping the door ring.

A hand reached out and clutched her arm.

"Who are you?" Åsa demanded.

"Don't go in," the stranger hissed again. "Tonight there will be a sacrifice for victory."

A chill passed through Åsa as she remembered Gudrød's threat. Heid protected her in the women's bower, but in Gudrød's hall…

"You must come, quickly. A place has been prepared for you."

Åsa jerked her arm from the bony grasp.

The stranger pulled back her hood, and Åsa recognized the old slave Sigrid.

"Did Heid send you?" she asked.

"Come," the old woman whispered urgently. "If you value your life, and the life of your child."

Asa's hand dropped from the door, and she let Sigrid pull her away.

She followed the thrall, hurrying across the moonlit yard to the verge of the forest and plunging into the undergrowth. Branches scratched her, twigs caught her hair, and her breath came in gasps as she fought her way through the forest, desperate to keep the dark cloak in sight. At last, Sigrid halted before a thicket of brambles.

An owl hooted.

"Down there." Sigrid held aside the underbrush. A dark opening showed at the base of the thicket.

Åsa hesitated. She was not sure she could manage to get down that low with her unwieldy belly, and she was certain she would not get back to her feet on her own.

"Go! Do not come out tonight."

Åsa knelt awkwardly. Sucking in air through her mouth, she stuck her head into the dark opening. She shoved in with her shoulders and began to crawl on hands and knees in the dirt. Her belly hung beneath her, hampering every move.

In the dim forest light, she could barely make out the passage as it wound through the thicket. Thorns grabbed her hair and clothes, making her stop to tear free with every move. At last, the passage ended in a wide spot. Crawling in, she found skins covering the ground, topped by a fleece. A lidded wooden pail stood in the corner, which she hoped held food and water.

She burrowed under the fleece and lay there, shivering.

~

"WHERE'S MY WIFE?" Gudrød roared, terrifying the girl who poured his mead.

"Let her be," said Heid. "She needs her rest. We must protect the child."

Gudrød scowled. "Go get her," he commanded the warrior closest to him.

Heid rose from her high seat. "You dare invade the bower?"

The húskarl flicked his eyes from his king to the sorceress.

"It's my property," Gudrød snarled.

"I cannot be held responsible for the consequences if a man enters."

"I'll get her," said Hrolf, rising to his feet. "I do not fear women's magic."

Heid glowered but did not interfere as Hrolf strode out of the room.

~

ÅSA PULLED the fleece tightly around her and tried to sleep. Instead, she listened. The night was quiet. All she heard was the wind in the branches and the call of the raven and the owl.

A sound made her eyes fly open and her heart lurch. Footsteps? Too heavy for a deer. There—definitely human. Twigs snapped. Brush parted. She clutched her knife and lay still, breathing shallowly.

Now she could hear someone breathing, heavy from the effort of plowing through the underbrush. Torchlight flickered through the brambles. Gripping her knife, she called in her energy and asked for the protection of the dís.

The hiss of drawn steel whispered in the night. Åsa's breath caught in her throat as she listened to the blade hack at the brambles. *Please, Mother, hear me. Keep me safe. Keep your grandchild safe. Make us invisible.*

She felt a wave of comfort wash over her, so strong she thought her hunter must have felt it.

The torchlight wavered. Åsa held her breath, heart hammering.

Then, abruptly, the light retreated. Branches snapped and the footsteps receded into the night.

Åsa exhaled.

CHAPTER 17

Hrolf returned without Åsa, and Olaf felt a jolt of relief that nearly brought him to his knees.

"Where is my queen, boy?" Gudrød roared.

"She was not in the bower, Father," said Hrolf.

"Go search for her!"

"I have, Father. I have combed the steading and the forest. Do you wish me to search again?"

Gudrød looked sour, but shook his head. "There's no time for your bumbling. Bring me the black stallion."

That night, the king sacrificed a good horse to Odin for victory.

"We sail in the morning for the Shining Hall," Gudrød proclaimed as he splashed the wooden gods with the horse's blood, then spattered the húskarlar. They raised a cheer that echoed in the night sky.

The warriors feasted heartily, knowing that soon they would see action. The younger lads made merry, singing and telling tales and engaging in mock battles, while their elders looked on more soberly, conserving their strength for what they knew was to come.

In the firelight, Olaf joined Knut in reciting tales of legendary battles. Hrolf skulked in the shadows, never taking his eyes from his half brother. But tonight, Olaf felt untouchable.

Hrolf drank more than anyone, growing incoherent as the evening went on. One by one, the men fell asleep, but Hrolf stayed awake by the fire, staring into the flames. Olaf did not want to be alone with his half brother, so he slipped out of the hall to sleep aboard *Sea Dragon*. His ship seemed to welcome him as he stepped aboard. He burrowed under his sleeping skins, and soon the mead and ale he'd drunk carried him off to sleep.

That quantity of drink woke him in the night to answer a call of nature. He struggled out of his furs and made for the rail, grumbling, but the night's beauty arrested him. The slightest breeze rippled the water, setting the moon's reflection dancing in a sea of stars.

Beyond the quiet, he became aware of a sound. Not animal but not human. It came from the forest.

Olaf stepped onto the jetty and crept ashore, penetrating the underbrush silently, following the sound that grew stronger, more menacing, like the hum of angry bees. Something moved in the periphery of his vision. He froze, peering into the darkness. Gradually he made out a figure hunched beneath an ash tree, rocking back and forth, chanting in a furious, low tone. Olaf stole closer, his stomach knotting.

Hrolf. Rocking rhythmically, chanting words that Olaf could not understand, repeating them over and over. Building like a pot about to boil.

A breeze rattled the tree branches.

I need to get out of here. Olaf eased his way back through the woods to *Sea Dragon*, where he huddled in his sleeping skins, trying to forget what he had seen. When he finally fell asleep, Hrolf's chants echoed in his dreams.

OLAF WOKE early and was already stowing *Sea Dragon*'s awning when the ship crews stumbled down the trail, bleary from the night's revelries. Hrolf was among them, red-eyed and evil-looking. Olaf felt his half brother's glare sear the back of his neck.

By the time the last ship was loaded and the last man seated at the oars, the sun was high.

"If the wind stays fair, we'll fetch Skiringssal before dark," said Gudrød, jubilation in his voice. "They'll be watching the sea. We'll approach by land, and circle around behind them, where they least expect an attack to come from."

The fleet of fifty ships spread out across the water and unfurled their sails in the freshening breeze. Legs braced against the surge, Olaf plied *Sea Dragon*'s steering oar, his heart lifting as the sail filled. The wind whipped his hair, the sea sparkled, and warriors sang at their oars.

He spotted Hrolf among the húskarlar in the stern of Gudrød's longship, *Dragonlord*. He seemed to be trying to impale Olaf with his glare. Olaf looked away, but the memory of what he had witnessed the night before caused worry to nip at the edges of his joy.

The warm day faded into a sparkling afternoon, and when they reached the coast of Skiringssal, Gudrød led them through the multitude of shoals and tiny islands that littered the shore. He brought the fleet in to beach in a cove to the north, hidden among the trees, to await the sunrise.

"Even so, we'll keep a cold camp tonight."

After a quiet meal, Olaf saw Gudrød in the prow of *Dragonlord* gazing out over the dark shore where the fishermen's fires had just begun to flicker. He went to stand beside his father.

"There, beyond the Shining Hall, at the base of the holy hill where the water flows in spring, is the gathering place of our forefathers," Gudrød said. "There they held the assembly from ancient times and made the laws we still live by. Beyond is the sacred lake where the land spirits dwell that give our family luck.

They will be glad to feel again the presence of those kindred who belong to this place. With their help, we will drive out the invaders."

He stood for a long time staring across the water.

AT FIRST LIGHT, they roused and made ready, the older men quieting the excited youths. As they stole into the forest, Olaf glimpsed the shoreside settlement through the trees. Square, sod-roofed wood houses lined a planked boardwalk that ran along the beach. Just as Knut had said, no warships lined the shore; only a couple of beamy merchant knarrs lay unattended alongside the wharf that jutted into the bay.

Gudrød led them to a trail that wound uphill through the trees.

"Move silently," he said. "Let us keep what surprise we may have."

They made their way through the underbrush with as much stealth as their armor allowed. Gradually the forest thinned and the hall roof emerged above the trees. Olaf caught his breath. Skiringssal was even greater than Borre. Dark timbers soared to unimagined heights, and at every corner, a carved dragon's head glinted silver in the early sun, jutting out to challenge the sky. No wonder his father dreamed of taking it.

Gudrød stopped, gazing up at the massive roofline. "At last, I will win the Shining Hall of my fathers. Long have I dreamed of this day."

The company fell silent, staring.

On the ridge above, men were watching.

The Danes were waiting for them.

Gudrød drew back his spear and hurled it at the Danes. A difficult uphill shot, miraculously it soared over their shield wall, as true as Odin's legendary spear, Gungnir. Every eye followed that spear's trajectory as it landed, quivering, in the earth beyond the enemy.

"I mark you all for Odin!" Gudrød cried.

The Vestfold men cheered at the sign of certain victory.

"Form the Swine Horn," Gudrød shouted. His men fanned out to either side, forming a great wedge to penetrate the enemy's defenses. Olaf brought his shield up and locked it to his father's for the first time. Shields went up on all sides, giving the formation depth and width. The archers gathered behind the Swine Horn's protection.

Olaf stared up at the ridge, where the Danes stood behind their own shield wall, claiming the advantage of the high ground.

"Nock!" Gudrød shouted. "Draw!" A hundred bows creaked. "Loose!" A hail of arrows whickered overhead, but the uphill flight sapped their power and few found their mark. The Danish volley passed them midair, the high-ground advantage giving their missiles deadly force.

"Shields up!" Gudrød cried, and Olaf's shield flew up with his neighbor's as the enemy missiles struck. A jolt ran through the formation as arrows quivered in linden, but no screams followed. They had survived the first volley.

"Shields down!" The row of shields came down as one.

The Danish line stood solid. Not one man had fallen yet on either side.

"Charge!" roared Gudrød, driving forward.

The Danes screamed a war cry and rained arrows down on them. Their shields flew up to meet the missiles. An iron point struck Olaf's shield with enough force to make him stagger, but the locked shields kept him steady. He was carried inexorably beside his father on the point of the wedge, striving up the hill to meet the Danes. They labored against the incline, weighed down by their heavy mail and weapons. Olaf's brynja seemed to have shrunk, his chest straining against the chain links. His arm ached from holding up his shield, and sweat poured from under his helmet, stinging his eyes and burning the back of his neck.

They closed on the Danish line, the enemy faces becoming clearer until Olaf could make out the color of their beards and the fear in their eyes.

"Tighten up!" Gudrød bawled. Shields knocked as they drew together. Olaf's eyes met the fierce glare of the Dane in front of him. A bead of sweat roll down the man's cheek.

"Charge!" Gudrød lunged at the enemy, pulling the entire formation with him.

Olaf's throat vibrated, roaring with the others as they slammed into the enemy shields. The Swine Horn shuddered. The men behind pushed forward, and they strained against the Danes, unable to take a step. Spearheads thrust between the shields, seeking flesh. Olaf shoved with all his might, and the strength of the men behind him, but still the enemy didn't move. Sweat broke out afresh under his helmet.

An unearthly shriek split the air. A figure leaped out of the shield wall, whirling his axe with one hand and sword with the other.

It was Hrolf.

He wore a wolf's head in place of a helmet. His eyes were wide and glazed, and he uttered another chilling shriek as he sliced and hacked. A Dane swung his axe and connected solidly with Hrolf's torso in a blow that should have stopped him in his tracks, but Hrolf cut the man down and kept going.

Hrolf's performance galvanized Borre's warriors. Locked in formation, they drove their wedge through the Danes' shield wall. Olaf raised his axe as he had a thousand times in practice, hooking the top of the Danish shield in front of him, pulling it down. Beside him, his father thrust his spear into the enemy's throat, jerking it out as the corpse fell.

The air stank of blood and bowels, resounding with screams of men on both sides as they fell. Olaf hooked his axe over the next enemy's shield, then pulled it down and stabbed his short sword into the foe's exposed throat. Step by step, the war party scaled a mounting pile of corpses.

And then they broke through the Danish line.

They whirled to face their enemy, both shield walls breaking into smaller skirmishes. Olaf belted his axe and drew Bear Biter, thrilled to be using it in battle at last.

A Dane swung his axe, and Olaf dodged, then swung Bear Biter into the man's throat. He yanked his blade free and whirled to catch a sword blow on his shield, slashing Bear Biter low to catch the enemy in the calves, bringing him to his knees. The Norseman beside him drove his short sword into the Dane's heart. He met Olaf's eyes and grinned.

The knot of men had drifted away from the main battle to the verge of the forest. Olaf started to move back to find his father, but the man beside him crowded in, so close Olaf didn't have room to swing his sword. He stepped left to gain fighting room, but another warrior blocked that side. Olaf sent him a glare, but the fool only grinned while the man on his right pressed closer still. Whoever's men they were, they were poorly trained in battlecraft. Fury rising in his throat, Olaf rammed his right elbow out. But instead of meeting ribs, it found nothing but air, and he stumbled. As he fought to recover his balance, a shape swooped in from the left. He ducked, but it caught him on the helmet with a solid clang that sent him staggering. Another blow hit the back of his head, and he fell. Someone jerked Bear Biter from his grip.

"Kill him!" A rough voice.

Olaf blinked and strove to focus on the group of men who stood above him. He recognized the two who had crowded him in battle. The eyes that stared back at him were cold as stones.

"The young lord paid us good silver to kill him."

Olaf's heart drummed hard against his chest.

"That would be a waste. Look at him, a big, healthy boy. He'd bring a good price as a slave."

"We're supposed to leave him dead on the battlefield."

"Many corpses are never found after a battle. I say we take him to Haithabu and sell him in the slave market. We can be rich men."

"We're already rich. We have the silver, and his weapons and armor will fetch a good price."

"The boy will bring twice that in Haithabu."

"Lord Hrolf will be angry if we let this one live. He wants him dead."

"Lord Hrolf will never know. I say we put in to Haithabu, sell him in the slave market, then disappear. We can be out of everyone's reach, even Hrolf's."

"I say we kill him."

Olaf sat up just as a spear drove into the ground where his head had rested. He reached for his axe, but it was gone. He rolled to the side as a blade whispered by his throat.

Eyes glittering, a husky man thrust at him again, but Olaf dodged the blow. He looked up in time to see Bear Biter in the other man's hands raised to split Olaf's skull.

The attacker's eyes widened and he pitched forward. He lay at Olaf's feet, a spear quivering in his back.

Olaf gaped at his captors. Bristling with weapons, their eyes gleamed like wolves'.

"Lars seemed to think he could appoint himself our leader," said the man who had just killed Lars. Planting his boot on the corpse, he jerked his spear free. "He always was a backstabbing bastard. Fitting he should end that way. Now let's secure our merchandise."

Olaf flushed, aware of many pairs of eyes on him.

Lars's killer grinned, displaying teeth with grooves filed into them. He took Bear Biter from Lars's hand and tucked the sword into his belt. The other men surrounded Olaf. Laughing, they took hold of his arms and yanked him to his feet.

"We'll make for Haithabu, and sell this young lord to the highest bidder," said the man who had killed Lars.

"I agree with Anders," said another. "We sell the boy at the slave market. We need all the silver we can get." The rest of the men shrugged their agreement.

They bound Olaf's hands and hauled him through the woods to a tiny cove where a battered ship lay on the beach.

Three of them held him while others dragged his brynja over his head, then his fine wool tunic, even taking his breeks and boots, leaving him barefoot in his shirt. They threw him to the bottom of the boat, where he lay shivering on the floorboards, trying to grasp what was happening to him.

He had lost everything in a day.

CHAPTER 18

Borre

After her long night in the thicket, Åsa stumbled out into the chill dawn to watch Gudrød's fleet sail, praying to Freyja that he would never return. She begged the Valkyries to choose him for the corpse hall, or the sea goddess Rán to claim him.

Her mind reeled from the night's events. Why had Sigrid led her away from the feast? What did she know? Had the sorceress sent her slave, or had the old woman come of her own accord? When Åsa asked, Heid only smiled.

She shuddered, remembering Gudrød's threats to sacrifice her and the child in her womb.

Well, now he was gone to war. Skiringssal was only half a day's row to the south, but the battle could last days, or weeks. As queen, Åsa must take charge of Borre in Gudrød's absence, whether it was permanent or temporary.

After being closed up all winter, the hall was rank with soot

169

and mold. Åsa threw the great doors open to let the spring breezes rush through, scouring the air. She set the maids to take down wall tapestries and scrub the sooty timbers. Women plied their brooms in every corner, chasing out the ghouls of winter with the spiders and the mice. They dragged the bedding to air in the weak sunlight and replaced the old straw in the mattresses.

The sheep and goats tottered out of their byres into the yard, where the women washed their winter coats and sheared them. Newborn lambs chased each other in mock battle, their cries potent with indestructible life after winter's silent death.

A week went by, and a messenger brought word of Gudrød's victory. He had driven the Danes from Skiringssal. Åsa hoped fervently that he would stay there.

Åsa stood beside Heid's cart while thralls loaded the carved wooden image of the fertility god Frey. It was time for the sorceress to visit the district farms in her role as representative of the goddess Freyja, driving the cart around the new-sown fields to bestow the god and goddess's blessing.

"I wish we didn't have to go and leave you here alone," said Astrid.

"Brenna's here, and the other women," Åsa said, keeping her voice calm and confident. "I'll be fine."

The apprentices gathered to help their mistress into her cart. Heid climbed in and took up the reins, allowing her acolytes to fuss over her, fluffing the down cushion and tucking a sheepskin lap robe around her legs.

The gentle sunshine could not dispel the foreboding that rankled deep in Åsa's gut. It must have shown on her face, for the völva leaned down and patted her arm. "Your child is not due until midsummer. I will return in plenty of time for the birth." She shook the reins, and the horses took a strain on the loaded cart.

Åsa fell in beside Astrid as the young people followed their mistress up the trail, singing softly. Slaves came behind with two more horse-drawn wagons carrying tents and cooking gear and supplies for the journey.

The trail led inland where it joined the re, a moraine road made by giants long ago that ran from north to south through the entire district. As they turned off onto the re, Åsa lingered at the crossroads. She watched the entourage dwindle in the distance until they were out of sight and only their voices floated back to her across the hills.

She turned away at last. She had thought she would be glad to be out from under Heid's merciless stare, but the silence seemed to bear down on her as she trudged down the path to the hall.

At the steading, she shook off her gloom and threw herself into the everyday work with the women, tending the crops of barley, and flax. Each day, she made the long trek to the saeter in the summer pastures to work with the dairy maids. Fed on the lush grass, the cows and goats produced milk generously. Some of it was set aside for buttermilk. The rest they separated, skimming off the rich cream to churn butter, straining the skimmed milk to sour into skyr.

She set a small amount aside in linen-covered troughs to make gammelost, the pungent cheese. This was Åsa's specialty. After the milk had soured for several days, she set it to simmer in a cauldron over an outdoor fire until curds began to form. She poured the molten curds into linen-lined wooden molds and left them to set for a few days. When the cheese was firm, she wrapped it in dried grass and aged it in the dairy hut for one cycle of the moon.

During this time, the cheese had to be rubbed daily to help it ripen properly. Åsa loved working in the cool dairy hut with its earthy scent, sunlight from the open door warming her back. But when her simple tasks were done and she went to the bower to rest, images of her mother's final labor crowded her mind. When she closed her eyes, she saw the still, cold, beloved face. If she dozed, the screams started in her head.

Her mother had screamed for hours until Åsa prayed for her to stop. But when the screams finally did stop, the silence was far, far worse. The wise women had prayed to the family dísir for protection, chanted their spells, and made offerings to the mother goddess Frigg. They untied knots and unbuckled belts, traced birthing runes on her belly, and still the child would not come. Only blood came, so much blood, soaking everything, flowing off the bed onto the floor, leaving the still, white face of her mother on the pillow. It was the longest night of Åsa's young life, and it ended in the greatest loss she had ever known.

The women only shook their heads sadly and said, "That's the way of it."

Now Åsa dreamed that it was she who was laboring alone in the dark with a child who would not come. She opened her mouth to cry out for help but found no air in her lungs.

Waking drenched in sweat, she rose in the dark, threw on her shawl, and went out into the night.

She appeared in the smithy silent as a ghost. Ulf roused himself from his cot and brewed her a soothing potion over the dimly glowing forge. He sat with her while she sipped it, giving silent comfort.

Soon it will be over, she told herself, without believing it.

She wished Heid would return.

$$\approx$$

Skagerrak Sea

SOMETHING WOKE HIM—A sound, a movement, his fylgja, something. Olaf tried to sit up, but his head pounded in warning and he sank back. Beneath him, the ship rose to meet the seas. Above, the sail billowed and cracked.

For a moment, he thought he was aboard *Sea Dragon,* but then it all came flooding back. How he'd been a fool, betrayed, taken captive. Now he was on his way to Haithabu, to be sold as a slave. His face burned at his own stupidity.

His hands were numb in their bonds. Wriggling into a sitting position, he looked over the side, and a wave of dizziness swept him. Everything was backward. The land lay to the east, and open sea to the west. His heart gave a lurch as he realized they must have crossed the Skagerrak.

His captors sat on their sea chests eating dried fish and bread. Olaf's stomach growled. He cleared his throat to let them know he was awake. "I would like something to eat. And some water."

The man Anders looked at him, startled. Then he laughed.

"Certainly, my lord," he said, picking up a bucket. He dipped it in the bilge and flung cold seawater over Olaf's head. The others broke into laughter as Olaf sputtered.

He realized he was not going to get any food.

After his captors had finished their breakfast, Anders approached. Olaf steeled himself for more torture. Instead, the man cut Olaf's bonds.

"If you want to eat, bail," he growled, handing him the bucket.

The old ship had taken on a lot of water. The bilges were full. If he wanted to stay afloat, he'd better bail. Olaf heaved himself up and grabbed the bucket. Sensation seared back into his hands and legs, but he kept moving. He scooped water from the bilge and dumped it over the side. After a few rounds, his hands stopped burning and he fell into a rhythm that made the work easier. For a while, it seemed as if the old tub took on water faster than he could bail, but slowly the water level lowered.

When he could see the hull planks, he set the bucket down and said, "Now may I have something to eat?"

"We don't feed slaves!" Anders laughed and shoved him into the bow where he crouched, shivering in his wet shirt.

A fair wind drove the ship south. Olaf kept an eye out behind, hoping to sight his father's fleet, searching for him. They would make short work of these outlaws. Olaf would have to explain to his father how he'd been duped, but that embarrassment was a small price to pay to see his captors punished. And Hrolf. He imagined Gudrød disowning Hrolf, outlawing him, driving him into the forest.

Toward evening, they beached the longship on a deserted stretch of coastline. The cook, a man named Odd, sent Olaf to gather firewood. He stifled the overwhelming urge to run, knowing he wouldn't get far without boots, and he had no chance of survival without a weapon. He must wait for rescue.

He watched the outlaws feasting around the fire. When they set aside their dishes, he eagerly collected them, scavenging the leavings before he cleaned them. His hunger was barely blunted when he huddled in the bow. His shirt had dried stiff with the salt water. He scrounged a ragged tarp that was at least dry and wrapped himself in it.

A dark shadow of despair grew in his mind. Perhaps no one would come for him, after all.

OLAF'S STOMACH stabbed at him. He had been dreaming of food. He knew he must find a way to get something to eat or he would not last. When rescue came, he would have to fight. The cook fire wafted the scent of porridge his way. He forced himself up and stumbled toward it, drawn like a magnet. Gathering wood, he built up the fire and stood watching hopefully as Odd stirred the pot.

The cook glowered at him from beneath blond eyebrows. Olaf tensed to dodge a cuff.

"Here, boy, take over," said Odd, handing him the spoon.

Olaf kept his eyes lowered as he took the spoon and began to stir, feeling better just being near the porridge. He restrained himself from shoveling it into his mouth. His mouth would burn, and the outlaws might drive him away from the pot. Stirring all the while, he cast about for a way to get some for himself. He spotted a flat stone nearby. He glanced at the others, who were chatting around the fire. Quick as lightning, Olaf dipped some porridge out of the cauldron and onto the stone to cool. He resumed stirring, watching the outlaws. After a few minutes, he risked scooping a handful of the porridge from the stone into his mouth. Just in time, for the men began lining up with their bowls.

Dishing out the porridge, he made sure there was a generous serving left in the bottom of the pot. As soon as the crew sat down to eat, Olaf took the pot off the chain over the fire and carried it down to the shore. With his back to the men, he gobbled the cooling porridge, easing the stabbing pains in his belly.

The pots scrubbed and gear loaded, Olaf took his place at the oars. His heart weighed heavy in his chest as he helped row the ship farther from his home.

Two sails appeared on the horizon. Olaf's heart hammered as he strained to make out the sails.

"Looking for rescue?" Anders jeered. "Your brother hired us to kill you. He's sworn he saw you fall in battle. Everyone thinks you're dead, your body lost, and you would be, except that you might be worth something as a slave."

Olaf stared at him. Would his father believe that? With a sinking heart, he realized his father would have no reason to doubt Hrolf. Olaf looked miserably at the ships. By now he could make out the checkered patterns on their sails. They were not from Vestfold.

"We're in the Kattegat now, boy." Anders cackled. "You'll see no Vestfold ships in these waters."

They ran down the eastern shore for two days, putting into one of the myriad coves at night. The old ship needed constant bailing while under sail, the seas working the old caulking out of its seams. The work kept Olaf's mind off the despair that rode in his gut like a stone. He made himself the best cook's helper Odd had ever had, finding better ways to purloin food, and got hold of a ratty old sheepskin to warm his nights.

On the third morning, land appeared to starboard, and Anders set a southwesterly course. By early afternoon, they anchored at the mouth of a narrow passage, waiting for slack water. As soon as the current slowed, they manned the oars, pulling for all they were worth. In the flat, calm water, the old tub didn't leak as much, so Olaf stopped bailing and took his turn at the oars.

Anders drove them hard all afternoon, negotiating the reefs and currents in narrow passages between skerries and islands, making as much progress as possible before the tide turned. When they could no longer pull against the foul current, and it threatened to flush them back, they put into a deserted cove for the night. Olaf was too tired even to feel miserable. Sleep came over him instantly, a blessing and a balm.

Anders kicked him awake at first light. They got underway and rounded a cape, then turned due west, heading for a broad bay on the mainland. Once inside the bay, they followed the withy markers inland, where the waters narrowed into a fjord that wended through dense forest.

Columns of smoke rose in the distance, and soon, dark roof timbers poked above the trees. As they closed the shore, a settlement materialized. Like the port of Skiringssal Olaf had glimpsed, square, thatched buildings lined a boardwalk that ran parallel to the shore. But this settlement dwarfed Skiringssal.

Ships were moored alongside jetties that stuck out perpendicular from the boardwalk. Anders rafted his old tub alongside a merchant ship.

He approached Olaf with a rope. "Come here, lad." Olaf backed away, but two crew members grappled him and held him while Anders bound his hands. Despair drained away the last of Olaf's strength. "Come along with you." Anders gave the rope a yank. Olaf stumbled along as best he could as Anders dragged him over the neighboring boat and onto the jetty.

Once they were on the boardwalk, Olaf got his feet under him. He could not help but gawk as Anders pulled him along. The air rang with the sound of hammers on metal and the cries of men and women calling out their wares. Goods were offered that he'd never encountered: heaps of aromatic spices in all the shades of sunset; smooth, shiny silks in vivid colors; booths stocking feathers and furs and honey and wax and walrus tusks, pottery and glassware, iron and amber, and piles of silver, more than he had ever seen in one place. Men hacked coins into pieces and weighed them on scales. Tantalizing aromas rose from the food stalls, striking Olaf senseless with hunger.

In the distance, he sighted a crowd gathered around a platform on which chained men and women stood. Anders dragged him inexorably toward it.

When they reached the spot, the crowd parted to let them through to the block. Anders prodded him up onto the platform alongside other slaves.

Olaf faced the crowd, his nose running and the breeze chilling his bare legs. Under the speculative stares, he hung his head, grateful there was no one there who knew him.

"Here's a strong, healthy young thrall who can do an honest day's work," Anders declared. "He's a biddable lad who won't give any trouble."

Olaf's face heated. Indeed, he had given Anders remarkably little trouble.

A man in the front row mounted the platform, his gaze on Olaf. "Stand still, lad."

Olaf's heart thrummed against his chest. He'd surely be better off with any master than with Anders's crew of cutthroats. But he'd be a slave all the same.

He forced himself to stand still while the prospective buyer looked him over as if he were livestock. The trader squeezed his muscles and forced his mouth open to examine his teeth, then lifted each foot as if Olaf were a horse. It took all of Olaf's will not to jerk out of the man's grasp.

I will never do this to another human being, he vowed.

The trader straightened up and looked at Anders. "I think I can make you a fair offer."

As the prospective buyer haggled with Anders over price, Olaf's hopes rose and fell like waves on the cliffs. When at last the two men reached an agreement, the trader took hold of Olaf's rope. To his surprise, the trader untied the rope.

"My name is Björn," he said. "You will work for me on my ship. Have you been to Birka?"

Olaf shook his head. He had never heard of Birka.

"It is a trading port, much like this one, but far to the east and north, across the Eastern Sea." Björn put a hand on Olaf's arm. "Come, lad."

Olaf stumbled after his new master.

CHAPTER 19

Borre

Åsa woke before dawn, full of energy. She rose, shedding her nightmares, dressed, and went out to make the trek to the saeter.

The days ticked off on the primstave, inexorably nearing the solstice mark, and still the völva had not returned. What if Heid did not return before her labor began? Åsa tried to calm herself with the knowledge that Brenna was here, and many other women experienced in the ways of birthing. But as she trudged through the fields to the saeter, dread burned in her stomach.

A piercing cry split the quiet morning. Looking up, Åsa saw the dark shape of a falcon silhouetted against the sky. With a pang, she thought of Stormrider.

At least the bird was free.

As the raptor soared across the sky, a bell tinkled. Ragged strings trailed from its feet.

Jesses.

What if it *was* Stormrider?

Impossible. Falcons never came back from the wild. And how would Stormrider find her in Borre, so far from home? She shook her head and sat down with the dairy maids, breaking her fast with a bowl of curds before she set to milking the cows and goats.

As the sun warmed the yard, dairy maids carried their brimming pails into the cool dairy and began to skim off the cream. Åsa was working the churn, listening to their chatter, when she felt a pinch in her abdomen. She must be too vigorous at the churn. She slacked her efforts, but the pain stabbed again, and she sat down. Just about the time she thought she could get up, another pang gripped her, harder this time.

One of the dairy maids looked at her in alarm. "Are you all right, lady? Your face is white as milk."

The next pain made her double over. Water gushed between her legs, and she said, "Get Brenna."

Wide-eyed, the girl took off at a run.

Brenna arrived, out of breath, while Åsa shuddered through another pain. Brenna wasted no time in getting Åsa to her feet. "Help me get her to the bower!" The girls clustered around Åsa, supporting her as they stumbled across the fields.

They hauled her into the bedchamber, and Brenna helped her onto the bed. The other women crowded in, busying themselves burning herbs on the brazier and boiling water.

"The first one always takes a while," Brenna reassured her, cooling her forehead with wet cloths.

It took a long while. The contractions came hour after hour through the day. Drenched with sweat, Åsa's breath rasped in her throat. Brenna kept hold of her hand while the other women bustled in and out.

Chanting birthing spells, Brenna traced the birthing runes onto Åsa's swollen belly: Berkana to ease the pain and give calm, Pertho to ensure a smooth delivery. Two women hauled her up and walked her around the chamber while others untied knots and loosened saddle girths, praying to Frigg and Freyja, beseeching the Norns for favor, and chanting spells to protect the mother and child. In the exhausted breaks between contractions, Åsa remembered all this from her mother's final childbed.

It didn't save my mother.

The labor continued as the night wore on, but still the baby would not come. Åsa fell into a profound sleep between contractions, only to be roused by the next pain. In her conscious moments, she realized that she was going to die. She didn't care. If only the pain would stop.

At some point, she became aware of a flurry among the women. Irritation pricked at her. Why couldn't they leave her to die in peace? Then the next contraction took her, rolling through like surf crashing on the rocks.

Vaguely, she knew that Heid stood over her, and Astrid held her hand. She felt the tip of the völva's knife on her palm tracing runes as she chanted, then Heid clasped Åsa's elbows, shoulders, hips, and knees.

Too late. From a great distance, she heard Astrid beg the dísir for help, calling on the goddess Eriu and the Valkyries, handmaidens to Freyja.

Åsa had no room for anything but the contractions. Each wave possessed her, body and soul. As she cried out, there was the tinkle of a bell and a flutter of wings in the open gable end. Across the sea of pain, she glimpsed a falcon perching on the roof beam, jesses trailing from its feet.

Stormrider.

The peregrine cocked her head, training a goldenrod eye on Åsa. As she met the falcon's gaze, the pain receded. Relief swept in and lifted her.

She found herself in the rafters.

She stared down on figures far below. With a shock, she recognized Heid's wild tangle of hair and the bowed heads of

Brenna and Astrid. Surrounded by a crowd of women, they bent over a figure on the bed.

This time, the shock jolted her into the air. It was her own body on the bed, white and still against the quilt. A corpse.

Dread rose in her. Nothing could make her go back down there, to that scene of death.

She turned to the open gable where the stars glimmered, calling her to leave all this pain behind.

Powerful shoulder muscles contracted, then pushed. She lofted into the air and flew out into the night.

HEID DROPPED Åsa's limp hand. "She can't last much longer. I must speak to the spirits." She rose and donned her shawl.

Brenna took the völva's seat, face white with worry. "I'll stay with her."

There was no time for the elaborate preparations the ceremony usually entailed. The völva burst into the bower hall and mounted the platform as the women formed a ring and raised their voices in the spirit-summoning songs. Men crowded the doorway, careful not to cross the threshold.

Heid seated herself and cast a seed of cannabis onto the brazier. Almost immediately, her head lolled onto her shoulders, her eyes rolled back in her head so that they showed white. She uttered strange words in a high-pitched, unearthly voice. Then her head snapped up and she stared.

"Bring the smith to me."

Ulf stepped from the crowd and stood before her, head bowed.

"Your lady is dying, and I cannot save her," she said.

"What can I do?" he said.

Heid stared down on his grizzled head, considering. "There is one thing."

Ulf met her gaze. "I will do anything you command."

"In my vision, the old king, Halfdan, came to me. He is angry. Gudrød has dishonored him, not only once, but twice. King Halfdan will not allow another son to be born unless his sword is recovered for the child, and the boy named after him. Otherwise, he will take both mother and child with him to the grave."

Ulf stared hard at the ground.

"You must bring me the old king's sword and his belt."

There was silence in the hall.

Finally Ulf spoke. "I am no mound breaker. Nor am I kindred to the mound dweller. What makes you think the haugbui will let me rob his grave and live?"

"It is the only way," said the völva. "I am old and can no longer perform such feats. But you are strong, and learned of the runes. If anyone can manage it, you can." She peered at the men gathered in the doorway. "Who will go with Ulf to help him dig?" she demanded.

No one spoke. Those that could ducked out of sight.

"I will go," piped a high voice. Ulf's assistant, Bram, stepped out of the crowd.

The völva looked down on the skinny boy and sighed. "Very well. You are small, but you have the heart of a boar. Bring me a pickaxe," she commanded. The crowd parted as Bram scurried out. Before anyone could leave, he returned, hefting a pickaxe as he made his way to the völva.

Heid took the pick from him. She drew her knife and carved runes on the wooden handle, chanting their names aloud as she worked. When she finished, she held the pickaxe out to Ulf. "These runes will give you some protection."

Ulf took the pick, bowed his head, and made his way through the crowd, Bram following.

~

THE MIDSUMMER NIGHT was almost as bright as day. The sun had dipped below the trees for a few hours, but a full moon shone down on them. Ulf shouldered the enchanted pick, a shovel, and an iron spike, with two lengths of rope looped on his belt. In his pocket he carried a squat candle and a fire steel. Bram trailed behind, lugging a wooden bucket with another length of rope coiled inside. They halted at the base of the mound and shifted their gear.

Ulf examined the surface of the mound carefully to choose his point of entry. Without a team of men, he must dig the shortest and easiest route possible. That meant locating the grave chamber and digging straight down to it.

The prow of the ship would be oriented to the north, the land of the dead. There would be a tent-shaped burial chamber of logs nailed to the mast. The mast would be under the highest point of the mound.

Ulf toiled up the mound's grassy side, beckoning Bram to follow. The boy struggled with the heavy bucket, but he still trailed his master. At the top, Ulf paused to catch his breath and let the boy catch up.

He chose what he hoped was the center of the grave chamber, and muttered a prayer to Hod, the smith's god. Then he set the spike in the ground and swung the enchanted pick, using the flat side to drive the spike deep. Tying one end of the rope to the spike, he knotted the other end firmly around his waist.

"This will take a while," he told Bram. "Probably the rest of the night. You will have to pull up the bucket and dump out the dirt, then lower it back down the shaft to me. Once I am inside the grave chamber, watch for the rope to jerk. That means I need you to help pull me up. Stay here, no matter what you see. And stay awake!" Bram nodded, his eyes huge. Ulf wondered if the child had the courage to stay by his post alone all night, and if he did, could he stay awake? Ulf could only hope for the best.

With his powerful arms and shoulders, Ulf broke the sod and

began to tunnel straight down into the mound. It was slow going in the sticky clay, heavy with moisture, but the stickiness also kept the sides from caving in. He dug out a space wide enough for him to swing the pick. Standing in the hole, he filled the bucket with dirt and handed it to Bram to dump. He fell into the rhythm of his hammer in the smithy. Before long, the tunnel was over his head and he could no longer reach Bram. He shoveled the loose earth into the bucket and gave the rope a tug. The heavy load rose slowly up the shaft above him as Bram hauled on the rope. When the lad pulled the bucket out of the shaft to dump it, Ulf could glimpse the night sky through the opening. Then the stars blacked out again as Bram lowered the empty bucket back into the shaft. The smell of damp earth, decay, and mold filled Ulf's nostrils, and he sweated despite the chill. The tunnel seemed to get narrower. As he dug, he muttered spells to keep the dead asleep.

Through the night, Ulf dug deep into the mound, the patch of sky ever farther away. He chanted his spells and wielded the pick hour after hour until he forgot what he dug for.

Then he hit something solid, and realized that he had found the roof of the burial chamber. He swung the pick to breach the rotting timbers. Each blow made him wince, and he chanted louder.

At last, he broke through the roof. The air that smote his face was cold and dank, with a foulness that made him gag. He lowered the bucket into the breach until it clunked on the bottom. A shiver coursed down his spine as he peered into the darkness. Taking a deep breath, he gripped the rope and climbed down into the chamber.

Inside there was no light at all. The close air reeked of decay. Fighting down panic, Ulf fumbled the fire steel out of his pouch. His hands shook so hard, it took a dozen tries before his torch flared.

The flame guttered in the stale air, throwing huge shadows on the walls of the grave chamber. By the flickering light, Ulf scanned the room before him. A massive bed dominated the chamber, and on it lay the dead king in hoary splendor, on a rotting feather mattress covered by a moldering tapestry. The wooden headboard was incised with a valknut, the corpse knot, a symbol of Odin, and the bedposts were carved into monster heads that looked alive in the wavering light. On the floor lay a jumble of rags and bone, a thrall sacrificed to be the old king's companion in his grave.

In the torchlight, gold glinted on the intricate brooch that fastened the dead king's red cloak. His bony hand clutched the jeweled hilt of his great sword. Tufts of white hair sprang from beneath his gleaming helm. His flesh had dried on the bone, curing like leather, making the old king look as if he might still rise up from the bed.

King Halfdan had not fallen in battle. An old man, he had chosen the only other way to enter Valhöll. He had gone into the mound while still alive, sacrificing himself to Odin. When the king sealed himself into the mound, everything he might need was buried with him, including a slave to serve him. A trestle was set with an oil lamp and gaming board to while away the time awaiting death with his companion.

There was plenty of food and drink: mead, ale, cheese, grains, and wild apples. The insatiable appetite of the draugr was well known and feared. While kings and queens were buried unburned in their mounds so that they could continue to bless the land with the fertility as they had in life, sometimes their corpses grew hungry and rose to walk the land in search of food. The draugr were filled with superhuman strength and mindless rage, murdering anyone in their path. The living sent them on their voyage to the other world well provisioned, in hopes that they would stay in their graves and not plague the living.

By the looks of the untouched food, the old king and his servant had eaten nothing during their years in the mound.

Before taking another step, Ulf scanned the grave chamber until his eyes lighted on the thing he sought. It was an unassuming object, merely a thin stick as tall as a man, leaning across the chamber wall. But in the dim glow of his torch, Ulf made out the runes carved on it, reddened with blood that had long since turned brown. He approached the staff cautiously. Without touching it, he examined the runes. They were in the elder form, containing ancient symbols that had fallen out of use.

When read, the passage appeared to be nonsense. But in the last position were five dots, telling the reader to count back five runes to discover the power within the phrase.

Ulf let out a hiss of breath as the obscured meaning became clear. It was a curse that upon touch would rouse the draugr of the dead king. Every mound had such a curse to protect it, hidden from the incautious eye. Ulf had found the one that guarded Halfdan's grave.

Planting the butt of his torch in the bucket of dirt, he drew his knife and whittled away the runes into tiny scraps. These he caught in the king's iron cauldron, setting fire to them with his torch. He hoped that would suffice to disable the curse.

He took a deep breath and approached the corpse, chanting softly, reassuringly, all the while. "Sleep, Grandfather, sleep," he chanted. "There is nobody here. What you hear is only the wind."

With utmost care, he reached out and touched the great gilded buckle that fastened the king's leather belt. He gingerly opened the buckle and laid it on the down mattress. Holding his breath, he put his hand under the skeleton's hips and lifted. The king's trews were all that held the bones together, and Ulf was careful not to misalign them and risk disturbing the draugr. With one hand, he held the dry, weightless pelvic bone up while he pulled the belt out from under it, then eased the pelvis back down to the mattress.

Without pausing in his chant, he pried back the finger bones and lifted the sword in its wood scabbard.

He wrapped the belt around his middle, testing the crumbling leather to make sure it would hold. Fastening the massive gilded buckle, he slowly backed away from the dead man. When his calves contacted the bucket, he reached back and pulled on the rope.

A clump of dirt plopped into the chamber.

He pulled again. More dirt fell. He poked his head into the shaft and connected with solid earth.

He was buried alive.

Ulf took hold of his enchanted pick. With the shaft blocked, he knew he would suffocate before he could dig his way out, and any effort he expended would just use up the air faster, but he had to do something. He couldn't just sit by the old king's corpse and wait for his own end to come.

He climbed up on the bucket and dug his pick into the hole. Loose soil caved in on his head. Sputtering and spitting, he mounded the sticky clay in the grave chamber so that he could stand on it and reach higher. It was slow going, and the air was beginning to taste stale. Ulf poked at the hole again, and more dirt rained down on him. He dug into the shaft, to the limits of his reach, until his head and shoulders were engulfed.

It took enormous effort to heft the pick and strike at the hole. His vision blurred, and he struggled more for each new breath.

Out of the corner of his eye, he thought he caught movement. *An illusion.* Ulf turned back to his work. A heaviness dragged in his chest at the whisper of sound behind him. Slowly he pivoted. Through the gloom, he saw the old king sit up on his bed, opening a leathery lid over an empty eye socket.

CHAPTER 20

Daylight pierced the gable end of the bower.

"The smith should have returned by now," Heid fretted. The girl was dying. After more than twenty hours of labor, her lips were chalky and her breathing barely detectable. Contractions wracked her body, but she did not react to them. She stormed into the great hall. "Get out, get to the grave mound," she shouted to the sleeping men. "Find the smith, bring him to me." Shaking her staff, she drove them into the dawn.

It was Toki who returned first, alone, carrying Bram. Blood streamed down the boy's head, but he breathed. "I stumbled on him lying unconscious in the weeds."

Heid took hold of the child and patted him awake.

"Tell me what happened, boy," she demanded.

Bram blinked the blood from his eyes. "I stood by while Ulf dug a tunnel into the mound," he began, his voice faint. "I pulled up the bucket when it was full of dirt and dumped it on the mound. I was waiting for Ulf to pull on the rope. I waited a long time. Then along came Arne the smith. He chased me away with a shovel. But I don't remember what happened after that."

Two men burst into the bower. "We have just come from the

old king's grave mound," said one. "It is sealed. No one has dug there."

"But I watched Ulf dig all night. He made a deep tunnel into it," said Bram, sitting up suddenly. He winced and sank back onto the pillows.

"The tunnel has been filled in, you idiots," Heid said. "He must be inside. This would never have happened if you cowards had gone with him." She seized her staff and turned on the men who gathered outside the bower. "Come with me now, or I'll make your manhood rot off." She stepped outside the door, staff raised, as they weighed the risks. The völva raged before them in the flesh, her curse a concrete promise. In the end, they decided it was better to chance the draugr's fury.

"Hurry, you useless louts," she cried, shaking her staff at them.

They ran before her, trying to escape her wrath. They grabbed up picks and shovels as Heid, hobbling at an alarming speed, drove them across the fields with her staff. At the base of the mound, she halted, unable to climb the grassy slope.

"Get up there," she cried, lashing about her with her staff, thumping head and limb.

The men swarmed up the grassy slopes.

"Find where he dug," Heid shouted after them. "Look for loose sod. Hurry, you fools!"

"Here," came a shout from the top. "It looks like the turf has been disturbed."

"Dig!" cried the völva, pounding her staff on the ground.

They fell to with picks and shovels, quickly throwing up the loose dirt of Ulf's shaft.

"Careful with your shovels, you idiots," she said. "Don't hit him." She clawed her way up the mound.

As they dug deeper, they broadened the shaft so that three men could work side by side.

"Look out," cried Toki. The diggers slowed down just in time. "There he is!" A patch of white scalp showed in the black dirt.

Toki dropped his shovel and knelt. With his hands, he carefully uncovered the smith's grizzled head.

Ulf's eyes were closed, his face a pasty white under the grime. He was very still.

Frantically, Toki loosened the soil with his hands until he could get a grip under the smith's armpits.

"We need ropes down here," he said. Men lowered ropes down into the crater. Toki rigged a harness under the smith's arms.

"Careful with him," the völva shouted as they dragged him from the loose dirt. Toki grabbed him by the hips and hoisted him up to the surface, then scrambled out of the hole.

"He looks dead."

"Lay him down here," Heid cried. She took off her cloak and spread it on the grassy mound. The men carefully laid the smith's body on the cloak.

The sorceress bent close to his face to see if she could detect breath. She felt his head, listened to his chest. At last, she shook her head. She unbuckled the sword belt from his waist. "At least he got what he went after. Bring his body back to the bower." She handed the sword and belt to Toki and crabbed her way down the mound.

Wrapping Ulf in the völva's cloak, the men carried him off the mound and across the fields. They brought him into the bower hall where Heid instructed them to lay him on a bench by the fire. The women removed the smith's muddy clothes and bathed away the sticky clay of the grave mound, then wrapped him in furs. During all this, he lay inert, limp and pale as milk.

The völva peered into his bloodless face. "I cannot detect breath or heartbeat," she said, "yet I have known men to live even so. If his body does not putrefy, then he lives. Keep him warm and watch over him." She turned to the men and growled, "Find the smith, Arne. Bring him to me."

Taking up the sword belt, she hurried into the bower. Brenna raised her head from Åsa's chest, tears streaming down her face. She shook her head.

"Oh, get away from her, you fool," Heid cried. Brenna stepped out of the völva's reach, but stayed close.

Åsa lay curled on her side, body white and still, her belly convulsing with each contraction.

"Get her up," Heid commanded the women who gawked in the doorway. They converged on Åsa's limp figure and hauled her to her knees.

"Hold her," the sorceress instructed, buckling the belt around the girl's heaving belly. She launched into the birthing chant, the women joining in.

Åsa's body jerked in a contraction. The women chanted harder, their voices swelling until the room rang.

Another contraction.

"The child is crowning," Brenna cried.

"Now!" the völva shouted, opening the massive buckle. The leather belt fell free. Brenna took a firm grip on the child's head and eased the baby halfway out. Another contraction clamped down. Brenna waited for the release and pulled again.

The child slipped free.

She held the naked infant in the chill air as he drew his first lungful and wailed.

The women eased Åsa's still form back down onto the bed.

Åsa soared out over a sunlit meadow. Far below stood a table. At the head of it, her father sat; beside him, her mother; and next to her, Gyrd. They all looked up at her and called out. A wave of joy suffused her, and she flew down to take her seat beside them.

Her mother took her hand and smiled into her eyes.

"I am so glad to see you all!" Åsa cried.

"We are glad to see you, dearest," said Gunnhild.

Over her voice came a wail. A child's cry.

"I want to stay here with you, Mother."

The wail came again. It pulled on Åsa, but she kept her sight on her mother's serene face.

Gunnhild smiled. "Not yet, dearest. You must go back. Our boy needs you."

Åsa let the cry pull her this time. She felt herself sliding away from her mother, back to the bower hall. She hovered in the rafters, looking down on her body prone on the bed.

Heid was staring up at her.

The sorceress took the squalling baby from Brenna's arms and held him up. The linen-wrapped package drew Åsa's gaze magnetically. His tiny face was dark, almost purple, wrinkled as a winter apple.

"Live," Heid commanded. "Live for your child."

The infant opened his mouth and wailed again.

The cry pulled Åsa down from the rafters, back into that sea of grief and pain.

Åsa's eyelids fluttered.

Heid's acerbic voice rasped. "Glad you decided to join us."

"Where is my baby?"

Heid leaned down and placed the warm bundle in her arms. The sorceress gave Åsa a piercing look. "He is a very special boy," she said. "He has a destiny to fulfill. You must raise him to be a great king."

Åsa's arms closed around the baby, and she stroked the wrinkled red little face. Then his eyes opened, and she caught a glimpse of her mother looking back at her.

She stared at her son in wonder.

THE HÚSKARLAR CAUGHT up with Arne the next day. They dragged him back in chains, his right eye swollen shut, his lip split, and a big hunk of his beard gone. They locked him in an empty cow byre to await judgment at the Midsummer Assembly.

Heid presided over the women's feast, celebrating the successful birth. Three men carried in the vat of birthing ale and fled as if Hel's minions were after them. The menfolk kept their distance while the song and laughter emanated from the bower. They knew from past experience that any man unlucky enough to be caught by the gleeful women could expect to be the butt of drunken mischief that would be difficult to live down.

Amid much song and laughter, the women of Borre fashioned a man of straw and made him suffer many indignities in postures that defied imagination.

"I'd like to get you with child," cried one of the women, shaking the straw man. "I'll bet you would squall like a stuck pig if you had to give birth."

The women cheered in agreement.

"Brave those warriors think they are. Bah! I'd take a spear wound over birthing pains any day."

"Men think they are so tough. They wouldn't last an hour in the birthing chamber. They'd faint at the sight of the afterbirth!"

The women howled with laughter.

Åsa, pale after her ordeal, watched the antics from a fur-covered bench along the wall. She kept a firm hold on her son, resisting the revelers' attempts to get him from her.

The only man allowed to attend the feast was Ulf, who still lay wrapped in furs, pale as a corpse. When the revelries had wound down, Heid examined him again carefully.

"He's unnaturally white," said Heid, "and I can't detect breath or heartbeat, but even after three days, his body shows no sign of corruption. He lives, yet he is dead. He is under the haugbui's curse. I must see if I can compel the mound dweller to release him back to us."

She mounted the seidr platform for the second time in a few days. Casting a seed of henbane on the brazier, she inhaled the poisonous fumes while her apprentices formed the ring and began the vardlokkur.

The seidr took her instantly, her eyes showing white as her head lolled back. Her breath came in rasps and strange, harsh sounds emanated from her throat.

Then her voice caught. Her hands flew to her throat as she choked. The women exchanged alarmed glances even as they continued to sing the vardlokkur, not daring to stop.

Heid's body writhed, her hands still clutching her throat. Her voice came in strangled gasps. Then she fell from her chair as if hurled, striking the platform hard enough to knock over the brazier. Coals spilled onto the platform as her body jerked and shuddered. Wide-eyed, the women sang with ever more force while the flames leaped.

Åsa thrust her child into Brenna's arms and scrambled onto the platform, Astrid behind her. The apprentices gasped as she righted the brazier and scooped up the burning coals with the iron tongs while Astrid beat out the flames, then turned to the writhing sorceress and called her name.

Heid's body gave a final jerk and lay still. The women fell silent.

"Help me," Åsa cried. Astrid took Heid's legs while Åsa gripped her shoulders. They picked up the sorceress and carefully lowered her down to the others, who laid her alongside Ulf. She looked as dead as he did.

"The haugbui has them both in his power," said Astrid.

"How do we get her back?" said Åsa. The apprentices were silent, gazing on the prone body of their mistress.

From her corner, old Sigrid raised her head. "There is only one who can help."

"Who?" Åsa demanded.

The old slave's voice rent the air harshly. "Hrafn," she croaked.

The apprentices shuddered.

"Who is this Hrafn? Where does he live?" Åsa said.

Sigrid replied, "Hrafn is a berserk of great power. He was once the leader of the king's húskarlar, but Gudrød came to fear his powers, and outlawed him. Now he dwells in the forest, where he is the leader of the outlaws."

Åsa's stomach clenched.

"How do I find him?"

The old woman said, "You don't. He finds you."

THE EVENING WAS COMING on when Åsa and Astrid made their way into a clearing in the forest. There they waited in silence as the tree shadows stretched across the glade. Nothing stirred.

"Will he really come?" Åsa said at last.

"Shhh!" said Astrid. "Can't you smell him?"

Without warning, a voice rasped like metal on metal. "Why do you seek Hrafn?"

They whirled to see a figure clad in gray rags. He threw back his hood, and they gasped at the sight of his crudely sewn eyelid.

He chortled, an eerie sound that sent a shiver down Åsa's spine.

"We need your help." Her voice came out as a squeak.

"Why should I help you? I was cast out of this place long ago. I owe nothing to those who live here."

"It is not for us," said Astrid, "but for the völva Heid. She has been taken by the haugbui."

Hrafn's laugh was a fractured scrape. "So the old witch has gotten herself in too deep? She knows better than to deal with mound dwellers," he said, satisfaction evident in his voice. "What makes you think I would help her?"

"We'll pay you," said Åsa desperately. "I have jewels."

Hrafn laughed. "What good are your baubles to the likes of

me?" He eyed her in a way that made her insides liquefy, but she kept still, face blank. "You," he said at last. "She saved your life. Now you want me to save hers."

Åsa's throat was so dry, she could only nod.

"Now, why would she take such interest in you?" he murmured to himself, walking around her. "You don't look like much. A girl..." He leaned in close and sniffed at her. Åsa pulled her cloak tight to hide her trembling. "A king's daughter...a new mother... What is she up to, that one?"

Suddenly he stopped in front of her and pinned her with his agate eye. "Oh...I understand..." he breathed. His voice was so low, she could barely catch his words. "If I do this, you will owe me a debt."

Åsa nodded, dread heavy in her stomach.

Hrafn grinned in a way that made her shiver.

"I will come tonight."

Åsa feared she would come to regret her bargain.

IN THE BRIEF darkness of the summer night, a gray-cloaked figure flitted from the cover of the wood to the bower door where Åsa and Astrid waited.

"Well, where is the old witch?" Hrafn demanded, throwing back his hood.

They led him to the völva's body where it lay on the bench next to Ulf.

"Two!" Hrafn said. His face broke into an unpleasant grin. "You will owe me double."

Åsa nodded. "Very well. Time is short. Get on with it."

Hrafn mounted the seidr platform.

The women began to gather. The old man glared at them.

"I don't need your silly songs," he said. "Scat!"

The apprentices scuttled to the corners.

Hrafn lit the brazier with his fire steel. From a pouch at his belt, he withdrew a pinch of herbs and cast them onto the fire, sending an acrid column of smoke into the darkness.

He began to croon in a cracked singsong voice. His head lolled, the song came in fits and starts. His arms rose, quivering, his head jerked from side to side. The chanting became the screech of eagles, strident and powerful.

Suddenly he lurched out of the chair. Eyes staring straight ahead, he began shouting until Åsa's ears rang from it. Then he stopped abruptly. He fell to the floor with a thud and lay still.

Åsa was beginning to fear she now had a third living corpse when the old man sat up. For a moment, he stared around him in confusion. Then he broke out in a grin and fixed her with his piercing eye.

"Remember, little queen, a double debt you owe old Hrafn."

Gripping his staff, he slid off the seidr platform and made his way unsteadily to the door while everyone in the room stood as if paralyzed.

"What was that old coot doing here?"

They all turned as one to see Heid sitting up on her bench, with Ulf blinking beside her.

CHAPTER 21

Eastern Sea
Midsummer

Olaf had never worked harder in his life. As they made their way through a welter of islands and narrows, he rowed Björn's beamy knarr, *Eastern Trader*, whenever the wind was absent or foul, which was most of the time. The vessel was a tub compared to the longships he was accustomed to, and the long sweeps bit the sea awkwardly. Under sail, the sea-hardened crew taught him quickly how to do things to their liking, and Olaf worked hard to please them. He was always the first one ashore when they made camp, gathering firewood and hurrying back to help with the cooking. The hard work and scarce diet made him sleep like a stone and claw his way back from dreams each morning when the crew rousted him. It kept despair at bay.

As soon as Anders and his crew had departed, Olaf approached Björn.

"I am the son of the king of Vestfold," he said in low tones. "If you bring me home, my father will reward you beyond your dreams."

Björn had laughed good-naturedly. "Boy," he said, "if I had a silver piece for every slave that has told me a story like that, I'd have retired from trading long ago."

"But it's true! Anders and his crew kidnapped me and took everything I had."

"And why didn't Anders ask your father for a ransom?"

"My enemy hired him to murder me, but his greed got the better of him. If he offered me for ransom, he would have to face the man who hired him. A man that Anders fears."

Björn said, "That's quite a tale. Can you prove any of it?"

Olaf realized that the outlaws had taken every trace of proof from him—his clothing, his armor, his sword. He hung his head.

Björn patted his shoulder. "You're a good boy, even if you do tell wild stories. My advice is, work hard, and I will treat you well."

After a cold meal of bread and reconstituted dried cod, Olaf dove into sleep like a falcon on its prey. Björn roused them before first light for one last pull through a narrow channel between two islands, then at last they broke free into the Eastern Sea. Raising sail to the favorable west wind, they rounded the headland and turned north. The beam wind let them rest, leaving little to do but trim the sail and dole out dried meat and flat bread.

As the knarr bowled along on a northerly course, the coast began to break up into myriad islands.

"That is Öland," Björn said, pointing out a long, low island to the west. He turned to the east and gestured to another large island. "And that is Gotland."

The white of a sail glinted against Gotland's dark shore.

"Looks like we have company," said Björn to the lookout. "Keep an eye on them."

The current was with them, and the boat shot between the two islands like an arrow from a bow.

The low-hulled ship slipped out into their wake.

"I don't like the cut of his sail," said Björn, staring astern. "Arm yourselves."

The crew members belted swords and axes, setting out bows and casting spears near to hand. No one offered Olaf a weapon. Slaves did not bear arms.

They broke into the open sea again. As the sun neared the horizon, Björn tacked into the coast. He squinted off to the west. "There they are," he said softly when the sun picked the sail out against the land. The other ship stayed to windward of them, as if looking for an opportunity. The crew fingered their weapons, and Olaf sensed their tension as they glanced over their shoulders.

At last light, they slipped into a snug little bay on the lee of an islet, hiding behind the headland as their pursuer sailed by. Björn had them set a stern anchor, then run the bow onto the beach and tie off to a tree.

"We'll set a good watch tonight, in case our companions realize we've given them the slip, and pay us a visit."

Björn wouldn't let them build a fire, but the night was warm enough. As they ate, Olaf kept glancing to the west. He noticed that Björn did the same, in spite of the two crew members he had set to watch.

"Lay out your sleeping skins on the beach," said Björn. "Stuff them with wool and other goods to make it look like your body's in there." Then he bade the crew slip on board *Eastern Trader* to sleep, where the knarr's high sides hid them from view.

After scrubbing the pots, Olaf climbed aboard and lay down in his rags. He stared at the men Björn had set watching from the rocks silhouetted against the stars. His eyes burned from the smoke of the cook fire, and he struggled to keep them open. The night was balmy and for once he wasn't shivering. It felt so good to lay down after a hard day's work. The boat rocked gently at anchor, the waves lapped soothingly against the hull. Sleep pulled him down.

He startled awake in the dark. Something was wrong. He looked to the empty rocks. Struggling to sit up, he was about to cry a warning when a hand clapped across his mouth. He thrashed against strong arms. "Hst, you fool!" Olaf relaxed when he recognized Björn's hiss. "They're behind that rise."

Olaf joined the crew, peering over the knarr's gunnel. Dark shapes appeared silently on the rise and crept toward the camp. Olaf shuddered as the pirates hacked their axes and swords into the empty bedding. Then a roar welled up from the crew, and he was up with the others, leaping over the side, splashing through the shallows.

Though Olaf had no weapon, he charged into the brigands. The pirates reeled in momentary confusion as the knarr's crew fell on them, but in an instant, they were fighting back.

Olaf, on the fringes of the melee, caught movement on the periphery of his vision as a pirate crept up behind Björn. Shouting a warning, Olaf shoved into the heaving mass of men and flung himself on the attacker. Björn whirled and drove his sword into the pirate's gut as he fell. Björn looked up at Olaf, startled, then grinned in thanks as he pivoted to meet the next attacker.

Olaf grabbed the dead man's sword and shield. He eyed the pirate's clothing, but a swish of air made him whirl, bringing up his shield in time to block a sword blow. He parried automatically and shoved, locking shields with his opponent. Then he yanked the pirate's shield wide to open the attacker's guard, and drove his blade in, penetrating the man's midriff. He put his foot on the man's stomach and jerked his sword out, sending the corpse reeling to the ground.

With the advantage of surprise, the merchantmen proved

every bit as lethal as the brigands and soon dispatched the last pirate to bleed in the sand with his mates.

They found the pirate ship abandoned on the other side of the islet. It was lean and low, with rowing stations for sixteen men. Björn eyed his crew.

"Well, we are close enough to Birka. With this fair weather, I think we can bring it in with six men." The crew agreed enthusiastically, and Björn had more volunteers than he needed to man the pirate vessel.

"The brigands must have had more success with other prey," he said, looking over the cargo.

While the others were sifting through the pirate's loot, Olaf hunted among the bodies until he found a tall one. He stripped off the dead pirate's breeks and pulled them on. They fit well enough. The boots were too big, but he could stuff them with rags. He added the warm tunic and a wooden scabbard for his sword. Buckling on the corpse's leather sword belt, he joined the others around the fire.

He tensed as he felt Björn's gaze upon him. For a moment, he faltered, not daring to look at the merchant captain.

Then Olaf met his gaze fiercely, hand tightening on the sword hilt. It was not a very good sword, but he would fight with his life to keep it.

"You fight well, for a slave," said Björn, handing him a cup of ale. Olaf reached out to take it and then did not know what to do. He stood frozen until one of the Svea crew moved over to make room for him. He let out his breath and took his place among the merchants.

He picked up a honing stone and drew it across his sword, trying to smooth out the worst of the nicks. It was a sorry blade. The pattern welding was clumsy and poorly finished. Even Arne could do better. He was lucky it hadn't broken in the fight. Still, the possession of it defined him as a man, not a thrall, and he would die before he gave it up.

CHAPTER 22

Borre

A few days before the summer solstice, Gudrød's fleet sailed into Borre in triumph, banners fluttering, painted shields lining the rails.

Åsa stood with Heid at the head of the eager crowd, clutching Halfdan so tightly, he began to fuss. She couldn't help scanning the ships' crews for a blond head that towered above the rest.

Her heart stuttered when she realized Olaf wasn't there.

She shoved her worry down hard. *Why should I care? He cares nothing for me.* She had more important things to worry about just now.

A cheer went up as the warriors disembarked and the crowd surged forward to greet them. They made way for the völva, who stepped into Gudrød's path, pulling Åsa with her.

"You have a new son," Heid announced.

Gudrød made no reply. He did not look up but busied himself with the ship's mooring lines.

Heid laid a clawlike hand on his arm. "We nearly lost both your queen and your son," she continued peremptorily. "But the smith Ulf risked great peril to save them. How will you reward him?"

Gudrød looked at her sourly. "The smith has failed to produce a Serkland sword for me. His life is forfeit. I will let him live, for now." He stalked away toward the hall, calling for mead.

TENTS BLOOMED among the burial mounds as folk set up for the Midsummer Assembly, the most important meeting of the year. Traders arrived overland and by sea, offering everything from dried cod to jewelry. Those from the north brought ivory and furs, and reindeer antlers for combs, while from the south came soapstone for cooking pots and schist for whetstones, Frankish glass and Eastern amber. The prattle of barter drowned out the bleats of livestock.

The hazel poles were set in a ring and the hallowed bands stretched between them. Five big men manhandled the high seats inside. Åsa swallowed hard as she entered the sacred ground and took her place beside Gudrød, the húskarlar gathered behind them. Hrolf stood at their head, in the place that Olaf should have been.

Two men helped the old lawspeaker to his place. He was a man of high birth named Grim, and it was his task to know by heart all the laws, to remember the cases of the past years and how they had been resolved. The lawspeaker was ancient, and profoundly deaf. These days he kept to his bed and was brought out only for the assembly.

Gudrød rose. "We have won a great victory against the Danes, and taken back the Shining Hall." Cheers rose from the crowd as the húskarlar beat their weapons on their shields. Gudrød waited while the hubbub subsided. "My son Olaf fell in battle.

Though we have not found his body among the dead, his brother, Hrolf, saw him fall. The Valkyries have taken him to Odin's hall."

Heat flamed in Åsa and she fought to keep a stone face. Through blurred eyes, she spotted Brenna making her way through the crowd, the baby in her arms. When Brenna reached the circle's bounds, she handed the child over the rope to Heid. Åsa tensed as the sorceress approached the high seat. The boy had survived the required nine nights, and now the völva brought him before his father. With Gudrød lay the choice of accepting the baby or rejecting him to be exposed in the forest—a thing unheard of for a highborn son, especially now that Gudrød had lost his heir. Still, worry gnawed at Åsa's stomach. Gudrød had no reason to love this child. He might do anything.

Åsa shrank back in her seat, trying to keep out of Gudrød's sight in case her presence reminded him that the child was not his. Her fingers worried the fringes of her shawl as she waited for her enemy to decide the fate of her son.

Gudrød's jarls had gathered to witness the event. Heid unwrapped the baby's swaddling clothes and laid him naked on the ground for inspection. The boy's eyes snapped open, and he stared intently around him. Then he squinched up his face and, sucking in a vast gulp of air, opened his mouth and let out an earsplitting squall. He kicked and thrashed in fury, demanding attention.

The jarls laughed at this lusty display. "He's strong enough!" they shouted over the baby's howls.

Unsmiling, Gudrød nodded. Heid picked the screaming child up and held him while Gudrød dipped his hand in the basin of water held by one of the apprentices. As he sprinkled water on the tiny, furrowed forehead, Åsa exhaled, realizing that she had been holding her breath.

Heid turned and faced the hall. Above the infant's dwindling cries, she announced, "There have been many signs and portents from the grave. It is the will of the haugbui that this child be called Halfdan, after the patriarch."

Ulf limped forward, carrying the sword he had recovered from the grave mound. He presented it to the völva.

"This is the sword of King Halfdan, known as the Mild, taken from his grave mound by the brave smith, Ulf," said Heid. "I now bestow it upon Halfdan, grandson of Halfdan, that he may bear the virtues of his ancestor."

She passed the sword three times over the baby. Halfdan fell quiet, reaching his tiny fingers up for the polished blade. The gesture won an approving shout from the crowd.

Gudrød's sworn men surged forward with their gifts, including an upland pony with fine gilt trappings, a richly woven blanket, and enough silver, furs, and ivory to bury the boy.

At last, the völva restored the child to Åsa's arms. Her blood quieted as she hefted his familiar weight.

I must bide my time until I am strong, and keep my son healthy.

Now was the time for lawsuits to be presented. Old Grim rose from his chair and recited the laws in a quavering voice. When he finished, he resumed his seat and stared into the distance. Gudrød alone judged the cases, some of which had been simmering since the last assembly at the spring equinox.

The first case was that of Arne the smith.

Åsa watched two húskarlar drag the smith before the assembly. The crowd thronged the hazel bounds, smelling blood.

"Who accuses this man?" Gudrød demanded.

"I do," Åsa declared.

He turned to her in surprise. "And what is his crime?"

"He attempted to murder the smith, Ulf, by burying him alive."

Gudrød leaned forward, a spark in his eyes. "And where did this occur?"

Åsa tensed, aware that the ground was becoming perilous. "In the mound of King Halfdan."

Gudrød's voice rose. "Do you say that Ulf broke into the patriarch's burial mound? That is a crime in itself."

Heid stepped forward. "The old king came to me in a vision and told me what must be done to save your queen's life, and that of your child. Ulf entered the mound at great cost to himself. If he had not taken this risk, your wife and son would both be dead."

Gudrød narrowed his eyes. "And what proof do you present that Arne buried Ulf alive?"

"The boy, Bram, was witness."

The crowd expelled Bram, who stumbled into the sacred ground.

"Tell us what happened, boy," Gudrød commanded.

Bram raised his eyes to the king fearfully. "I stood by to dump the bucket of dirt while Ulf dug a tunnel into the mound," he began, his voice faint. "Then along came Arne the smith. He chased me with a shovel."

"What happened then?"

"I don't remember," said Bram. "The next thing I knew, I woke up in the bower hall with a sore head."

Gudrød frowned at the boy. "So, you don't know how you came to be unconscious?"

"No, lord."

"Did you see Arne bury Ulf?"

"No, lord."

Gudrød cast his piercing gaze over the crowd, and Åsa shivered. "Were there were no witnesses to this crime?"

Heid spoke again. "We found Ulf buried in the mound. He was unconscious, prisoner of the haugbui."

Gudrød smiled coldly but did not reply. He turned to Åsa. "And you, his accuser. How do you know that Arne committed the crime? Where were you while all this was happening?"

"In the throes of childbirth," she admitted.

"So, we have no witnesses to the crime, only assumptions," Gudrød said.

The crowd murmured uneasily.

"It is obvious that Arne hit the boy with the shovel before burying Ulf," said Heid.

"Perhaps the haugbui, angry at being disturbed, caused the tunnel to cave in."

Cries of protest rose from those who had dug Ulf out of the mound.

Gudrød smiled at the crowd. "I see that you have strong opinions in the matter. Very well, I will not gainsay the will of the people." He turned to Arne, who was scowling in his chains. "What have you to say, smith?"

"They're all liars," Arne snarled. "I committed no crime. They just don't like me."

Gudrød turned back to the assembly. "Since no one saw Arne commit the crime, I cannot put him to death." The crowd surged against the hallowed bonds, making angry noises.

"Instead, I declare him outlaw. Arne, you have until sunset tomorrow to leave Borre. After that, anyone who sees you may kill you without penalty."

The crowd, mollified, roared their approval.

Arne glared at Heid and Åsa as the húskarlar removed his chains. "I'll make you sorry for this," he growled.

Heid shook her head as she watched him hurry away. "Now the outlaws have a smith."

Bile rose in Åsa's throat at the injustice of it, but she pushed it down and steeled herself for what she must do next.

Keeping her arms tight around Halfdan, Åsa turned to Gudrød. He scowled at her.

She drew a deep breath. "My lord," she said, loud enough for all to hear, "I have given you a son. I ask you to keep your Jóltide promise to me. Now that you have secured Skiringssal, I ask you to fulfill your responsibility to Tromøy. The people are unprotected, leaderless. I ask that you keep your word and send warriors there to defend it."

Gudrød smiled. Somehow, it was not a smile she liked.

"Very well," he said. "Hrolf!"

"Yes, sire," said Hrolf boldly, stepping out from behind the high seat.

Åsa watched in shock as he knelt before Gudrød.

"Hrolf, you have served me well. I now make you jarl over Tromøy. Go there and rule in my name."

Hrolf rose. He bowed to Gudrød, then inclined his head to Åsa with a sardonic grin.

Åsa felt as if she had been punched in the stomach. How had her plea gone so wrong? There was no way out of it now, since every jarl had witnessed the exchange. Her request had been fulfilled. Of course, Gudrød would have to award Tromøy to the protector. There would be no other motive for the warrior to care for the place. The newly made jarl would then owe tribute to his king, so Gudrød would profit from the transaction.

She had never thought of him giving her father's kingdom away to Hrolf. She'd been too naïve, and that would cost her people dearly. She must stop making mistakes.

CHAPTER 23

The barley turned golden, ripe for the harvest, and every adult in Borre swung a scythe. The children followed behind and bundled the sheaves, leaning them together in stoups.

As soon as the harvest was in, Gudrød gathered his warriors and set sail for his summer raids. He left women, children, thralls, and the elderly behind to care for the land and the live-stock, protected by a small band of Borre's elite household guards.

In his absence, Åsa was the undisputed ruler of Borre. She kept Halfdan swaddled and strapped to her chest, turning him over to the wet nurse only when he wailed with hunger. Even then, she jealously watched the girl's every move. Brenna slid naturally into the position of fóstra, hovering nearby to take the baby on the rare occasions that Åsa let go of him.

The bower rang at all hours with the infant's demands, but the women delighted in his presence. Even the völva hobbled over to pick him up when he fussed. The child's hair grew thick and black as a crow's wing, earning him the byname Halfdan the Black. Though he had Gunnhild's coloring, there were moments when Åsa would glimpse Harald peering out from Halfdan's tiny face, and sometimes Gyrd's mischievous eyes.

My family isn't gone; they survive, contained in this one small package.

The days were hot, and soon the barley stoups were ready to thresh. All the folk of Borre turned out to work under the late-summer sun.

Åsa was the last to leave the bower to join the threshing crew, lingering over Halfdan as she put him down for his nap. As she straightened up, her gaze fell on the old king's sword where it hung on the wall above the cradle. It had been so long since she'd held a weapon. On impulse, she reached out and lifted it down. The weight felt good in her hand. She tried a thrust and winced at the pain in her shoulder. She swung again, and the unfamiliar weight yanked her off-balance.

Shame stung her. *How far I've fallen from my dreams of becoming a shield-maiden. Big as a whale all winter, trapped indoors with no exercise but weaving—I've become a mockery.*

Gripping the sword, she strode into the woods. In an isolated clearing, she hefted the blade and began the routine that Jarl Borg had drilled into her and Gyrd since they'd been old enough to hold a wooden practice sword. She was glad no one could see how clumsy she'd become, but she kept at it, thrusting and parrying until her arm trembled.

Quit before you hurt yourself, fool. She made her way back to the hall, exhausted but happy for the first time in months.

She knew the old king's sword was too long and heavy for her to handle properly no matter how much she practiced. That evening, she paid Ulf a visit.

"I need a sword," she said. "Something light enough for me to train with."

"I wondered how long it would take you," Ulf said, smiling. He brought out a long, narrow bundle wrapped in sheepskin and laid it in her hands.

She opened the fleece and caught her breath. There lay Lightning, in perfect condition, its blade glistening with oil. Tears sprang to her eyes as she reached out for it. "How did you..."

"I found it in the armory. Careful, it's sharp."

She thrust and parried, delighting in the familiar weight and balance. *There may be hope for me yet.*

The next day in the clearing, she wore herself out. When she could no longer lift Lightning, she rewrapped it and made her way back to the bower, stowing the sword in her chest at the foot of her bed.

Rummaging in the armory, she found her old brynja and helm among the captured armor. They were too small to fit any man and so had been left to rust. She took them to the sand barrel and spent the better part of the morning polishing them.

When the helmet shone and the brynja's rings flowed like water, she hefted the chain-mail shirt over her head. The links cascaded down her torso and settled into place. She donned the helmet, picked up Lightning, and strode to the clearing. There she went through the drill Jarl Borg had taught her in childhood. Sadness weighed heavy in her chest at the thought of the old jarl, his bones picked clean on the battlefield.

Each day, she found time to slip away, working hard to regain her strength and agility. Her muscles hardened and she recovered some of her old speed. Before long, she had advanced as far as she could on her own. She needed sparring partners.

She donned her helmet and chain mail and approached the practice yard, where the house guard was hard at its drills. Hefting a blunted practice sword and a red-and-white-painted shield, she marched onto the field.

The warriors froze, staring.

Åsa clashed her pommel on the shield boss in the traditional challenge.

No one moved.

"What's wrong with you?" she jeered. "Afraid of a woman?"

Her remark stung their captain into speech. "We cannot raise arms against our queen," Olvir said.

"Since I *am* your queen, you cannot refuse my direct order," she countered. "I command you to fight me."

Olvir did not move. Again, she clashed her sword and shield together.

"Come on, man, I don't have all day!"

He took a step into the yard. Before he could change his mind, Åsa rushed him. In his surprise, he fumbled his parry and she got past his guard. Her blunted sword tip rammed into his midriff and sent him stumbling back, gasping for breath.

"First blood!" she cried. The warriors roared with approval.

She saw murder flare in Olvir's eyes. He bore down on her and, with a sweep of his foot, knocked her legs from under her. She slammed down hard on her back, his sword point at her throat.

She watched the flicker in his eyes as he remembered with whom he sparred. He jerked his sword back from her throat and held his hand out, head bowed.

"Lady, forgive me. I concede the field."

The blood still beating in her veins, she brushed him off and sprang to her feet. "Very well. Who's next?"

The warriors exchanged glances.

"Come on, it's an order!"

One of them stepped forward.

This time, she was more careful. These men did not dare to hurt her, and if she wanted them to trust her, she would have to respect that.

The next round was more a sparring dance, points scored carefully by each side. The húskarlar seemed reassured, and three more responded to her challenge.

From then on, she appeared in the practice yard every day. Soon enough, the warriors got used to working with her, and began to teach her their skills in earnest.

CHAPTER 24

Eastern Sea
July

The fluky morning breeze hurried *Eastern Trader* and the pirate ship into a ragged scatter of islets, which Björn navigated with a sureness born of experience. At midmorning, he turned into the coast, entering an inlet that led north and evolved into a passage. The narrow passage required them to drop the sails, and Olaf took his place at the oars.

The channel grew narrower, shoaling until they ran out of water. Björn beached his boat on the sandbar, the other two boats drawing up alongside. In the distance, Olaf could see the blue water where the channel resumed.

"Now we portage," Björn said, indicating a well-worn track across the sand that led to the channel beyond.

Björn's men grabbed hold of the heavy-laden cargo ship and began to heave. Olaf fell in with the others, taking hold of the gunnel and straining forward. For a moment, the knarr resisted.

Then, with a hiss, the keel broke loose of the sand and began to slide. Step by step, they coaxed the heavy cargo ship across the sand. At last, they reached the far shore and turned back for the other vessel.

The pirate's ship was much lighter than the knarr and slid easily by comparison. Even so, by the time they hauled it across the sandbar, Olaf's shoulders and thighs were throbbing, and he gratefully took his seat at the oars. After the slow drag of the portage, the boat seemed to fly through the water.

They followed the channel until the sun was low in the sky, then broke into open water. A fresh breeze filled in and they hoisted the sails. Olaf had never been so glad to boat his oar and lean against the gunnel, watching the sail belly out and the boat surge forward into the chop.

The ships wended through the shoals and islands under sail, making good time until they sailed into the lee of a sheer bluff that reared high above them, stealing the wind and the sun. Björn had them drop sail and sent them back to their oars. As they skirted the bluff, Olaf craned his neck and stared up at the earthen rampart of a hill fort. Helmeted men peered down at them from the walls, spears poised.

Björn waved, and one of the warriors waved back in recognition. The helmets disappeared behind the rampart.

They rounded the point to encounter a sandbar, water breaking all along the length of it. Björn steered them to a gap in the bar where the water ran smooth and deep. Beyond lay a broad harbor crowded with ships. Some swung at anchor, but most were moored to pilings, dozens of which sprouted from the water. It must have taken years to sink those pilings, and a lot of slave labor. Olaf shivered and gripped his sword hilt tighter.

Björn nosed into one of the wharves. There were no open spaces, but he signaled the crew of the pirate ship to come alongside.

"Björn!" A burly, dark-haired man hailed them, his black beard split by a grin.

"Skeggi!" Björn tossed him a mooring line.

"It looks like you have done well this spring," observed Skeggi as he tied the line off, looking over the pirate vessel as it rafted alongside the knarr.

"Yes, I've had some luck," said Björn. "A crew of pirates thought to take our ship, but we took theirs instead."

"Congratulations on your good fortune, and welcome home," said Skeggi. "Come to my camp when you are ready, we will feast you tonight."

"I thank you. We will be there."

Olaf lingered uncertainly as the crew stepped onto Skeggi's boat.

"Are you coming?" Björn called. Fear and excitement made Olaf's heart pound as he clambered over the boats and scurried after the crew down the wharf toward town.

Birka was a revelation. The island settlement was much larger than Skiringssal, rivaling Haithabu in size. Craftsman's wattle and daub cottages lined the planked walkways that ran along the shore, and timber halls loomed on the hilltops. Olaf followed Björn and his crew along the boardwalk, gawking at the merchant stalls that offered a variety of silks and silver he'd never seen, even in Haithabu.

They came to a crowd gathered around the slave block bidding on a naked man in chains who stood on the platform, head bowed. Olaf's stomach roiled. But Björn led them on until they arrived at an encampment on the beach. The aroma of roasting pork made Olaf a little dizzy.

Skeggi was tending the spit. "Join us!" he cried.

"After days of dried cod, that pig smells good enough to draw the gods." Björn took a seat on a drift log among the others and accepted the ale horn Skeggi handed to him.

Olaf sat next to Björn, who drank and passed the ale horn to him. As he took the horn, Olaf eyed the Svea merchants. He felt like a fraud. He didn't belong with these people. But to them, his weapons and clothing made him an equal, not a slave. He drank and passed the horn to the next man.

After the ale horns had made a few rounds, Skeggi leaned forward and slapped Björn on the knee.

"Have you thought about sailing to the Eastern Lands this winter?"

Björn took a drink before answering. "It's wild country there, filled with pirates and savages."

"That is true. But with danger come great profits. Those Finn trappers bring down piles of the finest furs from the far north. They are happy to trade them for axes and beads." Skeggi's eyes gleamed, but Björn looked dubious.

"If we formed a coalition," Skeggi continued, "we would be strong enough to take on most anything that might come. We leave here with a full cargo of axes and beads and whatnot. Crossing the straits this time of year shouldn't be too bad. We can dry-dock our ships in Aldeigja, and pick up sleds and dogs and wait for the rivers to freeze. We hire a guide who will take us into Finn country where we trade for a cargo of furs, then take the rivers east to the Itil River to Bolghar. Men come up from Serkland who have more silver than good sense. They'll pay anything for the best furs. In their country, it's so warm, they don't need furs, but they're a status symbol. After we make a killing in Bolghar, we load up the sledges with silks and silver, and head back to Aldeigja before the rivers thaw. We'll sail home in the spring, rich men."

Björn smiled. "You make it sound so easy."

"I won't make light of the dangers or the hardships," Skeggi replied, "but neither will I make light of the riches that stand to be gained."

Björn's eyes gleamed in the firelight. "Let me discuss it with my crew. We will give you our answer tomorrow. But in the morning, I have business in the slave market."

A cold shadow fell across Olaf's heart. He would not be part of this expedition. In the morning, Björn would sell him.

That night, he lay sleepless, the image of the slave market looming in his mind. Tomorrow he could be the one standing naked on the block, examined and bid on like livestock, to labor until he died from hard use and starvation. His whole body urged him to run, but that would not help him, here on an island. Even if he managed to steal a boat, he would not get far. The slave trade was big business in Birka, and he was merchandise, livestock. They would catch him and beat him within an inch of his life, and then sell him all the same. He longed for home, though Gudrød would not want him if he knew that he'd been enslaved. There was no other life for him but the one that lay beyond the slave block.

He lay awake all night, despair a heavy weight on his chest. He watched as the light crept over the land.

The crew convened to discuss the matter of going east while Olaf lurked by the fire.

"We could stand to become rich," said Erland.

"We could stand to become dead," said another. "You heard Björn, that country is nothing but wilderness infested with pirates and savages."

"The profits are greater in the east. Where else can we get silver? And as a part of a company of three ships and more than a hundred men, our odds of survival would be good."

"I think we should go, and come back rich men," said Ketil.

The others roared their agreement.

"All right, it's settled," said Björn. "We'll go."

Olaf busied himself with the pots. When a shadow fell over him, he didn't look up.

"Come, boy," said Björn. "We have business in the market."

Olaf's hand went to his sword, but what good was that? If he drew it, the crew would fall on him and bind him like an animal. Best to go like a man. With a heart of lead, he followed Björn.

They arrived at the slave market, and Björn mounted the block. Olaf took a deep breath to still his trembling and stepped up beside his master.

In a loud voice, Björn addressed the crowd. "This man is my slave, bought and paid for." Olaf closed his eyes and fought down nausea. "But even though he was a slave, he saved my life. I owe him a life, the life of a free man. Now I shall make him one."

At first, Olaf could not understand what was happening.

"I declare before you all that this man, Olaf Gudrødson, is a free man." Then Björn was clapping him on the shoulder and pulling him off the block while the crowd cheered. Björn's meaning penetrated Olaf's mind. Shock and relief coursed through him, making him dizzy. He clung to Bjorn's arm like a drunkard as they made their way through the streets in triumph.

Back at the camp, the Svea merchants seemed to already know what had happened, greeting them with brimming ale horns and congratulations. After they all drank, Björn bent down to take off his boot. He handed it to Olaf, who realized this was the ceremony that made him a free man. He numbly took off his own boot. As if in a dream, he pulled on Björn's boot while Björn slid Olaf's onto his foot, and arm in arm, they walked three times round the fire amid the cheering crew.

"You're one of us now, for better or worse," said Björn. "We are going to the East, and it's your decision whether you come with us or not."

Olaf didn't even stop to think. "I'm coming!" he cried, and the crew cheered again. His shipmates.

That night he lay awake in a delicious state of excitement and fear. He would be sailing to the East, to a land few men had ever seen. He might very well die a fearsome death in a foreign land, and no one would ever know what happened to him.

But he could return home with riches nobody had ever

dreamed of, and stories to amaze them. He imagined laying silver at his father's feet, and in his mind, Åsa sat at Gudrød's side. But she was smiling at Olaf, bathing him in her blue eyes as the silver cascaded into her lap.

A flame of excitement burned through the fear, and he realized he wanted to go more than he had wanted anything in his life.

East. He was going East.

Anything could happen.

CHAPTER 25

Borre
September

The days shortened and the evenings cooled. The flax began to yellow, and every able person descended on the fields to get the harvest in before it rained. They pulled up the whole plants by the roots and tied them in bundles, leaning them together in stoups to dry in the fields. After the flax plants had dried for a week, the women harvested the seeds with a ripple, then sank the bare stalks in a retting pond downwind of the steading, and left them to rot away the tough outer layer. A week later, a team of women who had drawn the short straws hauled the stinking flax from the water and laid them out in a field to dry in the autumn sun.

After a few days, they collected the plants and began the hard labor of breaking the stalks on a board and beating the outer husks away to expose the long, silky inner fibers, like fine blond hair but much stronger. These they combed with a heckle to make them ready for spinning.

Once the flax was safely in, the women turned to the fall shearing, after which the sheep would be turned loose to over-winter out of doors. Everyone pitched in as the women grappled the sheep and sheared away their wool, which was lush from the summer grass.

The spring wool came out of storage, and the women combed it together with the stronger fibers of the fall. From that moment, every female old enough to walk carried a distaff tucked in her belt wherever she went, spinning flax or wool any time her hands were not busy with other things. Even Heid dropped a spindle.

The days shortened, and the autumn equinox approached. People began to arrive from the surrounding countryside for the álfablót, the sacrifice to the álfir.

It was one of the most important occasions, yet there was no sign of Gudrød's ships. Åsa tried to ignore the unsettled feeling in her stomach.

Two days before the equinox, a messenger arrived with the news that Gudrød would hold the sacrifice in Skiringssal.

There was no time for the folk in Borre to pack up and reach Skiringssal before the equinox. Heid turned to Åsa. "Well, girl, you must preside in the king's stead."

Åsa's skin prickled. The queen took the place of the king at the assembly when there were no adult males left in the house-hold. With Hrolf in Tromøy and Olaf dead, it was up to her.

It dawned on her that if she were at home in Tromøy right now, she would be presiding over the assembly in her father's stead.

Brenna managed to pin up the sleeves and hem of Gudrød's robes so that Åsa would not look like a child playing dress up. But that was just what she felt like as she led the procession down the winding trail through the trees to the burial mounds. Surrounded by the house guard, she rode with Heid in her elaborately carved cart. Behind them walked the free folk of Borre, leading livestock for sacrifice and driving carts loaded with camping gear and Åsa's high seat. They erected tents in the fields surrounding the mounds, where everyone would sleep out of doors for a week while their dwellings stood open to the air one last time before winter.

Åsa took her place beside the völva at the base of old King Halfdan's burial mound while slaves unloaded the carved images of the gods and posted them around the mound, facing the four directions.

When the folk had gathered before the gods, Åsa and Heid sacrificed a boar and a goat, painting the mound red with the blood to bless the land and its people. The cooks carved up the meat and set it to simmer in cauldrons for the evening feast.

Men set the hazel poles in the field and roped off the law circle with the hallowed bands, setting a boundary beyond which no weapons could pass. Four húskarlar carried the high seat into the circle, along with a chair for the lawspeaker. They spread a wolf pelt on the seats and set a small table beside it on which Astrid placed a pitcher of small beer and a goblet of Frankish glass. She filled the glass and stepped back behind the chair.

Åsa swallowed hard as she entered the hallowed ground and took the high seat, the húskarlar gathered behind her. She did her best to appear confident while frantically trying to remember the debates and discussions her father had presided over, racking her brains to recall his decisions.

The men helped Grim to his chair. He stood and mumbled the laws in his quavering voice, then took his seat again and stared blankly ahead. Åsa suspected that he lived more in the next world than this one. She must treat him with appropriate respect while ignoring his advice completely. She would just have to brazen her way through, without any help.

Taking a sip of beer, she braced herself to hear the first dispute of the day.

Two red-faced men approached the law circle, backed by their friends and kin. The house guard flanked the antagonistic parties. Weapons were secured with peace bonds at the assembly, but murder and mayhem had been committed just the same.

Åsa straightened in the chair, glad she was within the hallowed bands, and stared directly into each man's eyes. She took a deep breath and fortified her voice with the power of her galdr training.

"Tell me who you are and why you are here," she commanded the one on her right, the plaintiff's position.

"I am Alf Thorvaldson," he replied, "and this man has taken my cow."

The other man interrupted angrily. "That's a lie. The cow strayed onto my land, and by rights that makes it my property."

"I was right behind her, trying to lead her back to my land!"

The two men's voices rose as they asserted their positions.

"Quiet!" said Åsa.

To her immense relief, the adversaries fell silent.

"You have not told me your name," she said sternly to the second man.

"I am sorry," he said. "I am Regin Odson. I own the farm next to Alf's."

"Have you and Alf quarreled before?" she asked.

"Alf insulted me at the assembly last year," said Regin. "Everyone heard him."

"I see, so you have waited all this time for an opportunity to get back at your neighbor, is that it?" she asked.

Regin reddened and opened his mouth to protest. Then he closed it.

Åsa pondered, glancing at the lawspeaker. Grim's penetrating stare was fixed on her, but he said nothing. She could not tell if he had even heard the statements. She did not want to ask his advice so soon, but the crowd was beginning to mutter.

"Did this cow step onto Regin's land with all four feet?" she asked, to buy time.

"Only the front two," said Alf defensively.

At this statement, her mind suddenly cleared. The decision was obvious.

"Since this was only a partial trespass, and you will agree no harm was done to your property, Regin"—she looked hard at the farmer, who nodded reluctantly—"then I decree that Regin should receive one half of the cow's milk from now until spring."

She stopped herself from looking at Grim, trying to show complete confidence in her decisions. Still, she listened for a tell-tale cough or clearing of his throat.

The lawspeaker remained silent while the assembly clashed weapons on shields, signifying their approval of her judgment. Even Alf and Regin had to admit that her decision was fair. They went away, if not completely satisfied, at least unable to disagree.

The assembly continued for six days, during which Åsa presided over divorces, settled disputes, and heard complaints. Grim sat through the proceedings, but he never intervened. In fact, she suspected that the elderly lawspeaker heard nothing.

Her confidence grew with every case. It was not really so hard. One just had to listen closely, and watch the adversaries' reactions, and the answer would come clear. Her biggest fear was that two plaintiffs would refuse to accept her decision, and demand their right to settle the dispute by holmgang. She dreaded presiding over a duel. But whether due to Åsa's judicial skill or pure good luck, there was nothing of that sort this time.

Divorces were the easiest, for every man and woman had the right to annul their marriage for any reason. They had but to declare it in front of at least ten witnesses, and the assembly was the logical place to do it. The woman took her dowry with her. Since it was so easy to dissolve a marriage, most of the divorces were amicable. The couples separated before bitterness festered.

Åsa was surprised to notice nods and smiles at her decisions.

People seemed to approve of her. For the first time in months, she felt almost at home.

In the evenings, Åsa sat among the assembly listening to bad poetry, or laughing at the insult contests and lying stories of folk inspired by mead. The fresh air gave her a good appetite, and she slept soundly on the collapsible bed in her tent. Halfdan seemed to thrive with the outdoor living. During the day, Brenna hung his cradle from a tree outside the tent, and he watched the birds and clouds in perfect contentment.

On the last morning, Åsa opened her eyes to see sunlight and leaves dappling the linen weave of her tent. For a moment, she thought she was in her bed on Tromøy, but the truth came into her mind quickly. Her family was still dead, she was little better than a prisoner, and Hrolf ruled Tromøy.

Those problems could wait. For now, she lay there savoring the sunlight.

Åsa took her place on the high seat and heard cases all day. That evening, tired but happy, she sat by the fire sipping ale with Heid and Astrid when a well-dressed stranger approached Åsa.

Astrid stared at the newcomer, and the small wooden box he held. "Greetings, Gunnar. What brings you to Borre?"

The man inclined his head to Astrid, then turned to Åsa with a deep bow. "Lady, I am Gunnar Halvorson. I am foster brother to Sigurd Brodison of Ringerike."

"Greetings, Gunnar Halvorson," said Åsa. "Your foster brother and his father, King Brodi, are valued allies of Vestfold. You are welcome at my fire."

Gunnar cleared his throat. "My foster brother sends me to speak with Lady Astrid."

Åsa nodded, though her heart sank. "Very well, Gunnar, speak."

Clutching the box, Gunnar turned to Astrid. "Lady, my foster brother, Sigurd, reminds you of the times you met when you were children. He remembers you well."

Astrid colored and lowered her eyes. "And I remember him."

"Fondly, I hope," said Gunnar.

Gunnar hurried on. "Lady, it has been my foster brother's wish to wed you for some time. He asks me present a marriage proposal to you."

Gunnar opened the box to reveal a glint of gold. The bride price. A rock seemed to drop into the pit of Åsa's stomach. Astrid gasped at the finely wrought necklace nestled in a bed of fleece.

"Sigurd asked me to present this to you as a token of his intentions," said Gunnar. "He stands to inherit all his father's lands, which, as you know, are considerable."

Astrid's mouth opened, then closed, then opened again. At last, she said, "I thank you, Gunnar. I will give you my answer in the morning."

"Until morning, then." Gunnar closed the box, bowed, and backed away from the fire.

When he had gone, Åsa turned to her friend and spoke in measured tones. "Do you want to marry this man?"

Astrid blushed. "I knew him well when we were children. He was a good friend then."

Åsa swallowed and kept her voice light. "It's a good match. You will be a queen when his father passes."

"But I don't want to leave you, or Heid, or my sister apprentices," Astrid said in a rush. "I would miss Halfdan and everyone here."

Åsa forced a smile. "Ringerike is not so far. You could come for visits."

Astrid nodded. "So you think I should accept his offer?"

Åsa stared into the fire. She wanted to say, *No, stay here forever.* But was that best for Astrid, or for Åsa? "Remember the runes. This may be the marriage they spoke of."

Astrid's eyes gleamed with hope. "Yes, it might."

"Heid will need to recruit another apprentice." Though she tried to sound playful, Åsa's voice came out as a croak.

They spoke no more on the subject but turned their attention to the skáld.

In the morning, Astrid accepted the proposal and took possession of the golden necklace. Sigurd would come and fetch his bride in the spring.

At least I have my friend through the winter, Åsa thought. But when Astrid left...Åsa turned her mind firmly to other matters.

CHAPTER 26

Gulf of Finland
Autumn

Björn steered *Eastern Trader* in the wake of Skeggi's knarr, *Sea Sow*, as they wended their way through the northern passage from Birka. When they broke into open water and the first swells hit, a few of the men were sick over the side, while their more seasoned shipmates teased them. Olaf was glad that he had always been a good sailor.

The rhythm of the days at sea set in as the little fleet bowled across the Eastern Sea. Everyone had gained their sea legs by the morning of the fifth day, when the lookout sighted land.

"It is the land of Finns," called Skeggi. "The locals will not show themselves, for fear of slavers."

The open sea became a broad gulf. They dropped the sail for the first time in five days, and took to the oars.

Skeggi kept them to the northern shore. "Keep a sharp

lookout for other ships. Pirates infest the southern shore, and they've been known to venture into these waters."

The four ships threaded their way through the skerry-littered waterway, sheltered from the brutal winds and southern pirates alike. They camped on the low-lying islands, which were crowned by birch trees alive with birds. All day, the birds raised a raucous carol, but as soon as the sun dropped, they fell silent. An eerie darkness invaded the land, and Olaf wrapped himself in his cloak and fell into a wary sleep.

At the first glimmer of the sunrise, the birds instantly took up their chorus. There was no danger of oversleeping. Stiff with cold, Olaf scurried to build up the fire and put on the porridge. He was working harder than he ever had as Gudrød's son, yet being the lowest member of this merchant crew made him happier than he'd ever been in Borre.

Taking to the oars again, they worked their way through the shoals. The gulf narrowed, and they began to fight the river current long before they reached the river's entrance. At the river mouth, the flow was strong enough to drive them backward. They fought their way upriver for an entire day, besieged by tiny insects that bit and flew in their mouths and noses with every breath. It seemed their sweat drew the little demons. That night, sore and tired, they made a rough camp on the riverbank. Olaf slept with his head inside his sleeping skins where the flies couldn't penetrate. At first light, Skeggi roused them and they struck out again, battling the current until, at last, the river slackened, spilling into a vast lake. Yellow-brown water lapped tranquilly on rocky beaches choked with willow and alder.

"Lake Ladoga," Skeggi said with satisfaction as they rested their oars. The going was easier as they worked their way along the marshy southern shore until the scrub parted to reveal another river mouth. Once again, the current was against them, and they spent another day pulling hard, choking on clouds of gnats.

Just as the light glimmered low behind the trees and gloom descended on the river, Olaf caught the scent of woodsmoke. In the half-light, columns of smoke rose above the trees, and he heard the ring of hammer and axe.

They rounded a bend and a settlement appeared.

Aldeigja.

The riverbank was crowded with longboats and knarrs. Farther inland sat rows of ships on blocks undergoing repair after the rugged passage across the Eastern Sea.

Björn nosed *Eastern Trader* in among Aldeigja's fleet. A man on board one of the ships waved him over to raft up. Olaf clambered over the knarr's side with a mooring line and made fast to the welcoming ship.

"Welcome!" said their host with a broad smile. "My name is Dag. After you have a look around, join us for some ale!"

Skeggi rafted *Sea Sow* to *Eastern Trader* and the pirate's ship, which Björn had renamed *Eastern Serpent*, tied up outboard.

"I need three men to keep watch on the ships," Björn said.

Olaf held his breath. To his delight, Björn's gaze passed over him, and three others were assigned to take the first watch.

The settlement of Aldeigja sat at the mouth of a brook in the midst of a vast swamp forest. Square log houses lined split log walkways that rode on the boggy soil. The ring of hammers came from a roofless smithy where workmen fashioned rivets and ship's fittings. Open workshops walled with woven branches housed craftsmen making trade goods: bone combs, glass beads, bronze amulets inscribed with runes, images of Freyja's and Thor's hammers, and iron fire-steel pendants.

The settlement was populated by a mixture of Svea, Finns, and Slavs. The Slav women strolled the boardwalk, gold rings dangling from embroidered linen head scarves, gilded pendants gleaming on their breasts. The men wore fox-trimmed tunics that hung to the knee over voluminous breeks that were gathered and tied below the knee.

Dag made the Svea crew welcome in his hall. When Björn and Skeggi told him of their plans to make for the Bolghar fur market, Dag invited them to team up with his group.

"The more we have, the safer our trip," he said.

They stayed in Dag's hall for the next month while they repaired the ships and laid them up on blocks. As they waited for the rivers to freeze, Björn and Skeggi felled some trees and set the men to building a dozen sledges.

They purchased dog teams to pull their sledges and supplies for the journey: dried meat and fish, sacks of barley, and barrels of ale, as well as the trade goods the Finns wanted: fish hooks, knives and axes, amber and glass beads, and bolts of wool and linen cloth.

Snow flew, and within a fortnight, the river had frozen solid. They loaded the sledges and set out on skis, Dag with his eight sledges and his crew of fifty men leading Björn and Skeggi's twelve sledges and crew of eighty.

The first week, they followed the river north through the forest. They traveled from first light until dark, taking turns driving the sledges and breaking trail in the new snow on skis.

Olaf was given charge of caring for one of the dog teams, and he loved them, especially one of the lead dogs named Eik. Eik was friendly and intelligent, a natural leader who kept the other dogs in order. When they made camp at night, Olaf staked the dogs out, and fed them before he ate, heating frozen meat over a fire. The dogs burrowed into the snow, leaving only their noses uncovered. Each dog had a set of leather boots to protect their paws from the ice. Olaf checked the boots every night, repairing them by the fire before he slept. As Olaf came by with strips of meat each morning, the dogs burst from the snow, glad to see him and eager to hit the trail.

After a week, they reached the frozen shores of Lake Onega. "Here we will trade with the Finns," said Dag.

They made camp beside the lake and waited, but no Finns appeared.

"They are here, watching us from the trees," said Dag. "They won't show themselves for fear of being taken as slaves. They engage in silent trading. You will see."

At dawn, they packed up the camp and got underway.

"There they are," said Dag, pointing. The shore was dotted with neat piles of bundled furs, sometimes accompanied by a pair of gleaming walrus tusks or a crock of honey and blocks of wax.

Dag examined the displays of goods. "The black fox is worth the most. In the south, to be seen as an important man, one must trim his robes with black fox. The Serklanders will pay almost any price for it."

As they made their way along the deserted shore, Björn and Skeggi followed Dag's lead, stopping to make offers at displays they liked.

"Pick one," Björn said to Olaf.

Olaf looked at him in astonishment. "But I have nothing to trade."

Björn smiled. "I will stake you. You can repay me when you make a profit in Bolghar."

Björn helped Olaf choose an offering that included a pair of walrus tusks and a bundle of black fox pelts. He laid an axe and knife, a handful of beads, and a length of woolen cloth in the snow beside it.

When they made camp in the evening, they still had not seen a single Finn, but Olaf's neck hairs prickled. He knew they were being watched.

The following day, they retraced their route.

"If the goods you laid down are gone, then your offer has been accepted. You are free to take the display."

When Olaf came to the spot where Björn had laid down the trade goods for him, only the pelts and ivory remained. A little jolt of excitement sparked in him.

"Congratulations on your first trade!" said Björn, handing him a sack for his new acquisitions. As he stowed the black fur and tusks, Olaf felt a tiny flicker of hope.

Dag had advised them well on their purchases in Aldeigja, for in every case, their offerings had been taken. By the time they reached the end of the shoreline, the sledges were heaped with furs, mostly black fox, interspersed with pelts of beaver, otter, mink, ermine, and squirrel.

Fully laden, they departed the trading grounds, following the river south and east. The sledges skimmed across the frozen marshes, the forest sheltering them from the winter gales. The journey took on a festive tone, with high hopes for trade in Bolghar.

They drove their sledges through the forest until the trees thinned into a vast grassland and they found the broad ice road of the Itil River.

The weather was clear, and the dogs ran effortlessly over the river ice under cloudless, vivid blue skies. But when Olaf looked back, he saw a dark cloud loomed on the horizon, racing toward them across the steppe. Though the dogs fairly flew along, the storm cloud gained on them all morning.

Dag called a halt at midday and set them to building a snow wall against the sledges. They had barely finished when the wind shrieked down on them. Olaf gathered the dogs in the lee of the wall and buried them all under furs while the wind howled and the snow piled up over them. Olaf heaped snow in a pot and brought it under the furs until the dogs' combined body heat melted it. He let the dogs drink first and then fed them chunks of frozen meat. After the dogs gulped their meal, Olaf huddled with them under the furs as the storm shrieked down on them.

As the snow grew deeper, the air inside their little snow cave grew close. Olaf poked a spear through the leeward side for ventilation. In the thin air, the dogs went to sleep, but Olaf forced himself to stay awake to keep the air hole open. Time passed, how long he couldn't know, for it was impossible to tell day from night.

The snow piled up deeper and deeper until the spear could no longer penetrate to the air outside. Olaf's eyes began to flutter. It was too much trouble to stay awake. And perhaps that was a mercy. In the dark, he lay down among the sleeping dogs, and his hand found Eik's fur as he let his eyes drift closed. An inner joy suffused him, and he saw a vision of Åsa, her red-gold hair cascading over her shoulder, her blue gaze shining down on him.

CHAPTER 27

Borre
November

Asa woke in a sweat. She had dreamed of Olaf again. He'd been somewhere cold and dark, a place of despair. Was it Niflheim, the misty world of the dead? But Olaf had fallen in battle. Surely the corpse maidens had taken him to Odin's hall.

She shook her head, dispelling the grief that threatened to choke her. Olaf was dead, and she needed to forget him. There was much else to occupy her. It was Slaughter Month, when most of the livestock were butchered and the meat preserved for the winter. A few were kept alive, some for the Jól sacrifices, while the prime specimens would be housed in the byres through the winter for breeding stock. The winter ale must be started to be ready for the feasts.

Gudrød had sent word he would winter in Skiringssal. Åsa felt a huge wave of relief at the news. Borre was safe enough without him and his hird. The harvest was safely stored, and the winter gales would to hold the sea raiders at bay.

When Jól came, only local folk attended Borre's feast. A few nearby farm families joined Borre's small population of servants, the twenty húskarlar, Åsa and Halfdan, Heid and her apprentices. The atmosphere seemed lighter for the absence of the king and his hird.

Åsa presided with a new confidence. When she and Heid sacrificed a goat and reddened the carved figures of the gods, she could actually feel their power flow through her.

The men set the meat cooking in a cauldron over an outdoor fire while the women sang to coax a blessing from the álfir and the dísir. When the meat was cooked, everyone gathered around the longfire in Borre's great hall to feast. They passed the memory horn and toasted departed kin. That night, they set out the traditional meal and vacated their beds to sleep on the floor so that the dead could have a night on earth.

Wrapped in furs next to Halfdan's cradle, Åsa dreamed that Gunnhild stood over them, gazing down on her grandson with love and pride. She woke with tears blurring the darkness where her mother had appeared.

WITH THE END OF JÓL, the weaving season began. The men hauled the looms into the bower and nailed them to the walls.

Despite the darkness outside, within, the longfire crackled cheerfully and chatter filled the bower as the apprentices measured out the warp. Åsa joined in their chant as they warped the looms, and soon the room was ringing with sound.

A harsh call sounded over the women's voices. There was a flurry of dark wings in the gable end. Åsa looked up to see a falcon perched there. Her gaze met its golden eye, and she felt a familiar tug in her chest.

Stormrider.

A bony hand gripped her shoulder. She tore her gaze from the falcon to meet the völva's intense stare.

"Come, child, it is time for us to retire."

Åsa reached over to take Halfdan from Brenna.

"Brenna will sleep with him in the bower hall tonight," said Heid.

Åsa opened her mouth to protest, but the sorceress's determined gaze stopped her. She nodded to Brenna and followed Heid into their chamber.

Heid closed the door and gestured for Åsa to sit. The sorceress met her gaze with a penetrating look.

"You are shape strong."

Åsa stared at the völva. "I have never shown the signs before."

"No doubt you have, and passed them off as dreams. But during the birth, you left your body. I saw you."

Åsa shivered, remembering Heid's shrewd gaze on her as she hung in the rafters.

"Now that you have done it once, it pulls at your soul, and your tether to your body is light," said Heid. "You will leave your body again whether you will it or no, and at the most awkward times. We cannot wait any longer. You must learn to control it."

The völva leaned back and closed her eyes. She began to speak in a singsong voice. "The Allfather can lay as if asleep, sending his hugr into any form he wishes, a bird or animal, and it will do his will. Those of us with knowledge can also send out our spirit forth. This is what you have done without effort. Now you will learn hamfor, the spirit journey."

Åsa felt the beginnings of panic rise in her. The spirit journey was a dangerous art, reserved for the adept. She had never aspired to such a thing.

The sorceress continued. "The spirit journey must be practiced with care and precision. You must always be sure your body is in a safe place, with someone on hand to guard you. If any harm befalls you in your travels, the same will happen to your body. You must not be awakened while in spirit form, and you must be protected against spells that can cause your hamr to lose its way."

Åsa shuddered. "Is that what the haugbui did to you and Ulf?"

"Yes, it can happen to anyone, no matter how experienced," Heid said shortly. She uncorked a pot and poured a pungent brew into a cup, which she handed to Åsa. "Drink, but sparingly," she cautioned. "Too much, and it is a deadly poison, but with just the right amount, you can cross the veil between life and death."

Åsa stared into the cup, every nerve alight. "Why are you teaching this to me, and no one else?"

Heid gave her a hard look. "Because you can." The intensity in her voice made Åsa's stomach churn. "This cannot be learned, it is born into you, and it is my obligation to pass this art on to one who can use it. Few are capable of it. Most are so traumatized by the first sight of their own corpse, they never get over it. You overcame your fears. Your mother also had this ability. Sometimes it passes from mother to daughter. It seems this has happened to you. I trained your mother, and now I will train you."

"But I don't want this," Åsa faltered.

"You really have no choice. It will happen whether you will or no. But think of it, being able to leave this body and journey where you will. Take courage. Your hamr is strong. And I will watch over you."

Åsa felt the web of fate tighten around her. The urge to flee seized her, but equally strong was her desire to find out more. She wanted the power.

She took the cup and sipped.

The brew smelled of rot and decay. Panic gripped her as the liquid burned her throat. This was death.

Heid smiled and picked up a skin drum. "You're all right.

Close your eyes." She began to chant, beating a rhythm on the taut hide.

As Heid chanted, Åsa's feet began to tingle. The sensation strengthened, foaming up her legs and into her torso until her entire body vibrated. She felt light and free.

The room seemed to spin. She sensed a yawning pit with no bottom, and her stomach churned.

"Now open your eyes," Heid said.

Åsa looked down on a scene that made no sense. The room pitched as if she were on a ship in heavy seas. Struggling to bring her vision under control, she stared down on figures far below. She recognized Heid's wild tangle of hair. The other form slumped forward as if sleeping—or dead.

Her stomach heaved as she recognized herself. A powerful jolt flung her back into her body, and the room leveled out.

The völva laughed. "It's all right. It's a shock at first. But you've seen it before. Do it again. This time, try not to be so afraid."

Heid resumed drumming and took up the chant. In spite of her panic, Åsa wanted to explore this state. How was it that she could exist outside of her own body? She had to find out. Regaining control of her panic, she allowed Heid's chant to draw her back into the trance. She thought back to Halfdan's birth, when she had escaped her tortured body. The peace she had found. The freedom.

Opening her eyes, she found herself high up in the rafters once again. She clung to the drumbeat for stability.

"Now, look down," Heid said.

How could the sorceress know that she had left her body? Could she see Åsa's hugr?

"Look down at your body, seated there. It is only sleeping. See, the chest rises and falls with breath. You can return to it whenever you wish with only a thought. Stay up there now, looking down on yourself, until the fear has completely gone."

Åsa hung in the rafters and stared down at her still body, striving to master the terror.

Heid's voice drifted up to her. "This is not the first time you have experienced this, or even the second. Whether you know it or not, you have left your body many times in your dreams. Something in you remembers. It comes naturally. Now you will learn to do it according to your will."

Gradually, Åsa's fear subsided and a sense of well-being flooded into her.

"All right, come back now," the sorceress said.

This time, Åsa slid back into her body easily. She knew the way.

"Slowly, now, open your eyes," said Heid.

Åsa looked out of her own eyes once again, at a room that was as it should be.

"Breathe," said the sorceress. "Wiggle your fingers and toes."

Åsa sent her will into her limbs, settling into her body.

"That was a very good session," Heid said.

"I want to try again," said Åsa.

Heid smiled. "You must let a few nights pass before you attempt the soul journey again. Your spirit's tether is not over-strong. At this stage in your development, you could become permanently detached from your body. There have been tales of souls who wandered off and could not return. Their bodies lay in a trance for years while they wasted away. You saw it happen to me, and I am an experienced traveler."

Åsa shivered, remembering Heid and Ulf lying as if dead. She would do as her teacher commanded. For now.

"Drink this," said Heid, handing her a cup of a steaming brew. "It will restore you. Spirit travel can be very taxing. Now you must rest."

Åsa took the cup and sniffed. It smelled of clean herbs, not death. Sipping the hot drink, a little life flowed back into her limbs, but they were too heavy to move. Exhaustion swept over her.

She drifted into a peaceful sleep, and woke in the morning fresh and restored. For the first time in months, she had slept the entire night through.

Every third night, Åsa would leave Halfdan in the bower hall with Brenna and retire to her chamber with Heid. There, the sorceress would beat the drum, ushering her into the trance. Åsa began to feel comfortable outside of her body. Fear no longer rose when she looked down on her lifeless self. She began to look forward to the release. Her body may be imprisoned in Borre, but she was free.

After a week, Heid said, "You have gained strength very quickly. You may begin to practice every night. But do not think you are safe outside of your body. There are…things out there that do not wish you well. Remember that when you are free of the constraints of the body, your emotions hold sway. You must guard against a tendency to act rashly."

Åsa took her place on the bed. Questions swirled in her mind. What more could she do?

As if reading her thoughts, Heid spoke. "Each day, Odin sends out his two ravens, Hugin and Munin, Mind and Memory, to fly over the nine worlds and bring him tidings. It is said that those who have the skill can inhabit the form of their spirit animal. They can look through the animal's eyes, they can travel in its body."

"I don't have a spirit animal," said Åsa.

Heid replied. "You do. Your fylgja has been with you most of your life. You know it well. You have seen it many times, both waking and in your dreams. It follows you wherever you go. Call to it, and it will come."

Åsa tried to picture her spirit animal, but her mind was blank.

A bell tinkled. In a flurry of wings, Stormrider landed the rafters.

"You see," said Heid, "your fylgja comes when you call her."

Åsa stared up at the peregrine, who cocked her head and looked Åsa in the eye.

"You must take care when you occupy your spirit animal," the sorceress warned. "To animate the body takes a great force of will, and will deplete your strength faster than you can imagine. It is not an art to be taken lightly, or abused."

Heid picked up the drum and began to chant as she beat out a rhythm. Stormrider settled. "Now, hold the bird's gaze and project yourself into her."

Åsa focused on the falcon as the familiar trance came over her. She felt her hugr flow toward Stormrider. Just as she approached, the bird sidled on the rafter, and Åsa missed her entry, leaving her a shimmering mist in the air. She flowed back into her body and lay blinking as the peregrine flew out through the gable end.

"The bird can see your hugr very well. I think Stormrider likes to tease you," observed Heid. "But she will let you in eventually."

The next evening, Åsa waited tensely for Stormrider to appear.

"Call her with your mind," said Heid.

Åsa conjured the peregrine's image. With a rush of air and a tinkle of bells Stormrider landed in the rafters.

"Now, try to enter her body again," Heid instructed.

Åsa sent herself out to the falcon, to be rejected again.

"We'll try again tomorrow," said the sorceress.

And the next night, Stormrider repelled Åsa once again. But on the fourth night, Stormrider turned her predator's eye on Åsa's hugr, curiosity glinting in their golden depths.

Åsa slid into the raptor's body. The shock of success startled her right out of the bird, but this time, she gave a mental shove and propelled herself back into Stormrider's body. With triumph, she felt her talons grip the perch.

The world seemed to slow dramatically as intense color flooded her vision and details came in to sharp focus.

"Bird's eyes are not the same as ours," said Heid from below. "The world looks different to them."

Her range of vision had broadened. She saw Halfdan's empty cradle, almost behind her, as well as Heid on the other side of the room. Even from this distance, Åsa could make out the weave in the sorceress's shawl.

Åsa spent some time preening the falcon's feathers, allowing Stormrider to get used to her presence. She was keenly aware of Flosi the cat, who, tail twitching, watched her every move from Heid's bed.

At length the sorceress called her down. As Åsa slid out of the bird's body, exhaustion overwhelmed her.

"It takes some stamina to do this," said Heid. "Rest now."

Stormrider reappeared in the rafters the next night, and Åsa repeated the entry, inhabiting the body, grooming, getting used to the raptor's expanded vision and the speed of her reactions.

After three nights of this, Heid called up to her. "Try your wings."

Åsa worked the bird's powerful shoulder muscles and gave a tentative flap that sent her bolting up into the air. It was no more than a hop, and she stumbled back onto the safety of the beam, gripping with her talons, heart beating hard in her breast.

"Keep practicing," the sorceress instructed.

Åsa hopped again, and this time kept her shoulders working. She fluttered nervously in the rafters while an inner excitement bubbled. After two laps around the bower, she came to rest in the safety of the oak beam.

When Heid called her back, she was both disappointed and relieved, thrilled and afraid at the same time.

During the next session, she launched more confidently, and made several laps around the room. It seemed to come naturally, as if her mind had somehow merged with Stormrider's.

She flew around the bower every evening, until one night she found the courage to loft out through the gable end. She perched on the roof peak, gazing at the stars. Then she launched out into the evening sky.

The night air energized her as she flapped her way around the bower roof. The air currents lifted her, and she learned to angle her wings for loft and speed. Her spirits soared as she flew. For the first time since the fall of Tromøy, she was free to come and go at will.

She circled the roof three times, scanning the landscape with the raptor's vision. From high in the air, she spotted the glowing trails of shrews and mice, making her stomach growl appreciatively. She marveled at the strength of the falcon's broad wings. As the updraft lured her higher, her eye caught a movement and a fierceness possessed her. Without a thought, she folded her wings into her body, dipped her head, and dove. The rushing air blinded her as she hurtled toward the earth and a translucent lid slipped over her eyes. Through the protective veil, she tracked her prey, knowing the moment to lash out with her talon and seize the sparrow. She flung out her wings and spread her tail feathers, breaking her furious dive and flipping upright. The quarry was light enough to carry to the rooftop, where the peregrine fed with fierce joy under the stars.

From then on, Åsa entered Stormrider every night and flew out, ranging farther and farther over the sea, lured by the call of home.

One night, she flew south, to Tromøy.

CHAPTER 28

Asa followed the coastline, Stormrider's body knowing without thought how to seek the wind currents and ride them, resting, before working the powerful shoulder muscles again to flap the broad wings.

To the east, the broad waters of the Vik glimmered under the crescent moon. The endless dark forest stretched to the western horizon. Woodsmoke curled up to reach her, and she spied a clearing far below. Moonlight glinted on the sod roofs of houses clustering the beach, and tiny dots of light streamed from their smoke holes. With a thrill, she realized this must be the fabled seaport of Skiringssal. Wharves reached dark fingers into the shimmering sea. In winter, there were no ships tied alongside. They were all safely in the boathouse that hulked on the beach.

Inland, a column of smoke rose through the snow-clad trees. There lay the Shining Hall, its gilded dragons' heads guarding the four directions. Beyond lay boundless wilderness.

She glided out over forest and sea. When she grew tired, the falcon part of her chose a tall pine and flew down to roost. The talons of one foot latched on to the branch, and she tucked the other leg up under her feathers, and took a bird's dozing rest.

The weak dawn woke her, and she took to the skies again, flying across a never-ending wilderness of inlets and islet.

An island appeared, larger than any other, glistening white on the shimmering sea, and she knew from the shape of the harbor it was Tromøy. She began to recognize trees and rocks, and her heart beat harder. She soared on instinct to her father's hall.

There it stood, high above the harbor, roofed with snow. Joy sparked briefly, but she knew this was not right. Her father's hall had burned. This was Hrolf's new hall, raised over the ashes of her home.

A heaviness came over her as she glided down to the roof and lit on the open gable end, talons gripping the timber. Silently folding her wings, she peered into the gloom.

Hrolf was robed in a bearskin, silver glinting at his chest and on his bare arms. He sat enthroned on the high seat, in the place that had been her father's. But this was not her father's seat. The new posts had been set in their proper places, but the carvings were not the same as those from her father's day. Now one-eyed Odin hung from the world tree, the wolf Fenrir strained at his fetters. Loki leered from the shadows.

A huge gyrfalcon perched on the back of the high seat, scanning the room with a predatory gaze. A jolt of alarm shot through Åsa and she shrank into the shadows.

As she watched, warriors dragged in a ragged man and woman, trailed by three young children. The húskarlar threw the mother and father to the floor before the high seat. With a shock, she recognized a family of farmers she had known all of her life.

"What is their crime?" Hrolf demanded.

"Stealing food," replied the warrior. "We caught them in the storehouse."

"Lord, we are starving," cried the farmer.

"Silence!" roared Hrolf. "You stole from me."

The man cringed away from Hrolf, but still he spoke up. "You have locked up the stores. We are all starving. We won't survive the winter this way."

"I have a solution to that," said Hrolf with a grin. "We will sacrifice you and your family to the gods. That solves your hunger problem, and the gods will give prosperity to the rest of us."

The man and woman clutched at their children as the warriors tore them from their grasp.

Åsa claws tightened their grip on her perch as her heart swelled with fury. With a cry, she launched herself at Hrolf.

Everyone in the hall stopped what they were doing and stared up at her as she hurtled down from the ceiling, wings folded, talons outstretched. The father recovered his wits before the guards. He broke free of the warriors, grabbed his wife and children, and ran from the hall.

Hrolf's head went up, and his eyes blazed like coals. Diving full speed with talons outstretched, she aimed at those eyes.

He screamed in rage. His eyes rolled back in his head until the whites were showing. There was a blast of air and Åsa felt Hrolf's essence rush into the gyrfalcon perched on the back of his chair.

The huge falcon took to the air, heading for her.

Fear lanced through her. She spread her wings to break her dive and flipped in the air. Reversing direction in an instant, she shot out of the smoke hole. A rush of wind from huge wings beat the air behind her.

She dropped just before the talons gripped her. The bird of prey cried out in rage and swooped down on her. Pumping her shoulder muscles, she flung herself back up into the air.

She was smaller, quicker, than the gyrfalcon, so her evasive actions were effective. But the diversions were taking their toll. Her shoulders ached with every stroke. She was not fully recovered from her long flight.

The big bird came in for another attack. Åsa hung in the air, waiting, and managed to dodge once more. She put on a desperate surge of speed, but she could feel the beat of the gyrfal-con's wings close behind her.

A cry split the air. An owl swooped in on broad wings, talons extended. Looking back, Åsa saw the gyrfalcon wheel in midair to face the challenger. The owl hit the falcon at full speed and sent it tumbling, feathers flying. The falcon flapped its wings, stopping its fall, and took after the owl.

The gyrfalcon was the bigger bird and the faster flyer. It was gaining on the owl. Åsa wheeled around and shot back to join the fray.

The gyrfalcon fell on the owl, talons outstretched. Grabbing hold of its victim with one foot, the big falcon gouged at the owl's eyes.

Åsa struck hard, knocking the falcon off its prey. The owl slashed at the gyrfalcon's throat, but the big bird dodged, leaving the owl with a talon full of feathers. Åsa joined the owl in pursuit of the attacker.

With a frustrated cry, the gyrfalcon wheeled in the air and headed back to the hall. The owl veered off in another direction. Åsa kept going north, not daring to slow or look back. Only when dark finally fell did she come to roost in a tree.

At first light, she lofted into the air and beat her way back against a stiff headwind. The journey was hard work. She no longer played in the updrafts, and she looked at the earth below only for location.

At last she sighted the mounds of Borre, the column of smoke rising from the great hall. She labored through the heavy air to the bower roof. Landing heavily in the rafters of the bower, she looked down on the völva, seated by the fire, motionless in a trance. On the bed, she recognized her own body lying motion-less and pale beneath the comforter.

The völva's eyes snapped open, and she caught Åsa in her beady glare.

"So, you survived," she said.

Åsa flew down to the bed. She let herself flow back into her human form, peering through bleary, blinking eyes. She longed to hold Halfdan in her arms, but he was with Brenna in the other room.

Heid glared at her from across the room. She said harshly, "Don't ever be such a fool again."

"I went to Tromøy..." Åsa said weakly.

"That was not hard to guess, you foolish child," Heid retorted. "You put yourself in mortal danger."

"Hrolf took the form of a gyrfalcon and we fought. He nearly killed me. An owl saved me."

"Did it indeed?" said the völva. "That was more than you deserved."

Åsa tried to sit up, but pain seared through her head, forcing her back down. "Hrolf has rebuilt the hall. He sits in my father's place. He is sacrificing my people. I have to stop him."

The sorceress rose more slowly than usual and hobbled over. She gripped Åsa's shoulders with bony fingers and forced her back down to the pillow. With a start, Åsa saw that the völva's eyes were swollen, the skin around them livid with scratches.

Only Heid's voice held its customary power. "They are his people," she admonished. "He is the rightful jarl and can do as he wishes. There is nothing you can do against him in your spirit form. He is a powerful shapeshifter, more powerful than you, and now he is forewarned. All you will achieve by returning is to let him kill you. The only thing you can do is remain alive. Bide your time. Practice, grow stronger in your art. Raise your son to be a mighty king. Have patience."

Åsa stared at her bleakly. Patience was the one thing she did not possess.

CHAPTER 29

The Northern Steppe
December

Olaf opened his eyes to darkness. Where was he? He had been with Åsa...but she was gone. His hand fell on a furry body, a cold body that did not rise and fall with breath.

Memory flooded in. He was trapped in a snowbank, and the air was stale and close. The dog was dead, and soon he would be too. Whether the storm still raged outside or not, he had to get out.

He staggered to his feet and plunged his fists into the snow, shouting. Once he'd broken the hard inner crust, he hit powder.

He heard muffled shouting. With his last strength, he dug into the shifting snow, but it poured in around him. He was buried deep, maybe too deep. Still, he kept burrowing into the powder, holding his breath like a man swimming in heavy seas.

Rough hands jerked him out of the snow. Brilliant light assaulted his eyes, making him blink.

"There you are, boy!" Olaf's hands burned as Björn chafed the blood back into them. Olaf gulped in a lungful of air and squinted at a landscape transformed by new hills and valleys of snow. "We couldn't find you," said Björn. "We thought you and the dogs were dead for sure. But then we saw the depression where you'd made the air hole. The snow started caving in where you were digging. It's lucky we found you as fast as we did."

Three of the dogs had died in the snow cave, though, to Olaf's relief, Eik survived. The crew dug the sledges out, but they camped for a day to allow the surviving dogs to recover from their ordeal. When they finally got underway in the morning, men harnessed themselves up beside the weakened dogs to drag the sleds through the powder, taking turns breaking trail on skis. Olaf was still very weak, but there was no room for him to ride on the fully loaded sledges. He skied behind on the packed snow, keeping up as best he could.

"Only a few days to Bolghar," Dag said cheerfully.

Though the following days were clear, even when nothing fell from the sky, the smallest breeze stirred up a blizzard of hard snow granules, stinging eyes and shrouding the world in a haze. Olaf was grateful for the wind, however, for it scoured away the newly fallen snow to reveal the riverbeds that were the only trail in a blank white land.

The great Itil River meandered eastward across a vast, snow-covered steppe until it turned due south and was joined by another great river, the Kama, from the northeast. At the confluence of the two rivers, a wooden palisade rose up from the steppe. Here, at last, was the great fur market of the Bolghar.

The massive gates stood open. Before them spread a city to rival Birka. As they drove their sledges along the frozen street, Olaf caught snatches of familiar speech. A bearded man in tunic and trews waved them over. Dag stopped the sledges as the man stepped forward to greet them.

"Welcome! I am Ilke." Ilke gestured at the cluster of twenty or so tents and a horde of Norsemen. "This is the Svea camp. There's plenty of room for your tents."

They made camp among their newfound countrymen and spent the first night passing the ale horn.

"I see you have a good cargo of fur," said Ilke. "You arrived just in time. A caravan of Serklanders arrived two days ago. They've already started bargaining with us for our furs. If you join us, we can get a better price for our pelts."

In the morning, the market bloomed as stalls opened and merchants began their calls. The place made Olaf dizzy with its sheer size and noise. The scents of roasting meat and fresh manure mingled in the air. Caravans of Serklanders and Khazars rode in on tall, ill-tempered beasts that Olaf thought must be cousins of the moose. Arrogant Magyars swept by on their splendid horses. Children chased each other through the crowds, dogs yipping at their heels. The great market resounded with the cries of traders in a dozen different languages and the protests of their livestock. Color was everywhere, with silks more vivid than those Olaf had seen in Birka or Haithabu.

Merchants clothed in billowing robes and headdresses eagerly traded for the products of the north: slaves, honey and wax, amber beads, walrus tusks, and most importantly, furs. In addition to the sought-after silver dirhams, they offered bolts of silk dyed in vivid colors and piles of exotic spices. At one stall, a dark-eyed trader wrapped in furs presided over half a dozen iron ingots. They looked like dull-gray eggs. Olaf stopped short before them, staring.

The trader spewed out an unintelligible stream of words, waving his hands over the ingots, obviously expounding their virtues. Olaf caught one familiar word: "Wootz."

His hands began to sweat. Turning to Ilke, he asked, "Is this man a Serklander?"

"That he is."

"And are these ingots wootz?"

The Serklander nodded vigorously and repeated, "Wootz!"

Olaf could hardly breathe. If he brought wootz steel to Ulf, the smith could forge the weapons Gudrød demanded of him. Olaf would have his father's gratitude.

And Åsa's gratitude as well, for Ulf's safety would be assured.

He tried to keep his face bland. "I want to trade for these ingots," he said to Ilke. "Will you help me?"

Ilke frowned. "You don't want their steel. It's too brittle. It fractures in the cold."

Unless you know how to forge it. "Even so," he said. "I would like to bring some home."

The Serklander's harangue brought Olaf back to the present. The ingots were not yet his. He turned to his sledge and pulled back the tarp, revealing his load of furs.

The traders eyes widened for an instant, then quickly narrowed again. He gestured toward the entire load. Ilke shook his head, holding up five fingers. This brought on a torrent of words from the trader, and Ilke reluctantly raised a finger on his other hand. The Serklander pleaded vociferously, but Ilke folded his arms and gave him the stone face.

The Serkland trader choked off the flow of words and gave a curt nod.

"Looks like you've got a deal, boy," said Ilke.

The Serklander came out and fussed over Olaf's furs, at length choosing six of the finest sables. Olaf triumphantly loaded the ingots onto his sledge while Ilke shook his head, and they headed off to camp.

Two weeks passed as they traded by day and feasted at night. They celebrated Jól with the Svea traders. After another week of trading, their stocks of furs and ivory were gone, replaced with silver, spices, and bolts of silk.

And wootz steel.

CHAPTER 30

Borre
January

Night had fallen, and everyone was in bed but Åsa. The bower room was warm and snug. In her single bed across the room, Heid's bright frizz poked out from under her eiderdown comforter, Flosi beside her, purring in his sleep. High in the rafters, Stormrider roosted, beak tucked in her feathers. Brenna snored softly in the big bed she shared with Åsa. Halfdan slept in the cradle suspended from the beam next to the bed, a chubby fist flung over his head. Asleep, he looked so much like Gyrd. Åsa wished her brother had lived to meet her son. All the things Halfdan could have learned from his uncle—sword craft, hunting, seamanship. Åsa would teach him these things herself, but it was not the same. A boy needed a man to emulate. She dreaded the thought of fostering him out to another lord to raise him to manhood, although that was the right thing to do. Well, a few years remained before she needed to make that decision.

She tucked the blankets around the sleeping child and cast her eye on the basket by the door. They were getting low on food inside the bower. With a sigh, she picked up the empty basket and entered the bower hall. She padded past the sleeping apprentices, through the chill entryway, and into the frigid night. Clutching her shawl close, she trudged across the packed snow of the courtyard to the storehouse.

This was no one's favorite time of year. The deer herds had moved north in their search for food, and Borre's folk subsisted on dried cod that had to be soaked to make it edible. The livestock, on reduced rations too, had stopped giving milk, and it was time to break out the redolent gammelost, the rank cheese that kept for years.

With the key on her belt, Åsa unlocked the storehouse and scanned the dwindling stores. She made a mental tally of what remained of the barley, cod, and cheese, counting it out against the twenty warriors, Heid and her nine apprentices, Ulf and Brenna, and the thirty servants and slaves who lived in Borre. By Åsa's reckoning, careful rationing would see them through to spring.

She filled a bucket with dried cod, and loaded a basket with stinky cheese and a stack of flatbread from the pile they had baked last fall. The bread was so dry, it kept for years, but it was satisfying and it took a long time to eat. Halfdan was teething, and the flatbread was perfect for him to gnaw.

Åsa locked the storehouse and packed clean snow on top of the cod. She would set the bucket by the fire and let the fish soak overnight until it was soft enough to eat.

In the dark wood, a wolf howled. They were hungry too. With a shudder, she picked up the bucket and the basket and hurried back to the bower. Just as she reached the door, a noise stopped her cold.

The hiss of skis on snow. The crackle of fire and a breath of smoke.

Blood turning to ice, she peered back into the dark yard. The waning moon gleamed on pristine snow. Stealthy on skis, dark figures glided across the moonlit swathes, torches glimmering. Åsa caught her breath. Silhouetted against the light were pointed ears. A wolf's muzzle. The round ears and snout of a bear.

She rushed into the bower, silencing the waking apprentices. She ripped open her chamber door and yanked her sword and shield down from the wall. Making her way back through the hall, she crept to the entry door and peered into the night.

"Berserker and ulfhednar," Heid hissed in her ear, making her jump. "Hrafn's outlaws. They're after our food."

Blades glinting in the torchlight, the creatures swarmed the great hall where the húskarlar slept.

"They're going to burn it."

Flames already bloomed at the building's base. The outlaws surrounded both doors, ready to hack down anyone who tried to escape the fire.

Åsa did not want to speculate about what would happen when the outlaws turned their attention to the bower. She motioned the women who had crowded the entrance to withdraw, then yanked the door shut.

"They'll burn the hall, kill the warriors, and do worse to us," said Astrid.

"Bring the children to my chamber," said Åsa, holding the door while the women carried their sleeping children inside. She went to the cradle where Halfdan slept. She longed to scoop him up, but it was better that he slept.

"Try to keep them quiet," she said to Brenna, who nodded silently. Old Sigrid and two other serving women took their places beside her.

Back in the bower hall, Åsa turned to Heid and her apprentices. "They are concentrating on the húskarlar. They do not expect women to attack."

"We are sorceresses, not shield-maidens," said Astrid.

"That could be to our advantage," said Åsa. "These are no ordinary warriors. They are berserker and ulfhednar. We need more than steel to fight them." The apprentices' eyes grew wide. "It's our only chance. You either fight, or die."

The sorceress glowered at her apprentices. "I have trained you well. If you can't fight off a few berserkers, then I'll no longer call you mine."

Åsa watched their faces as Heid's power overcame their fear. With a wicked smile, she said, "Raise the seidr."

Heid mounted the seidr platform. She took her chair while the women gathered around. Throwing back her head, the völva began to chant the galdr to instill terror in an enemy.

The women joined their voices to hers, raising the unearthly sound that reverberated in the bower's high ceiling. Åsa's hair rose about her head as their voices charged the air. Every bit of metal in the room rang out. The raven banner in the corner lifted as if on a breeze.

Åsa raised her sword. It quivered with a magnetic power. "Attack!"

Nine iron staves rose in the air. Åsa kicked the door open, raising a battle cry amplified by all the women's voices. Eyes blazing, they stormed into the night.

The berserkers whirled on them in confusion.

Åsa charged the nearest wolf-clad warrior. He wore no armor, for a berserk believed his powers would protect him in battle. She swept Lightning at his legs, connecting with a solid slash, but he came on, wild-eyed, axe raised. Åsa sidestepped his downward blow and struck at his legs again. The berserker stumbled, then recovered and swung his axe.

Åsa dodged once more and let her opponent's momentum carry him past her, then pivoted and hacked into his back. As he recovered and rounded on her, she jerked her sword up, bashing the blade into his head with all her strength. Finally, he went down. She sagged against the wall, sucking in deep breaths.

The melee surged around her. Women shrieked, berserkers howled like beasts. The air crackled, smelling of hot metal. Sparks flew as Heid's apprentices battered the attackers with their iron staves, driving them away from the hall.

The berserkers rallied in the chaos and turned on the women. Now the air filled with women's shrieks as the dark forms surged over the apprentices. Åsa's guts clenched. *What have I done? These women are not trained warriors. I've led them to their deaths.*

Light flared from the hall door. Borre's warriors burst out with spears and axes and swarmed the outlaws' rear guard.

Whatever supernatural powers the berserkers had wielded vanished. Blades bit into their flesh, and they howled. The snow ran dark with their blood as the húskarlar cut them down from behind while the women crushed their front ranks.

When it was over, six outlaws sprawled on the bloody snow and a knot of survivors stood at bay. Among them lurked Arne, the blacksmith.

"Throw down your weapons!" Åsa shouted. Steel rained down upon the snow.

Still shaking with battle rage, she turned on Hrafn. The wily outlaw chief grinned at her.

"You owe me two debts, young queen," he said. "Now I will collect one."

Heid glowered. "He deserves nothing!"

"I saved your hide, witch!" Hrafn retorted. "You and the black-smith. If I hadn't intervened, you would still be trapped in the other world, living corpses, both of you."

"I would have freed us without your help," Heid said.

"Not before your bodies perished," he countered.

"Enough," said Åsa. "To pay my debt, I will spare your miserable life, old man."

"And my men."

"All but him." Åsa pointed to Arne. "You turn the smith over to me."

Hrafn regarded the outlaw smith. "Very well. I never invited him to join us anyway. But you owe me as second debt. We need food."

"That goes beyond my debt to you."

"What is the point of sparing our lives if you let us starve?"

"I can't make that decision for those who would have to do without." Åsa looked around at Borre's people.

"If you give us food, we will bother you no more," said Hrafn.

"We fended you off once, we can do it again," Åsa shot back, with more bravado than she felt.

Hrafn fixed her with a penetrating stare. "And I will be in your debt. And that of your son." He gave her a cryptic smile. "You will both have need of that favor one day. If I starve, I will not be able to help you."

Heid sucked in her breath. "Take the offer," she hissed.

Åsa searched the faces of her people. They all knew it meant hunger for the rest of the winter. Yet they all nodded. The alternative was to live out the rest of the winter under threat of attack by desperate men.

"Very well," she said, taking up the storeroom keys. "We have little to spare, but I can give you enough to keep you alive until spring."

The folk of Borre watched the outlaws carry off meagre bundles of dried cod and flatbread. Then they turned on Arne.

"You led them here," Åsa spat.

His eyes glowered from beneath his brows.

They dragged Arne to the world tree, and strung him up, a sacrifice to the dísir to help them survive a hungry winter.

CHAPTER 31

Bolghar
March

The days lengthened, and one night as they sat by the fire, Ilke said, "We plan to depart soon, so that we can reach Aldeigja before the rivers thaw."

"You are right," said Skeggi. "We can all travel together."

"It will be good to get home," said Björn. "We've been away long enough."

Home.

Olaf realized there was no stab of homesickness when he thought of his father, or Borre. Only relief to be away from the constant expectations, the criticisms, the rivalry with Hrolf. *Here, I am not Gudrød's son, the one who never lives up to his expectations. I am accepted for who I am, for what I have accomplished.*

But the image of Åsa popped into his mind. His throat constricted at the thought of seeing her again.

In the morning they began to take on food and ale for the trip.

On a day when the low sun shone briefly but brilliant, promising a stretch of good weather, they loaded up their sledges and departed.

The good weather followed them north, and the sledges skimmed along the river's frozen surface. Traveling with thirty sleds, with more than two hundred men and dogs, at night their camp was like a small village.

They crossed the steppes quickly, staying ahead of the storms, and entered the forest. It was darker among the trees, and the short days were even shorter. They made camp early and departed late, loathe to leave their fires.

At last, they found Lake Onega and crossed its white expanse in a day. They found the Svir River and finally heard the ring of hammers and scented the smoke of Aldeigja.

Björn set the crew to preparing the ships for the voyage home, re-caulking seams, replacing rusted rivets, mending walrus-skin ropes. Olaf threw himself into the familiar work, putting all other thoughts aside.

The river rumbled like thunder as the ice began to break up. As their departure neared, Olaf approached Björn. "If you take me to Skiringssal, my father will make it worth your while."

Björn smiled. "Wild story or not, we can stop in Skiringssal. The trading is good there."

Soon, the spring storms subsided, and the longships departed, their holds full of silver, spices, fur, and silk. Olaf stowed his ingots as ballast below the floorboards and slept on the deck above them, though the Svea laughed at him.

"You guard those useless ingots as if they were silver," said Björn.

Olaf shrugged. "To me, they are."

OLAF STOOD IN THE BOW, watching as the familiar islands of Skiringssal hove into view. Part of him couldn't wait to arrive, while the rest of him wanted to sail on by. What kind of welcome awaited him?

They arrived as the sun was setting. Though Olaf could have guided them in, Björn preferred to enter the unfamiliar harbor by daylight, so they anchored behind an outlying island for the night. Olaf was glad of the delay. He stared up at the familiar stars, not even trying to sleep. Was Gudrød in Skiringssal? How would he react to Olaf's return? And Åsa. Would she forgive him at last?

In the morning, he bathed in an icy stream, combed his hair, and trimmed his beard. He unpacked the fine clothes he'd acquired in Birka, dressing with care in the baggy trousers tucked into fine leather boots, fastening the red wool cloak with his silver brooch. Olaf intended to look the part of a sea king when he arrived in Skiringssal.

Björn's knarr skimmed into the bay on the morning breeze, the crew neatly dropping sail. Their timing was perfect. The ship kept just enough way on to slide gracefully alongside the wharf.

The warrior who caught the spring line gaped at Olaf's finery. Then his gaze traveled to Olaf's face, and his expression changed to shock. He stared as if he were seeing a draugr. "Lord Olaf?"

Heads whipped around at the name.

"Yes, alive and well, as you can see. I am no ghost," said Olaf, stepping onto the wharf with what he hoped was a regal manner. He forced a smile. "Is my father here?"

"He is, lord."

"Well, fetch him, man." Olaf stood tall as a lad set off running up the trail to the hall.

They had finished making fast and were unloading their trade goods when Björn looked up and stared. Olaf followed his gaze to see his father ride down the trail, mounted on a splendid horse, at the head of his húskarlar. He looked for Åsa, and bit back disappointment when she didn't appear.

Olaf met Gudrød's eyes and was surprised to feel…nothing. Not even fear.

Father and son stared at each other for a long moment. Olaf felt his father take in his exotic clothing, the silver clasp on his fine cloak, his soft leather boots.

"It's really you. Son, I am glad to see you alive." Though Gudrød did not get down from his horse, the emotion in his voice caught Olaf off guard.

Björn stared at the two of them. "So your wild story was true, after all," he murmured.

Olaf pulled Björn forward. "Father, this is Björn, a trader from Birka. I owe him a great debt. He saved my life and took me on as a member of his crew when I had nothing."

Gudrød inclined his head. "I thank you for bringing my son back to me. I will treat you well."

"Father, there is more." Olaf climbed aboard the knar and lifted a floorboard to reveal the gray cakes of steel. "I have brought you something you desire above all else. Wootz steel."

Gudrød stared at the six ingots, each one the perfect size to make a sword. When he looked at Olaf, his eyes gleamed.

"Well done, son."

Olaf forced a smile. Those words no longer lifted his heart as they once had.

Gudrød clapped him on the shoulder. "You must be hungry. Come to the hall, bring your shipmates. I will feast you."

As they entered the hall, Olaf expected Åsa to greet them. His gaze searched the room, but she was not there. He stifled the urge to ask about her, though worry gnawed at him. Where was she? Was she safe?

A serving girl came in with a horn of mead and Olaf's stomach lurched. Why was Åsa not bringing in the welcome horn?

"I am sorry to have you so poorly served, son," said Gudrød. "The queen is in Borre."

Olaf was glad the room was dimly lit, for the relief that washed through him made his hand tremble as he took the horn.

Over mead and food, Olaf told his tale. He said nothing about having been Björn's slave. He hoped no one would ever know that. To his relief, Björn kept silent about it. Perhaps the trader realized his rewards would be better if he didn't mention that incident.

When Olaf described his kidnapping, Gudrød looked grim. "Hrolf swore he saw you fall on the battlefield."

"He is a liar, Father. A liar, a kidnapper, a betrayer of his own kin. Those men had orders to murder me. I only survived through luck."

Gudrød winced. "Hrolf is Lord of Tromøy, with his own hird of warriors."

"We must get him out!"

"He has grown strong there."

Olaf stared at his father, his high spirits evaporating.

A shadow had fallen on the evening, and despite the abundant ale and food, the men retired early.

Gudrød went to his chamber while Olaf slept in the great hall with the warriors. It felt strange to be back among the men whose respect he had once so desperately longed for. Now they fawned on him, ensuring he had the bench closest to the fire with the softest furs. Despite the strangeness, he slept well.

The next day, Gudrød took Olaf to the boathouse. He opened the big double doors, and Olaf's heart leaped when the daylight fell on *Sea Dragon*.

Gudrød looked at him with glistening eyes. "It was to be your funeral ship, but I couldn't bring myself to burn it. I just kept putting it off. I'm glad I waited." He shook himself as if trying to rid his body of a spell. "Sail with me to Borre. We'll take the ingots to the smith, and he can forge new weapons."

Olaf's heart quickened.

Åsa is there.

CHAPTER 32

Borre
May

With the spring weather, Sigurd's ship arrived to claim his bride. Åsa tried to keep a smile on her face as they packed Astrid's chest with fine linens and wool and the implements a noble wife would need. On top of all they placed her iron distaff, blessed by Heid.

The chest was loaded onto a cart, and the women of Borre gathered to escort Astrid down to the jetty. As they trouped down the trail, their voices swelled in song.

Astrid embraced Åsa with tears in her eyes. "I don't want to leave you."

Åsa's smile wavered. "I'll be fine." She patted Astrid on the back firmly. "You deserve to be happy. And it's not as if you're leaving middle-earth. We'll see each other."

Astrid turned and stepped onto her husband's ship. The apprentices crowded the jetty, waving and calling out blessings as

JOHANNA WITTENBERG

the crew brought in the mooring lines and hoisted the sail. Åsa held Halfdan tight to her chest as she watched her closest friend sail away.

"Well, that's that," said Heid. "I must recruit a new girl." Leaning on her staff, she hobbled up the trail. Her eight remaining apprentices filed in behind, leaving Åsa to stare after the ship as it dwindled out of sight.

When the sail had disappeared over the horizon, Åsa settled Halfdan on her hip and set out for the hall, her spirit riding like a stone in her stomach.

"Ship ho!" cried the sentry. Åsa whirled in an instant of wild hope that Astrid had somehow changed her mind.

"It's *Dragonlord*!"

Åsa's heart plummeted. Shifting Halfdan to the other hip, she walked back to the jetty to meet the ships. Two sails glimmered against the sky, *Dragonlord*'s red-and-white stripe, the other striped blue and white.

Her heart gave a lurch. *Sea Dragon*.

A familiar golden head shone above all others, and she caught her breath.

Olaf. Alive.

Towering over his men-at-arms, Olaf looked every inch a king in a red wool cloak trimmed with black fox. Åsa stared, clamping down hard on the joy and confusion that simmered within.

He was alive. He was here, back from his adventures safe and whole.

And taking his place in his father's good graces once more.

Her joy turned sour.

~

OLAF'S first sight of Åsa struck him like a blow. He picked her out

268

in the crowd instantly, straight and tall, her red-gold hair lifted by the breeze.

He steadied himself as he brought *Sea Dragon* alongside the jetty. Åsa turned her head suddenly and trapped him with her eyes. He saw the accusation in them.

She looked down, and his gaze followed hers to the babe she carried. He caught his breath.

Of course. She was a mother now, a queen. His father's wife, out of his reach forever. He must accept that, as he had so many other things. The longing that roared in his veins had no place.

He didn't hear her stiff welcome, but followed her in a daze to the hall. He took the guest seat she led him to and accepted the ale horn from her, not daring to meet her eyes. He drank, then sat staring like a fool while the kitchen folk scurried to put together an impromptu feast.

Olaf watched her take the high seat beside Gudrød, regret gnawing at his stomach. If he had not bungled his father's proposal in the first place, she would have accepted and her family would still be alive. If he had explained things better to Gudrød, he would not have attacked Tromøy, slaughtered her family, taken her by force. If he had helped Åsa escape, instead of bringing her back like a calf to the butcher…

And now, because of him, Hrolf ruled her kingdom.

He wished there was some way for him to make amends. He longed to see her smile again.

Perhaps there was.

Before he could change his mind, he rose and hoisted his drinking horn. "My brother Hrolf hired thugs to murder me," he announced. "His actions put him outside the law. Yet he rules in Tromøy, where he abuses the people and the land. I cannot allow this to stand. If I fail to take action, I will be a coward."

Gudrød scowled at the implied insult. Olaf ignored his roiling stomach and turned to Åsa.

"Lady, I make you a vow," he declared. "I will drive Hrolf from Tromøy by summer's end, or die trying."

The húskarlar met his words with cheers.

Åsa stared at him, her expression full of hope, and Olaf felt the guilt slide off his shoulders.

He would save her kingdom.

~

GUDRØD WAS NOT PLEASED by Olaf's pledge. He made it clear next morning.

"Well, you made a foolish vow in front of everyone. Now I must make good on it," he growled. "You'd best get back to Skiringssal and muster the fleet. I will meet you there."

Olaf was in high spirits in spite of his father's displeasure. He hurried down to *Sea Dragon* to make ready for departure.

He was deep in the bilges when her voice reached him.

"Leaving so soon, Lord Olaf?"

Olaf hoisted himself up on the floorboards and met her blue gaze. His heart thundered. "I sail to Skiringssal to muster the fleet. Then we go south to drive Hrolf out of Tromøy."

Åsa set Halfdan on his feet and fussed with the boy's hood. "I came to thank you for your vow to liberate my people. And for bringing the wootz steel for Ulf."

He cleared his throat, groping for words. "I am glad to win your thanks, lady."

"May Thor keep you safe, and All-father Odin grant you luck," she said, a smile blooming on her face. Halfdan began to grizzle, and she bent to pick him up. She cast another fleeting smile before she fled up the hill, leaving Olaf staring after her.

~

ÅSA STRODE UP THE TRAIL, ready to burst. She needed to fight.

Brenna was puttering in the bower, and Åsa handed Halfdan off to her, then hurried to the practice yard. Shouts rose from the húskarlar, who were hard at their training games. She snatched up a practice sword and stormed onto the field to confront Olvir.

He grinned and launched his attack.

She fought like the storm that raged inside her, driving him back while the warriors cheered. Olvir defended himself with vigor and probed for an opening in her wild attack. So intent were they that neither noticed when the onlookers fell silent.

"What's going on here?" a familiar voice rang out. Olvir froze in midstroke.

Gudrød stormed up and ripped Olvir's sword from his hand.

"How dare you raise arms against your queen?" he roared.

Åsa bristled. "He is acting on my orders."

Gudrød whirled on her.

"How dare you give orders to my men?"

She glowered back at him. "As queen of Borre, it is my right and duty to give orders in your absence."

"Well, I'm not absent!" he shouted. "Get to your bower."

Åsa held her ground, the blood rising in her face. She didn't trust her voice.

Olvir seemed transfixed by the tension that shimmered in the air.

"I said, get to your bower," Gudrød roared again. His red face was so close that his spittle hit her cheeks.

She fixed him with her stare and did not move.

He reached out to grab her, but she was ready for that and jerked out of reach.

Gudrød raised the sword and advanced on her. Åsa watched him come, rage searing through her veins. Her own sword felt alive in her hand.

"Are you both mad?"

The völva hobbled onto the field with surprising speed.

Planting herself between the two of them, she struck the earth with her staff, glaring up at Gudrød.

He glowered back but halted his advance.

"Get her out of here," he snarled.

"That's what I intend to do," said Heid evenly. Without turning her back on Gudrød, she backed up until she stood beside Åsa. "Come, Halfdan is fussing."

The mention of her child's name penetrated Åsa's fury. She drew a breath and lowered her sword. Clamping her arm with steely claws, Heid drew Åsa with her as she backed away from Gudrød.

"You'd better keep out of his sight," the sorceress whispered. "Stay in the bower for a few days."

Åsa knew Heid was right, but her spirit raged. Why should she be confined while Gudrød roamed free? He was the one who should be locked away.

She turned and stormed to the bower.

SEA DRAGON WAS ready to sail. Olaf stood at the steering oar, looking up the trail as the crew cast off and took their seats on their sea chests, running out their oars.

She hadn't come to see him off. He was disappointed and a little surprised. Åsa had expressed heartfelt gratitude, and he thought she would say goodbye, but the trail remained empty. He didn't expect to see his father, who was still in a huff at what he considered Olaf's rash vow.

Olaf really had no choice in the matter, and Gudrød knew it as well as he did. If Olaf failed to go after Hrolf, he would be forever branded a coward. And Gudrød really had no choice but to help him. The law was clear: Olaf must take vengeance for what Hrolf had done to him. But he was doing it for Åsa as well as himself.

He shook off his disappointment. She owed him nothing. He was doing what he must do. He turned his back on Borre and set a course for Skiringssal.

BRAM LUGGED in the cakes of wootz steel, each one the perfect size to make a sword. Ulf watched the growing stack. He'd never thought to see their like again.

"Wootz requires special handling," Ulf lectured Bram. The boy's eyes gleamed with interest, and Ulf warmed to his instruction. "My master taught me many years ago when I was a slave in the East." The master who had left no slave alive to tell the tale. Except Ulf. "The forge must stay at a lower temperature than for bog iron."

With tongs, Ulf gripped an ingot and hefted it from the stack. Controlling his excitement, he thrust the cake into the fire. Bram trod the foot bellows, watching Ulf carefully for nods and shakes of the head to tell him when to increase his efforts and when to slack off to keep the furnace at just the right temperature. Another boy ran back and forth, feeding charcoal into the fire. Ulf kept a close watch as the metal glowed dully, the red brightening to orange and finally a yellow white.

The moment a few sparks flew from the ingot, Ulf pulled it from the furnace and laid it on the anvil. Holding his breath, he gingerly hammered the precious metal, just a few light blows, before returning it to the furnace. He watched the steel change color, then pulled it out and again forged it lightly just until it cooled. "Steel must be coaxed into shape, never forced."

In the warmth of the smithy, Ulf was overcome with a vision of himself back in Serkland, working under his master's cruel gaze and the imminent threat of death.

Not so different from his present situation.

The wootz steel made countless trips from furnace to anvil as

Ulf drew the ingot out into a bar, which he folded back on itself and twisted to create the pattern. Day after day, he worked until he couldn't lift his hammer, transforming the bar into a blade, tapering to the edges and the point. On the day he forged the fuller channel down the blade's length, it had become a sword in truth.

Ulf heated the blade for the last time to return the metal's flexibility. He hovered over the blade while it cooled in the air, his ears attuned to any sound of cracking. When he could pick it up with his bare hands, he examined it minutely for any flaws.

There were none that his exacting eye could find. It was beautiful. It was perfect.

Satisfied, Ulf began the painstaking process of polishing the metal. When it was finished, he rubbed the blade with vinegar, watching the steel surface anxiously as the wave pattern emerged.

He spent an entire day grinding the edge sharp enough to slice Serkland silk in midair. Then he carved the blade with secret runes that he inlaid with silver wire so they would flash in the light.

At last, he riveted the cross guard and hilt in place. Holding the finished weapon up in the firelight, he uttered galdr spells to give the blade its nature. No longer would his life hang on the whim of his master.

Finally he named the sword.

"Gudrød's Bane," he cried.

The steel rang out in response.

~

ÅSA FOLLOWED THE COASTLINE, flying without effort. In the past, she had been helpless to intervene in Tromøy's fate, but now she went to scout for Olaf's war.

Halfway to Tromøy, she sighted a column of smoke rising

above the trees. Skiringssal. The moonlit roofs came into view. Before, they had been no more than a distance marker, but now Olaf was there. A longing possessed her to land there, just to look at him.

She must focus on her mission to discover Tromøy's status: How many ships did Hrolf have? How many men? Were his defenses ready for an attack?

She flew over Skiringssal's harbor, where Vestfold's fleet had gathered, and counted fifty ships at anchor.

The settlement receded into the distance, the land swallowed by the forest once again. The steady beat of her wings carried her on. The sun rose and she flew through the morning. By midafternoon, her island came into view.

She circled Tromøy's hall, striving to maintain the consciousness of a bird, to relegate her human mind to the shadows, to observe but not be noticed. Just another bird.

Her wings ruffled the air as she glided silently down to the roof, where she lit on the gable end and peered inside.

Hrolf sat enthroned on the high seat, the gyrfalcon perched on the chair back. Åsa stilled, shrinking into the shadows. The big raptor did not look her way. The bird appeared unsettled, distracted, perhaps by the two well-dressed men who occupied the guest seats across the longfire. They listened attentively as Hrolf spoke.

"My spies tell me that my brother is alive and well, and our father has made him lord of Skiringssal." Hrolf's face was expressionless, but his eyes blazed with fury.

One of the guests spoke. "That is to our advantage, Lord Hrolf. It will be much easier to take Skiringssal from your brother than from an experienced war chief like your father."

Åsa's talons dug into the beam as she recognized the accent. This man was a Dane.

"When will we attack?" Hrolf demanded.

"On the first full moon after midsummer, lord," said the Dane.

"How many ships will your king send?" Hrolf asked.

"He has promised seventy-five dragons, fully manned with seasoned warriors," the Dane replied.

Hrolf nodded. "Enough to take Skiringssal, and get rid of my brother once and for all." Åsa held her breath as he leaned forward, looking at the Dane keenly. "Then I will rule Skiringssal as well as Tromøy."

"Yes, lord. You will hold both in allegiance to the Danish throne. Then we'll attack Borre."

"My father won't like that," Hrolf reflected.

"Your father will be dead, lord."

Hrolf barked a laugh and raised the mead horn.

Her bird's heart thundering in her chest, Åsa launched herself from the eaves, hoping Hrolf was distracted enough not to sense her presence.

She had to warn Olaf.

A stiff headwind challenged her flight north. It seemed to take forever, but at last she spotted the roofs of Skiringssal. Her heart thrummed as she lit on the gable end. Peering down into the walled-off sleeping room, she made out a massive, carved oak bed.

Fair hair gleamed on the pillow. His scent, fresh as new grass, wafted up to her, reminding her of his lips on hers, his arms holding her so long ago.

She found herself beside him. Her form was human shaped, though no more substantial than sunlight. His body was warm, the flesh and muscle firm under her touch.

He opened his eyes, and she saw her own longing reflected in them.

"How many times I have thought of you," he murmured, reaching out with one finger to trace a fiery path down her cheek. "I have wished a thousand times that I could hold you and tell you I am sorry. I would do anything to change what happened."

At his words, Åsa felt her tension run out like water, leaving her light, a little dizzy.

He drew her face to his, breath quickening. Her heart beat harder in response.

But she could not stay. She struggled to focus. "There is danger," she said urgently. "The Danes are coming. They will attack Skiringssal on the full moon."

Olaf's eyes widened. "Wait... Stay..."

She must get to Borre and warn Gudrød. With a great effort of will, she tore herself from Olaf's arms and flung herself into the rafters, where she gripped the beam with talons, a falcon once more. Olaf sat up and looked around the empty bed, bewildered.

"Another dream," he said aloud. The grief in his voice lured her. But if she went down there again, she might never leave. She hopped to the gable end and flew out with the smoke.

The dark forest seemed to stretch on forever, the wind fighting her as she beat her way north. But she sighted smoke rising above the trees at last. Mustering one final surge, she flapped her way to the bower hall. Landing in the eaves above her chamber, she saw Heid drowsing in her chair by the brazier and her own sleeping form motionless on the bed.

The völva's head snapped up as Åsa slipped into her body.

"What news from Tromøy?"

Åsa forced her lips to shape words. "Hrolf has made an alliance with the Danes."

The sorceress rose from her chair and hobbled over to the bed. She gripped Åsa's shoulder with fingers like iron. The touch brought Åsa fully into her body.

"Tell me what you heard."

"They plan to invade Skiringssal with a fleet of seventy-five ships. They're going to kill Olaf and set Hrolf up as their puppet king, then attack Borre."

"When will they attack?"

"At the full moon," said Åsa.

"That's only a week away."

"I've warned Olaf," said Åsa. "But Gudrød will never believe me."

"He can't know of your abilities." Heid picked up her staff. "I'll tell him I've had a vision. He'll believe me."

The crippled sorceress was out the door, moving faster than Åsa thought possible.

CHAPTER 33

Skiringssal
Full Moon, May

As the sun rose over the sea, Hrolf stood in the bow of *Wave Steed*, exulting in the spray on his face as the ship beat into the northerly breeze. In his wake sailed two longships, each manned by thirty-five sworn men. They had departed Tromøy under cover of darkness, sailing all night to rendezvous with the Danish fleet. And now he could see them, seventy-five sails fanned out across the water. His dream was within his grasp. He would soon be lord of Skiringssal, and his brother would be dead.

He would see to it himself this time.

Sighting Malmøy, the island that guarded the southern entrance to Skiringssal's harbor, he signaled the helmsman to close the coast. As the ship's bow fell away from the wind and the crew eased the sail, a signal fire flared on Malmøy. The shore watch had seen their change in direction. Little good it would do

Olaf. It was far too late for reinforcements to arrive before the Danes overran Skiringssal. Hrolf would personally burn the Shining Hall, with pleasure.

As his ships entered the channel between Malmøy and the mainland, the crews dropped sail and ran out the oars. With a lookout stationed on the bow, they threaded their way between the islands, keeping under cover as long as possible.

They rounded an islet, and the harbor opened before him like a treasure chest. He gaped at the size of the fleet crowding the anchorage. Trade had picked up since his brother's return. He smiled at the thought of all the plunder soon to be his.

As they drew closer, his stomach dropped. These were no merchants. They were ships of war, long dragon ships with painted shields racked along their sides, teeming with armed men.

Every ship in Vestfold must be here.

Had they been forewarned? But how? Hrolf had maintained utmost secrecy. He glared back at his men. One of his own people must have turned traitor. He would find them.

"Fifty ships, lord," reported his lookout, bringing him back to the problem at hand.

Hrolf's stomach eased a bit. "The Danish fleet still outnumbers them. We'll win easily."

Vestfold's fleet upped anchor and ran out their oars, making their way toward Hrolf's ships. He grinned, thinking of their shock when the Danes swarmed out from behind the island.

Hrolf's steersman maneuvered upwind of the Vestfold fleet, and his other two ships flanked *Wave Steed*. From the corner of his eye, Hrolf glimpsed the first Danish ships enter the channel. Time to distract the enemy.

The archers had already picked up their bows and gathered in the center of the ships, within a protective shield wall of warriors.

"Archers!" Hrolf cried. "Nock."

Bows flew up on all five ships.

"Draw!" Hrolf felt the breeze freshen on his cheek. "Loose!"

The archers loosed a volley into the Vestfold fleet, arrows flashing past enemy missiles.

"Shields!" His warriors flung up a roof of shields. The enemy arrows, straining against the wind, had lost much of their force by the time they clattered harmlessly on the wooden shields. But the cries from the Vestfold fleet told Hrolf that his own arrows, bolstered by the wind, had taken their toll.

But that toll did not slow the Vestfold ships. The vanguard closed on Hrolf's little flotilla amid a storm of casting spears from both directions. Linden chips flew and men screamed. Grappling hooks shot across as the ships crashed together and the fight began. Shouting war cries, warriors hacked over the gunwales at each other with sword and axe.

A grappling hook thunked over *Wave Steed*'s gunnel, biting into the wood while three more hooks landed and caught. The Danes had better get here soon. Swinging his axe with his left hand and sword with his right, Hrolf drove the boarders back. The crack of steel on bone set his blood afire as his axe bit into the neck of the enemy before him. Gore splattered his face, and he tasted blood, feeling the frenzy come over him. Howling, he jerked his axe from the corpse and turned to eviscerate the next man.

"Hello, brother."

The voice sent a chill through Hrolf, the battle ecstasy leaking away.

Olaf stood smiling, one foot on the gunnel, sword and shield in hand.

"Seems your friends have deserted you," he said, nodding toward the harbor entrance. Hrolf glanced back, seeing a dozen Danish ships in the passage as he'd expected. Then he looked again.

The ships were sailing in the wrong direction. Instead of

entering the harbor, the Danes were retreating back to the open sea. Beyond them, Hrolf glimpsed the rest of the fleet sailing past the entrance. Heading north.

His stomach dropped again. Bile seared his throat as he realized what must have happened.

"They're going on to Borre," he said, trying to sound as if he were privy to the plan.

He was rewarded when the blood drained from Olaf's face. His brother's shock confirmed his suspicions. The bulk of the Vestfold fleet was here, leaving Borre poorly defended. The treacherous Danes had surmised as much when they saw the number of ships in the harbor, and now they were bypassing Skiringssal for easy pickings in Borre. Angry as he was, Hrolf had to admit the Danes' tactics were sound. It was what he would have done.

Yet here he was, abandoned to his fate.

The enemy had cleared the decks of Hrolf's other ships and cut them adrift. Now the Vestfold fleet descended on his flagship, ensnared by Olaf's grappling hooks. Hrolf knew he'd better get away while he could.

Hrolf feinted his axe in a killing blow at Olaf's neck, forcing his brother to raise his shield and sword. But Hrolf pivoted and, with a downward sweep of his axe, cut the lines and shoved the two ships apart with his foot. Olaf leaped back from the gunnel as the gap between them widened.

Hrolf smiled at his brother.

"I'm heading south, to Tromøy. You can pursue me, brother, and perhaps you'll catch me. Meanwhile, Borre will fall. Or you can lead your fleet after the Danes right now and hope you get there before it is too late."

Hrolf savored Olaf's tortured expression as he wrestled with his choices. He held his brother's gaze with a taunting grin as *Wave Steed* pulled away.

Hrolf smiled and turned to his men.

"Row, you bastards! Row for your lives!"

They plied their oars under a hail of arrows, heading for the harbor entrance, the Vestfold fleet hot on their stern. But Hrolf had gained a few precious seconds of surprise, and rowing away from certain annihilation gave his men special vigor.

With a few more strokes, they cleared the entrance and headed south, while the Vestfold fleet turned north in pursuit of the Danes.

THE MORNING DAWNED cold and still over Borre.

Bram spotted Gudrød on his way to the smithy and rushed to warn Ulf, who managed to hide Gudrød's Bane before he arrived.

"I've come for my sword. I leave for Skiringssal today," said Gudrød.

"I'm sorry, lord, it is not yet ready." Ulf showed him a half finished sword.

"You have disappointed me, smith," said Gudrød. "I must depart to war today, without the sword you promised. I will deal with you when I return."

Ulf bowed his head to hide the glint in his eyes.

Gudrød stormed to the jetty where Heid and her acolytes waited beside *Dragonlord*, a bound goat ready for sacrifice.

"Mount the dragon's head," he bellowed at his crew. They scurried to the prow. As they struggled to fit the carved head onto the stem post, the lookout dashed onto the jetty.

"My lord!" Gasping to recover his breath, he croaked, "Danish ships—on the horizon..."

"How many?" barked Gudrød.

"More than fifty, lord."

Gudrød paled. "Any sign of our fleet?"

"No, lord."

Gudrød's jaw tightened. "Our ships are no doubt in pursuit of the enemy. Until they arrive, we'll have to defend Borre with the forces we have." His voice was harsh with fear. "We cannot hope to survive without the gods' favor. Take that goat away. I must make a sacrifice that will ensure us victory."

"There is a fine stallion in the stable," said Heid.

Gudrød shook his head. "That won't be enough to gain victory against such great odds. The Danes sacrifice to the gods too. We are asking for a miracle. The corpse god will require human blood."

"You have many thralls to choose from," the sorceress offered.

"Bah! Do you think the gods are stupid? They know a thrall's life is not a fair bargain for such a victory. The kingdom hangs in the balance. It must be a great sacrifice, the sacrifice of royal blood. Bring me the boy. Bring me Halfdan."

The völva stared at him. "You would sacrifice your own son? After all we have done to ensure his survival?"

Gudrød gave her a wolfish grin. "I have a grown son and heir at Skiringssal. What need have I of an infant? Bring the boy!"

"I'll have no part of it," said Heid.

"Then I'll get him myself," said Gudrød, stalking toward the bower.

IN THE QUEEN'S CHAMBER, Åsa sat on the floor with Halfdan as he raced the tiny wooden horses Ulf had carved for him. She smiled down at his dark head. She could stare at him for hours.

The door burst open and Gudrød stormed in. Åsa leaped up, grabbing her son.

"I thought you had departed for Skiringssal, lord."

"I have need of this boy," Gudrød said.

She backed away, clutching Halfdan to her chest. The child whined and struggled in her grip.

"Give him to me," Gudrød snarled.

"Come and take him," she said, setting Halfdan down and shoving him behind her.

Gudrød advanced on her. Åsa looked desperately around the room for a weapon. Her sword was on the wall across the room, and Halfdan's sword hung over his cradle, behind Gudrød.

Her gaze fell on a pair of sewing shears on the table beside her. She grabbed them, holding them in front of her like a knife.

Gudrød bared his teeth. "You have tried to kill me with sewing implements before."

Åsa backed to the wall, pinning Halfdan behind her. He was quiet now, as if he knew this was not the time to fuss.

"Do not resist me," said Gudrød, closing the gap between them. She rammed the shears up under his ribs.

He pivoted, the blade glancing off his chainmail. Then he slammed his fist into her head, knocking her to the floor, where she lay stunned.

Halfdan's shrieks brought Åsa's head up. Before she could reach him, Gudrød snatched the boy and strode out of the bower.

Åsa dragged herself to her feet and threw herself at the door as the key clicked in the iron lock.

CHAPTER 34

Åsa ripped Lightning down from the wall and raced back to the door. Hacking furiously at the oak, she knew she'd never get through the thick wood in time. Gudrød would kill the last of her family, and there was nothing she could do to stop him. Screaming in rage, she beat the door with the sword, sending chips flying.

"Stop!" came a cry from the other side of the door.

Åsa roared in fury and hacked with the sword again.

"Stop!" came the cry again.

"You can't stop me!" Åsa paused to draw breath.

The lock clicked.

Åsa stared as the door swung open. Heid stood there, grinning as she hooked the key on her belt.

"Come, child, Ulf is waiting."

Sword in hand, Åsa raced to the smithy, Heid hobbling behind.

Ulf and Bram waited for her with armor and shield. They helped her into the mail shirt and helm, and Ulf brought out the new-forged sword.

Åsa stared in awe at the blade. The watered steel shimmered in the forge light, silver runes flashing.

"I carved Gudrød's death runes into the steel," said Ulf.

Åsa gripped the sword. The blade was longer than Lightning's but seemed to weigh no more than the shorter sword. She swept it through the air. It was perfectly balanced.

"It's named Gudrød's Bane," Ulf said, eyes gleaming.

Åsa bared her teeth in a wolf's smile and ran from the smithy.

Breathing hard, she reached the jetty where Gudrød's men gathered. Their attention was focused on the end of the pier, and no one noticed as she slipped into their ranks. She edged her way toward the front where she could see Gudrød standing before the carved wood altar, his ceremonial robe over his armor. Two of Heid's acolytes held ready the brass bowls to catch the blood.

Åsa stood on tiptoe to peer over the shoulder of the warrior before her, searching for her child. Her heart lurched when she spotted him lying face down on the altar.

He was so quiet—was she too late? But his little back rose and fell with breath. He was alive—for the moment.

She forced her way to the front of the crowd as Gudrød drew his knife and turned toward the altar, beginning his incantation.

She gripped Gudrød's Bane and took a deep breath.

Then she lunged from the crowd, driving her sword at Gudrød's back. He whirled, dodging instinctively as her blade slashed through his robe, skidding on chain mail just below his ribs.

Swords slipped from scabbards.

Åsa cast off her helm. The warriors froze, hands on weapons.

She raised her sword and cried, "I am Åsa Haraldsdottir, and I claim right of vengeance on this man, for the slaying of my kin!"

The warriors let their swords drop back into their sheaths. They knew she had the right of it.

Gudrød drew the Serkland sword and advanced on her, grinning.

"So, little queen, you wish to join your father?" he taunted. "And your brother?"

She donned her helmet and took a firm stance, gripping Gudrød's Bane in both hands, scowling to banish images of the past.

"And soon your son," he said. "Your line ends today."

She tightened her gut against the roiling fear. "It is you who will join my father in the corpse hall today," she declared, charging the words with power so they rang in the air. She thought she saw uncertainty flicker in his sneer.

Yet his first charge drove her back and made her heart pound as if it would leap from her chest. She gritted her teeth and planted her feet, but he was grinning again.

He swung the Serkland sword in a glittering arc. Her shield flew up to meet it, the impact jarring down her arm. She braced herself, trying not to stagger. Before she could recover, he swung again, his blade coming down from above at an angle she could not parry. His sword scraped across her brynja, popping rings. She felt the sting as the edge sliced along her ribs.

She sprang away, but he charged after her, fetching her helmet a blow that made her head ring. She clutched her shield and struggled for balance.

"You're like your father. Weak." His breath was hot on her face. "I killed him. I killed your brother. Now I'll kill you."

The vision sprang up of her father, the light dying in his eyes. *Father, help me. Help me save my son.*

Gudrød's sword edge had found the breach in her chain mail. He brushed the blade across her skin, almost a caress. Visions of their wedding night flashed through her mind: his body pressing down on her, the blade pricking her throat.

Yet he did not prevail.

She met his gaze. "You're impotent." Her voice was low, soft as a lover's, but loaded with scorn.

Gudrød's eyes widened.

"You're a cuckold." His face reddened. She nodded toward his men. "They would kill you if they knew." His cheeks were purple now, his breath rasping. The sword trembled in his hand.

Now.

She flew forward, out of the grip of fear. Sliding under his guard, she drove her blade into his midriff, ramming the wind out of him. Steel scraped steel. Three rings shot into the air.

She saw shock drive the doubt from his face. Years of battle experience took over, and he swept his sword in an arc aimed to take her head off. But he seemed to move so slowly. She had plenty of time to duck while his momentum carried him around, exposing his back. Without hesitation, Åsa sliced her blade low across his calf. She felt the resistance of muscle and tendon give, then steel scraped bone.

He roared in pain, his leg buckling for an instant.

Then he recovered and rounded on her.

She pivoted before he could square up to the new direction, dancing away from his slicing blade. Propped on his good leg, he straightened and gripped his sword in both hands, raising it above his head.

So slow. It seemed like she had hours to react.

His sword came hurtling down. Hers flew up to parry. His blade met hers with a resounding crack.

And shattered.

Warriors gasped as shards of steel shot into the air.

Gudrød stared at the stub of his sword, his face a mask of fear.

Åsa did not hesitate. With all her strength, she drove Gudrød's Bane upward into his throat. His eyes widened as blood gushed from the wound. His lips moved in a red froth.

Åsa reached her son before Gudrød hit the ground. Snatching Halfdan from the altar, she smelled the sleeping herbs on him, but his breath was steady.

"I'll take him." Brenna materialized from the crowd. Åsa handed Halfdan to her and turned to the warriors.

She ripped her sword from Gudrød's throat and raised it high over her head.

"I am your rightful queen."

Every man knelt before her.

Åsa stared down on their bowed heads. *Is this what I want?*

The sentry came pelting down the jetty. "The Danes! They're closing on the shore." The warriors leaped to their feet, drawing weapons.

"Wait!" The völva stepped forward. "Royal blood has been spilled. We must complete the ritual to ensure our victory."

Heid picked up the sacrificial knife where Gudrød had dropped it. Her acolytes brought the brass bowls and caught the blood that still seeped from the corpse's wounds. Heid dipped the twigs and showered drops on the sea. "Njord and Rán, grant us victory over our enemies."

She dipped the twigs again and turned to Åsa, sprinkling her with blood. "I consecrate you queen of Borre."

The húskarlar clashed swords on shields, and Heid anointed them with the last of Gudrød's blood.

As the thunderous acclaim subsided, Åsa raised her sword.

"To arms!" she cried.

～

ÅSA STOOD ON THE JETTY, Olvir and Ulf beside her, watching the vast Danish fleet descend. Counting *Dragonlord*, Borre had less than a dozen ships.

High on the patriarch's mound, the raven banner snapped in the breeze as if it would take wing. Beneath it, Heid and her apprentices chanted. Snatches of their battle charms carried on the wind.

Their presence gave Åsa a confidence that defied logic, but it freed her mind to concentrate on the problem at hand. If nothing else, they stood between the enemy and Halfdan, safe with

Brenna back at the bower. Åsa knew if the worst happened, Brenna would flee into the forest with the child.

The offshore wind forced the invaders to drop their sails and man the oars to reach the shore, buying her a little time. Staring out over the steel-gray sea, Åsa wracked her brains for some advantage, some weakness to exploit.

The Danish longships closed on the shore, bucking in the brisk chop. An idea formed in her head. She had no time to ponder. She must act.

"Archers," she shouted, "To the jetties!"

Olvir looked up, startled, then grinned.

"Archers!" he echoed. "We can pick them off from before they land."

Åsa stationed Borre's archers and spearmen on the jetties behind a contingent of warriors forming a shield wall. Bonfires flared behind them. As the Danish ships closed in, the defenders launched a volley of flaming arrows into the enemy fleet. The offshore wind boosted the arrows, fanning the flames as the furled sails and rigging caught fire.

The Danish crews battled the flames, unable to stop and return fire while Borre's archers bombarded them from the jetties. Smoke thickened the air, mingling with screams as the arrows found their marks.

Engulfed in flame, the first ranks of Danish ships drifted down on those behind them and set them afire. Soon, twenty ships were ablaze. Those who weren't killed outright leaped into the water, where Borre's archers picked them off.

The remains of the Danish fleet retreated from the flaming ships.

The air fell eerily silent. Smoldering hulks clogged the blood-red water, filling the air with rank black smoke. Ravens and gulls shrieked as they fought over the bodies that bobbed in the gore.

As the hulks burned to the waterline, the enemy fleet turned and flooded in, thickening the air with spears. Quivers empty, Borre's archers retreated to the beach.

Åsa drew Gudrød's Bane, watching the first Danes land. Behind them came more ships than the eye could take in. Beside her, Ulf hefted his battle-axe. They did not say it aloud, but they knew they wouldn't last long.

"Shield wall!" she cried, and the warriors rattled into formation.

The Danes splashed ashore, their chain-mail brynjas and helmets glinting. They roared, clashing swords on shields. Åsa's stomach roiled. Through force of will, she managed to stand straight and keep her gaze fixed on the enemy.

The Danish archers sent up a silent flight of arrows. "Shields up!" Åsa cried as the thicket of bolts thwacked into their shields. They withstood the first volley, but how long could they hold out against a concentrated assault? The Danes could keep hammering them until they smashed Borre's defenses.

But the Danes did not wait that long. As soon as the last arrow landed, they charged. Hundreds of feet pounded the sand, war cries clashing with the chants Heid's women howled from the mound. Åsa gritted her teeth against the chaos and held with her men. A Dane charged her, and she bashed his head with the metal edge of her shield, making his helmet ring and stunning him long enough for her to plunge her sword into his throat.

As the defenders fell, the shield wall broke up. Åsa fought on beside her men, enemy corpses piling up without seeming to stem the hordes that surged from the sea.

The metallic smell of blood underlay the pervasive stench of spilled entrails. A lull came in the onslaught, but she could see yet more Danes swarming ashore, rafting up to the beached ships and clambering over them. Her sword arm was leaden, her throat parched, her eyes raw. The battle lust had drained away. They couldn't last much longer.

A shriek split the air behind her. She whirled to see a two dozen men clad in animal skins come screaming out of the trees.

Hrafn.

The outlaw chieftain loped up, grinning.

"Today, we pay our debt to you," he said as the outlaws joined the defenders.

A fierce joy flooded her, and she screamed with them, shaking Gudrød's Bane at the sky. The blood lust surged into her. *This is how my father felt... This is how a shield-maiden feels.* New strength flowed through her veins as she thrust and parried. She could keep fighting until the last Dane lay bleeding at her feet. The men around her were a blur, and time slowed again as the battle frenzy came over her. As each new foe appeared, she had time to size up the attack. Gudrød's Bane claimed every man that came within its reach.

Hrafn's outlaws were reaping a red harvest of their own, but even so, she knew the defenders were vastly outnumbered. Danes poured from the ships that surged up onto the beach.

Cries came from the sea, and she realized it was not the sound of feasting gulls.

Åsa looked up from the Dane she had just gutted. New long-ships surged into the corpse-choked water. Her heart sank as the vessels ploughed through the smoking hulks and drifting bodies. Was there no end to the Danish fleet?

It was only a matter of minutes now, and it would all be over. She faced a charging Dane, one last enemy to take with her to the afterlife.

Her target drew back his spear arm, ready to throw his javelin. Åsa gripped her sword and charged, eyes searching the sky for Freyja's swan-maidens.

The Dane pitched forward, an arrow in his back. Åsa instinctively flung her shield overhead.

From the new ships came a flight of arrows, piercing the

backs of the charging enemy. The Danes faltered, stumbling over their fallen comrades.

The Vestfold fleet had arrived.

The ships beached among the Danish fleet, and their warriors splashed ashore. As the Danes turned in confusion to face the new threat from the sea, Åsa saw her chance. "Charge!" she screamed, and Borre's remaining defenders fell on the attackers, butchering them as they struggled to regain their footing among the corpses while the new arrivals attacked from the shore. Caught between the two forces, the Danes lost courage and fell like barley stalks beneath the scythe.

And then there was no one left to fight.

Åsa stood with her few surviving men in a tangle of bodies, numb with exhaustion.

"Olaf!" came the shout.

She spotted him in the crowd and stepped over a body toward him.

She blinked up into hazel eyes.

"Lady, are you wounded?" Olaf looked at her with concern.

She realized she was covered with gore. Smiling up at him, she said, "No, it's all Danish blood."

CHAPTER 35

The folk of Borre burned the dead in two giant pyres, one for the Vestfold defenders, the other for their enemies. As the greasy smoke rose over the shoreline, Heid and her women chanted spells to ensure the dead departed the earth and did not trouble the living.

Olaf interred Gudrød's body in a temporary grave. A king's burial required careful planning. The survivors of Borre made special clothing for their lord to wear in the afterlife while Heid's apprentices carved runes and rehearsed ceremonies.

"My father would wish to be buried in *Dragonlord*, at Skiringssal with his forefathers," said Olaf.

Åsa started the funeral ale. Through the brewhouse's open door, she watched Olaf in the yard selecting which of his father's horses and dogs would accompany Gudrød into the mound. He looked up, and his expression brightened when he saw her, making her heart quicken. He had changed so much in his time away, no longer the unsure boy, now a warrior confident in his abilities. But through everything, he had somehow retained his sweetness.

Beside him stood Halfdan, who followed him everywhere. Olaf still thought of the little boy as his half brother.

She wanted to tell him the truth. But if Halfdan was exposed as Olaf's son, the boy's rights of inheritance would be at risk.

She was free of Gudrød at last, free to be with Olaf. But her joy was fouled with blood and betrayal. She couldn't forget her fear and shame when Olaf dragged her back to Gudrød in bonds. She didn't forgive him for it and couldn't trust him, even while she understood how powerful his bond with his father had been. There was so much between them. She had killed the father he now mourned. She knew he understood her right to vengeance, but could he forgive?

That night when they were alone, she broached the subject that hung heavy in the air. Gudrød had made Olaf heir to his land, and that claim stood, but Borre's hird had sworn to Åsa and followed her into battle. It was up to the jarls to choose between them as the new ruler of Borre.

"I must return to Tromøy," she said. "Tromøy is in a shambles, easy prey. I must claim it from Hrolf."

He bowed his head. "As you say, lady. My vow still stands. As soon as my father is in the mound, I will escort you to Tromøy with Vestfold's fleet. We will destroy Hrolf."

She took a deep breath. "And I will remain there."

Olaf looked at the floor as the color seeped up his neck. "I had hoped you would stay here and rule Vestfold with me."

"Tromøy needs a full-time ruler. It is my land and I must protect it. It's my home."

Her heart tore as she watched despair come over Olaf's face. She went on to say what she must. "I do not relinquish my son's claim to Vestfold."

Olaf stared at her.

"You will rule alone until Halfdan becomes a man," she said. "Then I will send him to you to claim his share of the kingdom."

Olaf nodded. "As you say, lady."

∼

BORRE'S HÚSKARLAR exhumed Gudrød's body and carried it aboard *Dragonlord*. Olaf took command, and Vestfold's fleet fanned out around their king's flagship. Åsa and Halfdan joined Heid and her acolytes on board *Freyja*. Brenna was with her, and all the Tromøy folk.

The fleet arrived in Skiringssal, and Olaf took up residence in the hall with the lords and húskarlar. Åsa stayed in the bower with her son and the other women.

Olaf chose the burial location on an estuary. Slaves hauled the ship into the shallows, where they tied *Dragonlord* off to a boulder. Food was laid in along with cooking gear, and the ship's sail was folded on the foredeck. They built a burial chamber on *Dragonlord*'s foredeck, and set up the king's great bed inside. Olaf laid his father's corpse out in state, ready to meet the afterlife. He clothed Gudrød in ritual garments and propped him sitting up on richly embroidered bolsters, the hilt of the broken Serkland sword in his hand.

Then the ritual began.

Åsa remained in the bower house, taking no part in the ceremony. It was time to visit Tromøy, to see what they would face. She lay on the bed, Stormrider perched above her on the headboard, Brenna watching over her and minding Halfdan. Åsa let herself flow into the falcon's body. She lofted into the air and flew out of the gable end, heading south over the endless forest, to Tromøy.

The peregrine's flight from Skiringssal took barely half a day. As she flew over the north end of the island, she saw no sign of a lookout at the signal fire. Vestfold's fleet could attack by night, as Gudrød had done, though she was sure Hrolf expected that. He would be patrolling the waters daily in falcon form, and he would spot their ships long before they arrived.

She soared over the steading and lit high in a tall pine, settling in to watch.

No ships lay on the beach beside the boathouse. She watched from the pine all morning, and no one stirred. She flew to the gable ends of the hall. It was empty.

She flew back to Skiringssal and described what she had seen to Heid.

"It seems Hrolf has gotten away."

"Yes. Olaf will be very unhappy about that."

"I don't know what we can do. It's not practical to hunt him in that forest."

Their words trailed off as they pondered.

Another subject rose in Åsa's mind, something she'd wondered about for a long time. She drew a deep breath and turned to the sorceress. "Tell me of the prophecy."

Heid did not speak for a long time before she replied.

"I suppose I owe you that much." The old sorceress fell silent again. "My dream has long been to unite this land, and cease the endless warring. I had a vision. The gods spoke to me." She drew a deep breath. Her voice deepened with the resonance of prophecy. "From the Gudrød the Hunter and Harald Redbeard will spring the greatest king of all. The lords will unite under this king, and cease their strife. This I saw in the darkness."

Now it was Åsa's turn to take a deep breath. "Halfdan is not Gudrød's son."

The völva laughed, a natural laugh Åsa had never heard from her before. "Yes, I made sure of that. But Gudrød's blood runs in Olaf's veins. So the prophecy was fulfilled."

"But it happened when I escaped. I drugged you…"

Heid looked at her in mock severity. "Do you really believe I am so careless with my sleeping herbs? And how do you think that boat came to be there on the beach, just waiting for you to get enough nerve to take it? Gudrød was right when he suspected you had help, but it wasn't Ulf."

"But, the wedding night? How could you be sure that it would be Olaf's child and not Gudrød's?"

Heid smirked. "Who offered Gudrød the wedding cup? I made sure that he would not be capable of fathering a child."

Åsa sat awhile, trying to take it all in. But there was something more she needed to know.

"You once told me that my father's death was payment owed."

The völva looked away, staring into the distance. "When I was fifteen winters, there was a raid on my village. I was the only survivor. They killed my husband and my child. One of the raiders trampled me with his horse and left me for dead." She sighed. "Perhaps death would have been better than a lifetime as a cripple. But the gods did not see fit to take me that day.

"I lay by my family's bodies for two days. I would have died there beside them, but the völva Solveig found me. She decided I should live. She and her followers nursed me for weeks until I could walk. Then she taught me the ways of the sorceress. I have followed that path all my life.

"Eventually, I discovered who was responsible for the deaths of my family." She said nothing for a long time. Then she began again. "The raid was led by two young men who later became great kings, Gudrød the Hunter and Harald Redbeard."

Åsa stared at her, the missing pieces of the story falling into place like boulders in a landslide.

Olaf and the warriors finished the funeral rites, bloody and exhausted. They crowded the benches of the great hall to eat a meal and then slept. In the morning, they rose and bathed.

Åsa waited in the great hall to greet Olaf. When he walked through the door, he looked different. He was still tall and fair. It was his bearing that had changed.

As the warriors gathered, he took the heir's customary place on the step before the high seat. Åsa brought him the first horn of funeral ale, on which he would make the heir's toast. He took it from her and raised it to the company.

"This land is mine by rights of inheritance. In my father's stead, I swear to keep the Danes from our shores so long as I live." He brought the horn to his lips and drank to seal his vow.

The men clashed their weapons upon their shields in approval.

Åsa mounted the step beside him and raised her horn. "As queen of Vestfold, I delegate my right to rule to Olaf Gudrødson. When my son, Halfdan, comes of age, he will claim his share of the land."

Olaf took the high seat amid cheers and clashing weapons. He was king of Vestfold. One by one, each of the jarls and warriors in the hall approached the high seat and swore his loyalty to Olaf.

When everyone had made their vows, Åsa declared, "I maintain my right to my father's lands on Tromøy, and I go to claim them."

Olaf said, "I have sworn that I will drive Hrolf from Tromøy. I go with Queen Åsa to fulfill that vow. As my sworn men, I bid you sail with me."

Again, the hall echoed with cheers and the drumbeat of weapons clashing on shields.

Åsa stepped up to the high seat and took her place beside Olaf. The toasts to the honored dead went late into the night.

After the festivities ended, Åsa retired to the bower. She entered Stormrider's body and went forth to see how things lay in Tromøy.

As before, she found the great hall empty, the hearth cold.

Hrolf was out there somewhere in the wild, with what remained of his men.

That was a worry for another day.

~

HALFDAN IN HER ARMS, Åsa watched from *Freyja*'s bow as the longship slid onto the gravel beach. Beside her stood Brenna and Toki, Heid and Ulf. Olaf sailed beside them in *Sea Dragon*. Behind, Vestfold's longships filled the harbor.

Olvir jumped down and set the gangplank. Holding Halfdan close, Åsa walked down the plank and set her feet on Tromøy's soil for the first time in two years.

Vengeance had claimed her father, and Olaf's, in an endless cycle. *Let it end now.*

Åsa looked up the hill, where the folk of Tromøy gathered in front of the hall, nearly one hundred strong. They were cheering.

She set Halfdan down on his sturdy legs, and he started up the trail.

GLOSSARY

Álf—elf, male, often considered ancestors (plural álfir)
Berserker—warriors said to have superhuman powers. Translates either as "bear shirt" or "bare shirt"
Bind rune—three or more runes drawn one over the other
Blót—sacrifice. i.e., Álfablót is sacrifice in honor of the elves, Dísablót is in honor of the dís
Brynja—chain-mail shirt
Dís—spirits of female ancestors (plural: dísir)
Draugr—animated corpse
Fylgja—a guardian spirit, animal or female
Fóstra—a child's nurse (foster mother)
Fyflot—magical symbol
Galdr—spells spoken and sung
Gammelost—literally "old cheese"
Gungnir—Odin's spear
Hamr—"skin"; the body
Haugbui—mound-dwelling ghost
Haugr—mound
Hird—the warrior retinue of a noble man
Hugr—the soul
Húskarl—the elite household warriors of a nobleman (plural: húskarlar)
Itil—the Volga river
Jarl—earl, one step below a king
Jól—Yule midwinter feast honoring all the gods, but especially Odin
Karl—a free man
Karvi—a small Viking ship
Knarr—a merchant ship
Lawspeaker—a learned man who knew the laws of the district by heart

Longfire—a long, narrow fireplace that ran down the center of a hall

Mjölnir—Thor's hammer, a symbol of fertility

Norn—the supernatural sisters who weave fate named Skuld, Verdandi, and Urd

Ørlög—personal fate

Primstave—a flat piece of wood used as a calendar. The days of summer are carved on one side, winter on the reverse.

Ragnarök—the end of the world

Runes—the Viking alphabet, said to have magical powers

Seidr—a trance to work magic

Serkland—the middle east

Skáld—poet

Skyr—a dairy product similar to yogurt

Small beer—a beer with a low alcohol content, a common drink

Thrall—slave

Ulfhed—"wolf head"; another warrior like a berserker (plural ulfhednar)

Urdr—the web of fate, one of the Norns

Valhöll— "corpse hall", Odin's hall

Valknut—corpse knot, a symbol of Odin

Valkyrie—"choosers of the slain," or corpse maidens. Magical women who take warriors from the battlefield to Valhöll, or Freyja's hall Folkvang

Vardlokkur—a chant to draw the spirits

Völva—a sorceress. Literally, "wand-bearer"

Wights—spirits of land and water

Wootz—crucible steel manufactured in ancient India

Characters

Tromøy
Harald Redbeard, King of East Agder, Norway
Gunnhild, his queen, a noblewoman of Lista (deceased)
Gyrd, their son, age 16
Åsa, their daughter, age 15
Brenna, their nurse (fóstra)
Toki, Brenna's husband, steward of Tromøy
Jarl Borg, trusted ally and battle commander
Ulf, blacksmith of Tromøy
Astrid, daughter of the king of Grenland, foster sister to Åsa and Gyrd

Borre
Gudrød, king of Vestfold, Norway
Alfhild, his queen (deceased)
Olaf, their son, age 16
Hrolf, Gudrød's natural son, age 17
Heid, a famous völva (sorceress)
Knut, a famous skáld (poet and historian)
Arne, blacksmith of Borre
Hrafn, an outlawed berserker and sorcerer
Halfdan the Mild, Gudrød's deceased father
Halfdan the Black, Åsa's son
Sigrid, Heid's slave
Grim, lawspeaker
Olvir, captain of the household guards
Alf Thorvaldson, farmer
Regin Odson, framer, Alf's neighbor
Solveig, Heid's mentor (deceased)

Ringerike

CHARACTERS

Gunnar Halvorson, Foster Brother to Sigurd Brodison
Sigurd Brodison, son of Ringerike's king, Brodi

Outlaws
Lars
Anders, the leader
Odd, the cook

Eastern Lands
Björn, a Svea merchant
Erland, crewmember of *Eastern Trader*
Ketil, crewmember of *Eastern Trader*
Skeggi, a Svea merchant
Dag, a Svea merchant
Ilke, a Svea merchant

Author's Note

The Norse Queen is based on the life of Queen Åsa, a woman who seized power and held her realm for twenty years at the dawn of the Viking Age. Nothing is known about her reign, though her existence is confirmed by scant but tantalizing references in ancient historical accounts and archaeological evidence.

Of special interest is the Oseberg ship, one of the richest Viking-age burials ever found. The ship was discovered by a farmer ploughing his field in 1903 in Vestfold, Norway. Archeologists excavated a mound containing the most elaborate ship burial from the Viking age. Analysis of the bones revealed that the grave occupants were two women, one in her fifties and the other in her seventies. Both women were contemporary with Åsa, and many consider the Oseberg burial her grave.

The grave contained household equipment including looms, kitchen gear, and food, as well as mysterious tapestries portraying a ceremonial procession. There were carved sleighs, beds, a cart, and magical items such as cannabis seeds and a wooden staff carved with mysterious runes. Horses, dogs, and an ox had been sacrificed as part of the burial ceremony.

Whether the Oseberg burial was really that of Queen Åsa, we may never know. The grave chamber timbers have been dendrochronologically dated to 834 AD, and both women have been proven to be from Agder, where Åsa was born. Her burial would have been very much like this one, and the objects found in the grave tell us much about her life—what she ate, what she wore, how she spent her time.

A scant paragraph exists in written history about Åsa. The writings, done about four hundred years after her death, do not paint a particularly heroic view of her. Yet much evidence today suggests that women of the early- to mid-Viking age were combatants themselves. I have chosen to portray Åsa in that light.

I've explored the mystery of the enigmatic Ulfbehrt sword, a weapon of crucible steel far superior to the pattern welded blades common in northern Europe at this time. The blades were inscribed with the Latin letters +VLFBEHR+T. Nobody know where, when, or by whom these swords were made. The commonly held theory is that weapons of this caliber could only have been produced in Francia, perhaps in a monastery. But more of these weapons by far have been found in Norway than anywhere else in the world.

In the ninth century, the nomadic Bulgar people split into two waves, one group settling at the confluence of the Itil River (now known as the Volga) and the Kama River. There, on a spur of the Silk Road, they established Bolghar, a trading post catering to the Middle Eastern lands, trading furs and slaves for the silver of the caliphate. It is known that Scandinavians navigated the Volga during this period, reportedly as far as Baghdad. It is very possible that they traded for wootz steel, and certainly possible that the knowledge to forge Ulfbehrt swords had been acquired by a Scandinavian. I have woven the tale of an accomplished smith named Ulf into my tale.

I have also chosen to weave magic into my tale, because to the people who lived in these times, the world was an enchanted place filled with sorcery and spirits. To portray it otherwise would not bring a true picture of the world as the Norse saw it. I have tried to make these experiences as real as possible.

In the end, this book is a work of my imagination and my fascination with the research that has been done of the early medieval period, also known as the Viking age.

ACKNOWLEDGMENTS

I have so many people to thank in bringing this novel into being: My beloved mother who first introduced me to Åsa and the Viking world; Ruth Ross and DV Berkom, who gave me the swift kicks I needed with the first attempts and had the patience and fortitude to keep reading draft after agonizing draft; my wonderful fellow writers at Kitsap Writers, each of whom contributed so very much and kept me going. A special thanks to my critique partners Meghan Skye, Carrie Lawrence, and Roland Boykin, who spent endless hours reading and critiquing. Thanks to my dear husband Brian who is always on my side and eager to read more, and beta readers Yelena Strickland, Ali Mosa, Jennifer Conner, Colleen Hogan-Taylor, and Paula Gill, all of whom gave me priceless insights. I owe many thanks to developmental editors Ruth Ross and Laurie Chittenden, and to Michelle Hope for her meticulous copy-editing. Any errors that exist in this book are entirely my own.

ABOUT THE AUTHOR

Like her Viking forebears, Johanna Wittenberg has sailed to the far reaches of the world. She lives on a fjord in the Pacific Northwest with her husband, whom she met on a ship bound for Antarctica.

Thank you for reading! If you enjoyed this book a review would be appreciated.

If you would like updates of forthcoming titles in the Norsewomen Series, as well as blog posts on research into Viking history, visit www.JohannaWittenberg.com and join the mailing list.

Coming in Summer 2020: THE FALCON QUEEN, Book 2 in The Norsewomen Series

Åsa has avenged her father and reclaimed his kingdom—but can she hold it?

Follow me on Twitter, Facebook, and Pinterest.

Made in the USA
Columbia, SC
27 December 2020